THE O'CONNOR PROTOCOL

FRANK BURKETT

Published in Australia by Sid Harta Books & Print Pty Ltd,
ABN: 34632585293
23 Stirling Crescent, Glen Waverley, Victoria 3150 Australia
Telephone: +61 3 9560 9920, Facsimile: +61 3 9545 1742
E-mail: author@sidharta.com.au

First published in Australia 2023
This edition published 2023
Copyright © Frank Burkett 2023

Cover design, typesetting: WorkingType (www.workingtype.com.au)

Frank Burkett
The O'Connor Protocol
ISBN: 978-1-922958-18-1

About the Author

Frank Burkett lives in tropical Queensland, which is the setting of his second novel, *The O'Connor Protocol*. His previous novel, *View from the Clock Tower*, was shortlisted in 2006 for the British Crime Writers' Association Debut Dagger award. Although raised in Queensland, Frank has travelled extensively, including three years in the United Kingdom where he studied at The University of London for a Diploma in Dramatic Art. He spent three years in Rhodesia (now Zimbabwe) where he worked in the field of land conservation. In 1980, back home, he completed a journalism major at The University of Queensland. Following a successful career in news media, Frank wrote and published *The Tropical Son*, a biography of country music singer Graeme Connors. Frank is now retired and currently working on his third book in which, once again, sugar cane, rainforests and coral reefs provide an exotic setting.

Also by Frank Burkett

Fiction

View from the Clock Tower

Non-Fiction

Graeme Connors: The Tropical Son

Acknowledgements

During the writing of this book, I spoke to many people about details and ideas. I asked odd questions out of the blue. I would like to thank the many friends, acquaintances and professional people who cheerfully engaged with my questions and, without realising, helped me clarify my thoughts.

My thanks also go to my editor, who patiently dealt with my inexperience in the publishing field.

CHAPTER 1

On the wall of my office hangs a photograph that I took from the upstairs balcony looking across Pioneer Bay and the moored yachts, past the islands we call Double Cone, then out to distant Hayman. It might seem odd having the same view on my office wall as I do from the flat, but I have good reason. This place is my home, which in 1990, I almost lost.

Tuesday in mid-April of that year began not unlike the day preceding it; a cool, tropical morning creeping towards noon and the suggestion of a warm, lazy afternoon. I turned my back on the photo and grabbed a handful of media releases for Pixie, the new girl setting copy on my weekly paper the *Whitsunday Post*. I was partly done when Heather, the middle-aged receptionist, called from the office kitchen, 'Coffee, Tom?'

'Love one.'

I heard her dress rustle as she moved from the kettle to the fridge.

'I can fetch it,' I said.

Leaving my desk, I strolled through the office where my staff had their heads down, banging out ads, banging in editorial, setting the classifieds. It was a healthy sound. While I relieved Heather of the coffee, I glanced out the window. A two-masted yacht was edging through the gap that protected Abell Point Marina from the swells of the Coral Sea.

'Whose boat is that?' I asked.

She followed my glance. 'Could be the *Calvados*.'

My pulse quickened. 'Thought it wasn't due for another month.'

'I'm only guessing.'

'Then I'd better investigate,' I said, and set my coffee on Pixie's desk. 'Here, save you getting up.'

'Is it sugared?'

'Yes.'

'I don't take sugar.'

'Sorry,' I said, collecting my Panama as I disappeared out the back door.

The yellow Moke stood under a lean-to at the rear of the office, sharing the space with my only male employee, Billy Thompson, who was propped against the car reading a letter. Billy was part-Aboriginal who had joined the staff within weeks of the paper's launch four years earlier. With his warm smile and knockabout manner, he was my star all-rounder.

I threw my hat into the back of the Moke. 'Run out of work, Billy?'

'My barrow is never empty, boss. You take one brick out, I load two in.'

'Bricks? You're in the wrong game. Appears the *Calvados* has arrived. You coming?'

'Why not? See if Jade has a long memory.'

'I hope not. And don't call me boss. It looks bad.'

I drove around the inlet separating Shingley Beach from

Abell Point, then down to the marina. This was the choice side of my work, rushing to the waterside to check on new arrivals. I reported on handsome yachts weary from a long haul across the Pacific, retirement cruisers up from Sydney and Melbourne, or tattered wind jammers down from New Guinea and the Pacific islands. They all had a story, and the *Whitsunday Post* was full of them.

'You ought to buy one,' Billy said.

'You say that every week.'

'And you never answer.'

'I don't need a reason.'

'To me you do. We've fished in boats since we were kids. You now have enough money to buy the marina.'

'Crap I have money. Maybe if I had better staff.'

'Don't change the subject.'

'I don't know, Billy. It's one of those things. Like marriage, really. Too easy to make a wrong call. And then what?'

As I pulled into a parking bay at the front of the marina, Billy leant under the seat and dragged out a tattered sailor's cap. He fixed it jauntily on his head, rolling his eyes at my Panama.

'Hope a tourist takes a photo,' he said.

'You'll be upstairs selling ads. No tourists there.'

'Your hat's outdated, boss.'

I glanced around. 'Don't call me boss.'

'You are the boss.'

'Hell, Billy, I've told you a thousand times. You're black and I'm white. That's why you can't call me boss. People will think I pinched you from the missions.'

Billy chuckled as he jogged up the stairs to a line of shops overlooking the marina. These southern traders provided our bread-and-butter income. They took the same twenty-square-centimetre ads every week, paying their bills without a quibble. And they liked Billy, the local who fitted in well with their pursuit of a *dolce vita*.

I edged past a line of tourists who were queuing to board the latest reef cat, the *Coral Wanderer*. Apart from a few who'd rather be in a bar, they sported cheerful hats and smelt of sunscreen and deodorant. Young couples held hands while the pensioners wore a face of great patience and low expectation. Abell Point Marina had three long arms stretching out from the marine office to the rock wall. Private craft were tied to two of the arms, while the third was for tour boats and the yachts with bowsprits twice the height of a man. From the top of the ramp, I watched the ketch slide into a berth and knew for certain it was the *Calvados*. The ship's owner-skipper, Jade Wilson, stood on the deck supervising his crew, who were handling lines fore and aft. Jade swore as a cruiser surged through the channel and washed his boat against the timber.

'Get that line on fast,' he called to the young woman who struggled at the bow. Then he saw me. 'Tom, come and help.'

'Look, there's a knack,' I said to her, looping one end of the line round a bollard. Each time the *Calvados* plunged forward we drew up the slack, then held tight as she pulled away.

'Quick, one more turn,' I said.

When the young woman lifted the rope, she slipped on the decking and fell across me. I caught her by the waist and pulled her upright before the *Calvados* jarred against the tyre protectors. Dropping a second hitch over the bollard, we steadied the yacht as it heaved and tossed like a spirited horse. Within seconds she began to settle.

'Thanks for that, it could've been nasty. I'm Lisa by the way.' I detected an English accent.

'You okay now, Lisa?'

'Yes, I'm fine. Bit shaken.' She smiled. 'But that's life on the ocean.'

I thrust out my hand. 'My name's Tom.'

She took my hand in a firm grasp. 'Hi Tom. I don't normally meet strangers like this.'

'I'm not a stranger. I'm local,' I said, pointing to the *Whitsunday Post* logo on my shirt.

Jade had finished securing the wheel and came to the rail. 'Tom O'Connor. Never expected to see you again.'

'Then you should find another marina.'

He leant over the rail and we shook hands. 'I see you're wearing the same old hat. Newspaper gone broke?'

'I like the hat, Jade. And what's that round your neck? A gold anchor chain?'

Jade laughed comfortably. He was a tall, sun-tanned Sydneysider with bleached hair and a mouth of strong white teeth. His big hands were confident as they rested on the polished teak rail, and he looked the part with his all-girl crews and easy swagger. Airlie gossip said he never bought a drink or slept alone, but I've known the ugly side of him, caught his reflection when people have seen him for what he is, when a girl has refused to fall into his bed or a man buy a drink because Jade was not his best friend.

Which I had discovered the previous year when I

committed an error, and grudgingly owned up to it. We had run out of news for the paper and Billy arrived at the idea of giving wings to a persistent rumour about drug trafficking. As a result, page three led with words to the effect: *A southern-based tourist vessel visits Shute Harbour each year to liaise with drug couriers.*

To our dismay, the *Calvados* was the only southern vessel anchored in Shute Harbour on the morning of publication. That afternoon, Jade marched into my office demanding compensation and an apology. He received the apology but I stood by our article that a trusted source had released the information; the trusted source being local farmers and their wives. By the end of the season, he had thawed at the edges and I was less offhand about printing rumours.

'You're back early, Jade. How come?'

'I heard this is the best season in years. So, I said, *bugger old habits*. I raised the sails and came straight through. No stops.'

I glanced at Lisa. No wonder she had slipped on the marina. Exhausted from all that sailing, not to mention wobbly sea legs. She guessed what I was thinking and shrugged. She was a handsome woman if you overlooked the blemishes: the scar on the forehead, the hair cropped unfashionably short and the tiny creases from too much sun. But her smile was warm and her eyes friendly.

Jade nodded to her. 'There's a hose connected to that reel. Start washing down the back deck. Avril can help when she's tied off the lines. And tell Ingrid and Freja to get busy with the sails. Nobody will be eating in the galley tonight.'

'See you, Tom,' Lisa said.

'Magnums bar at seven. They'll put a table aside for the *Calvados*. Always do.'

'Okay, but I need to find digs first.'

'After you've finished here,' Jade said. 'Not before.'

'Right, Cap'n!' she answered, unrolling the hose.

I climbed over the rail and ducked into the saloon where Jade had opened a bottle of Jamaican rum. Selecting two glasses from a timber cabinet, he mixed the rum with soda and ice.

'Make it a small one,' I said. 'The day's still young and I have work to do.'

'Yeah, tough life.' He threw down the drink and poured a second.

'You cost me with that drugs story, Tom.'

'I've apologised and this is a new season. Let's move on.'

After a pause he clinked my glass. 'Okay, what's happened in the last five months?'

'Nothing much. A couple of cyclones, work has started on the airport extensions, and the mayor's on a study jaunt to Darwin. Left his missus at home and took the secretary.'

'Be damned. I didn't know Abdul had it in him.'

'Seems otherwise.'

'She must be a rocket.'

'Not what I've seen.'

Mayor Abdul Nader wasn't a fool in most things. He had worked on his father's Lebanese farm since walking age, and would be still there except a neighbour said he was a gifted speaker. Abdul rolled the word *gifted* about in his mouth until election time then ran for Proserpine Shire Council, winning the seat from an ex-hippie. But if he had a gift for language, he kept it hidden. Meanwhile, his wife never attended official functions. She was a dumpy, shy woman who refused to leave the farm despite the more glamorous life on offer. As the months passed, Abdul took his secretary to Council events and — discreetly at first — select functions that were out of town. She was unmarried, half his age and attractive in a prim, horsey way. Rumour flourished about their sleeping arrangements, but Abdul appeared not to care.

Now back on deck, glass in hand, Jade was in a mood for talking. Too many days at sea.

'I don't know if I'll do another season, Tom. Even without your crap the years are getting harder. The boat is old and the crew too smart for their own good.'

'And whose fault is that? All girls, and never the same one twice.'

Jade's ketch had worked the Whitsunday tourist scene for more than fifteen years. It began life as the *Torres Mail*, servicing the archipelagos that spread eastward from New Guinea to the Solomons. When the Pacific War ended in 1946, a steam ship took over the route and the *Torres Mail* was sold to a Canadian who refitted it as a private yacht for the Mediterranean summer. The Canadian lost his fortune on the share market, and the yacht drifted to Sydney where it passed through several hands, none of whom spent a dollar on upkeep. When Jade bought the yacht in the seventies, he renamed it the *Calvados*. He knocked out three cabins, turning them into bunks for twelve passengers. Another cabin was fitted out for his crew, and he kept a master cabin for himself. Jade was a so-called 'character' of the

Whitsundays. His yacht was well known and rival skippers mimicked his dress: baggy white shorts and bare feet, a Hawaiian shirt, a bleached sailor's cap and a gold chain round the neck. He played to the image, as did his female crews in their smart, blue-and-white outfits. Other skippers tried the all-girl look but the experiment rarely lasted; no thanks to a mistrustful wife. However, according to Jade, the system worked because with foreign young women there was no need for promises. After one season they returned to university, the boyfriend or the home country, and they rarely expected more. Around Easter each year, with his ship ready to sail, he would pin a notice on the wall of a Sydney backpackers' hostel seeking a female crew for the winter season in the tropics. He had no shortage of replies and usually selected British or European women. *Do you get seasick?* No. *Can you cook?* Yes. *Do you enjoy hard work and long hours?* Yes. *Do you have ties in Australia?* No. Then, provided they were reasonably attractive, he hired them. First day on board he handed out uniforms, sat them down and laid out the law. This was not a holiday cruise — it was a working boat and they were the sailors. He added that a sail change could happen in the middle of the night or in a blowing gale. Any sign of unwillingness and they would be dumped at the next port. When they were not on watch, they could do as they pleased although one place was out of bounds, the master's cabin. The crew were not permitted in there, *ever*. Finally, and contrary to local gossip, Jade never slept with his crew. After a couple of days when the new crew discovered his law was as fixed as his routine, they relaxed, even peeling off their tops to sunbake on the forward deck.

He was an unforgiving teacher, and expected they would be competent sailors by the time his first passengers walked aboard at Abell Point Marina.

This was back in the days when I admired him, myself barely twenty-one, the age I started the paper, and him old enough to be my father. I was fascinated by his self-control, the pressure of being alone at sea with four attractive women.

'Common sense, Tom. Nothing else. There's only four crew aboard. If one of them is in my bed when a squall hits, I'm no longer boss to the other three. Besides that, Airlie is a honeypot worth the denial.'

CHAPTER 2

had often thought about Jade's description of Airlie Beach: a honeypot. I knew he meant available young women, but the phrase had deeper significance. Jade wasn't a local as I was. My great-grandfather had grown sugar in Proserpine a hundred years ago, and the land he acquired over the decades was still in the hands of my family. Because I was raised in this environment of stunning beauty, I never regarded it with awe. In the wet season we grew our cane that was then cut and milled in the dry season. In the wet, with the monsoonal rains driving in from the north and farms under sheets of water, we took our holidays, mostly fishing and crabbing along the creeks that fed the Proserpine River. Sometimes, when the wind swung round to a south-easterly, we took our boats to Airlie Beach and fished in the lee of the Conway Range. But we never looked back and saw Airlie as the developers did. We never viewed the green of the rainforests or the blue of the ocean, and beheld a millionaire's paradise. Grandpa said it was because we hadn't lived in other places, but deep inside we knew both faces of tropical Queensland; the magical, sparkling winters and the cruel, dangerous summers that could destroy a person. Indeed, the awesome mystique of the Whitsundays was our honeypot, not the abundance of exotic flesh.

After school I left the farming to my older brother Patrick, and found a job with the *Mackay Mercury*, one-and-a-half hours to the south. I started as copy boy, and within two years I was a journalist in the small, exciting world of a daily newspaper. One morning, the general manager called me into his office, and asked if I would like to travel.

'Yes, sir. Travel appeals to me. Always has.'

'If you could choose, where would you go?'

'Never really thought of it, sir. Maybe Hawaii or London.'

'How about Hervey Bay?'

I assumed he was making a corny joke, and laughed.

'You know Hervey Bay, O'Connor?'

'Vaguely, sir. That's all.'

'The town is three hours north of Brisbane. Pretty spot by all accounts.'

I stared at him, waiting. Was this a test of my geography? What came next? Goondiwindi?

'The company has bought a free weekly in Hervey Bay, *The Observer*. They want a young manager. We thought you should go there and cut your teeth.'

'Me?'

'Why not? You're keen.'

'Yes, sir, but I like the *Mercury*.'

'You need the experience. The job is yours if you want it. Start Monday week. We need an answer tonight.'

I didn't leave the GM's office in a state of excitement. What the devil was at Hervey Bay? Besides, I had a life in Mackay. I played in a rugby team and had started making headway with a girl in accounts.

I decided to talk it over with my chief sub, an elderly

man who not only treated young journalists with respect but encouraged the use of his first name.

I approached his desk. 'Dave, can I have a word?'

He paused with the blue pencil mid-word over someone's copy. 'Yeah, Tom. Go ahead.'

'Not here. It's personal.'

'A girl in trouble?'

'No, nothing like that.'

'All right. Out the back.'

He dropped his pencil and visor on the desk and led the way to a loading dock at the rear. Settling himself on a crate, he pulled out a Chesterfield and said, 'Okay, Tom, what's the drama?'

'The GM wants me to manage a weekly in a place called Hervey Bay. I have to give him an answer by tonight.'

'So?'

'Honestly, I don't know. I like Mackay.' I told him about my footy and the girl I was close to inviting out.

He sucked on the Chesterfield through brown fingers. 'Well, Tom, you don't need my advice. You only wanted to talk about it. See if I'd laugh or cry. You know what you have to do.'

'Say yes?' I groaned.

'Of course. There'll be more football and girls in Hervey Bay, and in the office you can play at being a tyrant. If the powers didn't see a future in you, they wouldn't have asked.'

'You serious?'

'What did you think? They wanted to piss you off because you're a nuisance?' He tossed the spent cigarette into the lane. 'Enough time wasted, and we need those mill figures by two.'

*   *   *

I was dragged back to the present by the sound of the Moke's horn, on which I suspected Billy was resting his elbow.

'Will you be at Magnums tonight, Jade?'

'Of course. Same table, same people.'

I walked through the bustle of the marina to where Billy leant against the car, chatting to two young women who had their homes on their backs. As I approached, they smiled politely.

'Please, mate,' the taller one said to me in a foreign accent, 'can you take us to Airlie Backpackers?'

'Just wait here, miss. A bus will be along in ten minutes.'

'Crikey, Tom. How can they fit into Jack's little bus with those packs?'

'They should have thought of that before leaving Munich.'

'You know München?' the woman asked.

'Course he does,' said Billy. 'He'll tell you about it on the way.'

'Billy, I have work to do.'

'And I have a meeting at Todd's Real Estate. You could save everyone a fare.'

'Jack's is a courtesy bus,' I reminded him. 'Okay. Climb aboard.'

'Sank you, mate,' the woman said, and the pair jumped into the rear of the Moke with their great packs.

At the entrance to Airlie Backpackers, Billy helped them onto the pavement, brushing aside their gratitude with a huge smile. They were tall and bosomy, good health bursting from their pores, but clever and guarded with it.

'Going for a drink tonight?' Billy asked.

'Ve vill see,' the spokeswoman replied, thrusting her arms through the pack's straps.

'That's the last you'll see of them,' I said to Billy when we pulled out from the kerb.

'Couldn't disagree more, Tom. The one doing the talking is Matilda, and the one who secretly likes me is Teresa.'

'Teresa? That's a fake name.'

'Says a man of the world.'

*   *   *

I dropped Billy outside Todd's Real Estate, knowing I was unlikely to see him again before morning; however, by then he would have collected his ad copy and a news photo or two. Billy was great value and a close friend. As a kid he lived with his family in a neat home near the mouth of Saltwater Creek. His father had worked on our farm with Dad and Grandpa, and had taken his holidays on half pay during the long wet. Unlike other kids around that area, Billy never missed school. He and I sat together on the bus that took us into St Catherine's Primary and then the State High School where we studied together until Year Ten, at which time he found a job at the electricity board and I continued on to Year Twelve.

Although Billy and I were friends, we had history that went deep into Queensland's unsavoury past. He came from the Juipera tribe that had been hunted from their lands round Mount Mandarana in the 1860s. He claimed through his father that one of his forebears, Kowaha, had actually leapt, or been chased, to her death off the mountain. Somehow her daughter survived. It was Kowaha's statue that now stood outside the Leap Hotel, north of Mackay. According to hearsay, my great-great-grandfather Paul was involved in the hunting party. When his brother, the magistrate Michael O'Connor, shielded him from prosecution over the woman's death, a new phrase entered the family lexicon — the O'Connor Protocol — which simply meant brothers were expected to cover for each other.

When I raised the incident with Grandpa one night, he replied obliquely, 'Pop was a good man.'

'How could he be a good man if he hunted Blacks over a cliff?'

'Some of the men did, but not Pop. He wasn't like that.'

'Drew back at the last-minute sort of thing?'

'No, Tom, he wasn't near that tragedy.'

I plodded on. 'If Pop was blameless, why did he leave the district?'

'Because his farm had poor soil. This land you're standing on is alluvial. You think he made a mistake?'

Mum had sharp ears. She called from the kitchen. 'Enough now, Tom. Go off and do your homework.'

Another time, while helping my brother Patrick strip cane for planting, I asked, 'Do you believe in the O'Connor Protocol?'

He straightened from his work. 'Yep. Don't you?'

'I mean about Pop's narrow escape from jail.'

'Who said he did anything wrong? It's all rumour. Anyway, there's a second account that makes good reading. It relates to two of Grandpa's uncles who enlisted for the Great War.

They were twins who got up to serious pranks, even black-market stuff, then lied for each other. As a result, no charges were laid because you can't hang two men for the same crime. One of their senior officers called it the O'Connor Protocol.'

'So, nothing to do with The Leap?'

'I fancy both stories, don't you?'

Later, as we were washing up, I said, 'What was the Steele family's role in the saga?'

'The details are vague, but good friends Blake Steele and Paul O'Connor went along for the ride. What they did exactly I wouldn't know, but after the woman's death, Blake Steele ended up in jail while Paul was found to be innocent. You ought to investigate it, Tom. Two families were implicated in the crime, but only one emerged smelling of roses.'

*   *   *

Back at the office, a mountain of faxes and press releases covered my desk. All staff apart from Heather had left for the day. I glanced at the work in Pixie's tray and saw she had left a sport story for next morning. She had also left my cold coffee on her desk. 'Ungrateful girl,' I muttered, taking the cup out the back where I washed it.

'You ought to be careful how you treat her,' Heather said.

'Are you talking about the coffee?'

'She's at a sensitive age. Doesn't appreciate your cavalier attitude.'

'My what?'

'You heard. You think that as long as she completes her work on time, everything is okay. Well, it isn't. She's not a machine, and she's not invisible. She was almost in tears tonight. Cavalier attitude. Do you know what that means?'

'I'll look it up.'

'Or have coffee thrown in your face.'

I sighed. 'I shouldn't have given in to her father. She won't hang around. Far too bright for this place.'

'Tom, do yourself a favour. Look in the mirror.'

CHAPTER 3

Heather's lesson over, I chased her out the door so I could lock the office and make my way upstairs. This was the time of day I enjoyed most. Everything quiet, the sun more red than gold, and the distant sound of lanyards slapping against masts. I had run the *Hervey Bay Observer* successfully for two years when I heard the *Mercury* was starting a new paper on the Northern Beaches. I applied for the job, but was outgunned by a man who was older, smarter and more ambitious. As my time in Hervey Bay was drawing to a close, I took a fortnight's leave and drove to Airlie Beach, which was now buzzing under its new name The Whitsundays: the circle of reefs, mountains and rivers bordering the Whitsunday Passage that Cook had named in 1770. Mum and Dad owned a small shopfront on Shingley Beach just over the hill from Airlie. Years earlier, when cane prices were ordinary and real estate even worse, Mum said she would like to run a fish and chip shop. They bought the premises for a song, and leased it out to an Asian couple who turned it into a convenience store. When the Asians baulked at renewing the lease, and I had just resigned from corporate newspapers, I moved in and started my own paper using the money I had saved.

Heather was my first employee, followed soon after by

Billy. With Billy it hadn't been easy to start. He was keen enough, but two of the original traders — who'd been in Airlie since it was a fishing village — felt that dealing with a Black salesman was somehow beneath them. Which angered me. Not that I lectured them on racism or equality. I spoke to them about the valuable service we provided, and I finished with the line, 'Billy will be here tomorrow to see you, and again next week and the week after that. Nobody else. Just Billy.' I didn't expect the leopards to change their spots, however, I wouldn't deal with anyone who treated Billy as less than an equal. We lost both traders but, like Heather said, 'Good riddance.'

Meanwhile the fresh arrivals loved him, as did the real-estate crowd who valued everything against the colour of money.

'Billy is your new face at the *Post*,' I said to Todd Steele one morning, following introductions.

'Reliability and accuracy, Billy. That's all I ask,' Todd replied.

'He's reliable and accurate, but he can't do much with late copy.'

'You don't give up on late copy, Tom. They teach that mantra at paper school? Sorry, Billy, I didn't catch your surname.'

'Thompson.'

Todd frowned. 'Billy Thompson? Should I know you?'

'I don't think so,' Billy said genially. 'I come from Saltwater where there's no prime real estate. Only crappy old houses and prickle farms.'

'No such thing as crappy real estate,' Todd said.

I wasn't convinced Billy was as laid back as he appeared. Before driving across to see Todd, I had asked if he had any concerns.

'Concerns? What do you mean, Tom?'

'I've learnt part of the story of The Leap — your family, my family, Todd's family. And your family drew the short straw.'

'Let's have a coffee, Tom.'

We pulled into one of the coffee nooks that faced the beach. A haughty foreign girl came to take our order. No smile or hello, just a pencil hovering over the pad. I tapped the cappuccinos on the menu, held up two fingers and pointed to my mouth.

She stared at me. 'You vant two menus to eat?'

'Oh, you do speak. Sorry. Two cappuccinos, please.'

She wrote it down. 'Sree dollars eighty.'

After paying for the coffee, I said, 'Billy, if you prefer not to deal with Todd, I'm okay with that.'

Billy laced his fingers together and cracked his knuckles. It meant I should listen. 'Tom, most of the folk in Airlie are new, which is a refreshing change. You know, no prejudices. But for you and Todd it's different. I've pushed The Leap behind me but your families haven't, or won't. They say Blacks can't move on, but the real problem is with Whites who cling to the past. Yes, I know Todd Steele — everyone does — though I've never met him, and he probably doesn't know I exist.' He sipped his coffee. 'That's all.'

I waited for more.

'There is another point, I suppose. You and Todd are a match. Looking back at your first paper, his was the only real estate. He took a quarter page, then a half page and finally the back page.'

'He got them cheap.'

'Maybe,' he said, stirring sugar into his coffee, 'but I don't have a problem with Todd Steele.'

It was a fair comment that Todd and I had a symbiotic relationship. Even so, I had never let on about The Leap or its effect on our families. I know he and Grandpa had niggles in the early days, but that was when they both hungered after the best land. Grandpa wanted to farm it and Todd wanted it for real estate. As the years passed Grandpa felt increasingly threatened by the appetite for new estates. Anything with a view was cut into quarter-hectare blocks or squared off for apartments, and our current farmhouse had one of the best views in the Whitsundays. One hundred years ago the original house was built on a rise near the river, which was the district's only highway. However, Mum said she didn't want to stare at mangroves all her life, and a new house was built at the foot of the Conway Range, overlooking the farm, the river and distant mountains. The original house stood empty but it was kept painted, and the gardens and lawns cared for. Grandpa was proud of that house. He called it Pop's Place, and had us down every Saturday doing maintenance. Since most of the original furniture was still inside, Pop's Place at Christmas reverted from being a museum to accommodation for visiting family. Undoubtedly, Todd would have loved to get his hands on the two houses. Their real estate value was priceless.

*   *   *

My two-bedroom flat above the office was neither modern nor roomy, but it was comfortable. I poured myself a beer and strolled onto the balcony. In the distance, tiered catamarans were returning from the outer reef, and at the marina buses queued to take passengers back to their resorts. Closer to hand, two girls collected shells from the water's edge. They shared a joke and their laughter could be heard above the screeling of gulls. I was lucky to have bought this place from my parents when I did. In those days, Shingley had been the poor cousin to Airlie Beach, but as the years passed and the two villages melded into one, Shingley's land value had risen prohibitively.

After downing the beer, I changed into jeans and followed the path towards town, stopping to admire the *Calvados* at its berth. Although wider in the beam than a traditional ketch, it reeked class like an old dowager who's never lost her allure. From the marina I strolled past Captain Morgan's Bar, then along the boardwalk to the village centre and Magnums. Tables labelled for each boat were already full, and the big torches along the front cast a glow over the wooden building. I elbowed through the crowd to the *Calvados* table where Jade and his crew sat over a jug of beer. Jade saw me and beckoned.

'Hey, guys,' he yelled. 'Meet Tom O'Connor, the town's media baron.'

Then he introduced his crew. 'This is Ingrid and Freja and Avril, and you've already met Lisa.'

The girls certainly looked different. Out of their stale polo shirts and into festive dresses, their hair washed and gleaming, and the first signs of booze brightening their smiles.

'Hi, Tom!' Lisa shouted, and twinkled her fingers at me.

'Hi Lisa. How are the legs tonight?'

'You don't waste time.'

'I meant your sea legs.'

She smiled. 'They're great.' She pushed one of the girls to the end of the bench. 'Here, sit beside me. I owe you a drink.'

I held up a hand. 'No, old native custom. What do you want?'

'Gin and tonic, if that's all right.'

Five minutes later I reappeared with a jug of gin and tonic and two glasses.

Her eyes widened. 'Is that to get me drunk?'

'Sorry, you'll have to speak up.'

After sharing a pizza with the table, I steered Lisa outside where the evening was cooler, and her forehead scar less obvious.

'Did you find any digs?' I asked.

'Yes, the four of us have taken a house. Ten-minute walk to the boat, not far from the village. And where do you live?'

I told her about my flat above the shop.

'That must be handy,' she said.

'Yes, for lots of things.'

After a time, I gathered Lisa was from Devon and had been in the country three years. Supposedly she came out to marry an Australian she had met in London, but the romance ended a year later when she returned home to visit family. It had hurt at first, but she soon recovered. Now she was free and followed the sun.

'What do you mean free? No house, no boyfriends?'

'That's right. And that's how I mean to keep it. I'll stay

in Airlie one season then move on, probably back to Sydney and over to New Zealand. After one disastrous affair, I'm not rushing into another.'

'I'm in no hurry either,' I said. 'I've had bad experiences too.'

'Like what?'

'Long story. Could take all night.'

'I bet,' she said, picking up her glass. 'Let's join the others.'

I followed her into the main bar where a swarm of boys crowded the *Calvados* table, happily plying the girls — and Jade — with whatever drinks they chose. Out of the dimness of the bar I saw Billy coming towards me.

He tipped his cap to Lisa. 'Good evening, miss. Do you mind if I have a word with the boss?'

She thought he meant Jade. 'Go ahead.'

But he turned to me. 'Outside, boss. Won't keep you a minute.'

I touched her shoulder and smiled. 'Sorry, Lisa. Work.'

As I stepped through the exit, I swore. 'Billy, this had better be good.'

He grinned. 'She ain't your type, Thomas. And she needs to hide that scar.'

'Okay, let's hear it.'

'Pixie ran into an old school friend this afternoon. She's given us a lead story.'

I stared at him. 'Can't it wait until morning?'

'This one's hot off the wire.'

We found an empty bench against the wall.

'What do you know of the Giya tribe?' he asked.

'More than most people. Why?'

'Pixie's friend works at the courthouse. She told Pixie that the Giya have registered a site of cultural significance.'

'Registered a what?'

'Site of cultural significance. In other words, sacred. Probably on Crown land.'

'That'd be a first for Proserpine. Is it genuine?'

'I guess so. A race can't live thousands of years in one place and not have sacred sites.'

I studied Billy, who seemed unconcerned by the news. 'How does this affect you, Billy? Why don't you write the story? Add a Black perspective.'

He shuddered. 'They'd say I was making it up. Give the job to Pixie.'

'Pixie? She's a copy setter.'

'She could do the research — track down the locality … which Giya signed the papers, all that stuff. And give her a byline. She'd love it.'

Billy climbed to his feet. 'Come, let's find that chick from the *Calvados*. What was her name? Geisa?'

'Lisa.'

When we returned to the bar, Jade had departed and Lisa was at a table near the window, talking to a group of older men who had the tough, hard look of professional divers.

Billy and I edged into a gap. 'Hi Lisa,' I said. 'I'd like you to meet Billy. He's my deputy chief of staff.'

They shook hands. She smiled. 'Nice to meet you, Billy. No more secret men's business?'

'You'll have to read the paper.'

She yawned. 'It's been a big week. Time for an early night.'

'I can walk you home,' I said.

'I'm fine thanks, Tom.' She nodded towards the girls from her crew. 'We agreed to go home together. Thanks for looking after me.'

I kissed the cheek she offered. 'Night, Lisa. See you around.'

As Billy and I exited via the front door, he laughed, 'Walk her home? She saw that one coming.'

CHAPTER 4

Next morning, I wandered in around eight. Since the office didn't open until eight-thirty, I was surprised Heather and Pixie were already at work. Heather was sorting through cards for the monthly invoices, and Pixie was typing up her sport story.

'Good to see two dedicated staff,' I said cheerfully.

'Morning, Tom,' Heather said, and nodded in Pixie's direction.

Dragging up a chair, I sat in front of Pixie's desk. 'Like a fresh coffee if I got you one?' I asked.

'No thanks. I've tasted your coffee.'

I picked up the receiver on her desk and dialled the Koffee Kings. 'That you, Dave. Tom here. Two cappuccinos and a long black, please. Pronto.'

Five minutes later the coffees arrived. I put one near Pixie's hand and sat again in front of her.

'Is there something you want to tell me?' I asked.

'Thanks for the coffee. It's very kind of you.'

'Anything else?'

She paused with her fingers above the keyboard, and for the first time that morning looked up. She had pretty eyes that couldn't lie if they tried. They were miserable.

'I'm okay,' she said.

'You're not. Bring your coffee into my office.'

Leaving her keyboard, she followed me. I was about to sit behind the desk, but thought better of it and cleared papers off the two visitors' chairs in the room. We sat facing the panoramic photo, which gave us space to marshal our thoughts. The framed glass also mirrored the image of an attractive, intelligent girl who dressed unpretentiously, wore a small chain and cross at the throat, and affected a simple, girl-next-door hairstyle. In retrospect, I had dropped her into a box with square corners and a fixed lid. Heather's advice came to mind.

'I'm sure you have potential, Pixie, but I don't know what it is.'

'I want to do more than set copy all day.'

'You have to start at the beginning.'

'I've done little else for six months.'

'Okay, we'll try with basic subbing.'

'I would like that, but … please, why can't you be nice to me?'

I could feel the eyes. Nothing like a direct question. I faced her. 'What do you really want, Pixie? When your father came to see me, you'd just finished high school. And at our interview you said you had matriculated. I assumed that inside six months you'd be gone.'

'Dad shouldn't have spoken to you.'

'He did what he thought best. You would earn money before uni starts.'

'I don't want to go to uni. I want to stay in Airlie.'

'Doing what?'

'Here, at the *Post*. You could teach me to be a journalist

and do page layouts.'

'And who'll set the copy?'

'Me. It's not difficult.' She leant forward, holding her coffee in both hands. 'Please, Tom.'

'Okay,' I said. 'We'll give it a try. But a word of caution, not all days will be fun.'

'Thank you. I won't let you down.'

At once she was nervous. Draining her cup, she set it on the floor under her chair.

'There is a story I could help with,' she said.

'Nothing to do with sites of cultural significance?'

'How did you know?'

'Billy told me last night, so I've had this idea. You, Pixie, track down the Giya applicants and where this site is. That sort of thing.'

She smiled. 'Yes, boss.'

There was a briskness in her stride as she returned to her desk and picked up the phone. In no time Heather walked past my office and said, 'You could've done that weeks ago.'

*   *   *

As I shuffled through the copy on my desk, I found the Aboriginal story we had planned for next week's page three. The story was about a heritage centre under construction in Airlie's main street. I glanced at the five paragraphs:

STEPS will be taken this week to preserve Aboriginal culture in the Whitsundays when the first sod is turned on a heritage centre in Airlie Beach. Chamber of Commerce president, Steve Redmond, said the State Government, Shire Council and Chamber had provided backing for the project.

'Aboriginal tribes lived in this region long before we arrived,' Mr Redmond said.

'As a community we have a duty to safeguard their culture.'

The official launch will take place this Friday at two o'clock, opposite the ANZ Bank in the main street.

Steve Redmond had thrown the press folder on my desk, but in his haste had misspelt the names of local donors, of which my paper was one. He called it the *Poste* with an 'e'. Annoying, but not a surprise. Steve was chasing pre-selection at next year's state ballot, and was yet to learn that enemies can propagate quicker than friends. Adding to the insult, our name was in small print at the bottom of the page, unlike Todd Steele Real Estate in bold capitals at the top. Since its inception, the *Post* had actively supported Aboriginal heritage while tight-fisted Todd Steele, to my knowledge, had never backed an honest cause. Yet with one flourish of the cheque book his name was in bold. Time to pay the philanthropist a visit.

Shop doors were opening when I drove into the village, avoiding traffic that jostled to enter what Council blithely called a public car park. I zipped into the rear of Todd's office and parked behind his white Mercedes with the number plate — *AIRLIE 01*. Climbing the narrow stairs, I passed through offices where clerks and sales reps were already at work. Todd was seated on the corner of his desk, riffling through a pile of photos. Some he threw in the bin, others he passed to a young woman who sat at the desk writing numbers on the back.

He glanced up at me. 'What can I do for you, Tom?'

Todd Steele was a gaunt, well-dressed man with red hair that had turned to grey at the temples. His skin was blotched from years under a tropical sun, and the backs of his hands were like hairless crabs in white crumpled suits. Todd and my grandfather were the same age, which I knew was over eighty, but while Grandpa Henry spent his days on the farm verandah, Todd was still one of the who's-who of the Airlie business set.

'I'm about to run a story on this heritage centre, Todd. I was studying the guest list for the launch: a cabinet minister, the mayor, a dozen bigwigs, yourself and "the press". Do you see anything odd in that?'

'You've been relegated?'

'No. Where are the Blacks? Not one.'

He reached into his in-tray and lifted out a sheet of embossed paper. 'It says here: "The State Government, Shire Council and Giya people kindly request your attendance at the official launch of the Whitsunday Heritage Centre". There's your Blacks. Maybe one of the Giya, maybe the whole tribe. That's for them to sort out.'

The young woman who had been numbering photos picked up the stack and slid them into an envelope. As she was about to depart, Todd handed her his empty cup. 'You want a coffee, Tom?' he asked.

'No thanks.'

After she had left, he said, 'So what's the issue with this heritage centre? You sore about the personal invitation?'

'No. I'm surprised at your generosity. You've not mentioned the Giya before, ever.'

'You keeping a file on me?'

'Don't be daft. And while on the subject of the Giya, did you know a site of cultural significance has been registered?'

'A what?'

I spoke slowly. 'A site of cultural significance. Which means, it's sacred.'

He shook his head. 'Whose land is it on?'

'No idea, but more sites could be identified. Are you ready for that?'

'I wouldn't know. If a city boy spots a rock on my land and reckons it's sacred, I'll take him to court. I respect Black people, Tom, and do what I can to help, but claims for cultural stuff have to be genuine. You can print that if you like.'

The young woman returned with two coffees. 'Do you take milk and sugar, Tom?'

I hadn't wanted coffee, but said, 'Thank you ...' as I remembered her face, *Lola Brunetta*. 'Yes Lola, milk and two sugars, please.'

'My pleasure, Tom,' she said, and stirred in the sugar before facing the handle towards me.

'She never stirs my coffee,' Todd grunted when the door had closed behind her.

'You didn't do homework together after school.'

He lifted himself off the corner of his desk and walked around to his chair. 'So why the long face, Tom? You bothered by this sacred site?'

'Of course not. It should dovetail nicely with the heritage centre.'

We drank coffee while he explained the different colours on a wall map. Red land for development went all the way to Bowen, and much of it contained his signature. The man was a big shark in a wide ocean, and I wondered how the Giya administrators processed that reality. Enough to send him a gold invitation? I would.

CHAPTER 5

Back at the newspaper, Pixie was waiting for me. 'What have you discovered?' I asked her.

'Interesting things. Can we go into your office?'

I entered the office reluctantly. A couple of hours ago the space was sacrosanct and she was a miserable copy setter. Now she had a story that demanded the boss's private ear.

'What is it, Pixie?'

'I saw my friend at the courthouse and she gave me copies of the registration. This is the map. Take a look.'

I held the map up to the light. I could see where Conway Road turned off the main road, and I could see where Palm Creek met the Proserpine River. Three kilometres further downstream was a square marked *Cultural Significance*. My heart raced. That was my grandfather's land.

'How big is this site?' I asked.

'A quarter hectare.'

'Well, that's not unmanageable.'

'Look at this other map,' she said. 'It's a close-up.'

I took the map from her. In the centre of the square was another square with the words *Farmhouse — Unoccupied*. This can't be true. That was Pop's Place.

'Are these maps genuine?' I asked.

'I guess so. They came from the courthouse.'

'Am I the first to know about this?'

'Not any more. They were filed on the land owners this morning.'

I winced.

'Will I do the story?' she asked hesitantly.

'Um … not sure. Put together the facts, that's all.'

As she hurried out the door, I said, 'And Pixie, be discreet.'

This was crazy. Pop's Place registered as a sacred site? As kids we had climbed over rocks near the back door, but Grandpa said they were part of Nana's rock garden.

Jumping into the car, I called out to Heather, 'See you in two hours.' I drove past cane fields towards Proserpine, left into Conway Road, then over the tram line and along the track to my parents' house. At the cattle grid I passed a government sedan headed in the opposite direction.

Mum, Grandpa and my brother Patrick were in the kitchen when I arrived. Patrick had the papers in his hand and was reading them aloud. Mum had taken a seat, hand to her mouth, while Grandpa leant on the sink staring out the window.

'You heard about this, Tom?' Patrick asked as I burst through the door.

'Yes, just now.'

'Who's behind it?'

'I don't know.'

'What does cultural significance mean?'

'It means important to Aboriginal people — even sacred. Their culture. Their history.'

'And what determines a site?'

I couldn't answer. I had no idea. Questions poured

out of him.

Grandpa turned from the sink. 'Some dirty prick's behind this.'

'Maybe not, Grandpa. Blacks have lived here for millennia.'

'When I find him, I'll string him up by his nuts.'

'Hey!' I shouted, and thumped the table. 'Let's calm down. Mum, make a cup of tea. We have to think it through … get some advice. It's only a registration, remember.'

'Registration be damned,' Grandpa said. 'I knew this would happen.'

'What do you mean?'

'It goes back to The Leap. Has revenge written on every page.'

'We don't know that, Grandpa. The Giya might be filing a legitimate claim.'

I expected him to ask who the Giya were, but he didn't. The name was no surprise.

'Get on the phone to Marvin,' he said to Patrick. 'We'll give the lazy bastard some work.'

Patrick and I turned to Grandpa. 'Marvin? You mean Marvin Fumbleton?'

'Who else would I mean?'

I laughed. 'What would Marvin know about native registrations?'

'Then who do you suggest?'

'Not sure. Somebody from Brisbane who deals in these things. Marvin is a small-town lawyer. He wouldn't know a sacred site from a mozzie bite.'

'Don't be a smart arse, Tom. Get him on the phone. If he doesn't know, he can find out who does.'

Patrick put the call through to Marvin's office, obtained his secretary, and waited an age for the man himself. Patrick explained the documents we had received, then listened, saying 'yeah' a dozen times. Finally, he made an appointment for Friday and hung up.

I walked across the living room and looked down on the original farmhouse where it had stood for a hundred years. Apart from dominating a low rise, there was nothing unique about the house's position. To the right were a couple of sheds that had survived white ants and cyclones, to the left were cane fields, and to the rear was Nana's garden, the clothesline and a row of camellias.

'Why do you think they chose Pop's Place?' I asked.

'The rock garden,' Mum suggested.

'Rock garden, my arse,' Grandpa snorted. 'Half those rocks were turned up by the plough. Pop and I carted them there, one by one. How can that make them sacred?'

*　　*　　*

When I returned to the office, Billy was seated on a bench under the mango tree writing up notes. I brushed ants aside and sat next to him.

'Did you know the registration is on Grandpa's land, Billy?'

'Yes. Pixie told me.'

'What do you make of it?'

'Could be just a formality.'

'But the registration includes Pop's Place. Were it only the rock garden at the back, nobody would care. What do you know of the Giya?'

'The name is local, of course. I thought their lands were around Bowen, but you know me, Tom, I was raised as a white kid. Went to a white school from since I was little. In any case, Giya families could be living anywhere from Mackay to Townsville. There's an old Aboriginal couple in Proserpine called Harvey and Thelma Nicholson. He'd be genuine, and he'd know who these Giya are.'

We were about to leave when Lisa came through the door. She was dressed in the *Calvados* uniform of blue top and white skirt.

'Hi,' she said. 'Your lady on the front counter told me I'd find you here.'

'Visitors are supposed to wait in the chairs we bought for them.'

'Then you ought to buy decent furniture.'

I wiped down a stool and sat on it, making room for her next to Billy.

'More secret men's business?' she asked.

'No. Are you off to work?'

'I'm on a late lunch. Been walking the town selling berths for Sunday. That's when we start our cruises. The day has been fun, and better than scrubbing decks. So, what's up?'

I told her about the native registration.

'We don't have those things at home,' she said. 'Is it serious?'

'Serious enough.'

'I'm glad I'm not asked to judge. But that isn't why I am here. I finish work in two hours, and I wondered if we could hire one of those little catamarans for a sail round the bay.'

'I'd love to, Lisa, but midweek is always busy.'

'Come on. It will take your mind off things.'

I looked into those eyes, then out to the ocean.

'Sure. I'll see you at Mick's Cat Hire at three-thirty. And bring a change of clothes. Afterwards we can try one of Captain Morgan's antipastos.'

After she exited, I turned back to Billy. 'Okay, Billy, I'll track down these Nicholsons while you keep loading your barrow. Bricks, wasn't it?'

CHAPTER 6

When I arrived at the beach mid-afternoon, Lisa had already negotiated an hour's hire with salt-in-your-veins Mick who had run his catamarans for years. After folding her spare clothes into a pack, she joined me wearing a long-sleeved shirt over her bathers. She then helped push the cat into deep water, climbed to the front and said, 'Okay, Cap'n, show me the sights.'

The little cats were easy to handle with their main sail and jib. They liked to fly with the wind up their tail, but were stubborn as four-legged cats when asked to turn. Under the warm sun and a light breeze, we sailed across the front of Airlie, looking at the apartments swarming up the hill, and Mount Conway blue and majestic in the distance. Dozens of people walked the foreshore, and several more played in the water near the yacht club. Lisa asked lots of questions about Airlie, but she seemed more interested in what I knew of the yachts moored along the front.

'Where do they come from, Tom?'

'All over the world. Airlie would have to be one of the best anchorages in the north. If there's bad weather, yachts can take shelter at the marina. If it's really foul weather, like a cyclone, they can anchor in Shute Harbour. Jade always prefers the harbour.'

She had unbuttoned her shirt to reveal a light-coloured bikini. The sun's afternoon rays were soaking into her tanned skin. 'He knows every inlet, I believe,' she added.

'That's right. Been doing it for years. Takes guests cruising or diving, then mid-November sails back to Sydney.'

'Why November?'

'The cash dries up.'

The air was much cooler when we pulled the catamaran onto the sand beside Mick's tent, which he called a booking office. We changed from our beachwear, then strolled around Coral Cove to Captain Morgan's Bar and Restaurant. By the time we had found a table, the sun was glowing crimson across the bay. A cloud dumped showers out to sea, and the line of boats returning tourists from the reef had begun to tail off.

'It's beautiful here,' Lisa said.

'It's why all the beautiful people come.'

'Are you one?' she asked.

'I play my part,' I said modestly. 'But we can't all be beautiful. Some have to be characters.'

'What am I?'

'You need a wooden leg and an eye patch to be a character. You don't have the props.'

'Is that a compliment?'

Captain Morgan's wife came by and slid a plate of antipasto onto the table. 'I've been wanting to talk to you, Tom,' she said.

'Business or pleasure, Maggie?'

'Business. That invoice of yours is still wrong. We were shut four weeks in February, so no advertising. I told your woman a dozen times.'

'Heather doesn't make those mistakes.'

'She has now.'

'You saved any copies of the paper?'

'Yes, in that box near the wall. Some have bits torn out, but they're all there.'

When she returned to the kitchen, I excused myself and dug through the box until I found a February edition. Although worse for wear, the dining section was intact. Across the bottom was Captain Morgan's advertisement.

I took the paper back to the table, and when Maggie came by, I showed her the page.

'Heather didn't make any mistake. Your ad never stopped running. It's been in that spot twelve months.'

Maggie curled her lip. 'I told your Blackfella we were closed. He should've pulled the ad.'

'His name is Billy, and he followed your instructions.' I folded up the paper. 'And Maggie, you have just placed your last advertisement in the *Post*.'

'That's unfair,' she whined. 'I didn't want to pay a whole month for nothin'.'

At that minute Dan Morgan emerged wearing an apron like he was the executive chef out for a quick smoke. In many ways, Dan was the opposite to his wife. While she was sharp-faced and bitchy, he was everybody's friend. While she was involved with the accounts and ordering, he was out front shaking hands and remembering names. He was also good-looking in a, well, Captain Morgan kind of way with his bright eyes, dark beard and rumbling laugh.

Dan was halfway across the floor when Jade entered and threw an arm over his shoulder. The strong, friendly voices of the two characters (one a hearty sea captain, the other a cook-cum-pirate) carried to all parts of the bar, interrupting guests who had been instinctively drawn to the popular eatery.

Dan noticed me and waved. 'Hey, Tom, I saw you sailing that little cat. You should crew for Jade.'

'I'd need to grow tits first!' And we laughed.

When he caught the scowl on Maggie's face, Dan said, 'Haven't broken up the party, have I?'

'Of course not.' I handed the paper back to Maggie. 'I'm a reasonable man. Apologise to Billy in my office, pay fifty percent of the February debt, and you'll keep your space.'

'All right … but it's not fair.'

Remembering my manners, I turned to Lisa. 'Lisa, meet Dan and Maggie Morgan. They own everything here but the view.'

'Lisa, eh?' Dan said. 'You must be Tom's latest.'

I rolled my eyes. 'Time for a new line, Dan.'

Everybody stood about awkwardly, then Dan said, 'Come on, Jade. We have business to attend to.'

When they left, Lisa and I returned to the antipasto that had lost its zest.

'I suppose work never ends,' she said.

'With Maggie it doesn't. She hasn't stopped complaining since they arrived here. But Dan's okay. He likes people to be happy and eat his food. And it helps having Jade as your buddy. Jade has a studio behind the kitchen where he camps. Though you have to wonder why. He sleeps rough and can't afford a drink, but he isn't short of funds.'

Lisa had her chin on her hand watching me. The sun's

rays had exaggerated the scar on her forehead. Billy was right; one day she'd need to get it fixed.

'How do you know Jade is wealthy?' she asked.

'A couple of rentals in Airlie. Some kind of business in Sydney.'

'Is that all?'

'Wouldn't think so. Money makes money.'

She drained her glass and handed it to me. 'Have we time for a second?'

'Yes, then we find a meal.'

'Do you have food at the flat?'

'Bits and pieces,' I said.

'If you open the wine, I'll cook dinner. Suit you, Cap'n?'

Taking her hand, I stood her up. 'Here's the arrangement. You organise a meal while I work on the paper.'

I walked her back to the *Post*, showed her into the kitchen upstairs, then started laying up pages for that week's edition. Still no front-page story, and nothing on my desk from Pixie. An hour later I heard the shower run, then Lisa's voice calling me to dinner. The sounds were very homey.

She had set the balcony table with plates and cutlery, and stood a bottle of wine on a tray with two glasses. Coconut palms and the Coral Sea whispered in the background. It was like a promo for a holiday resort.

I turned back to the kitchen, and blinked. She was wearing my old *Mercury* tee-shirt that barely reached her thighs.

'I don't have fresh clothes with me, and as the night's so balmy I thought you wouldn't mind.'

'Um … no, of course not.'

'Pasta for dinner,' she said. 'Shower first.'

I had forgotten I was still gritty from the hour on the water. 'Good thinking.'

I walked through to the bedroom and found the bed neatly made and my washing picked up. *What's going on?*

'Hey!' I shouted. 'I can't find anything.'

'Like what?'

'The clothes I left on the bed.'

'You shower. There'll be something clean under the mess.'

I tugged off my shorts and stepped under the water. This was all kind of fast. And tomorrow was production day; out of bed before daylight and no respite until the last page at five.

When I emerged from the shower, she was in the bedroom holding up a pair of shorts. She tossed them to me. 'Dinner's hot and on the table. Bring the baby lighthouse with you.'

It wasn't quite the calm, laid-back meal I had expected. I think the pasta was nice but I don't recall tasting it. Lisa ate slowly like she was at an expensive restaurant, chatting between each mouthful, seemingly unaware that her outline could be seen through the cotton. She talked about life in England, and how as a little girl she used to visit her aunt who lived on a ravine … or was it a river?

'Hurry up and eat,' I said.

'Don't you like the view?'

'It's killing me.'

'No, I mean out there. Look the moon's coming up. Can we turn off the light?'

Not waiting for a reply, she walked across to the wall and doused the light. A pale glow fell across the balcony. Lisa faced me and removed the tee-shirt. She was utterly nude — all brown skin apart from the white triangle of her bikini bottom, and inside that triangle a softer, darker one.

'You like beaver?' she asked.

'One guess.'

Later while lying in bed, I reflected that this is tropical paradise as it ought to be, not newspaper deadlines and bad debts. After a time, I rose, dressed, and returned to my work. Around five I heard footsteps on the stairwell. She was there wrapped in one of the sheets. Padding across to my desk, she pressed her face against my back.

'That was wonderful.'

'Yes, easily four stars.'

'Tommy want more practice?' She stroked my hair. 'Come to bed. We'll soon have to be up.'

Shutting down the computer, I followed her to the bedroom. She dropped the sheet on the floor and said, 'My turn.'

After another round of shock and awe I fell asleep, but the last thing rolling through my head was the meeting we had booked with Marvin Fumbleton for Friday morning.

CHAPTER 7

When I stirred at daylight, Lisa was already dressed. She made two coffees while I showered, then we drove back to her house in Cannonvale. As I pulled up to the kerb, she kissed me.

'Thank you for the lovely night, Tom.'

'We should give it another try.'

'The pasta or the sex? We leave for our first cruise on Sunday. I think Jade wants to do a shakedown tomorrow night. You ought to join us.'

'Your bunk would be a tight squeeze, and besides we're meeting our lawyer tomorrow. Let's aim for Saturday night.'

'I'd like that. Nice clothes, nice restaurant.'

'And a nice …'

She placed a finger on my lips. 'Shhh …'

The sun was already clearing the tip of Mandalay when I returned to the office. The rear carpark was full of staff vehicles, and the clatter of keyboards and printers drifted into the still, humid air. After fixing a plate of cereal, I brought it downstairs and ate at Pixie's desk.

'Okay, ace reporter, what have you got?' I said to her.

'I spent all night trying to write the story,' she said

unhappily, 'but nothing worked.'

'That's why journalists start as cadets. Show me your notes.'

While she flipped through a couple of pads, I reviewed last night's extraordinary events. I must have been thinking out loud because I said, 'Funny word that … beaver.'

'What's a beaver?' Pixie asked.

'Little creature that builds dams. Furry thing.'

'What made you think of a beaver?'

'Saw one last night.'

'Oh, here it is,' she said, thrusting a page of notes in front of me. 'And this is the story I tried to write.'

She had all the information on the cultural site: places, dates, people.

'Who is this Lenny Watkins?'

'He represents the Giya people. I couldn't find anywhere that he's a tribal elder, but that's not to say he isn't. Titles are a bit vague.'

'Is he a local? Can we talk to him?'

'There's no address on file. Everything is being processed through their lawyers in Sydney.'

I turned her screen towards me. She had made a good start but the assignment was tough, not helped by references to her boss's family.

'You've done well, Pixie, though it needs reworking. Copy it onto a disk and leave it on my keyboard. Another thing, I'll give you an hour's tuition every Friday morning. Write it on the calendar.'

'Thanks, Tom,' she beamed.

'Right, finish setting your copy then help Mandy with the paste-ups.'

I still couldn't decide what to run for a lead. The story on the Main Street heritage centre was the easiest. No dramas there. However, by Friday night all the media would be publishing articles on Grandpa's sacred house and garden. I looked through Pixie's story. We didn't have a choice. Flipping her disk into my computer, I started editing:

WHITSUNDAY residents woke to the news this morning that a site of cultural significance had been identified on a local farm.

According to court records, the Giya tribe has filed the registration on land belonging to the pioneer, cane-growing family of Henry O'Connor.

Sydney law firm, Mason Edelstein and Birch, is representing the Giya in what is thought to be the first listing of its kind in the Whitsundays. Previous registrations have all centred on Crown land or places of iconic value, such as Ban Ban Springs.

Mr O'Connor was unavailable for comment yesterday, but a spokesman said the family would cooperate with authorities.

'The O'Connors have always encouraged the preservation of Aboriginal heritage. They would be happy to respect any site that has cultural significance,' the spokesman said.

The article went on with more detail, even identifying the land in question. Grandpa would not like hearing his name mentioned, but it was an element of the story that couldn't be suppressed.

When I put the edition to bed on Thursday afternoon,

the article on the sacred site filled the front page. On pages two and three we had thrown in fragments of background about cultural sites and the Giya people. We had also included a photo of the rock garden behind Pop's Place.

As was our custom after finishing the paper, we sat around in the office, drinks in hand while I made a point of thanking Pixie for the story. And yes, had everyone seen it was her byline? She was quite thrilled, her face animated as she chatted with other staff who didn't know what to suddenly make of her.

Billy came across and parked beside me. We clinked bottles. 'The phones will ring off their cradles tomorrow, Tom.'

'Maybe, Billy. But what could we do? I just wish the land wasn't Grandpa's. He doesn't need this in his eighties.'

While the staff collected their bags, Heather came over and whispered, 'Pixie has something she wants to give you.'

'She ought to wait for the right bloke,' I whispered in reply.

'Why do I even bother?' she groaned.

'Okay Pixie, what have you got for me?'

She took a newspaper clipping from her folder. 'When I was researching the article, Tom, I found this in the library, and I thought you might like to post it on the wall.'

As she handed me the clipping, the staff watched. It was a photo of a wrinkled baby in a crocheted bonnet and booties. Under the photo ran the caption: *Jennifer and Joseph O'Connor yesterday welcomed a boy, Thomas Henry, who weighed in at seven pounds, fourteen ounces. Thomas was born at Proserpine Hospital and is a brother to three-year-old Patrick Joseph.*

'You can hang it on your wall at home, Pixie.'

'No, this copy is for you. We already have one.'

At this, Heather unpinned a large wall map to reveal a blow-up of baby Thomas. Staff applauded like they were at an art exhibition.

'Thank you, thank you,' I said. 'It just shows how a little gargoyle can grow up to be a handsome adult. Now go home before I dig up unsavoury things from your past.'

Heather was about to speak. I raised my hands. 'Enough. Go.'

Pixie said, 'Thank you, Tom,' and that was it.

When they had left, I stood at the door for several minutes gazing over the marina. That last scene with my staff was the most intimate the *Post* had experienced. Over the months we'd had our highs and lows, like Airlie itself, but we were now Team O'Connor. From the door I could see the *Calvados* preparing for her sail the next morning. Blue-shirted crew moved across the deck, and I guessed one of them would be Lisa. I made my way upstairs, fixed a drink and wandered onto the balcony. Soft pinks and greys ran across the water, and tiny willy-wagtails dived at insects devouring the last of the light. I wouldn't say I am prone to melancholia, but that night I felt the opposing sentiments of Grandpa's anxiety and the staff's unexpected warmth. I sat on the balcony and drank my rum, and although it was Thursday night, I fell asleep alone in a chair overlooking the Coral Sea.

CHAPTER 8

The *Post* hit the streets at six-thirty next morning and Grandpa was on the phone at six-forty. Not that he saw the paper. Somebody had rung him.

'What the hell do you think you're doing, Tom?'

'Grandpa, I didn't have a choice as you'd know.'

'What's this shit about cooperating with authorities? I told you I'll find the prick behind this registration and string him ...'

'... up by his nuts. You're repeating yourself, Grandpa. But this isn't the wild west. By dark tonight everyone in the state will know about this sacred site. We'd look idiots pretending it's a surprise.'

'The story didn't warrant that huge friggin' headline.'

'The headline wasn't huge or friggin', so don't swear at me. Better still, swear at nobody. Putting folk offside won't help.'

'I don't need a lecture from my grandson.'

'You need it from someone.'

At which he snorted and dropped the phone in my ear.

Grandpa wasn't the only one on the line before breakfast. One of the SOW (Save Our Whitsundays) ladies from Airlie Beach spoke in an unusually subdued tone. She wasn't sure to be happy or sad. Her first thought was a sacred site had to be good. No land development could occur on a sacred site, but what if one sacred site led to another, and the Whitsundays filled up with sacred sites and homeless Blacks, right next to her own house? I assured her that the registration would have no impact on the region's appeal or status, and could even help improve the place.

The phone rang several more times. Local residents had formed a queue behind the SOW lady asking what it meant, and did they need to lock their gates. Then just before seven-thirty came a call from the *ABC*, followed by *Channel Seven* wanting an interview at one, and then the *Mackay Mercury* who considered sending a reporter, but as there were no photos, they could do the interview by phone.

Billy wandered in at eight munching on a sandwich. He made himself comfortable in front of my desk. 'I don't like this at all, Tom.'

'You're not the first to cheer me up.'

He looked around for somewhere to throw his crust.

'Eat it,' I said. 'Ants are already crawling over the place.'

'Tom, I spoke to Dad last night about these Giya. He said their story does go back to the land bordering Mount Mandarana, but he doesn't think they were caught up in The Leap affair.'

'Thanks, Billy. That's reassuring.'

'It seems their connection with the woman who died is through marriage.'

I leant back in my chair, and stared at the ceiling. 'Billy, you are a Juipera descendant, same as the woman. Is there any chance your family is involved in this registration?'

'Give us a break, Tom.'

'Well, …'

He sat upright, his face angry. 'Tom, cut the bullshit. Our folks have respected each other for a long time. My dad and yours worked together on the farm. You and I went to school together. We're like family, and family don't spite each another. If we thought there was a sacred site on the farm, we'd talk to you.'

'Sorry, Billy,' I said. 'Grandpa thinks this business does originate with The Leap, and so do I. Have you heard of the O'Connor Protocol?'

'Yes, sort of. Two men who were brothers. Always stood up for each other.'

'That's right, more or less. I've only heard bits of the story, but apparently Grandpa's grandfather Paul was involved in the chase. When the shit hit the fan, he was rescued by his brother Michael, who was a magistrate.'

'Is that for real?'

'It would appear so.'

'Where does the registration fit in?'

'If I'm reading Grandpa correctly, the link is our friend Todd Steele. From what I understand, Todd's ancestor was implicated in the woman's death — even went to jail for it — while Paul O'Connor walked free.'

'Crikey. That does alter things.'

'Not for Grandpa. He's wound up like a spring.'

By eight-thirty the rest of the staff had arrived. All had their own stories to tell about the front page. Heather said her mother (who shared her house) thought the O'Connors were a family of principle. Ethel, the woman who set the ads, said her old man hoped the Blacks would find a sacred site on his land so he could claim compensation. Meanwhile, Pixie sauntered into the office with a new hairstyle and wardrobe. She said that after the paper closed, she had gone into Proserpine where she visited a hairdresser and bought new clothes for interviewing cabinet ministers and the like. She now wore a short tartan skirt and a blouse with tartan on the collar.

'Is that the O'Connor tartan?' I asked her.

She did a little twirl for the staff. 'No, it's McLeish who were Scottish lords on my mother's side.'

'You serious?'

She laughed. 'Who's to say?'

'Okay folks,' I said, bringing the office back to order. 'Excellent paper last night. Fun's over.'

I was about to return to my office when Pixie tapped her watch. 'Boss, we start my training in twenty minutes, remember.'

'Sorry, Pixie, I have a lawyer's appointment at ten. We'll aim for straight after lunch.'

'You promised.'

Heather's word *cavalier* sprang to mind. 'All right, at nine we'll sub a couple of articles, then once the lawyer is done you can meet an Aboriginal family.'

'Interview Black people?'

'Observe, actually.'

In the minutes before nine I sorted papers on my desk, signed a wad of cheques for Heather, and explained my agreement with Maggie Morgan.

'You should've closed their account months ago, Tom. Old fish-face will play you for a fool until you're dead.'

'Not any more, Heather. One dropped payment and Finnigan will take their spot.'

'Does Billy know that?'

'He does now, and he's also got an apology coming.'

I then took a handful of news stories off the fax machine and showed Pixie what to look for.

'Anything that doesn't relate to the Whitsundays goes straight in the bin. Government and Council media releases come in by the truck load, and most of it is spin. You know what I mean — spin a yarn. Learn to separate the wheat from the chaff. Here's one. *State Government Improves Road Safety*. So what have they done? First par is all about how much they love us.'

'Par?'

'Paragraph. The second and third pars are more chaff. The story starts about nine lines down. Government will spend five million on upgrading Shute Harbour Road. Read further and it's not an upgrade, but overdue road works. So really the story is the fourth, sixth and seventh pars and is only about rescheduled work for this financial year. Bugger-all to do with road safety and upgrading. Right, cut down the original twelve pars to three, give the story a new lead and tail, and condense the minister's five titles because that's another par on its own.'

Glancing at my watch, I picked up the car keys. 'Right, come with me to Proserpine. Bring those faxes to edit while I'm in with the lawyer.'

She shoved the faxes into a briefcase, then hurried out the door and hopped jauntily over the Moke's sill into the passenger seat. 'You wouldn't get away with that in the city,'

I remarked to the back of her head.

'You say something?'

'I did.'

As we roared along the country road that led from Shingley to Proserpine, she took a tartan cap from her bag and pulled it over her hair.

'Is that part of the ensemble?' I shouted.

'Yes, I bought everything together.'

'The full set?'

'Yes, every single piece. Except the bra, of course.'

I concentrated on the road ahead, thinking how much she had changed in a few days; the miserable ex-schoolgirl who was bored with type setting, now a trainee journalist, compositor and fashion model. She also had her first byline, and her hands on a story she instinctively knew was breaking from its shell.

'How long have you owned this car?' she shouted.

'Five years.'

'It's a wreck. Noisy, windy, unsafe.'

'It's a Moke. Made for beaches and people with flair.'

'Maybe for teenagers with surfboards. Not for senior editors.'

I glanced across at her. Wind was whipping the fine hair around her face. She was loving it.

'How old do you think I am?' I asked.

'Normally I'd say thirty, but you and Billy are the same age and I know Billy is twenty-five, though he looks younger.'

'Younger than his years, or me?'

'You both look young when you're happy. Like the days you're together. Two schoolboys, really.'

'Yes, some days are like that.'

CHAPTER 9

We eased off the highway into Proserpine's main street, then right into Chapman Street where Marvin Fumbleton's office was in a run-down, 1930s-style brick building. *Marvin Fumbleton LLB — Solicitor* was barely legible on a brass plaque that missed two of its four screws. Earthen pots, one with colourful petunias and one with marigolds, stood on plinths either side of the entrance.

Patrick's late model Holden was already parked outside.

'Don't sit out here,' I said to Pixie. 'Marvin has a spare office you can use.'

I pulled open the glass door and let Pixie through first. Three leather chairs were gathered in one corner, shielding a coffee table that carried a dozen glossy brochures. Across from the chairs stood a timber cabinet with a jug of water and a tray of glasses. Oak panelling ran about a metre high around the walls, and ended at a doorway near where a secretary sat behind a cluttered desk. She was the only other person in the room.

'Hello, Tom,' she said. 'The others are waiting. Is this your stenographer?'

'No, Helen, she's a journalist from the *Post*. She has a couple of articles to write up. Okay if she uses your spare office?'

'Um, I'm not sure. Don't know if it's empty.'

I turned the handle of a door to the right of where she sat. A table and two chairs stood alone in a dark, cavernous room. Switching on the light, I said, 'This will be fine, Helen. No ghosts that I can see.'

Pixie shivered. 'I'll sit out here, thanks.'

'No, you're an ace reporter. Work in there, but keep the door open. Shan't be long.'

Pushing open a second, heavier door, I walked into Marvin's office where Grandpa and Patrick drank tea out of prissy little cups. They were discussing a canvas that had hung on the wall from when Marvin's father started the practice after the great depression. Marvin was in his mid-sixties — a stout, ruddy-faced man who loved the peaceful life. Esoteric jokes, Latin roots and golf's idiosyncrasies were his staple conversation — and that canvas of his father's. It was of a classic English village that seemed full of children, horses, cattle, sheep, birds and flowers. Clothes flapped on a line and a wintry blue sky held a wintry sun to its breast. To my mind the only thing going for the canvas was that it had belonged to Marvin's father, who was born, apparently, in one of the cottages.

When I arrived, the men stopped admiring the work and took their seats.

'Hello, Marvin,' I said, and shook hands.

'Hello, Tom. We always seem to meet on these formal occasions. *Quis erit erit.* What will be, will be. Okay, Henry, you'd better fill me in.'

'You know as much as we do.'

'Well, some of it.' He picked up a pre-war handset. 'Helen,

do you have the O'Connor file nearby?'

'It's in your front tray. Left side.'

'In my front … left? You're quite right. Sorry.'

After scanning the introduction, he pushed up his glasses. 'What do you want me to do, Henry? It'll be awkward taking this through the courts.'

'We're fighting it,' Grandpa said. 'It's Pop's house we're talking about.'

'Exactly what are we fighting?' Marvin asked. 'The registration? The Aboriginal tribe? The government?' He dropped his glasses back onto his nose, and read another few lines. 'Well, the Geeyah …'

'Giya.'

'Yes, the Giya don't seem to have identified any previous sacred sites. At least, not in Proserpine. That weakens their case, I would think.'

'You think?' Grandpa spluttered.

'Give us a break, Henry. I was up late reading this stuff. Everything's rather vague, you know. The relevant Act is still at committee stage, and it's not like they built a church or something.'

'Okay, what's your advice?'

'Let the registration go through. The house is empty.'

'Piss off.'

Marvin recoiled. 'If you don't like my advice, you can find another solicitor.'

'Sorry, Marvin,' Grandpa said grumpily. 'I'm not crawling out of here like a whipped dog.'

Patrick chimed in. 'No disrespect, Marvin, but who is this law firm of theirs, Mason Edelstein and Birch?'

Marvin studied the head of the document. 'Sydney crowd, I'd say. Top shelf.'

'Well, somebody means business,' Patrick said. 'They probably specialise in this sort of thing. Money no object.'

'What are you getting at?' Marvin frowned.

'We're a bit outgunned in this. If we object, legally that is, and it ends up in the High Court, they'll have twenty silks on one side of the table, and we'll have Marvin on the other.'

Our lawyer was not impressed. 'You can hire a Sydney firm for all I care.'

'Okay, okay,' I said, raising my hand for calm. 'What if, instead, we could prove that an ulterior motive is behind the registration?'

'Bang on, Tom,' Grandpa cried. 'Some prick has it in for us.'

Marvin's face reddened. 'That's … that's a serious accusation, Henry. You're jumping to conclusions.'

'Crap. How long have we got?'

'Um, I read somewhere three months to lodge an appeal.'

'Right, you get to work on the legal shit,' Grandpa said. 'Outplay these Sydney yobbos, and in the meantime, we'll find the bastard who's trying to nail us.'

Grandpa jumped up from his chair, slapped the lawyer's back, then headed outside with Patrick and me in a line behind him. When Pixie saw us go past, she grabbed her papers and followed.

On the footpath Grandpa said, 'If old Fumblebum thinks we're lying down on this, he's got another think coming.'

He glared at the door through which we had just come, then noticed Pixie and gave a little jump. 'Shit. Where did you spring from?'

'I'm … I'm with Mr O'Connor … him, sir,' she stammered, pointing at me.

Grandpa eyed her up and down, glanced at me, then back at the girl. It wasn't hard to read his mind.

'Has your bit of skirt been eavesdropping?' he demanded.

'Show some respect, Grandpa. Of course she hasn't. Pixie is a journalist at the *Post*. She's in town with me to write an article.'

'Okay. Tell her to bugger off and write her article while we drink coffee, and talk tactics.'

'Grandpa, she's not buggering off anywhere.'

Patrick had better manners. He thrust out his hand. 'Hi, Pixie. I'm Patrick, Tom's older brother. You're welcome to join us for coffee.'

'No, thank you. I'm all right. I'll … um … stay here, thanks.'

I smiled for her. 'Come, Pixie. We all need a breather after Marvin's gloomy cave.'

She glanced at Grandpa who hadn't softened, then kept well clear of him as we sauntered up the street towards a café. Patrick chatted to her about newspapers and farming while I tried to distract Grandpa, who was having none of it. When we reached the café, I ordered four coffees, then gave Pixie ten dollars to buy some stationery we had genuinely run short of.

As she walked down the street, I said to Grandpa, 'Listen, Pixie is a terrific girl …'

'Yeah. Knock your eyes out.'

'She does, but that's not what I'm saying. She's local, she's keen, and she's a great employee. You know her father Terry

Hanson — the same man who's worked on our farm for years.'

That widened Grandpa's eyes. He swung in his chair and studied Pixie's body from the rear. 'That is Terry Hanson's daughter?'

'She should be at uni, and will probably end up there. In the meantime, she's a friend of the O'Connors. Spent half the night writing a positive article. Look at poor old Marvin. Happy to say a prayer for the cause, but stand up in court? Not if he can help it. So, learn to be kind to her.'

Patrick was more direct. 'Great asset,' he said. 'You screwing her, Tom?'

'Of course not. I'll repeat that clearly. NO, I AM NOT. Now, while she's absent, let's talk about the case. Grandpa, what's on your mind?'

'We've got three months to nail the bastard.'

I turned to Patrick. 'That was helpful. And you?'

'Well, apart from Todd Steele, who else is in the frame? We all know he's carrying baggage from the past, but why target us now? Not to mention you can't invent sacred sites just to annoy people. What about you, Tom?'

The café owner delivered four coffees to the table. I waited until he had left. 'I'm trying to chase down the Giya people. Find out what's prompted this. Are they sincere or being manipulated? I will drive out this morning to interview a family called the Nicholsons. They seem to be the oldest Black residents in Proserpine.'

Patrick stirred two spoons of sugar into his coffee while Pixie's lone cup glowered at us. I looked down the street. She was nowhere to be seen.

'Grandpa,' Patrick began, 'do you remember years ago the Black family who camped on the river at the bottom of our farm? Where did they come from?'

'Can't say exactly. They were already camping there when I was a kid. They stayed for the winter months, fishing mostly, then when summer came, they moved inland away from the floods. I think Pop had an agreement with them. If they didn't bother us, we didn't bother them. Why do you ask? Not another sacred site?'

'No. I want to do some research.'

'All right,' I said. 'I'll follow up the Giya, Patrick can check out the folk who camped on the river, and Grandpa can stay with Marvin.'

'And who's looking for the bastard that caused it all?'

'Three of us, Grandpa. And go quietly. Be careful what you say to people. We don't want to look foolish if the site is genuine and Todd is innocent.'

After collecting our hats, we rose from the table. Pixie was still nowhere in sight. Grandpa looked at her untouched coffee and said, 'What a waste,' and drained the cup.

Back outside the lawyer's office Patrick and Grandpa climbed into their car and left for home, while I waited near the Moke for our frightened puppy to appear. After a time, she approached warily from the opposite direction.

'Has he gone?' she asked.

'Yep.'

She shivered. 'The old grouse wanted to eat me.'

'Sorry, should've warned you. He's taken the registration badly. Right, let's say hello to our Aboriginal elders.'

We drove up past the golf club, and took the last exit

out of town. A few kilometres later we ran out of bitumen, then followed a rough, pot-holed track to where a half-dozen fibro houses stood on the bank of a gully. Everything about the houses was clean and neat: the grass mown, gardens tidy, chickens in roomy pens. A couple of Black children too young for school were playing with a ball. Pixie waited in the car while I knocked on the first door. An elderly woman came out and pointed to the home of Harvey and Thelma Nicholson, two doors up. I returned to the car and drove fifty metres.

As I cut the ignition, I said to Pixie, 'Come inside with me, but not everything you hear is for the newspaper. Okay?'

'Maybe I shouldn't even listen,' she said.

'Look, I told Grandpa you were behind our effort to get to the truth of this matter. I apologise for not having asked first. You can tell me now if you want to stay in the car. It won't affect your job.'

She gazed out the open door, controlling her emotions, then faced me. 'Tom, I'm sorry if you think I could be disloyal. I'd give anything to convince you I'm grateful for where I am now and that I want to be useful. If you have any doubts, I'll remain out here. I won't say or do anything silly.'

I was tempted to hug her, but checked myself. Instead, I said, 'Right, ace, we have work to do. Let's go.'
I knocked on the door and retreated to the bottom step like a weekend Mormon. An old man opened the door and peered at us.

'Mr Nicholson?' I asked.

'Yes,' he said cautiously.

'My name is Tom O'Connor and this is Pixie Hanson.

We're from the *Whitsunday Post* doing an article on the sacred site downriver. Do you know about it?'

He nodded.

'We'd like to talk to you because we understand you are an Aboriginal elder in this region. I'm sorry I don't know what tribe you're from, but the registration is being made by the Giya.'

'I'm not from that mob,' he said.

'Mr Nicholson, is there somewhere we can sit and talk?'

'Yes, come inside. And my name is Harvey.'

Reaching up, I shook his hand.

Inside the house was as clean and tidy as outside. Big hopper windows were thrust open, casting light onto a polished lino floor and furniture that was a mixture of styles. An elderly Black woman sat at the table stitching ribbons on a baby's jacket.

'Tom and Pixie, this is my wife, Thelma. Make tea if you would, love, and bring it onto the verandah.'

Harvey led us through screened French doors to a wide timber verandah that had a hammock stretched between two posts, a squatter's chair, and a table setting for six. Motioning us to chairs at the table, he sat opposite. When Pixie drew out a notebook and pencil, he glanced at them without comment.

'How can I help, Tom?'

'Does my name O'Connor mean anything to you?'

'Yes, the site is on land owned by Henry O'Connor.'

'He's my grandfather. As you can imagine he's not happy about the registration. It is on land that includes his pop's old house.'

'I didn't realise that,' he said softly.

'Do you know much about the Giya people?'

'They have been on this earth since the Dreamtime, like all Black people. Their ancestral lands run from Bowen to Calen. Now they live mostly around Collinsville.'

'So, they're not from the Proserpine River exactly?'

'Well, the river — any river — is a tribe's lifeblood. Where there's a river there will be a sacred place.'

'Are you aware of many such places?'

'A few, though not on any farms. Once the tractors have been through, sacred places disappear.'

'Do you know where my grandfather's farm is?'

'Not really. Only that it is on the river.'

His wife Thelma brought out four cups of sweet, black tea and a chocolate mud cake with multicoloured icing. She offered the plate to Pixie who shook her head and patted her stomach.

'Try some, Pixie,' I said. 'It's yummy.' When I cut a large slice, Pixie selected a morsel, which she picked at like a bird.

'Harvey, I'd like to find the Giya who applied for the sacred site. If it is genuine, I'll do everything I can to support it. But if it's phony, I'd like to know who is behind it and why.'

'I'm with you there, Tom,' he said surprisingly. 'It might be a good thing if this registration goes to court. Sort out the boundaries and bloodlines of all the people who live round here: the Giya, Ngaro and Biri. I am from the Juipera mob further south, but our family has married into the Giya and their kids have married white people and Chinese and islanders, then back into the Juipera.'

'What are you saying? There is Giya in your blood?'

He was squirming. 'No, I am Juipera.'

'Do you know any Giya round here?'

'Sorry, Tom, can't say I do. The Giya elders live at Collinsville.'

Thelma set down her mug. 'That's not right, Harvey. The family at Woodwark Bay are Giya. I saw them in town yesterday. Shopping for clothes and stuff. And in a big flash Land Cruiser. They think they're sumpthin' but they're not.'

Harvey was angry. 'They're good people. Leave them out of this.'

Thelma snorted her defiance but said no more.

Not wanting to be involved in a marital dispute, I decided I would check out these folk myself. Although Woodwark Bay was about four inlets north of Airlie, I had never been there. In fact, I thought it was only accessible by boat. I seemed to recall Jade Wilson had a jetty and shed in Woodwark Bay where he took the *Calvados* for his occasional boys' night out, but I never imagined he shared his retreat with an Aboriginal family.

CHAPTER 10

We finished our tea and politely rose from the table. After shaking hands, we returned to the car and drove along the dusty, pot-holed road towards town. The time was now past midday and I asked Pixie if she wanted lunch.

She was chirpy again. 'I'd love a burger.'

'I thought you weren't hungry.'

'That cake was for her grandchildren. Didn't you notice?'

I hadn't … though on reflection … all that icing. 'Can you eat a burger on the road?'

'Do I look like a city type? Of course I can eat in the car.'

We ordered two takeaways, and as I drove, she spread a towel over her lap and ate hungrily.

'Tom, I took lots of notes and would like to write the story this afternoon. Give me time to work on it.'

'Okay, but what angle are you taking? Remember, there's nothing to be said about the O'Connors going to a solicitor.'

'We've found Giya people living in Woodwark Bay.'

'That's hardly newsworthy. Why not interview the local member … what's her name? Gloria Herbert, and maybe the president of the Chamber. Find out what they think.'

'I could phone the mayor.'

'Not yet. Council has a meeting this Monday. We'll ask him then.'

Back at the office, my first task was to help with the delivery complaints that were more raucous than usual. According to an enquiry Heather had made, the *Mercury's* night manager was forced — unwillingly, he stressed — to print their daily out of turn, which then shoved our paper into a midnight slot. When I rang and complained, he apologised with a cock-and-bull story about freak storms cutting power to the loader, which then delayed the ... blah blah blah. Adding to our woes, a bloke named Allan threatened to sue the paper for identifying him as a convicted drink driver when the real culprit was his brother, Allen. Why did parents do that sort of thing?

Late in the day, I rang Patrick, but Mum said he was out tilling plant cane and wouldn't be in for tea until six. I could try him then. She then asked how I had progressed with the Nicholsons, whom she remembered from school. Harvey and Thelma had two sons, twins she thought, one had been quiet and studied hard, the other was a bit of a tearaway. The good one had taken an apprenticeship at the mill, but the other one hung around camps and pubs. She didn't know what happened to him but with lots of those drifters they just disappeared. Could she remember his name? Benny. Something like that. When she hung up, I thought about old Harvey and Thelma. Beneath that dignified exterior lay a sore that might never heal. Although one of the twins did well, the other was a problem, which complicated an already difficult life.

Around four-thirty, Pixie brought in the story she had written, plus a fax she had edited, and a couple of advertorials for Billy and Roberta. She hadn't got to the television guide or community news yet, but would have them finished before the Council meeting on Monday.

'Your job description says the TV guide and community news are to be completed by Friday night.'

'Sorry, but I did start on them.'

'The reason they're done Friday is to free you up for editorial the following week. Isn't that right?'

'I am sorry. It won't happen again.'

'Pixie, you can't do everything. You are a copy setter. That's why I hired you. But you also want to cover news, edit press releases, and attend Council meetings. I don't know if it's possible.'

She sat on the chair in front of my desk, biting her lip. 'I don't mind arriving early, working Saturdays if necessary. It won't cost you.'

'This is not a matter of cost. And weekends are out of the question.'

'You won't take me off the news?'

'I'll see.'

'Thanks a lot,' she muttered, and used the distraction of a ringing phone to flounce from the office. If not a flouncing exit, it was a good imitation.

Several minutes later Heather opened my door and dumped a pile of letters into my tray. Her mouth was set in a line I knew well.

'Okay, what is it this time?'

'Tom, you're in and out of the office and can't see

everything. Pixie busted her heart today. What do you think Ethel has done?'

'This morning she filed old copy. In the afternoon she helped Mandy set regular ads.'

'That's right. Her entire day's work could've been done in three hours. There's your answer. Let her set the community news and TV guide, and let Pixie chase articles for next week's paper.'

'Heather, it'll cause a riot. Ethel will think jobs have been dumped on her because Pixie is the office favourite.'

'Of course she won't like it, but Fridays have been too cushy. Explain that you need to even out tasks in order to improve business efficiency. On top of that, you and Billy hardly write fresh stories anymore. Billy's advertising account has doubled in the last six months, and you're on every second committee in town. Everyone will love seeing Pixie out and about. She's such a bubbly, attractive girl. It can only be good for you, for her, and the paper.'

'Thanks, Heather. Your concern has been noted. Now, it's gone five o'clock. Good night.'

I heard her moving round the office, checking computers were off, the fax on standby, the windows shut, the safe locked. 'Bye,' she called from the rear door, and was gone.

Around six I finished sorting through the debtors. Some I would phone myself, some would be a job for Heather, Billy or Roberta, and the really tough ones would be handed over to a debt collection agency who, if successful, took thirty percent of the debt, leaving me with the remainder, which was better than zero. The sun had already dropped behind the mountains when I stepped outside. Taking a beer from the fridge, I sauntered across to the beach at the front of the shop. A pink glow filled the horizon and wavelets swished over the sand, sweeping pebbles into thin, ragged lines. Down at Abell Point the arc lights bathed crews preparing their boats for the morning, while nearer to hand a security light showed the gap where the *Calvados* normally berthed. Lisa would be on board right now making somebody's day perfect; maybe fetching a drink, hauling in a sail, cutting a lettuce for dinner. There was even a chance her day had ended, and she was up in the heads taking a shower, the salt sluicing from that exquisite body.

I walked back into the office and phoned Patrick who sounded very tired. Last month's rain had brought on the cane faster than he could till it. In some places the weeds were higher than the drawbar. Once dinner was over, he would return to the field and work under lights. Midnight should see the bottom paddock done. I asked if he had discovered anything about the Blacks who had camped along the river in Pop's day. He would see tomorrow. I told him quickly about my meeting with Harvey and Thelma Nicholson — that they were friendly though a bit guarded. One thing they did mention, however, was a Giya family living in Woodwark Bay. With Saturday morning likely to be quiet, I intended making a visit.

In the background I heard Grandpa's mantle clock strike seven. Patrick said he'd better get moving.

'Do you need a hand?'

'I'm right thanks, Tom. Talk to you tomorrow.'

'Okay, Patrick. And don't fall asleep at the wheel. Remember what happened to Dad.'

'I won't forget. Good night.'

The phone clicked and there was silence. Patrick and I always said, *Remember what happened to Dad* if we needed to work a tractor at night. On occasion during the harvest when the pace was hectic, I helped with the tilling, sometimes to midnight like Patrick was doing now. Just on nine years ago, late in the afternoon, Dad had been fertilising ratoons when a stanchion on the tractor broke. As it was too late to fetch a mechanic, he found a bolt in the toolbox for a temporary repair. According to Mum, he'd lost almost two hours and refused to come home until the hopper was empty. Around nine-thirty he still hadn't returned. Mum and Patrick climbed in the ute and went searching for him. That night had been Mum's worst nightmare. Her husband dead under the tractor where it had rolled on him, the bolt snapped like a carrot. And all because he was anxious to complete a job he could have left until morning.

Patrick had a lot of his father in him: good looking, dedicated to the farm, and impatient. He had a girl he should've married years earlier, but had never asked. Glenda was around my age, desirable in a homely way and a teller at the local bank. It had become standard practice at dinner to remark on how a man so busy around the farm could be a dawdler when asking for a woman's hand. Grandpa didn't have an explanation, he had an aphorism. 'The bull quickest to the molasses is slowest through the shute.' Although Patrick had heard the saying a hundred times, his pace never altered. In the meantime, Glenda waited.

*   *   *

Upstairs, I showered and dressed, then strolled down to the Airlie Beach Hotel, which was quieter than Magnums and the best venue in town for televised sport. The evening was pleasant, and several couples sat on the deck that overlooked the beach and sailing club. When I entered the bar, I was delighted to find Billy watching football on the big screen. I pulled up a stool beside him.

'How's life, Billy?'

'I've laid ten dollars on the Broncos to beat St George. I might have done my money. And yourself?'

'This is my Friday night out. If I stay in the flat, people think I'm a hermit. If I go down to Magnums, I'm lonely and after crumpet.'

'Doesn't sound like you.'

Once the barmaid had poured two schooners, I sat quietly as St George hung on for a narrow first-half lead.

'Didn't your brother trial with St George?' I asked Billy.

'That's right. Played in two off-season matches.'

'He did all right, I hear.'

'Yes, he could've made the grade.'

'Not *could have*,' I said. 'He should have.'

Billy had lost his young brother in a car crash in Sydney two years earlier. His parents were devastated. They hadn't wanted Frankie to leave his north Queensland home, but Sydney was the centre of the universe, and that's where a talented young footballer needed to be.

During the interval, Billy sat with his back to the television. He nudged me. 'What do you reckon those blokes are doing over there?'

Carefully, I swivelled my head, and watched five young

men drinking in the corner. 'Talking girls, footy. I've no idea.'

'The bloke in the white tee-shirt is selling drugs. Those two on stools are buying.'

Trying not to appear obvious, I studied them. Everything looked normal.

'How do you know, Billy?'

'Watch his right hand. It's in his pocket. When he pulls it out, they'll slap palms like old mates. But a tab or sachet will change hands.'

'Might be weed,' I said.

'No, they sell weed at Magnums to the backpackers. Our friend is trading in serious stuff.'

I hadn't known this side of Billy. I turned to him. 'Where did you learn about drugs?'

He shrugged. 'They've been here for years.'

'Speed maybe.'

'No, hard drugs. Not big quantities like in the cities, but they're here. You can buy anything you want.'

I was intrigued. I had lived in Airlie most of my life and run the newspaper for four years, but not once heard of drugs stronger than cannabis.

'Where do they come from?' I asked.

'Don't know, Tom. We could write a story like before, but everyone would give you hell. Even the cops.'

'The cops are involved?'

'Who's to say? But what I mean is that nobody wants this pretty tourist town linked to drugs. Keep the dirty linen out of sight.'

'Here, Billy, I'll buy another round. This drug talk has depressed you.'

'No, it hasn't. Well, … it has a bit.' He cracked his knuckles and faced me. 'Tom … my brother didn't die in a car crash. He died of a drug overdose in Kings Cross.'

'Good Lord. How long have you known?'

'Always.'

'Go on.'

'Frankie was taking drugs before he left for Sydney. Not much. Mostly weed but the occasional shot of acid. And he liked his party drugs. After a game he and his mates would load the cars with booze and girls, and head down to Dingo Beach. That's when the drugs came out. I learnt about it early, but Mum and Dad never switched on to his highs and lows. One day he said he wanted to fly to Sydney and trial for St George. I wasn't the only one who tried to change his mind. But off he went. As you know he didn't make the grade in footy, didn't like the hard work, thought natural talent was enough. He picked up odd jobs round the Cross and spent his nights in seedy joints. He was in a car accident right enough, got knocked around, but I was the only one in the family to see the coroner's report. Frankie was dead before the car hit the pole. Full of badly cut heroin. Some mongrel in Sydney killed my only brother.'

'Shit, Billy. Sorry, mate. I never guessed for a minute it was anything but a car crash.'

'You're not the only one, Tom.'

'Maybe we should print something. No mention of Frankie, of course. Just a short editorial telling parents that serious drugs could be doing the rounds in Airlie, and to watch their kids.'

'Yes, it might do some good.'

'Billy, that story we wrote on drug trafficking last year. Was it a chance idea of yours?'

'No, Tom. Sorry.'

'Don't be. They're scum of the earth. Anyway, let's eat.'

The Airlie Hotel was known for its Friday night seafood dinners, and the best plate of all was coral trout with salad and chips. After ordering the meal, we bought another two schooners and sat at a table near the window. Dinghies were ferrying people out to a trimaran that was moored off the beach.

Billy ignored the scene on the water. 'One day I'll find the man who killed Frankie. That young bloke over there is at the end of the chain, funding his own habit. He will have a supplier — somebody addicted like himself — who in turn will report to a bloke making the stuff or importing it. They're the mongrels we want.'

Soon the meal arrived and we ate in silence, then Billy said he was going home, back to Saltwater Creek. When I said it was also my bedtime, we stood up from the table and shook hands. Maybe I should've offered to embrace him, let him know I cared, but hugs and kisses were not in our DNA.

We walked together as far as the main street intersection where Billy caught a lift to Saltwater. As I passed Magnums, a couple of Telstra boys I'd known from school were seated on the deck. They saw me and waved. Over the next two hours we got half-drunk, talked rubbish and played a round of darts. Around ten, I said goodnight, and trudged over the hill to my flat where I sat upstairs reflecting on Billy and

Pixie. In the space of one day, both had shown a dimension I never thought existed. Billy and his loathing of drugs, Pixie and her maturity. I was in bed by eleven and asleep five minutes later, though my sleep was anything but dreamless.

CHAPTER 11

Next morning, Saturday, was picture perfect; exactly like the photo I had hanging in my office downstairs. I took coffee onto the balcony and watched the tourists crowd onto the reef cats, envying them for the beautiful day that lay ahead.

Returning inside, I ate breakfast then wandered into the office to study the map I had pinned over baby Thomas. A bright red line, indicating a sealed road, led to the inlets opposite Airlie, followed by a dotted line that traversed the spur into Woodwark Bay. Although I hadn't known the bay was accessible by car, I had seen it from the ocean many times. Woodwark was arguably the prettiest of the many bays that dotted the coast from Cannonvale to the Gregory River. Protected by a shoal that had a single unmarked passage, the bay was of clean white sand with a grass frontage and a backdrop of tropical rainforest. A handful of squatters' shacks were clustered at the southern end of the beach in the lee of a headland, while at the northern end a jetty ran out from a building which, I understood, was owned by Jade Wilson. As I studied the map, I couldn't recall seeing any houses that might be home to a Giya family.

I left the office and drove through the housing estates that encircled the inlets across from Airlie. Each community was serviced by a narrow road, had a rocky beach of its own and a stunning outlook. At the end of the third inlet the bitumen stopped abruptly, and a two-wheel track led into the trees. The little Moke found the going hard as it scrabbled for grip across a spur that was covered in wash-outs and fallen branches. Then I was out of the trees and into a clearing that ran down to the water. Ahead of me was the reef partly exposed at low tide, the passage leading to Jade's jetty and the huddle of shacks. But most surprising was the house that stood in the shelter of trees at the edge of the clearing. Corrugated iron extensions had been added to the main frame, with more sheets of iron providing a verandah along the ocean front. Rocks and tyre rims held down the roof, while bits of discarded machinery provided buttress support for the walls. A few abandoned cars augmented the scene, and the clothesline bore a massive fish carcass that two dogs were stripping of flesh. At odds with this one-house shanty town was a gleaming Toyota Land Cruiser.

I parked the car under a tree and knocked on the wall. Soon a lean, middle-aged Aborigine came to the doorway. Behind him stood three or four Black women and a group of children. Work boots and hats were piled into one corner of the porch, and a drum overflowed with tins and papers.

The dogs paused in their feeding to bark at me.

'Lie down, you mutts,' the man shouted, then stepped outside. 'How can I help you, bro'?'

I thrust out my hand. 'Hi, my name is Tom O'Connor.'

'I'm Lenny. Lenny Watkins. What you here for, Tom?'

I took a deep breath. 'I'm looking for the Giya mob.'

'That's us. Or some of us.'

'Well, Lenny. I'm from the *Whitsunday Post*,' and pointed to the writing on the side of the Moke. 'As you probably know, a sacred site in Proserpine has been registered with the government.'

'Yeah, sure. I know all that, Tom. You doin' a story?'

'I guess so. But actually, I'm wearing two hats. My name is O'Connor.'

'You be one of the sons, I reckon.'

'Grandson, to be exact. The alleged site is on my grandfather's land.'

'It's not *alleged*, Tom. The site is real.'

'I'm not saying it isn't, but that's not the only reason I'm here. First, do you represent the Giya people?'

He held up his hand. 'Come and sit down. This sounds heavy stuff. Missus, bring out a pot of tea, and youse kids piss off. This is adult business.'

He led me to a bench under a Leichhardt tree. 'Yeah, I represent the Giya in this registration. I am a tribal elder. Don't have to be old to be an elder, but there ain't many of us left in Whitsundays. That's why I registered the site now. While I'm still kickin'. Kids today don't care about their culture. They want flash cars and flash clothes.'

'Where do the rest of the Giya live?'

'Oh, some to the north, some south. Others in Collinsville.'

'Lenny, apart from being a tribal elder, how do you know the exact location of the site? Have you walked on my grandfather's farm?'

'Of course, Tom. As a kid, my uncle took me in canoe up the river. We fish, we hunt crocodile, and he shows me sacred sites of the Giya.'

'Your uncle wasn't even born when the last Giya trod on that land.'

He clamped his jaw. 'We know sacred sites. They be powerful places for Black men.'

'Did you know there is a house standing on the sacred site?'

'Of course, Tom. But that's just bad luck for the O'Connors. Should never build a house on sacred land. Anyway, house is empty, so no harm to anyone.'

'What do you mean by that?'

He waited until mugs of tea were placed on the table and his family had retreated.

'Well, nothing can happen to a sacred site. What is already there, stays there. History lives in our sacred site, and history lives in your old house. We respect each other's history, nothin' more.'

'So, the old house is safe?'

He grinned. 'That be right, bro'. No need to fight the registration. The house is safe.'

'If you don't mind, Lenny, what's in it for you?'

'Nothin'. I'm a custodian of Giya sacred land, that's all.'

'And you're the man behind the heritage centre in Airlie's main street?'

'Yeah, Tom. You like it?'

'I think the centre is a great idea.' I turned to where the Land Cruiser stood in the clearing. 'That must have set you back a few quid?'

His grin was sly. 'My boys work in the mines. At Blackwater. Earn big money, over one hundred grand a year each. They buy new cars, new clothes, new TV, heaps of things. They be good boys.'

'Will you always live in Woodwark Bay?'

'Sure will. Fishin's good, life's peaceful, no worries.'

'Well, you're a lucky man, Lenny. Thanks for your hospitality. I'll see you at the launch of the heritage centre.'

We shook hands and I returned to the car, relieved that Pop's Place wouldn't have to be knocked down. All the same, I was unconvinced that Lenny's knowledge had come entirely from his uncle's memory.

Soon after lunch I phoned Patrick, who was in a better frame of mind having completed the tilling, and recounted my chat with Lenny. When I finished, he said he would take Grandpa in the ute that afternoon and explore the old Aboriginal camp on the river. Did I want to come over? Sorry, I told him, too much on my plate.

I actually spent the afternoon waiting for the *Calvados* masts to appear over the breakwater. When they did, around four, I grabbed my Panama and hurried down to the marina that was busy with afternoon traffic. The *Calvados* eased through the narrow channel, then slipped into her space like a graceful woman coming home to bed. Lisa jumped onto the marina and secured the boat aft while another deckhand did likewise at the bow. They then dropped a gangplank and helped their guests ashore. I waited until everything had settled before approaching.

'Hello, Tom,' Lisa said. 'Any surprises for me?'

'I've booked La Cucina, the best restaurant in Airlie. Overlooks the beach. Discreet. Perfect for lovers.'

'What does that mean? The lighting is poor.'

I laughed. 'See you at seven.'

After ninety minutes in the office filling time, I dressed and followed the boardwalk around the point to La Cucina. The restaurant owner, Giancarlo, met me at the door where we embraced like I was *casa nostra*.

He cupped his upturned fingers. 'Tom … Tom, my friend. Why you dine alone?'

'Giancarlo … Giancarlo,' I said, mirroring his gesture. 'Would I spend outrageous money alone?'

'So where is *bella donna*? She is late? Ah, women!' He sighed. 'Come, sit over here. You will be first to see lights on the water. Will you have candle, a drink?'

I folded my arms. 'You romantic old bastard. The cosiest table, a candle and drink. You don't care if I dine with a beautiful girl or an ugly toad.'

'Ah, *caro*, you insult me. I would never be happy if you bring toad to my table.'

'Giancarlo, just fetch a Jamesons, please. With ice.'

As he moved to the bar, the tables began to fill. I turned to the view. Palm fronds cut the dusk into shreds, a young man strummed a guitar at the water's edge, and children played under lights on the grass.

I heard movement at my elbow. '*Signore* Tom. May I present *Signorina* Lisa.'

Giancarlo stepped aside to reveal Lisa, who was attired out of a catalogue: the elegant dress, the leather shoes, the gold pendant. Her hair was brushed until it shone, and artful make-up hid the scar. I rose to my feet.

'Good evening, Thomas,' she said, and offered her cheek for a kiss. I smelt expensive perfume.

When I opened my hands in genuine awe, she said, 'Everything in order?'

'I thought you came to Airlie in a sail locker. Obviously not.'

'It was a big locker. Have you been here long?'

'Not really. First drink.'

For a time, we sat mesmerised, absorbing the atmosphere, fumbling with words. She ordered a Sémillon on ice, which she drank too quickly, and called for the bottle. I finished my whiskey. She told me about the overnight cruise on the yacht, and the little events that were funny and sad. I told her about a day's work on the paper while avoiding topics best kept for later. The mood held. We brushed fingers as we studied the menu, she flicked a moth off my shoulder, I refilled her glass. She ordered lobster and I ordered the mangrove jack. We emptied the bottle of white, started a second, and we touched knees under the table.

Lisa stroked my face. 'Tom, this is perfect. Too beautiful to end.'

'It will end ...'

'Don't say that.'

'I hadn't finished.'

'So how will it end?'

'I'll give a clue.'

'Oh, gosh,' she shuddered. 'More to the left.'

I returned my hand to the table. 'You haven't tasted your coffee.'

A half-hour later we stood on the footpath while a bubbling Giancarlo flagged down a taxi. When it arrived, we were taken back to my flat, the driver playing American blues on a portable cassette.

We had barely reached the top of the stairs when Lisa was undressed.

'Begin like you did earlier,' she whispered. 'Don't stop, ever.'

But it wasn't that easy, even for an O'Connor. Minutes later we plunged through the tape, seizing the trophy from an insatiable, fleeting deity.

*   *   *

On Sunday morning, we stirred when bright sunlight flooded the pandanus shading my windows.

'The *Calvados* sails this afternoon,' Lisa said. 'I have to leave at nine.'

With that announcement we climbed out of bed, made coffee and showered. I threw on casual gear while Lisa dressed in her nautical blue and white.

'Business attire,' she said.

When I drove her down to the marina, we said farewell and kissed.

'See you in three days, Tom.'

'If I survive.'

CHAPTER 12

I have always thought of Airlie as a stunning, fickle woman whose mood changes more frequently than a starlet refreshes her make-up. I have seen her angry when cyclones tear holes in the tree canopy. I have seen her sultry when grey, ominous clouds hang over the water. And I have seen her as a ravishing beauty like this morning, when, after leaving the marina, I drove up Conway Range and looked down on a green and blue vista that only a gracious god could have created.

Back on earth, around lunchtime, I followed my usual Sunday routine and motored out to the farm where I joined Grandpa, Mum and Patrick for the traditional roast.

'You look like a cat that's eaten the canary,' Mum said.

I wiped my face. 'Must be the meal I had last night.'

'Fried chicken or hamburger?' Patrick asked.

'Neither. Giancarlo's restaurant.'

'Not with that pretty little journalist?'

'What journalist?' Mum said.

'The one he took to the bloody solicitor's,' Grandpa answered.

Mum slapped him on the knuckles with her serving spoon. 'Your language is getting worse, Henry. Soon I won't be able to invite anyone out here.'

'Well, ask him about it. Turned up with a flapper who he's … he's …' The sentence died because he couldn't think of an acceptable verb.

'The prettiest creature you could lay eyes on, Mum,' Patrick said. 'And guess who she is?'

'Stop being silly,' Mum said.

'Pixie Hanson. Daughter of Terry Hanson.'

Mum stared at me. 'Thomas, I don't believe it. That's terrible. Pixie is still at school.'

'Mum, these apes need their heads banged together. Pixie left school last year and Terry approached me about giving her a job. So please, she's a cadet journalist … and she wasn't at Giancarlo's last night. End of story.'

Although Grandpa snorted, Mum said primly, 'I'm glad to hear it.'

'Pixie was with me in town to do the Giya story. We drove out to see Harvey and Thelma.'

That brought Grandpa's mind out of the gutter. 'So, is Harvey behind all this?'

'Not really.' I outlined the conversation, then added, 'I got the impression that Harvey has mixed feelings about the registration. While his wife was keen to implicate a family living in Woodwark Bay, he insisted that his bloodline is pure Juipera who, to his knowledge, have no cultural sites in Proserpine.'

'The Nicholsons are good people,' Mum said. 'Like I told you, Harvey and Thelma are Grandpa's age. I remember them from school. One boy, I think his name was Jack, took a trades job in the mill. The other, Benny or something, was a bit of a loss.'

'Do you know if they were Giya or Juipera?'

'We didn't notice that sort of thing.'

'Well, here's the good news. I drove out to Woodwark Bay yesterday and met the Giya family. Lenny Watkins was his name.'

Mum interrupted. 'That was it. Lenny.'

'I wouldn't think this is the same Lenny. Thelma talked about them like they were strangers. In any case, Lenny Watkins is behind this cultural registration, and he swears the house will not be touched. He said our history and Aboriginal history should coexist on the same land.'

'Are you sure?' Grandpa asked. 'That's only his word for it.'

'Then Marvin can include the house in one of the clauses. If they object, we'll know Lenny is untrustworthy.'

'Does this Lenny seem very bright?' Patrick said.

'Well, not book-educated. More cunning. Why?'

'Somebody smart has planned all this. That person is behind our Lenny. I'm convinced it's Todd Steele.'

'Okay, I'll put it to him on Monday at the Council meeting. He always attends. So, what did you find at the camp ground?'

'Nothing of interest. Floods have washed the place clean. There was no connection with a sacred site that I could see.'

'How far from Pop's Place was it?'

'Oh, maybe three hundred metres. They would've been invisible to each other before the land was cleared.'

We had finished our roast lunch and Mum was serving dessert.

'So, what's next?' Patrick said.

Mum knew what was next. She stabbed her wooden

spoon at me. 'You keep your eyes off that Pixie. I know what happens with pretty girls today. They don't want to settle down and have children. They want the bright life. Break a man's heart in a small town, then off to the city.'

'That's a powerful speech, Mum, and you haven't seen her in years.'

When Patrick laughed, I said to Mum, 'Why don't you lecture him? His poor Glenda will die of old age as a spinster. If he hasn't saved the money for a ring, give him Grandma's.'

'Well, I have popped the question,' Patrick said.

The three of us gaped at him. 'Truly?' Mum said.

'Yes, I was waiting for the right time to tell you.'

'Oh, Patrick!' she cried and threw her arms round his neck.

'Well done, brother,' I grinned, pumping his hand.

'About bloody time,' Grandpa said, and reached into the sideboard for his five-hundred-year-old bottle of whiskey that Captain Bligh had brought to Australia. He claimed his precious whiskey was worth a thousand dollars, but Patrick and I had swigged it secretly and were not that impressed.

'When's the big day?' Mum asked while we drank a miniscule toast.

'First weekend after the crushing. November the fifteenth.'

I had another toast with Patrick — beer this time — then helped Mum with the dishes before returning to my flat at Shingley Beach. I was thrilled with Patrick's announcement. Glenda was a kind, sensible blonde who would give Mum sensible grandchildren, one of whom would inherit the farm. Although Grandpa had made no comment — apart from the toast — I think he was genuinely relieved. The O'Connor line had been assured.

*　　*　　*

On Monday morning I was upstairs finishing my cereal when I heard noises in the office. The clock showed five minutes to seven. I hurried down to find Heather moving the furniture.

'What's going on?'

'Is your Council meeting at nine-thirty?' she asked.

I was angry. 'What if it is? Go home and rearrange your own house.'

'Sorry. Thought I would surprise you.'

'You have.'

'Do you remember how we talked weeks ago about the need to organise the office better? The ad reps here, production in the centre, and news along that side? You had forgotten? Never mind. This office at the front can be a proper interview room. I will need the other office for myself. The printers and faxes can go at the back near the kitchen, the paste-up benches stay where they are, Billy and Roberta across from them, Mandy over there with her production files, Ethel in the centre and Pixie at the side near your office. She doesn't need to sit in a cubby hole anymore, and she can be my support at the front counter.'

'When did you plan all this?'

'Over the weekend. See, I've made drawings.'

'What if the others object?'

'They shouldn't. Everyone's got more space, and Ethel will be where she's visible. That'll help when she's setting the television guide and community news.'

'Ah, you did have a motive up your dirty sleeve. Pixie gets

a desk near my office so she's in and out like a barfly, while happy Ethel toils away on the showroom floor.'

'Don't be a cynic, Tom. Now lift the end of that cabinet.'

By eight-fifteen we had swapped everything around. Sure enough, staff barged through the door then halted, hands to the mouth like in a TV home makeover. Billy didn't care what happened provided he stayed near the back, Roberta had no problem in front of him, Mandy was fine near reception, and Ethel … let's just say Ethel's nose picked up a suspicious odour.

'Yes, more space for my files, that's good. But I'm out in the open. How can I concentrate?'

'Well, you need to be more accessible to the ad reps and Heather.'

'More accessible? The whole floor wouldn't be a hundred square metres.'

'One hundred and thirty to be precise. But that's not all. I want Billy and Roberta to sell more ads, which means that I'll need Pixie to gather news and write their advertorials, which in turn means I want you to set the TV guide and community news.'

'When is this to start?'

'Next Friday, and every Friday from then on.'

Ethel's eyes narrowed to button holes. Billy, Roberta and Mandy buried their heads in their work, Heather stood firmly at my left, and Pixie was nowhere to be seen.

'Ethel, we have to balance out tasks,' I continued. 'Dynamics in the workplace it's called. You'll find inside a month that the new system works marvellously.'

'Last week Pixie was setting copy. This week she's doing

your job. What's her next move?'

'Sitting in your chair if you're not careful.'

When Ethel marched to her desk, Heather turned to me and shrugged. Only last week it had been a contented office. So, I did as I had with Pixie and dialled the Koffee Kings, ordering coffee all round. When they arrived, I took one to Ethel and reassured her that she was valuable, and that I couldn't keep up the late hours filing news stories. We had to share the load, truly.

After a safe interval, Pixie appeared at the back door and sat behind her desk, which faced the front counter. At once the clatter of her keyboard rose above the office murmur. Her profile was now in my line of vision, further across sat Roberta, and beyond her a glimpse of the foreshore reserve through a side window. Peaceful oceans seemed light years away.

At eight-forty I made noises that I had a Council meeting to attend. Pixie was on her feet and at my door. She said nothing but had that puppy look on her face.

'Sorry, Pixie, but TV guide and community news come first.'

'That's all done, boss.'

'When?'

Her eyes were pleading. 'Does it matter?'

'You set it on the weekend. What did I tell you about that?'

'Please, I'm ready for the meeting, and you promised.'

I yielded, but not without a martyr's sigh. 'All right then. Notebook, pencil, agenda.'

'And name tag,' she said, opening her fist.

Only last week Heather had ordered a new tag that read:

Pixie Hanson. Journalist. She wasn't leaving that behind. Again, she was through the back door, into the Moke, and her briefcase tossed behind the seat.

'It's not a picnic outing,' I said to her.

'Do I look dressed for a picnic?'

Another smart business outfit, but no tartan. She had sewn an embroidered koala to the skirt pocket; a small decoration that, admittedly, fitted the girl. However, I wasn't in the mood for Pixie's high spirits. Aside from the morning's quarrel with Ethel, I had a nagging fear that the O'Connors were being set up for a fall.

CHAPTER 13

As it turned out, Pixie's attendance at the meeting paid an unexpected dividend, which I redeemed some weeks later. We arrived early but rather than stand about sharing gossip, I took her into the chambers, and explained the scene.

'Okay, Abdul Nader sits up there in the centre, the town clerk on his right and the six councillors either side of them. These seats at the back are the public gallery, and that table in the middle is for the press. No matter how exciting something might be, and that's rare, we are not allowed to speak unless asked. Of course, we can talk quietly among ourselves. Everyone does. The mayor works from this stapled book, which is a detailed agenda. We are supposed to read our copies before the meeting starts. Ignore the run-of-mill figures, but look for things buried in reports. Afterwards, ask the councillor who submitted the motion. If you want real fun, ask the one who seconded it. They usually haven't a clue what the motion was about. Right, it's nine-twenty. Sit here next to me. Take whatever notes you want and save your questions. During the break I'll introduce you around.'

We sat at the table with Pixie to my left, Herb McBride from the *Proserpine Gazette* on my right, and the *Mercury* journalist at the end. Behind us, a dozen people filled the public gallery, including Todd Steele on his favourite roost near the door.

Right on nine-thirty, Mayor Abdul Nader opened the Proserpine Shire Council monthly meeting. The first hour was business as usual, the second hour was an unscripted morality play, which — as in medieval theatre — contained all the elements of sin and retribution. For a start, Abdul learnt there's no such thing as a free lunch, or in his case, a free viewing. While reaching blindly for his gavel, he knocked a stack of papers on the floor in front of the media desk. Without hesitation, Pixie jumped from her chair and began gathering up the files. Abdul apologised. It was clumsy of him. Damn work space too narrow. Leaning over his bench to supervise the clean-up, his eyes rested on Pixie who worked awkwardly on one knee facing him. Not a man to hide the images his brain computed, Abdul's eyes blinked like signal lamps.

Rising to her feet, Pixie stood the pile on his desk. 'They're all here, sir.'

Abdul swallowed. 'Thanks, um, miss ...'

'Pixie. From the *Whitsunday Post*.'

'Thanks, Pixie. Now where was I?'

Abdul failed to recall where he was at. He fumbled, forgot his lines, and flipped agenda pages two at a time. As the meeting descended into farce, he called for a break. Cups of tea were rushed from the kitchen, smokers headed for the verandah, and Abdul cornered me near the urinal.

'Bloody hell, Tom, what are you doing to me?'

'Hard to say, Abdul. Give me a clue.'

He glanced around. 'That girl of yours. She's got my old fella jumping a fence. I can hardly walk.'

When I looked closer, I saw he was indeed bent forward awkwardly.

'How did she do that?' I asked, astonished.

'Just by picking up my files. Nothing else. It was the way she knelt, crouched.' He closed his eyes at the memory. 'And I'll tell you another thing. Her pants are not … um … ordinary. Live rabbits were staring at me. I saw them, clear as day.'

'I'm guessing they were koalas,' I said. 'Big difference.'

'Hell, Tom. As a rule, I wouldn't care, even enjoy it, but I've got a missus at home and a secretary who knows when I've licked a stamp.'

'Leave it to me, Abdul, but you owe me one.'

He groaned. 'Whatever …'

I left him alone and uncomfortable in the corridor, and strolled into the annex where I found Pixie chatting to two councillors. She held a cup in one hand, a notepad in the other, and was trying to juggle both while jotting down facts.

'Hi, Tom,' she said excitedly. 'I've got all the councillors' names, and I've met the town clerk.'

'You're doing well. Be back in a minute.'

I walked outside to where Abdul's secretary was puffing on a cigarette.

'Hello, Tom,' she said. 'How's the newspaper world?'

'Fine, Hattie. I've come looking for you. Abdul needs you, urgent like. He's at the toilets.'

Alarm crossed her face. 'What's wrong?'

'Pain down below. Worse than cramp.'

Throwing her cigarette into the garden, she hurried along the corridor. I had done my best for him, now he was in the hands of a professional. After an extended morning tea, a bell tinkled for everyone to resume their seats.

'Enjoying it?' I whispered to Pixie.

'Love it,' she said.

'You're not the only one. Okay, here comes Abdul.'

Although his eyes bulged more than usual, he walked manfully upright. In his wake strode Hattie who shifted her desk to Pixie's side of our press table, but apart from that curious move, she didn't utter a word.

At five minutes after twelve when the meeting closed, Abdul and Hattie disappeared through their bolt hole at the side while the rest of the crowd drifted into the corridor. Pixie tugged at my sleeve with a handful of notes. With one eye on Todd Steele, I glanced over the points she wanted to raise with councillors.

'Take that one up with Li Yang,' I said. 'In the past he's always argued against access to the river through his property. Now he's okay about it. Find out what's going on. In the meantime, I want a little chat with Todd. See you in the café for lunch at twelve-thirty.'

Before Pixie could reply, I dashed along the corridor and grabbed Todd as he was about to knock on the mayor's door.

'Haven't got a minute to spare, Todd?'

'Sadly not, Tom,' he said, glancing at his watch. 'How about three in my office?'

I jerked my thumb at the mayor's room. 'Don't worry about Abdul. He's going nowhere for an hour.'

'Why's that?'

'Old complaint.'

Steering him into the committee room, I said, 'Do you

know much about this Giya registration of a sacred site?'

'Only what you wrote in the paper. It's on Henry O'Connor's land.'

'Actually, the site includes our original farm house. Do you know Lenny Watkins?'

'The name rings a bell.'

'He is a Giya spokesman. Calls himself an elder and lives in a house at Woodwark Bay with his family. Todd, be honest with me. When you financed the heritage centre, did you meet any Giya elders?'

'Yes, an old couple who came down from Collinsville. Where is this leading, Tom?'

'We've done a study on the heritage centre and sacred site. They're linked through Lenny Watkins, who is a cunning fellow. He has let on that someone is backing him, but he won't say who.'

Todd snorted. 'I don't believe this. A Blackfella says he's getting a kickback, and you think it's me.'

'I'm trying to eliminate the possibles.'

'Bullshit.'

'Todd, only somebody with a grudge against Grandpa would single out the block of land that includes his house. Give me another name.'

Todd had gone purple, and was clenching his fingers. He leant towards me. 'Tom, you're like the rest of your family. All nasty pricks. But we tolerate you because the town needs a paper. The same can't be said of Henry who should be in an asylum. If I hear anywhere that Todd Steele is behind this Giya business, I'll sue you for every cent you own.'

'Fair comment, and I'll add an amendment. If we discover

that Todd Steele put one cent into the registration on Grandpa's land, he'll be the second Steele to run foul of the law.'

'Don't push your luck, mate,' he said, and hauled himself out of the room. I leant back and tapped my nails on the armrest. Our little chat had got me nowhere.

From the Council chambers I walked up town to the café where Pixie flicked through her notes.

'Hi, Tom,' she said as I sat across from her at the rickety metal table. 'Guess what? I spoke to the mayor.'

'That was fast.'

'I didn't intend to. I just happened to be passing his office when the door opened, and his face appeared. It was like I gave him a fright. He was about to pull the door shut when he remembered his manners.'

'And?'

'So, I said, "Thank you, sir," and squeezed past him into the room. How was I to know his secretary was there? "Yes, girl?" the mayor says like he's papa bear. "Sorry, sir," I said. "I wanted to ask a couple of things from the agenda." Before he could answer, she snaps, "Sit down here where I can see you." Which I did, on a hard wooden chair in the middle of the room. Then she eyes me up and down like she's skinning me with a razor. "If you want to cover Council meetings, dress decently. And tell that to your boss, Tom O'Connor." Then she throws me out the door before I can collect my wits. She's an old prude if you ask me.'

I outlined the reason behind the woman's behaviour. 'Pixie, when you gathered up the mayor's files, he saw koalas in a place he would not have believed. The sighting caused his old fella … verbatim quote … to jump a fence.'

She giggled. 'That's awful.'

'Don't worry, cane farmers are tough. But you're correct about Hattie. She thinks she's the virtue warden … her own conduct excluded. So, what do we have for a Council story?'

'Only that item about Li Yang's river road. In return for access, Council will build a boat ramp. How did you make out with Todd?'

'Apart from calling me a nasty prick, nothing.'

CHAPTER 14

When Lisa returned to port late Wednesday, she found the note I had left inviting her to call by my office. She arrived at six and because staff had left for the day, we poured drinks and retired to the balcony.

'Any progress with the sacred site?' she asked.

'Not really. Too many ifs, buts and maybes.'

We were seated in easy chairs with our feet up on the railing. Lisa had changed into my *Mercury* tee-shirt, and I was in a pair of shorts.

'Lisa, have you seen any drugs round here?'

She sat upright. 'Of course not.'

'No cannabis, meths, acid ...?'

'Why do you ask, Tom?'

'Heard a rumour the other night about drug dealers in the area. Weed being sold at Magnums and heavier stuff in the street.'

'I've seen nothing, but it wouldn't surprise me. Airlie Beach is a young town.'

'Ever tried the stuff?' I asked.

'Oh, experimented like most kids. Though I don't mind the occasional snort of coke.'

'Good gear, is it?'

'Coke is fine provided you are sensible. If you come across any, would you tell me?'

'Of course.'

After finishing the pizza we had ordered, Lisa dragged on a pair of jeans and we strolled up to the sailing club to watch the lights of the big ships rolling through the passage far out to sea. The breeze had shifted ninety degrees to the north, bringing with it a late humidity and the scent of islands. Lisa nestled against me until staff made noises they wanted to close.

That was Wednesday. On Thursday, production day for the paper, Todd withdrew his back page advertisement. When Billy arrived to pick up the copy, Todd's assistant, Lola, said the firm would not be advertising this week.

Billy rang me. 'Sorry, Tom, but she says no ad, and Todd is uncontactable. Gone urgently to Mackay to see his doctor.'

'Tell Lola we'll run last week's copy, and he'll get invoiced for it. Apart from that, as of Monday he pays full price for colour.'

'Crikey, Tom, that's a bit harsh. He might be on death's door.'

'He's not sick, and I bet he's not in Mackay.'

A truce had existed between the O'Connors and Steeles for close to a hundred years. I could have been more diplomatic the previous Monday, but when I asked Todd about the Giya registration, he jumped straight to the high moral ground. Odd response for a man whose conscience is clear.

*   *   *

The paper came out on Friday with nothing dramatic in its content. All the usual things from baby photos to school reunions, plus an article on Councillor Yang's new road funded by the taxpayer. Half an hour before staff gathered for the team meeting, Heather burst into my office with a card to sign.

'What's this?'

'Pixie's birthday.'

'Pixie?'

'Yes, she turns eighteen today.'

'Today?'

'Stop parroting me. I left a note on your desk. Now give me twenty dollars. We've bought her a new briefcase.'

They had also bought her a cake with eighteen candles. When she blew out the candles like she was dousing a furnace, Heather told her to make a wish.

'I wish that ...'

'No, you mustn't wish aloud.'

'This one I will. I wish the *Whitsunday Post* becomes the best newspaper in the world, and everyone who works here is happy.'

With that she drove the knife right through the cake, spoiling the wish twice over, then popped a slice between her lips. As she did so, she turned to me and laughed. She was back into her original McLeish tartan, and not for the first time I reflected that life was as you made it.

Following the cake and chat, Heather gathered the dishes and said quietly to me. 'Her pay goes up two dollars an hour.'

'That can't be right.'

'She's worth every cent. The good news is that Todd phoned this morning. He wants you to ring him back.'

Since I was in no hurry to phone Todd, I called Pixie into my office and mumbled something about pay increases and her work schedule, including a tutorial on journalism.

'Tom, I really am grateful,' she said. 'I love my job and the paper, and everything.' Abruptly, she stepped across and kissed me, and was gone.

'No more birthday cakes,' I said to Heather, who missed nothing.

After a suitable time had passed, I picked up the phone and dialled Todd's direct number.

When he answered, I said, 'You asked for me, Todd?'

'You are an arsehole, Tom.'

'That's how Grandpa talks when he reads the paper.'

'I said no ad this week, but you went ahead anyway. So don't expect to get paid.'

'Todd, you know it's impossible to replace a full page at short notice. What is your game?'

'After that crap on Monday, I decided never to use your paper again.'

'Todd, your contract lasts another six months, so if you withdraw, it'll cost you and I'll fill the back page with another real estate. What you can do is assure me your hands are clean. Promise you know nothing about Lenny Watkins or the cultural registration on Grandpa's land.'

He was silent for a minute. I waited. 'Tom, you have my word. I am totally innocent.'

'Thanks, Todd, I appreciate that. Now phone my grandpa and tell him.'

'I've told you. Isn't that enough?'

'No. When he gets your call, we can all breathe easier.'

'Okay, and that's the end of the matter?'

'Yes.'

'And today's ad is free?'

'Good try. Free colour.'

With that he hung up and the truce was back in place. Two hours later I phoned Patrick who confirmed that Todd had indeed rung home, and given his assurance. Patrick then called Marvin Fumbleton who would draft up a Memorandum of Understanding between Henry O'Connor and the Giya people. We would do everything in our power to protect the site's cultural significance, while in return they would respect Grandpa's old house. The O'Connors would meet Marvin at ten on Tuesday to read the draft, and if satisfied, sign it.

That afternoon at one-thirty I attended the launch of the new heritage centre in the main street. At the entrance I was introduced to a gracious Aboriginal couple, Uncle Joshua and Aunty Tess, who were Giya elders from Collinsville, and whose children, they explained proudly, were at agricultural college. Despite her diminutive height and bad hip, Aunty Tess was almost regal as she moved from group to group, sharing anecdotes about her tribe's customs, including the dying art of gunyah construction. Uncle Joshua, less at ease, mostly smiled and avoided eye contact.

Ten minutes into proceedings, Lenny made his appearance in a suit two sizes too large. He came straight across and shook hands.

'Tom O'Connor,' he said warmly. 'Glad to see you. Your grandpa here? I hoped to meet him.'

'No, he's at home looking after the sacred site. This must be a wonderful day for you, Lenny.'

'Too right, Tom. Good day for everyone.'

The launch went as planned: three routine speeches followed by the minister cutting a ribbon, polite applause and a flurry of handshakes. Out of the event, the only observation I recorded in my notebook was: *Todd Steele and Lenny Watkins never acknowledged each other. Not a zip.*

CHAPTER 15

By five-thirty that Friday all staff had departed, and I was alone with the hum of artificial brains feigning sleep. I shut the computers down, locked the front door, and was about to head upstairs when the phone rang. Lisa had a surprise for me. 'Tom, grab a hat and change of clothes. Jade is taking the *Calvados* across to Daydream Island for a moonlight cruise. We have twenty people, all young, rearing to go. Cost includes your food and drink. We'll be home by lunch tomorrow. Can you make it in ten minutes?'

Snatching a pack, I ran down to the marina where the *Calvados* buzzed with activity. Lisa stood by one of the lines. 'Quick, Tom. Throw your kit on board and help load those boxes.'

After the boxes of beer and wine had been stored, Jade gave the order to cast off and we motored serenely into the channel. Drink in hand, I stood at the wheel with Jade who manoeuvred the ketch through the narrow waterway. A blue-clad young woman, whom I had not seen before, relieved me of eighty dollars.

'Surprised to see you here, Tom,' Jade said.

'Surprised to see you heading out,' I answered. 'Isn't Friday your night at Magnums?'

'Not always. Anyway, welcome aboard. Must be eighteen months.'

'Yes, all of that.'

When we reached the breakwater, he threw the wheel to starboard, pulling the timber vessel into the wind.

'Prepare to raise sails!' he shouted. As he held way, he called, 'Sails ahoy!' and the female crew began heaving on the bleached lines. Male guests sprang to their aid and rolls of canvas fed into the sky.

'Not giving a hand?' Jade asked me.

'No. Cricked my back loading boxes.'

He laughed, big white teeth gleaming like pearls.

Below me on both sides of the deck young people were spread out, quaffing plastic glasses of wine, laughing, shouting above the wind. The sun hovered over the *Calvados'* stern quarter, bright and warm, its glow turning the spray into red filigree.

'I ought to give up newspapers, Jade, and buy a yacht. Sail the oceans by day, and trawl Airlie's bars at night.'

'I ought to give up sailing,' Jade replied, 'and buy a newspaper. Eat with nobs every day, and screw the town once a week.'

'It's not that easy. Say the wrong thing and you get lynched.'

'Don't start crying, Tom. People might think you're dinkum.'

'You have lots of money, Jade. Where does it come from?'

'I run a tight ship. Nothing wasted.' He pointed to Lisa who was edging along the deck with a platter of savouries and a carafe of wine, her hair tousled and legs shining like gold. 'Great bang is she, Tom?'

I frowned. 'She's a fun girl. I like her.'

When Lisa saw us at the wheel, she came aft with the platter. 'I thought you might be hungry. What are you talking about?'

'Life's little enigmas,' Jade replied. 'Tell Ingrid to start cooking. I want dinner finished before we reach the island.'

'Aye aye,' Lisa said and returned to the forward deck.

'Can't be a lot of money in this, Jade. No matter how tight the ship.'

He was silent for a time, the wind tugging at his cap. His eyes swung from the compass to the sails and back to the compass. 'I received a bit of money when I was young,' he said. 'My dad was a ship broker who did all right. Died of a heart attack. Lots of posh money in Sydney Harbour, and he knew how to extract it. I had seen the *Calvados* over the years, but everyone, myself included, thought I should follow in Dad's footsteps. Buy and sell boats. Watch for investment properties. So, I purchased a handful of waterside blocks before prices went crazy. I sold a couple, which bought the *Calvados*, and now I do what I enjoy ... sail the best companion I've ever had.'

'You must want for a real companion though? The one and only woman in your life?'

'Not for me, Tom. No complications. The women up here crave the mystique of the Whitsundays ... and I oblige them.'

'What about Sydney in the summer? What happens then?'

'I let Sydney look after itself.'

With that, he closed the book. I sat on the rail, content to feel the power of the ketch through the swell. Down below, the crew organised guests, smiling as they moved from group to group.

Lisa, the brightest of them all, was an asset to Jade, and I could not believe he hadn't wanted to sample her wares.

Around eight we finished eating, and by eight-thirty we had dropped anchor off the short beach at Daydream Island.

Jade called the passengers together, many of whom were fuzzily drunk. 'Right folks, these are the rules. Rule One: I know there's a big moon, lots of light, but nobody goes in the water without a life vest. Rule Two: Nobody jumps off the deck. Beach only, no exceptions. If you want to go ashore, we have a zodiac that'll run back and forward until late. Rule Three: Nobody in the water after ten-thirty. That gives you two hours to snorkel and swim. When I blow the whistle, everybody out. You can sleep on the beach or onboard, that's up to you. We have plenty of bunks. The first zodiac leaves for the beach in five minutes. Food, wine, life jackets and blankets will be taken ashore. Have a good night.'

For the next couple of hours crew attended to guests, then at ten-thirty Jade blew his whistle. Lisa helped round up the strays, those who wanted to remain ashore and those who wanted a bunk, and made her final run with passengers. She motored to where I sat on the beach, feet buried in the sand, sampling one of Jade's chateau-de-cardboard reds. Lights bobbed on the *Calvados* as she rose and fell in the choppy waves, music drifted across the water, and the moon basted the ocean in streaks of silver.

Lisa fixed the anchor, then sat beside me. 'Enjoying yourself, Tom?'

'I couldn't be more relaxed.'

'Not helped by the wine?'

'Yes, amazing stuff. You sharing my blanket tonight?'

She took off her cap and ran fingers through her hair. 'Well, that's foreplay out of the way.'

'Are you all right?'

'Sorry, Tom, I thought this would be fun. I haven't seen you all night.'

'That's how it is, Lisa. I pay eighty dollars to lie back and dream. You get paid eighty dollars to cook and clean.'

'What did you dream about?'

'A life with no commitments, like Jade.'

'Forget about Jade,' she said, and rolled onto her elbow. 'Can I have a glass of your wine?'

'Sure, I found a whole box of the stuff,' and lifted my life jacket to reveal a cask.

'You naughty boy. That's meant to be shared.'

We dragged the zodiac above the high tide mark, and wandered along the beach to a quiet spot where we spread out the blanket.

After a time, Lisa said, 'Stand for me, Tom.'

I did as asked, all silver and shadow.

'I wish I could paint. You're so handsome like that. A Greek statue in the moonlight. And the moon does you a kindness, softens the edges, stylises the fancy bits … like in a comic book.'

'Done with the poetry?'

'Don't be a sceptic, Tom. Life is a poem really … lots of different verses … some fast and happy, some slow and sad … until the last line and a peaceful ending … one always hopes.'

Before sunrise, Lisa and I were awake, the blanket folded,

then a quick swim in the ocean. I helped drag the zodiac into the water, then remained on the beach while she fetched two coffees from the *Calvados*. We sat together, savouring our coffee, warmed by the rays that filtered through the casuarinas in the dune behind us.

'Have you settled into the Whitsundays?' I asked her.

'Yes, I like the place. At first, I thought it was a bit shallow, too pretty for its own good. But I'm changing my mind. Some nice people live here.'

'I have an idea.'

'Yes?' she said cautiously.

'Why don't you share my flat? Lots of positives. You'd have a short walk to the marina, and our time together would be more relaxed.'

'And sex twice a night,' she added.

'If it helps you cope.'

'I'll think about it, Tom, but I'm not sure the plan would work. Apart from the sex, we know nothing about each other.' She kissed me on the cheek. 'Let's not change things. Neither of us is going anywhere.'

Her response wasn't quite a snub. 'Okay Lisa, we have ten minutes, so let's open a few cupboards. Before catching Jade's ship, what did you do?'

My timing could not have been worse. At that moment Jade blew his whistle, and she jumped to her feet like a retriever.

'Breakfast on the beach. Give us a hand with the boat, Tom.'

As we puttered back to the ship, Jade leant on the rail watching us. A blonde came up and rubbed against him like a cat but he shrugged her away. The mystique of the Whitsundays, she just discovered, ended at daylight.

'Get cracking, you,' he said brusquely to Lisa. 'We have to be out of here in an hour.'

While Lisa helped the crew with breakfast dishes, I wandered downstairs to the toilet, but pretended to miss the sign and sidled aft to Jade's cabin. The door was pulled shut but not locked. I slipped the latch. Bigger than a master bedroom, the cabin had polished oak lining the walls and two picture windows that were thrust open. The bed was neatly made — probably the blonde's last task — and everything shipshape. Because nobody had seen me, I eased inside and quickly tried a few cupboards. All locked. Wardrobe, locked. Matching drawers under the bed, locked. A small drawer on his dresser was ajar. I slid it open. Inside, a watch inscribed with J. T., some jewellery, a few papers and a wallet. I opened the wallet and the top card was Seamus Carney, barrister-at-law. So even Jade needs a lawyer. I was about to flick through the remaining cards when I heard a noise in the passage. I closed the drawer, and gazed nonchalantly out the window.

Jade was at the door. 'What the hell are you doing here?'

'Sorry, Jade. I missed the turn. Was admiring the view. Awesome.'

He looked around. Nothing was amiss.

'Damn it, Tom, this is my private space.'

'My apologies, Jade. The mistake was genuine. Sorry.'

'That's all right,' he said grumpily. 'You'd better move if you want breakfast.'

On the beach I ate ham and eggs while sitting next to Jade's blonde, whose face was on her knees. After giving her best effort, she had been tossed aside like a spent toy. I felt sorry for her.

CHAPTER 16

We arrived back at Abell Point Marina shortly before lunch on Saturday. It had been a quiet trip home with every second passenger nursing a sore head. Jade had remained at the wheel, talking in monosyllables to anybody who opened a conversation, which included me. At the marina, Lisa said she would be delayed an hour before coming up to my flat. Furthermore, she couldn't stay because the *Calvados* was sailing to Whitehaven next day, and she had chores to do.

I replied, 'That's fine. Drop in and I'll give you a lift.'

Although tired from the previous night, I sat at my desk and trolled through the papers demanding my attention: debtors, creditors, insurance brokers, tax collectors, letters to the editor.

When Lisa called by at two, I drove her to her house. She was silent all the way.

'What's eating you?' I asked.

'Nothing.'

'Come on. Speak up.'

'That was wrong of you to snoop in Jade's cabin.'

'Who said I was snooping?'

'He did.'

'I strayed there by mistake. No harm in that.'

She grinned. 'What did you find?'

'Not a lot. Every drawer and cupboard was locked, though I did peer inside his wallet. A business card for a lawyer named Seamus Carney. Mean anything to you?'

The way she reacted, I thought it had, but she shook her head. 'The name's not familiar, but lawyers are like doctors. You never know when you need one.'

'I guess so.'

'Anyway, Tom, he called you a pest. I'm not to take you on board again. He was really angry. Said people like you need therapy.'

'He's mixing his metaphors. Pests need pesticide, and people like me don't need therapy.'

'How would you know?'

'Because I'm not crazy. Well, not the barking-mad type.'

'You don't have to be crazy to need therapy.'

'Good point. Any chance of a session tonight?'

She giggled. 'Sorry, all booked out. Besides, there's a beaver full of sand to wash.'

*　　*　　*

That Saturday night I felt uncharacteristically down. Something was missing, and I assumed the *something* was what people called home. I was twenty-five, had lived in the Whitsundays most of my days, yet I had acquired nothing of value except for a small newspaper and an empty flat. Adding to my misery was the admission that a woman had entered my life, and I was lonely without her. When I asked Lisa to move in, my intentions were noble. I did want a companion to share my flat and provide the makings of a home. I also wanted … well … in truth I didn't know what I wanted. But it wasn't loneliness.

The hand on my watch said the time was now seven, and I was in a dilemma. Either sit on the balcony with the black dog for company, or follow a custom inherited from my father. Choosing the latter, I took bait from the freezer and motored down to the rivermouth where I cast for salmon. Without doubt, I loved that suck and gurgle of the mangroves, the distant plop of a jumping fish, the magnetic red lamps of crocodile eyes. I never felt alone when down on the river.

*   *   *

Next morning, I drove across to the farmhouse for Sunday lunch. Paper clippings, guest lists and photos were strewn across the living room table where plans were in hand for the wedding. Glenda bent over the table sorting through bridal catalogues. Whenever she came upon a dress she liked, she took it to the kitchen for Mum's opinion, which followed in the vein: 'That's beautiful, love. Green suits you.' After giving my view on bridal gowns, I joined the men on the verandah where Grandpa sat in his favourite chair nursing a whiskey and soda. A pair of frosted beers stood in a tray. Patrick snapped the cap off one and handed it across.

We touched bottles. 'Cheers.'

'How are you today, Grandpa?' I enquired.

'Lousy.'

'Sorry to hear it.'

I wandered back to the kitchen where Mum was trying to read a recipe without her glasses. 'What does that say, Tom?'

'No brussels sprouts or cabbage.'

'Be sensible. The meal will never get cooked.'

I read out the ingredients then said, 'What's up with Grandpa?'

'He's frightened. This sacred site business is killing him. I know everyone thinks it will turn out all right, but not your grandfather. To him we lost Pop's house the day the papers were served.'

'What can I say to reassure him? Todd Steele has sworn he's not involved.'

'Try a different approach. It might cheer him up … and ask him to slow down on the grog. At this rate, he'll be blotto by lunch.'

After passing by the living room where Glenda's happy glow illuminated every corner, I sat with Grandpa on the verandah and reminded him of Todd's statement.

'I wouldn't trust that prick as far as I could boot him,' Grandpa declared.

'We sign the MoU on Tuesday. Did Lenny's lawyers object to any of the clauses we requested?'

'Not at all,' Patrick said. 'Marvin claims we have negotiated a good compromise. The sacred site becomes a legal entity on the condition we retain access to the house.'

'So, Grandpa, why the glum face?'

'Something's not right. I can smell it.'

When I glanced at Patrick, he suggested the three of us stroll down the hill and look over the old house. Better than watching Grandpa moodily sink tumblers of whiskey.

Pop's Place was a compromise between the grandeur of a Queenslander and the practicality of a worker's cottage. Bush-sawn weatherboards clad the house on opposite sides, while the back was a closed-in sleep-out at one end and kitchen at the other. On the fourth side an open verandah faced the river. Because of the slope of the land, the rear of the house sat at ground level while the front was on one-metre stumps. Behind the kitchen, a rainwater tank squatted against the outdoor laundry and a brick path led to the clothesline. Further back, a pile of rocks was the inspiration for an ornamental garden.

Grandpa pointed to the camellias. 'That's where my father died. Did you know that?'

'No. What happened?'

'He shot himself.'

We stared at Grandpa. I heard myself saying, 'You serious?'

'Everything became too much for him. Aged just fifty-two and saw himself as a failure. Cane was doing poorly, his wife had left home for a man in town, and I had found work at the mill. It didn't help that his two brothers had gone to war, won medals, and since left the district. One afternoon he fed the animals, doused the fire in the stove, and put the gun to his mouth. Right here where these camellias grow. I came home late from a night shift, and found him with a lamp. Bloody terrible. And I had no idea. I knew things were tough but never imagined he wasn't coping. It was left to me to work the farm, which I did. I found a nice girl, your grandmother, who I married and we had a son. Sadly, your grandma died of TB eight years later but your father grew up to be a strapping young man. So, you can see why this sacred site business hurts me. O'Connors have a powerful attachment to this chunk of land, even stronger than Lenny's family.'

Patrick and I were silent as Grandpa told his story. Although we had heard countless myths and legends about the O'Connors, we knew nothing of suicide.

Grandpa read our thoughts. 'We never talked about such things, even to one another. Folk knew of the O'Connor Protocol where you covered for your brother, but they didn't know we also hid the truth about my father. He had done everything right except make things right. And now he's about to get screwed again.'

My instinct was to walk Grandpa back to the house, cheer him up, but I stood rooted to the camellias where my great-grandfather had shot himself. His life had turned out to be so awful, his view of self-worth so diminished, that he had put a gun to his mouth. And what of Grandpa who had become increasingly erratic of late? To have come home and found his father's brains scattered through the garden. Was the pain still cutting into his heart, the monstrous thought that he should've been aware, that he ought to have done something? Patrick had found our dad lifeless under a tractor, but that was a tragic accident. Was suicide no less a tragedy, or was it the chronic debt paid by a family who recklessly invoked the protocol?

When we returned to the house for lunch, we were in a sober mood, which Glenda's wedding chatter failed to lighten.

Tuesday morning in the office was again spent with Ethel who had not warmed to her change in circumstances. In her mind she had been singled out for punishment when Heather and I reshuffled the desks. I began by ordering her a new chair, which arrived at morning tea.

She eyed it suspiciously. 'Thanks, Tom. But since I'm the only one with a new chair, there must be a catch.'

'No catch, Ethel. Some time back you said your chair was uncomfortable. We've bought you a new one.'

'I also said I'm not paid enough.'

'One thing at a time.'

I left her unwrapping the plastic and returned to my office, calling for Pixie as I went.

'Have you done that article on the heritage centre?'

'Yes.'

'Good. We need a follow-up to the airport extensions. Phone the manager.'

'Tom, can I make a suggestion? There's a second lead on Li Yang I want to pursue. He runs a shoe shop at the end of town. I've often been there. I'd like to find out what he knows about repairs to the levee bank.'

'Any reason in particular?'

'He has submitted a tender to do the earth works. Why

would a shoe man do that?'

'How do you know about the tender?'

'I saw his name twice in the agenda, once for the boat ramp and once for the levee bank. So, I read through the committee minutes.'

'Nice work. Get on the phone to him.'

'Why not face to face?'

'You won't have time.'

'I will if I join you in town this morning.'

'Who said I was going to town?'

'You did, last week. Said you had another meeting with the solicitor. While you're busy with him, I could stroll up to Li's shop.'

This was not the first occasion Li Yang had walked a tightrope with his conflicts of interest. Like any resilient politician, he shook hands with the right people and had a powerful mate in Todd Steele. But there are mates … and mates. There are tightropes … and tightropes. It wouldn't hurt for Pixie to give the rope a shake.

'Okay, I leave in twenty minutes. Be ready.'

After telling Heather I would be absent for two hours, I collected my file on the sacred site and made my way out the back door. Under a lean-to where I housed the Moke, I kept a few tools and a bottle of engine oil. As I squeezed between the car and office to access the bonnet, I overheard Ethel say to Mandy, 'She's off with him again, and it ain't news she's chasing. We oughta start flashing our knickers.'

I checked the oil, let the bonnet close with a bang, then walked via the front door to Heather's desk. 'Tell Airlie Office Supplies to come back and fetch their new chair. It's wasted here.'

Heather frowned. 'She'll leave.'

'If I'm lucky.'

Returning to the car, I waited for Pixie, who for some reason now wore a jacket despite the mild weather. Yellow banksias had been stitched to the jacket and skirt. As she jumped over the passenger sill, she tossed her briefcase into the back and tugged a cap over her hair. She turned to me and smiled.

'What are you so cheerful about?' I asked.

'I'm off to town to do a job. Why can't I be cheerful?'

'It makes people suspicious.'

At Marvin Fumbleton's office the little procession of Grandpa, Patrick and myself filed into his inner sanctum.

'*Qui totum vult totum perdit,*' he said.

'And I'll have coffee. Two sugars,' Grandpa replied.

'Sorry, Henry. Don't serve coffees here. *He who wants everything loses everything.*'

'It was only a bloody coffee.'

'No, I meant folk in general … greedy folk.' He wiped his nose. 'Are we … um … ready to sign?'

'No last minute changes?'

'Everything is in order. Here is their fax.'

He handed the two pages to Grandpa who passed them to Patrick.

'Read them aloud, son.'

When Patrick reached the end, he said, 'That's it. "Yours faithfully, Seamus Carney for Mason Edelstein and Birch".'

I came awake. 'Who is their lawyer?'

'Seamus Carney.'

'I know that name. I saw his card on the weekend. It was in the wallet of a boat skipper.'

'So what?' Marvin said. 'Nothing unusual about a skipper keeping his lawyer's card.'

'Maybe, but quite a coincidence given the thousands of lawyers in Sydney.'

At ten-forty Lenny Watkins arrived at the solicitor's office in his Land Cruiser. He was back into jeans and a cowboy shirt, and looked every part the tribal elder.

'I'm here to sign the papers,' he said to Marvin's secretary at reception.

'Yes, of course, Mr …?'

'Watkins. Henry O'Connor knows me well.'

Because we had been waiting in the office with the door open, Grandpa heard the exchange. 'I've never met you,' he called out.

Lenny entered Marvin's office and thrust out his hand. 'Course you have, Henry. My family camped on your river flat for years. As a little kid I fetched barramundi to your missus, and you gave us tea and flour.'

Grandpa had reluctantly taken Lenny's hand. 'I don't remember that.'

'Maybe I change too much. Anyhow, this sacred site is good for everyone. Your dad's house is safe and our culture is safe.'

'But why there?' Grandpa asked. 'You could've had anywhere on the whole farm.'

Lenny laughed, shaking his head. 'Because it is sacred to Giya. Many secrets in that patch of earth.'

Grandpa sighed. 'All right then, let's sign the damn thing. Is your signature the only one needed?'

Marvin intervened. 'Henry will sign for the O'Connors, Lenny for the Giya. I will witness both, then the paper goes to Lenny's legal firm who will file it in Canberra with the … um … Australian Heritage Commission.'

Once the formalities were complete, Lenny saluted cheerily and returned to his Land Cruiser. The three O'Connors shook the hand of Marvin, who beamed. 'I told you we could pull it off, Henry. Who said Proserpine lawyers are country bumpkins? The law is the law.'

'Don't look so pleased with yourself.'

As we filed out the door, I asked, 'Coffee?'

'Bugger the coffee,' Grandpa replied. 'I want a real drink.'

We walked around the block to the Metropole Hotel where we perched on stools and Grandpa ordered three whiskeys. We had downed the first and were toying with the idea of a second, when Pixie entered the bar and stood at my shoulder. The place went quiet.

'Hello, Mr O'Connor,' she said awkwardly.

Grandpa wasn't the only one studying her. 'Oh, yes, I know you. You're Tom's …'

'Journalist, Grandpa.'

Patrick sprang up fast for a man about to get married. 'Hello, Pixie. Nice to see you again. Sit here. I'll fetch another stool. Sorry I can't offer you a drink.' And pointed to the underage notice.

I set my empty glass on the bar. 'You're right she can't accept a drink, Patrick. She's at work, and the office calls.'

'I am over eighteen,' she said.

The barman eyed her carefully. 'Let her stay, Tom. I'll buy youse all a drink.'

'Thanks, Jack, but we're out of here. Bye Grandpa, bye Patrick. See you on the weekend.'

As we walked down the footpath, Pixie asked, 'How long were you in the bar?'

'You sound like Heather. Why the question?'

'You could've bought me a small wine.'

'No such thing as a small wine.'

As we motored back to Airlie Beach, Pixie filled me in on Li Yang and his interest in levee banks. Years earlier, the town of Proserpine flooded every wet season when the river poured out of the mountains and met the incoming tide below the bridge. A levee bank was constructed but in recent years had collapsed, and Council had secured a state government grant to repair the damage. Councillor Li Yang had bought himself an excavator, loader and tip truck — all registered in the name of a niece — and tendered for the work. Although the tenders were still at committee level, the public had not been informed of Li's finger in the pie. Clever Pixie had discovered this anomaly from research into Council records, and had been keen to test her theory.

'Catch him off guard?'

'Yes, like I'd touched him with a wire. Then he clammed up.'

'Did you tell him you were from the *Post*?'

'Sure did. He was all smiles at first. Sat me down on his

fussy little couch and described the wonderful things he'd done over the years.'

'Then you hit him with the ownership thing?'

'Sort of. I was running out of time.'

'Is there an article in it?'

'We would need more facts. And honestly, I don't know how to go from here.' She turned to me. 'Sorry, Tom, I'm out of my depth.'

'Never mind. You've done the town a service. I bet in the next agenda you'll find he's declared a conflict of interest and resigned from the works committee.'

'Really?'

'Yes, but he'll still win the tender.'

'So, what's the point of exposing him?'

'Life in the media is about finding a balance between the decent and the decadent. Sometimes we are right, sometimes we are not. Sometimes we publish, sometimes we don't. But remember, my child, we are always on the side of the good.'

She gazed at me in astonishment. 'Where did you read that?'

'Just made it up.'

And we laughed at the hubristic nonsense.

*   *   *

From his bench under the mango tree, Billy signalled me to join him. After waiting until I was alone, he said, 'The cops have arrested two men for selling crystal meths at the pub. I'd like to do a story.'

'What kind of story?'

'One that requires answers. Where did the stuff come from? Is there a local supplier? This arrest goes deeper than two young blokes slapping palms at the bar.'

'Billy, you're a salesman with weekly targets. We now employ Pixie to chase news.'

'I know, Tom, but my sales are fine and this story is a bit heavy for Pixie. The night I told you about my brother you said, let's warn people. Now we can. We've got evidence.'

'Very well, you have two hours on it. Take Pixie but look after her.'

Inside the office I found everyone busy, and Ethel still on her new chair. When Heather caught my scowl, she walked over and said quietly, 'Leave her alone, Tom. These things take time to settle.'

'Like my blood pressure.'

I turned to Pixie. 'Complete those notes later. They've arrested two men for selling meths. Go with Billy up to the police station, and don't let him out of your sight.'

She frowned. 'Why would I?'

'Just do as you're told.'

After she had left, Heather cornered me, 'Just do as you're told ... *please.*'

CHAPTER 18

Over the next five weeks, the heritage centre attracted tourists as predicted. Southerners learnt how the Aboriginal tribes ate fruit from the black bean and stinging trees. They learnt how they caught giant turtles and made fish traps. They discovered the names of local tribes and the Dreamtime origins of the Proserpine River, and they also heard snatches of the Giya-Bumburra dialect. At the same time, when no further reference was made of the site at Pop's Place, we all relaxed, including Grandpa, who dared to hope his fears had been imaginary.

At the paper, we held back on the meths story until the two men had been tried and convicted for selling drugs. The article raised no eyebrows until the final paragraph, in which Billy implied that police suspected a meths lab was operating in the area.

The usual Friday morning calls came in. First were the SOWs concerned for their safety, then the town Doh-Doh who insisted drug labs were a papal conspiracy. The third caller, a husky-voiced woman, said, 'Tom O'Connor, you watch yourself. Bad men get angry when they see their names in the paper.'

'How can they get angry? Their names are public knowledge.'

'I'll tell you a secret,' the woman continued. 'One boat in the Whitsundays is trafficking the stuff, and one person here knows more than you think.'

'Go on.'

'Look around you, Tom O'Connor. Don't be hoodwinked.' And hung up.

Friday morning calls were taking a turn for the worse. I'd hardly caught my breath when the mayor was put through.

'What the hell's going on, Tom? I rang Chief Inspector Gudinski and he's not heard of a drugs lab. Are you playing silly buggers?'

'No, Abdul. Billy and Pixie swear by their facts.'

'Pixie? That's not the girl …?'

'Anything else you wanted, Abdul?'

'Just call the inspector and get the official line.'

Around mid-morning the phone rang again. Heather lay her palm over the handset, turned to me and mouthed, 'Todd Steele.'

I took the call guardedly. 'Hi, Todd. Haven't seen you in weeks.'

'That's right, Tom. Been up to the eyeballs with work. Care for an early lunch?'

I picked myself up from the floor. 'You buying lunch? What's the catch?'

He laughed easily. 'No catch. Thought it was time to mend fences.'

'Sure. Eleven-thirty at Captain Morgan's?'

'Sounds perfect. See you there.'

I looked at my watch. Ten o'clock. Time for the staff meeting. I went to the kitchen fridge and drew out a bottle of cheap sparkling wine and a half-dozen glasses.

When everyone was assembled, I said, 'I've broken a rule of our ancestors and will toast today's paper with a bottle of wine.' I held up the bottle. 'This Trevi has cost me a day's pay, but it's for a good cause. Billy and Roberta have achieved new sales figures, Ethel and Mandy have set record levels of copy, and Heather has clawed debt back to a manageable level.' I poured the wine into the glasses.

'As for our ace reporter …' When I turned to Pixie, she was like a puppy sitting by the food bowl. '… Abdul Nader will never be the same again. Nor will Li Yang. Nor my grandpa. They have, well, entered the age of enlightenment.'

'You might too one day,' she chirped, sipping her drink.

'Everyone has done a great job,' I continued, ignoring the aside. 'We're a team to be proud of.'

When I arrived at Captain Morgan's, Todd was already seated over a glass of gin and tonic. He had his hand to his eyes, gazing across the bay to where a moored lightship harassed a yacht that was forced to tack awkwardly on its run to Gloucester Island. I climbed through the rail and perched on a stool beside him.

'Hi Todd.'

He jumped. 'Damn it, Tom. Use the door like everyone else.'

'You move fast for an old man. Guilty conscience?'

He was at once the old Todd Steele. Ageless, charming, shrewd. 'Conscience? Can't even spell the word.' And we chuckled like two priests after Saturday confession.

I then ordered a beer while waiting to hear the purpose

of our lunch. After munching his ice into fragments, he said, 'We haven't always seen eye to eye on your articles, Tom. Most of the time you do a great job. Give the town its fix of gossip and thrill.'

'Come to the point, Todd.'

'Your front page this morning on drugs. Two young blokes breaking the law, naughty boys but harmless really, unless you're an idiot. Like me selling you a kitchen knife. If you stabbed yourself with the knife, does that make me the bad guy? I'm a bit concerned, Tom, that you ran the story on page one. Frightens the crap out of investors. They think we're in a crime wave. I lost three sales this morning.'

'Sorry to hear that, Todd, but it's vital we crush these dealers early. How would Airlie look as the nation's drugs capital?'

'That's most unlikely, and you know it. I'm not asking for much. Just tone down the hype.'

'Okay, I'll consider the idea over lunch. Any objection to that?'

At which point I ordered mud crab for entrée and grilled snapper for mains, all washed down by two glasses of excellent pinot noir. While I ate heartily, he sipped his drink and toyed with a chicken salad.

'Best lunch I've had for months, Todd. You picked a great restaurant. Now about this drugs business. A friend of mine lost his brother to heroin in Sydney two years ago, but it started in Airlie … a few pills here, a shot of acid there, a snort of coke. He didn't buy the drugs from so-called harmless young boys. He bought them from people who knew he was addicted, or soon would be, and they would have a customer for life, short as it was. So, I can't agree with you that a drugs story should be buried inside the paper. And another thing, we didn't invent the story. It came after a police conviction. I don't like sensationalism any more than you do. In fact, I avoid it. Todd, thanks for the lunch, but my view on drugs won't change.'

Todd threw back the last of his gin. 'Might as well talk to the wall.'

'Don't play the angel with me,' I retorted. 'This town is a Todd Steele gold mine, nothing more.'

After glaring at each other, we sensibly shook hands. We both knew that in regard to the expression *gathering into barns*, Todd helped fill my barn and I filled his.

*   *   *

At the office I found Billy at his desk, sorting through the advertisements for next week's paper. From those ads he would create a dummy layout, around which we would fit the news.

'Billy, be truthful with me. Did the police actually say we have a meths lab in the area?'

'Yes, Tom. The dealers claim they bought the stuff up north, but they hadn't been north in a month.'

'Is that their only proof?'

'Sort of. They are hoping we flush out a rat.'

'Did Pixie hear any of this?'

'No, a young cop was showing her through the office.'

'I told you to stay together, Billy. You know what this means? Your lab story is only hearsay.'

'Don't you believe me?'

'I do, but that's not the point.'

'Sorry, Tom. It won't happen again.'

'Okay, what else is there?'

'In the past two weeks I have run down more leads. Enough to feel confident to write a second article. Mostly tips from the pub … one about the meths lab, one about couriers. No real proof, but it will keep the topic alive. What do you reckon?'

'Just go easy. I'm already nervous. After your article this morning, I took a call from a nameless witch. She said a Whitsunday boat was trafficking drugs, and that somebody here has information they are not sharing. Do you think that's gossip or fact?'

'Both are possible. Dozens of boats use Airlie, and any number of women could be holding back on you.'

'Why a woman?'

He shrugged. 'Sounds like a female thing.'

Although Billy's remark about the fair sex was a throwaway, it made me reflect on the expression 'pillow talk'. To my knowledge, only one man — Jade Wilson — had slept with every obliging woman in Airlie, and in doing so would have mined countless secrets. Because we hadn't spoken since the contretemps on his yacht, it was time for a conciliatory drink.

Around four-thirty on Friday I saw the *Calvados* masts enter the channel. Sails neatly furled, she chugged huffily against the tide. A few gulls on the afternoon shift trailed in her wake, squabbling over the uneaten food that the crew tossed overboard. When the yacht slowed to enter the breakwater, I hopped into the Moke and jostled through the cabs and buses to my 'reserved' space, from where I watched her glide into her berth.

Lisa spotted me and frowned. 'Don't stir him up,' she mouthed.

While the yacht was being tied fore and aft, I called out, 'Hi, Jade. Have a good run?'

'Yeah, Tom.'

He presented his back as the gang plank went down, guests departed and crew packed the sails. After he had secured the wheel, I climbed on board.

'Care for a drink, Jade?' I ventured.

'What did you bring?'

'Nothing. I figured maybe a beer at Captain Morgan's, or even one of those mixes in the box behind you.'

'Help yourself,' he said.

'Join me?'

'Sorry. Lots to do.'

'Jade, I was out of order straying into your cabin. I've said I'm sorry. Now, we've been sharing bottles of rum for years. Old pals in the Whitsundays. Let's not kill the friendship.'

He studied me hard, then with an effort, plastered on the toothy smile. 'Sure, Tom. Give me twenty minutes and I'll see you at Morgan's.'

When I returned to the deck, I said quietly to Lisa, 'Tonight at the *Calvados* table,' and sauntered along the boardwalk, admiring the season's new boats and noting those that hadn't been out all week. From the top of the ramp, I counted the vessels. More than one hundred, and anyone could be a drugs courier. Not to mention the hundred moored outside the breakwater. The information given me by the witch was next to useless.

For the second time that day I sat on a barstool at Captain Morgan's and watched the ocean traffic around Airlie. When a squall began marching towards us from the direction of Flame Tree, staff in bright Calypso shirts rushed to secure the umbrellas lining the jetty. Soon the squall was upon us, punching the deck with fat stinging drops, then the squall was gone, and staff reopened the umbrellas like mushrooms after rain.

I was into my second beer when I saw Jade on the timber

ramp. Disregarding my wave, he greeted me loudly for the benefit of friends and admirers. 'Hi, Tom. How's Mary?'

I laughed dutifully. 'Shot through. Like a virgin.' It wasn't all that funny but Jade enjoyed taunting me with it. One night at Magnums, he had attached himself to a girl named Mary who looked barely fifteen. In the toilets Jade had confided, 'She's a virgin, Tom, and she's hot for me.' I was scandalised. When I cornered her back in the restaurant, she said she had only wanted to sleep with him because she was homeless. I took pity on her and let her spend the night on a mattress at the flat. Next morning, Mary and my wallet were gone, and when I reported her to the police, they expressed no surprise. She was nineteen and had been lifting men's wallets for years.

After I had ordered two beers, Jade said, 'You wanted a chat, Tom?'

'That's right. This morning I took a call from a witch … well, she had a scratchy voice … who said there's somebody in Airlie — a woman, we think — who is holding back on me. I don't know why, but it spooked me. Now, as half the population are women and you entertain them in bed, I wondered if you could throw light on the call.'

He shrugged. 'Sounds daft to me. What was the context?'

'We ran a story on two blokes convicted for selling meths, and we implied that cops thought a lab was operating in the area.'

'So, an old hag rings to say a woman, or maybe not a woman, has a secret?'

'That's right. I suppose it does sound ridiculous.'

His eyes narrowed. 'We all have our secrets, Tom. Even

you. Did she say anything else?'

'A Whitsunday boat is trafficking drugs. That was no help either. More than two hundred yachts use Airlie in the season. You can't think of a skipper acting suspiciously?'

'If I did, I'd drown the bastard. Drugs are a pet hate, as you know.'

We finished our drinks, had another, and chatted with seafaring folk who called by our table. When we departed — Jade to his accommodation behind Captain Morgan's and me to my parked car — we agreed to stay in touch, and left it at that.

The light had faded from the sky and the street lights meandering up Shute Harbour Road glistened in the dusk. A second squall followed the first, dumping its rain in cold, horizontal streaks. After mopping out the water from my car, I drove back to the flat, which stood in darkness. A woman emerged from the lean-to. It was Lisa, still in crew uniform and dripping wet.

She was shivering. 'I thought you would never come.'

'Why didn't you wait at the car?'

'What good would that do? It doesn't have a roof.'

'It's not hard to put up. In any case, Jade and I are best mates.'

'Thank goodness. Now for a hot shower and warm clothes.'

I opened the back door, switched on the stairs light and led her up to my flat. After stripping off her wet clothes, she wrapped herself in a blanket, and poured a large whiskey.

'What will you have, Thomas?'

'Therapy, if it's still available.'

Half an hour later we showered and dressed, caught a taxi down to Magnums, and sat at the *Calvados* table with Jade and his female entourage, not one of whom appeared in the least bit secretive.

*   *   *

Next morning, Saturday, the rain had passed and the bay sparkled. While Lisa reclined on the balcony, I made toast and coffee, then took the tray outside. A willy-wagtail flew down to the rail, chittering for the crumbs that Lisa offered.

'I'm not the only one eating out of your palm,' I said.

'Don't say that, Tom. I'm the fly in this ointment. I caused the friction between you and Jade. You're my lover and he's my boss.'

'You didn't ask me to snoop. So relax.'

After buttering her toast, she said, 'Yesterday at the bar, did you talk about me?'

'Hardly at all. Compared a few anatomy notes, no huge detail ... put that fork down, I was only joking. To be honest I wanted Jade's help. After running a story on drug dealers, I took a call from a witch about somebody in Airlie keeping a secret. We assumed the somebody must be a woman, and that Jade, being the town's super stud, might provide a clue to her identity.'

'All because he's a super stud?' she asked, puzzled.

'Yes ... you know, pillow talk. He probably thinks the same of us ... passing secrets in bed.'

'We don't … do we?'

'Not really. I told you about his lawyer's business card, but that was in the car. The witch also said a local boat is trafficking drugs. Have you heard of that?'

'No. Crews don't interact, and if we did, drugs are the last thing we'd discuss. We are here for the tourists. You writing another article?'

'Possibly. Cops think there's a meths lab in the area. Might as well keep stirring.'

'If I can help, let me know.'

'I will. So, what are your plans for the weekend?'

'Our next trip is not until Monday. Any suggestions that don't include bed?'

'Why not come for lunch at the farm tomorrow? Mum does a great roast, and you can see the Giya sacred site.'

'Your family might get ideas,' she said warily.

'My family? Never.'

That afternoon I rang Mum, and told her she'd have an extra mouth to feed on Sunday.

'Who are you bringing, Tom? Not the Hanson girl!'

'Of course not. Pixie's on my staff. This is a woman who works one of the boats. A casual friend.'

'Doesn't sound very casual,' Mum said. 'Try not to be late.'

Over the years I've observed Mum gather facts — or part thereof — on the people around her, and collate them into a book. With those she rarely meets, a sentence or two is adequate, but with family members the chapters can run to hundreds of pages. The book then becomes an encyclopaedia. So when Mum rang late Saturday and asked if the friend preferred chicken to roast pork, or potatoes to beans, I could refer to earlier pages in her book. Mum wanted to know if the friend was Jewish or Greek, Irish or vegan; or — safest of all — a cane farmer's daughter.

'Has this friend got a name, Tom?'

'Yes, Mum. Lisa. And she'll eat whatever you put in front of her.'

'That's a big help. I hope she's a nice girl.'

'And if she isn't?'

'I'm sure she is. It will be so lovely. Six of us seated at the table together: you and Lisa, Patrick and Glenda, me and Grandpa. I don't think that's happened before.'

'Slow down, Mum. Lisa and I are casual friends.'

CHAPTER 20

When I collected Lisa on Sunday morning, her antennae had received Mum *en clair*. The woman who slid her legs modestly into the Moke was the 'nice girl': cute summer dress, restrained jewellery, a hint of make-up.

And edgy as a kitten.

'For heaven's sake, Lisa, it's only Sunday lunch.'

'I know, Tom. I've been saying that all morning.'

'Just be yourself.'

'You mean, polish your trumpet under the table?'

'Smart thinking. Grandpa likes brass.'

After calling into the bakery at Cannonvale, we drove out to the farm. The rain had freshened up the cane that grew three metres tall. Soon the harvesters would roar into life, fires would light the sky at night, and dusty, smoky air would replace the autumn humidity. Many farmers, including Patrick, had prepared for the fires by slashing their headlands, which gave the farms a semi-urban appearance. As I drove, I pointed out the features of the landscape: Mount Dryander that hunkered in the distance like a huge bear, Mount Marlow with its scrubby face, and Mount Julian whose foothills were disappearing under bricks and mortar. When we topped the rise on Conway Road, I traced the line of the Proserpine River where it snaked through the valley.

'And see, across there from the river to Palm Creek, that's Grandpa's farm, and you can just make out our home on the ridge.'

'Where's the old house and sacred site?'

'They're not visible from the road. You'll see them from our back verandah.'

Soon I turned off the main road, bumped over the tram line and drove along the gravel track to our house.

'Wow!' exclaimed Lisa. 'I thought cane farmers were poor.'

'We are. The bank owns everything.'

'Is this where you grew up?'

'Yep. This is O'Connor country.' I laughed at the glamorous take on what was, in reality, a tough existence.

Mum's watchdog face appeared at the kitchen window. Moments later, people spilled onto the porch and crowded round the car.

'Lisa, this is my mother Jenny, my grandpa Henry, my brother Patrick and Patrick's fiancée Glenda.'

'Hi,' Lisa said nervously.

'It's okay, they've all had their shots.'

Mum and Glenda took charge of Lisa, and led her inside to the wedding showroom that was now divided into four compartments: clothing, accessories, nuptials and reception.

Grandpa leant against the verandah rail and scratched his back on a post. 'She's got a damn good body, Tom. I worried the O'Connor genes might've leached out of you.'

'Thanks, Grandpa. All criteria safely met.'

'Is she for marrying or screwing?'

'Back off. I've spent the last six hours saying what nice people you are.'

'Well, it is a fair question,' Patrick said.

'Okay, she comes over every Friday night and we play scrabble.'

'I thought as much,' Grandpa said. 'A smart cookie.'

Inside, we had drinks and sat down to lunch; Grandpa at one end of the table, Mum at the other, and the happy couples on either side. Mum had correctly picked Lisa was Anglo-Saxon, and prepared an English roast that included dumplings, sprouts and turnip. Another page for the book.

Grandpa was eyeing Lisa's cleavage, when she asked, 'When does the paperwork go through for the sacred site, Mr O'Connor?'

He glowered. 'Too damn soon.'

Although he probably hadn't meant to swear, Mum shook her finger. 'Henry, mind your tongue. We have guests.'

But Grandpa was not contrite. The dread had taken hold. 'In about two months, I reckon. Some drongo in Sydney has written to say they've received the papers. If all conditions are met, which should take about six weeks, we'll receive an official notice. And that's it. The Blacks will own my house and land.'

'It was theirs first,' Lisa ventured. 'Maybe nothing will change.'

A silence descended like an unwelcome fog, then slowly dissipated.

'So which boat do you work on, Lisa?' Patrick asked.

After describing the *Calvados* and crew, she told anecdotes about the people who sailed with her, and even threw in a few juicy tales to show she was a woman of the world. Pretending nothing was amiss, she engaged Grandpa in her narration, and like an old walrus swimming out of the Arctic he slowly thawed.

When sweets were finished, the men cleaned the dishes while the women took glasses of Moscato to the verandah.

'Is she with us or against us?' Grandpa demanded.

'Neither. She didn't realise you were so touchy.'

'Touchy? You wait until Watkins gets his hands on the loot.'

'Grandpa, she made a reasonable point. No harm in that.'

'Lisa's okay, Tom,' Patrick said, 'but guess what happened yesterday? Lenny and his family set up camp on the river like in the old days. It's true. We wouldn't have known except we saw their fires. What's he up to? I thought he lived in Woodwark Bay.'

'He does.'

'So why is he on our farm?'

'How would I know? Maybe he likes to camp in the school holidays.'

'We don't want him there.'

'Then tell him to piss off.'

'You come too. It's a family thing. We'll do it now.'

'All right,' I said. 'Just the two of us. Grandpa, you go onto the verandah and talk to the ladies. Patrick and I will drive down to the river.'

'Take a gun with you.'

'Don't be mad, Grandpa.'

While I steered, Patrick listed off the points he intended raising: trespass, common courtesy, arable land, dangerous crocs.

'Leave out the last one,' I said to him. 'They know more about crocs than we do.'

'Duty of care,' Patrick replied. 'If we don't warn them about the crocs and a kid gets eaten, they'll sue us for millions.'

We followed Palm Creek to its mouth, then cut through the cane until we met the old track that fishermen had used in the days when giant bass were hauled from the river. On a flat grassy area known as The Gums, Lenny's family had set up their camp. Lengths of nylon cord were strung between trees to support blue poly tarps and dung fires burnt in a circle, incensing the swarms of mosquitoes. Two small tents for a shower and toilet stood a distance off, and a large green tarp provided shelter for the Land Cruiser. In the centre of the camp a fire smouldered under a rack that hung with billy cans. Lenny and his family sat around the fire drinking like it was a Christmas rehearsal, while the kids played in the river in an inflatable canoe.

We drew up to the edge of the camp and walked over to the fire.

'Hi, Lenny,' I said.

Lenny turned and squinted at us. 'Howdy, bro'. Come and share a drink. Good fellas.'

'No, we haven't come to drink.'

He laughed. 'Then youse can piss off.'

'No, Lenny. This is our grandfather's land. What are you doing here?'

'Drinkin' and eatin' and sleepin'. What ya think I'm doin'?'

Patrick stepped forward. 'You're trespassing. This is private property. Pack your junk and bugger off.'

Although Lenny was drunk, his voice turned cold. 'Hey, Whitefella, this land belongs to Black people. You bugger off.'

'If you don't start packing in five minutes, I'll throw you and your junk in the river.'

'Take it easy, Patrick,' I said. 'They can leave tomorrow.'

'Like hell! They can piss off now. Back to wherever they came from.'

Lenny jumped to his feet and seized a stick from the fire. He held it in both hands. Others in his family grabbed sticks, and crouched in a half circle like warrior cavemen. 'You're a prick,' Lenny said. 'White prick.'

Patrick didn't need hearing twice that he was a prick. He took two steps forward and smacked Lenny hard in the chest. Lenny yelped and broke his stick on Patrick's arm. Grimacing, Patrick deflected a second blow to his head and punched Lenny in the stomach. Four hours of cheap wine spurted onto the grass as Lenny sank groaning to his knees. A stick came whirling through the sunlight and caught me on the hip. As I stumbled, more sticks flew through the air. Suddenly we were back-to-back, warding off the storm.

'We need a distraction,' Patrick yelled. 'Set a tent on fire.'

We grabbed burning sticks and threw them into the nearest poly tarp that erupted in flames. All this time Lenny squatted on his haunches, watching in bewilderment as the mayhem swirled around him. Patrick seized him by the collar. 'Be out of here by two,' he said, 'or I'll be back with the cops. Do you hear me?'

When Lenny nodded, we ran to the Moke, reversed out of

the clearing and drove wildly up the track. Sticks continued to rain on us while acrid black smoke rose above the trees.

Near the end of the track, I pulled over. 'Bloody hell, Patrick! Great diplomacy.'

'That bastard wanted to kill us. Did you see him?'

'You went at it like Attila the Hun. What did you expect him to do?'

'You're getting soft, Tom. Chat over a pot of tea, that's more your style.'

'They'll be mad as hornets. God only knows what's coming next.'

'I reckon they'll disappear to the peace and quiet of Woodwark Bay. They wouldn't be that stupid to damage anything. The cops would nail them inside an hour.'

'Let's hope you're right,' I said as I let out the clutch.

'Oh, Tom, one other thing if you don't mind. Keep me out of this.'

I stared at him. 'You're covered in bruises, two cuts to the head. You think if you look angelic, nobody will notice?'

'I don't mean that. You remember that assault charge from a few years back?'

'Go on.'

'Glenda knows nothing about it. Let's just say they were legless when we arrived. Started throwing sticks. Went berserk. When we calmed them down, they promised to leave. Then we drove out of there.'

'Not even your dog would believe that.'

'It will if you sound convincing.'

When we arrived at the house, Grandpa and the three women were on the verandah gibbering at the smoke rising above the trees. They ran down to the car to meet us, Mum in the lead. 'Patrick, Tom. You're hurt. Good Lord, what happened?'

Patrick waved them off. 'It's not serious, Mum. If only we'd known they were blind drunk. We tried to reason with them, then next minute, *wham*, a stick came flying through the air. They went crazy, so we jumped in the car and came home.'

'This is terrible. Henry, ring the police. And Glenda, fetch the first aid box from the laundry.'

'Damn the police. I'll ring the army,' Grandpa replied.

'Steady on, everyone,' I pleaded. 'We've got a few minor bruises, that's all. When Lenny's family sober up, they'll leave. I promise.'

'Did either of you hit anyone?' Mum asked.

'Only in defence. I punched him when he came at me with a stick, but like Patrick said, we backed out of there pretty fast.'

'I thought Lenny's family was all women and kids,' Grandpa said helpfully.

When Glenda returned with the first aid, they eased off our shirts and lay us on stretchers on the verandah like in MASH. Mum and Glenda cleansed our wounds with antiseptic as Lisa watched in horror.

'It's like this every Sunday,' I said to her. 'Rarely the same tribe twice.'

'It isn't funny,' Mum snapped. 'You could've been maimed, or worse, and what a shocking display for our guest. Makes us look like hillbillies.'

'Yes, sorry. We should've gone down in the morning when

everyone was sober. Still, they're leaving and nobody was hurt.'

After Patrick and I had been mended, we took coffee on the verandah, and in a deliberate attempt to play down the incident we talked about the upcoming harvest and the weather. Meanwhile, smoke died from the river bank and the view across Pop's Place to the mountains was restored to its Sunday serenity.

*   *   *

'What really happened down there?' Lisa asked on the ride home. Her eyes were still big with fright. 'We could hear the fighting from the house. It was like people were being murdered. Shrieking and screaming. Then we see you two come flying out of the smoke.'

'Settle down, Lisa, you'll burst an artery.'

'You can't take the law into your own hands, you know. If they were squatters, you should've called the police.'

'We didn't have time. They were onto us before we got out of the car.'

'At the house, you said you tried reasoning with them.'

'I did.'

'And Patrick's knuckles were bleeding yet he hit nobody. Your case is full of holes, Tom.'

'I didn't know I was preparing a case. For a deckhand you're well informed on the law.'

'For a newspaper editor you know very little.'

After travelling in silence for ten minutes, she said, 'Sorry, Tom. It must've been traumatic.'

'It did have its moments.'

'Are you still shaking?'

'No, heart's back to normal.'

She sat facing me in the Moke, one hand on the dash, the other on my shoulder. She didn't know whether to laugh or cry. 'It was like in a Western movie. Your grandfather even went inside and loaded a gun. I feared we might get scalped.'

'Lisa,' I said calmly. 'It was nothing, really. Grandpa always over-reacts and they were so drunk they won't remember anything.' My fingers started to explore. They touched warm, soft cotton. 'So relax. What did you think of Glenda?'

'Lovely girl,' she said, and put my hand back on the wheel. 'Not while you're driving.'

CHAPTER 21

After delivering Lisa to her house, I returned to the flat in a troubled mood. Talk about fiasco! Patrick's bout of idiocy aside, I had imagined a few words in Lenny's ear would send him back to Woodwark Bay. But what was the man's game? Why leave a house with an enviable view for a few sheets of poly tarp? And I was also concerned that his family had the upper moral ground.

White Landowners Assault Homeless Blacks. What a great headline it would make. My only thought as I went to bed was that if people kept their mouths shut, the incident might blow over.

No such luck.

The Monday edition of the *Daily Mercury* carried the article on page three with a photo of several blacks lying on the ground, and "tribal elder" Lenny Watkins propped against his burnt-out tent swathed in bandages. The headline read, *Old Scores Settled In Fight For Sacred Ground.* Apart from the staged photo, the article was thin on details. All the information had come from Lenny, who implied the assault was payback on his tribe for registering a site of cultural significance. And the article finished with the usual line, "Police are investigating".

I picked up the phone and dialled Jacinta Marano, the *Mercury*'s editor. 'Hi, Jacinta. Tom here. I've read your story on the Blacks who got assaulted at Proserpine.'

'Yes, Tom. Just appalling. When they say Proserpine is the deep north, they aren't wrong. Give production a ring if you want to use the photo. They'll send it up.'

'No thanks, Jacinta. The story is more fiction than fact. That's my family mentioned in the paragraph about sacred ground. The tribe's people were blind drunk, and they were trespassing on my grandfather's farm. Nobody got hurt save the tribal elder who clobbered me with a stick, and it had nothing to do with Aboriginal culture. Another thing, why didn't your journalist phone the land owners?'

'Shit, Tom. Are you being straight with me?'

'Of course I am.'

'Hold the line.' After playing tinny music for five minutes, Jacinta came back. 'Sorry to keep you, Tom, but I spoke to the journalist. She said Lenny didn't know who his assailants were, but there were four or five men wearing masks. And his family were camped on a piece of O'Connor land they had occupied for centuries.'

'That's crap. And where did you get the photo?'

'The film was dropped into the *Mercury*. Apparently taken on the victim's camera.'

'You've been duped, Jacinta, and so have we.'

'Damn it all. How hard did you hit the fellow?'

'Not hard enough. Can you do another story tomorrow? New angle, that some fresh details have come to hand.'

'Sure, Tom. This makes everyone look silly.'

My chin was propped in my hands when Heather came through the door.

'Morning, Tom. Glad to see you're in one piece.'

'Thanks, Heather.'

'No broken teeth or anything?'

'No. Everyone is safe and well. Emergency services have taken their chopper off standby. Now do me a favour, and write your question and my answer on the whiteboard. Others will be in soon.'

'Tom, I've been with you long enough to know you wouldn't start a fight with Blacks.'

'Thanks, Heather. I welcome your support.'

'You're going to need it. The police are already at my desk. They want to see you.'

She returned with two big cops wearing a ute load of gear on their belts. I wasn't likely to run.

'Good morning, sir,' the sergeant said. 'Are you Thomas Henry O'Connor?'

'Phil, you know he is,' Heather said.

'Make us three coffees please, Heather.'

'Not for us, thank you, sir,' Sergeant Phil Manning said gruffly. He had known me since I was a kid.

'Okay, Heather, just one for me,' I said. 'And take your time.'

'Sir, were you on the bank of the Proserpine River in an area known as The Gums at or around two-thirty p.m. yesterday?'

'Yes, Sergeant.'

'We have a complaint that you and your brother assaulted a group of Aboriginal persons at their camp at the said time. Do you have anything to say on the matter?'

'Yes, we assaulted nobody. During lunch yesterday we noticed Black people were camped on our land. As we hadn't given permission to anyone, we drove down to ask why they were there, and to explain they were on private property. That's all. When we arrived, I discovered we had been ambushed. They had cameras in place, they pretended not to understand us, then started throwing sticks they had grabbed from the fire. One of them, a man called Lenny Watkins, hit me with a stick here, …' I showed the bruises on my arm and hip '… and he also hit my brother. In defence I struck back, then we ran for it. Meantime, they had set fire to one of their tents, and were trying to burn our car.'

While his partner continued to scribble notes, the sergeant showed me the photo from the *Mercury*. 'Have you seen this?'

'Yes, this morning. The picture is a fake. Look at all the bandages on people. Why would a group of friendly campers have a boot full of clean white bandages. Did you see the wounds under these bandages? Did anybody? We should be charging them for assault and trespass.'

'Do you have any witnesses?'

'My brother Patrick.'

'Where is he now?'

'On the farm.'

'And he'll corroborate your story?'

'Of course, he will. Sergeant, I don't know why my family was set up. The sacred site, which is nowhere near the bank of the river, has been registered and approved. That book's closed. Everyone left the table happy. Yesterday, we find Lenny Watkins camping on our land. We try to talk to him, he provokes us. What's going on?'

'I have no idea, sir. I'll discuss this with my chief inspector and get back to you.'

Then he said quietly, 'Strewth, Tom. This isn't looking good.'

'Don't I know it.'

Pocketing their notebooks, Sergeant Manning and his constable filed out the door, watched by my staff who had since arrived for work. As their broad backs disappeared, the eyes turned to me.

'Haven't you lot seen coppers before?'

'Not in your office like that,' Ethel said.

'Is that what you wanted? A shoot-out? Sorry to disappoint. Okay, today's not a show holiday. Let's get to work.'

'Tom, can I write a story on it?' Pixie asked.

'I'll pretend I didn't hear that lunatic question,' I said, and stormed back to my desk.

Shortly, I heard a knock on my door. I didn't look up. 'Yes.'

From the corner of my eye, I watched Pixie move to the chair at the front of my desk. Not a word. The silence became unbearable.

'What is it, Pixie?'

'Morning, Tom,' she whispered.

I threw my pen on the desk and glanced up. She was holding in the tears — only just. I waited.

'I'm sorry,' she said.

'That's okay.'

'I guess it was a daft question, and besides, I saw the photo in the paper this morning. It was horrible. You would never do anything like that.'

'Thanks, Pixie. I appreciate the thought. Is that all?'

She nodded.

'You look a mess. Grab that box of tissues on your way out.'

As she stood from the chair, she said, 'I did have an idea and it's not silly.'

'Try me.'

'I overheard what you said to the police. Why don't you go down and sneak a photo? If they are still on your land and their bandages are on the ground, it will show they are lying.'

'Pixie, that's brilliant. Fetch me a camera.'

I grabbed my keys from the desk and hurried out the door. As I ran to the driver's seat, she jumped in the opposite side with the camera and her bag.

I looked at her. 'Where are you going?'

'Please, Tom, the story's mine too.'

'What about the airport follow-up?'

'That's done.'

'All right. Buckle up.'

We drove through Cannonvale, along the main road past the cane fields, and turned off a kilometre before our house. After following a headland as close as I dared, I parked behind tall cane then changed out of my office clothes into fishing gear I kept in the back.

'Phew! Those clothes stink,' she said.

'No need to get personal.'

Using cane for support, I climbed onto the bonnet. 'Let's

see what our friends are up to. Yes, there's the Land Cruiser and one of their tarps still tied in a tree.'

When I returned to the ground, I said, 'You wait here. I won't be ten minutes.'

'No, I'm your back-up.'

'They'll see you and run.'

'They'll smell you first.'

She reached into her bag for a set of clothes.

'What are you doing, Pixie?'

'It's a gym outfit. I go to aerobics after work.' Turning her back, she replaced her blouse and skirt with a green tee-shirt and shorts. Finally, she laced up a pair of joggers.

'Is that it?' I asked, bewildered.

'What more do you want? Lead the way.'

We dodged from bush to bush, at times crawling through the long grass. When we reached camera range, we parted the grass. The family sat in a circle eating a late breakfast. While they ate, they talked happily. Bandages were strewn on the grass and broken sticks lay where they had fallen. To one side, the burnt-out tent stood as a charred reminder of yesterday's skirmish. Remarkably, the broken and bleeding Watkins family had healed overnight. As quietly as an SLR camera allows, I took a series of photos, making sure the date and time were printed on each image. But when I was about to retreat, I put weight on my bruised hip, which collapsed under me.

I handed Pixie the camera. 'Quick, back to the car. Stay out of sight. The office phone is under the seat. Contact Heather. Tell her to come. I'll talk to Lenny. Go.'

I waited a minute for Pixie to slither backwards, then rose to my feet and hobbled forward. 'Hello, Lenny.'

'What you doin' here?' he snarled.

'This is my land. You promised you would leave this morning.'

'That before you come here kickin' us, burnin' down our tents.'

'We came to talk. Anyway, we've recorded on tape that we tried reasoning with you. I have spoken to the police and shown them my injuries. Unless you're out of here by eleven, they'll press charges.'

'What bloody rubbish. I have photos.'

'I've already seen them. Obvious fakes.'

He became cunning. 'Why you sneak up on us?'

'I wanted to hear you joking and laughing. No injuries that I can see.'

'You make big mistake, Tom O'Connor. Lenny's no fool.'

He stepped up and punched me in the ribs. 'That's for yesterday.'

When I recovered my breath, I said, 'Fair enough,' and punched him in the head. 'That's for my brother.'

Lenny glared at me. 'You're bad news, white prick, and I don't believe you. Sit down.'

'No, sorry, I have work to do.'

'You're goin' nowhere.'

After pushing me onto the grass, he dragged his family to one side and argued with them about my fate. He couldn't do anything too foolish, and the longer they argued the more time it gave the cavalry. I checked my watch. Almost ten minutes had passed.

'Hey, O'Connor prick,' Lenny said from the centre of his conference, 'you come here alone?'

'Of course. Like when I saw you at Woodwark Bay.'

'Why are you on foot? Where is your car?'

'At the house. I walked down from the house.'

One of the women rose to her feet and began retracing my steps through the grass. 'Hey, Lenny,' she called.

When Lenny hurried across, she knelt on the ground then pointed back the way I had come.

'Liar, you have girl with you. Why a girl? Who is she?'

'Sorry, Lenny, your bush skills are out of whack. Maybe one of your kids went in there?'

'Don't play games with me.' He held up a strand of Pixie's long Caucasian hair.

'Lenny, all the O'Connor family wants from you is peace and quiet. We gave the Giya their sacred site, and we thought that would be the end of it. This is not a public camping area, nor is the ground sacred. Please, go back to Woodwark Bay so everyone can relax.'

'You never relax with Blacks.'

'That's not true.'

He snorted. 'Where is the girl?'

'She's at the house.'

One of the women tilted her head. 'Bro', car comin'.'

Moments later we heard a car shifting through the gears as it drove along the track.

'Might be the police,' I said.

'Quick, clean up camp,' Lenny said. 'Make it tidy.'

While the Watkins family dashed about the grass picking up bandages and rubbish, the car drew nearer. A white sedan halted at the edge of the clearing, and out stepped Heather and Pixie.

'What's going on?' Heather demanded in her no-nonsense voice.

'Nothin',' Lenny muttered. 'Just mindin' our own business.'

'Doesn't look that way to me, sir. You all right, Mr O'Connor?'

'Yes, thanks. Do you mind hanging about while Lenny packs his bags.'

'We're goin' nowhere,' Lenny said.

I whispered loudly. 'Lenny, this woman is from social security. A wise man doesn't upset social security.'

'Never seen her before.'

'And you won't again if you're out of here in ten minutes.'

Lenny and his family took less than five minutes to pack their gear and load the Land Cruiser. Sullenly they climbed aboard and drove along the track towards town. When the sound of their engine had faded, I said, 'Thanks, Heather. I was ready to stroll out when you arrived.'

'What were you thinking, Tom? You trying to die young?'

'No, but we've taken great photos. Good for a news page, even better for evidence. We're not the bad guys in this.'

had driven the track from the house to The Gums many times over the years, and before that, Patrick and I had taken our push bikes to the river where we spent afternoons fishing or crabbing. Even further back, I remember my parents driving to an area where we picnicked on sandwiches, and I recall Grandpa walking us toddlers past a goanna that observed from the safety of a tree. All those memories were happy, but inside twenty-four hours the place had turned ugly.

Mum came out to the verandah of the house, and watched in astonishment as the Moke drove up from the river.

'What's up, Tom?'

'Nothing, Mum. We did photos for the paper and checked the family had left. Everything's all right now.'

'Your grandfather has worried all night. And that picture in the *Mercury* this morning. Just dreadful.'

'Yes, that's partly why we needed our own. Where is Grandpa?'

'On the verandah. He's writing a letter to the editor.'

'That'll be a scream. Mum, this is Pixie Hanson. She's a bit scruffy from doing the photo. Okay if she takes a shower?'

'Pixie Hanson? My word, you have grown. Do you have a change of clothes?'

'Yes, Mrs O'Connor, in my bag.'

'You go and shower, love, and I'll run an iron over them.'

After I had directed Pixie to the bathroom, I said, 'Mum, stop fussing. Girls wear rumpled clothes today. It's the fashion.'

'What nonsense.' Then she held me in her gaze. 'I hope you're being careful. She's prettier than I thought.'

'Listen to yourself. Lisa was here only yesterday.'

'I haven't forgotten. Make sure you don't either.' With that, she bundled me to one side. 'Change out of those smelly clothes, then say hello to your grandfather.'

Grandpa was at the verandah table scratching laboriously on a notepad. He lifted his head at the sound of my footsteps. 'Did you read today's paper, Tom? Damn scandalous.'

'Grandpa, I've spoken to the editor. She'll run our side tomorrow.'

'And where will she get that?'

'From me. We don't want conflicting stories.'

'You'll downplay Lenny's mob. Make them look innocent.'

'And you'll inflame things. I've already had a visit from the cops. I don't need a second.'

'Tell them to interview me.'

'That'd make their day.'

He returned to his letter just as the kettle whistled in the kitchen. Pixie, in one of Mum's robes, came onto the verandah carrying a tray with four cups and a plate of biscuits.

'Newspapers give me the shits,' Grandpa muttered. 'They print nonsense then expect their victims to respond with pissy little letters.'

Pixie said, 'Ahem,' and set the tray on the table. He looked up at her. 'Aren't you the girl from town?'

'Yes, sir. Pixie Hanson.'

'You and Tom sleep here last night?'

'Of course not!'

At that moment Mum bustled onto the verandah with her clothes. 'Here, love, they're ready to wear. I adore the tartan.'

'Thank you, Mrs O'Connor,' she said, and escaped inside.

'Grandpa, I've been down the river to check Lenny's family have gone. Everything seems okay, and hopefully they won't return. The police already know that Lenny started the fracas. Please don't send your letter, whatever the content. It won't help things.'

'Who says?'

'Here, give it to me.'

Grandpa crouched over the page like a gnome over his toadstool.

'Do as you're told, Henry,' Mum said, 'and put an end to this nonsense.'

Grumpily, he handed the letter across. 'Wasted my bloody time.'

Ignoring the tea tray, I headed out the door to where Pixie waited near the car. Mum followed. 'Bye, Tom. Bye, Pixie. You take care now.'

'Bye, Mrs O'Connor,' Pixie replied, and slid into the passenger seat.

A couple of minutes later as we turned onto the bitumen she said, 'Your grandpa's mind is warped. His first thought just now was we had slept together.'

'You were half dressed.'

'I was in your mother's robe … if you don't mind. But Tom, why is he so unpleasant? He was the same in town. We're on his side, can't he see that?'

'Pixie, his universe is wobbling on its axis. I hardly recognise him myself.'

'That's awful. I'm sorry.'

She was quiet until Shute Harbour Road then said, 'Do you mind if I ask a personal question?'

'What sort of personal?'

'I wanted to say that you're … um … well … rather good looking, but you don't have a girlfriend. Why?'

'How is that relevant?'

'I just wondered.'

'I'm too busy running a paper. Six people to keep in jobs.'

'You could end up like your grandfather.'

'Pixie, you've played cowboys and Indians all morning. It's affected your head.'

'Your mum is really lovely. She's nice to me and she has good taste. She likes the McLeish tartan.'

'What she saw of it.'

'She saw enough.' When Pixie laughed, her mood was infectious. For the first time that day I felt better — girlfriend deprived, or not.

*   *   *

It was a pity Todd Steele hadn't heard Pixie's laugh. A blunt message in Heather's hand lay on my desk: *Todd wants you to call and he's not happy.*

When I dialled his number, he answered with the usual

gruff, 'Todd Steele.'

'All right, Todd, you've seen page three of the *Mercury*. What else bothers you?'

'Damn it, Tom. How many Blacks did you expect to kill?'

'Not one. Disappointed?'

'Your family is wacko. I thought you were different.'

'Listen, Todd, the story was a beat-up and the picture a phony. The *Mercury* is doing a retraction tomorrow, and the cops will probably charge the intruders for wasting their time.'

'Good luck with that. Which leads me to the reason for my call. The plaque for the heritage centre is with the engraver now. Some people want your name removed.'

'Who are these people?'

'Can't reveal sources, you know that.'

'Well Todd, do whatever you please. I won't lose sleep over a crappy plaque.'

'The situation needn't descend to that. I can fix it.'

'This'll be interesting. How?'

'No more hypotheticals about drugs in Airlie?'

'I'm sorry, but you're too late. A second article is to run at police request.'

'Tom, you've built yourself a successful paper. Don't go ruining it.'

He rang off, and I asked Billy and Pixie into my office.

'Right guys, you'd better show me the latest drugs story.'

Billy opened a small folder he carried, and laid a sheet of paper on my desk. Half a dozen neatly typed paragraphs were at the top of the page with the date June 28, and nothing else. I read them.

AIRLIE police confirmed this week that illegal drug use is on the rise in the Whitsundays.

Five years ago, in the six months to June, police had arrested seventeen people for a variety of drug offences that ranged from cannabis use to selling heroin.

Last year in the same period they arrested thirty-six people, most of whom were selling or using hard drugs. Only two of the offences were for cannabis.

A senior officer said that owing to Airlie's international appeal, the supply of drugs had become more exotic.
'Ten years ago, our biggest problem was alcohol and cannabis. Now it's heroin, cocaine and methyl-amphetamine, otherwise known as meths.'

The officer said police were searching for a commercial-sized meths lab believed to be operating in the area.
He asked residents to watch for unusual activity, or the smell of chemicals that had a caustic or hydrochloric type of odour.

'Our fear is that the bulk materials are coming in by sea, which makes our job more difficult.'
Police have asked anyone with suspicions of a drugs lab or illicit dealing to contact Crime Stoppers on 1800 800 400.

'There's nothing original in that,' I said to Billy. 'Apart from two impressive stats, there's no fresh evidence. It's a fishing trip.'
'Not entirely, Tom. We're putting the suppliers on notice.'
'What's your thoughts, Pixie?'
'The story might trigger someone's conscience. Alert an

old lady to funny behaviour next door.'

'The phones would never stop ringing. Okay, we'll go with it on Friday.'

'Pixie did the research,' Billy said. 'Give her a byline.'

In the newspaper industry, bylines had always been like ink stamps that children received on their wrists for performance. Over the year, the bylines (the reporter's name at the top of a story) were collected in a scrapbook and shown to one's grandmother at Christmas. They also emerged when the reporter was seeking more money or a new job. Billy never wanted a byline, but Pixie now had three. And she was proud of them because they proved she was a writer, not a copy setter.

When Billy and Pixie left my office, I pulled the letters tray towards me and began the thankless task of editing. My phone buzzed. Heather's voice sounded at the other end. 'Jade Wilson for you. Same complaint as Todd.'

I counted to ten. 'Hi, Jade. I thought you were on the high seas.'

'Not today, Tom. We don't leave until Wednesday.'

'So how can I help?'

'Your family and the *Post* make us look like buffoons. Drugs and Blacks. Does it get any worse?'

'I've stated my case fifty times, Jade, and I don't mind repeating myself. The article in today's *Mercury* was a set-up. The editor will run a correction tomorrow. As for drugs, I get the impression your loathing last Friday has since turned to approval.'

'That's rubbish. I had clients flying up from Melbourne

but your newspaper gave them the jitters. Gone to Cairns instead.'

'Jade, why are you and Todd harassing me when you should be on the side of the law? Like I said to Todd, the Aboriginal issue has been sorted and we're obliged to stay with the drugs lead. If nothing comes from this week's article, that's the end. Finish.'

He grunted. 'Too late by then.'

'Sorry, the decision's already made.' When there was no answer, I said, 'See you at Magnums.'

But the line was already dead.

CHAPTER 23

My mother shares a premise with the readers of *Women's Day* that life's foibles always happen in threes. Not twos or fours, but pre-ordained threes. In her family encyclopaedia — provided one knows the code — one can easily find the triple events in the O'Connor saga.

Which leads me to the third call I took that Monday morning.

Following my conversations with Todd and Jade, I had settled back to work when the outside line rang. Since other staff were occupied, I picked up the receiver.

'*Whitsunday Post*. Tom O'Connor speaking.'

'You're a jerk, O'Connor.'

'Sorry?'

'I'll finish you one day, jerk.'

'Who are you? What have I done?'

'Just read your last paper. That drugs stuff is all bullshit. Total shit. Print another word and you'll have an accident. Bad friggin' accident!' And with that advice, the call ended. Clunk. I closed my eyes and took several deep breaths.

When Heather walked past moments later, she said, 'What's wrong?'

'A maniac let me have both barrels.'

'The country is full of racists, Tom.'

'Nothing to do with Black people. It was our drugs story last Friday.'

'Maybe we should leave drugs alone. They are police business.'

'Heather, did you know about Billy's younger brother?'

'Do I want to?'

'This is not for public airing but you ought to hear. Frankie died from a drug overdose in Sydney. Billy never told anyone, not even his parents. He let people think Frankie died in a car accident, but it was drugs that killed him. He started taking the stuff here in Airlie. Not a lot, but enough to get hooked. So, you can see why Billy owes it to his brother. He can't bring Frankie back, but he can save others.'

Heather sat her bulk on the edge of Roberta's desk, and gazed through the window. The sun had crossed the mango tree shading the car's lean-to, and was now blanching the slats along my balcony. Heather's plump, homely face was deeply troubled. She had never married and for some reason regarded Billy, Pixie and myself as her surrogate children. She didn't work for me or the *Post*, she was the *Post*.

'You take care, Tom — all of you. Gangsters stop at nothing.'

On impulse she hugged me, and as I disappeared into that massive softness, I thanked God for people like Heather. Embarrassed, we retreated to our desks though the move was unnecessary. Staff were at lunch and the place was empty.

Late that afternoon I rang Patrick to check if Lenny Watkins and his family had returned to the farm.

'What did you say to them, Tom?'

'I told them we didn't enjoy being set up. That's after I had taken a few pics to show theirs were fake.'

'So why are they still niggling us? They've got their sacred site. We did all the right things.'

'I wish I had an answer, Patrick. Anyway, the cops saw me today. Have they been out home?'

'No.'

'When they do, lock Grandpa in the storeroom. Our stories have to coincide. I said we tried to talk to Lenny's mob, but they already had cameras on us and started throwing sticks. Lenny hit me on the arm and hip, and I punched him in self-defence. Then they grabbed sticks from the fire, pitched them into the tent and tried to burn our car. We backed out real fast. You hit nobody and we threw nothing. Understand?'

'Thanks, Tom. Apart from the Land Cruiser, did you notice Lenny wore a gold watch?'

'It might be phony.'

'Sure. And where are the sons who earn big dollars? The boys toiling in the mines?'

'At work, I imagine. They do long shifts at Blackwater. On another note, tell Mum I'll be out home on Sunday.'

'Consider it done. Who is the lucky girl?'

'You choose. No, that's inviting trouble. Consult Glenda.'

Glenda had been Patrick's devoted girlfriend since high school, but one day she'd need to learn the truth about him. Most of the time he had all the right attributes: thoughtful, generous and charming. However, he was a bad drunk who should never be allowed near rum. After one or two rums he was every man's friend, three or four he was the leprechaun tucking a club under his arm, five or more he was serious trouble. To my knowledge Glenda had not seen this side of him, and would have been upset to discover he had a problem. She would be even more upset to learn that Patrick had been charged with assault when his football team, the Whitsunday Brahmans, met their opposition, the Mackay Brothers, for drinks after a match in Mackay. As the Mackay team had given the Whitsunday boys a football lesson, the losers were in a sullen mood when they met at McGuire's Hotel. Patrick downed a few quick doubles, then king hit his opposition centre who had taunted him throughout the match. Because the offence took place in another town, it missed the local news, and I certainly kept it out of the *Post*. Patrick went to court in Mackay where he pleaded guilty, paid a fine and was given a good behaviour bond. How he kept the incident from Glenda I wouldn't know, but successful marriages were not built on secrets. For my part, I ought to have been more alert when we confronted Lenny's family at the river. I thought Patrick was sober but obviously he wasn't.

*　　*　　*

The next two days passed quietly enough. The *Mercury* ran a small paragraph on page five, distancing itself from Lenny's claim that he was a helpless victim. The retraction was one of those squirming, back-to-front, inside-out apologies at the end of which you had no clue to its purpose or meaning.

On Wednesday I received a call from the chief inspector who'd had forty-eight hours, feet on the desk, mulling over whether to charge or ignore the brawlers.

'Hello, Tom. Seb Gudinski here. Spot of bother with trespassers, I understand.'

'That's right, Seb. They walked in and camped on our land. Not so much as a hello.'

'Yes, I heard that.' He lowered his voice on the phone. 'Whose brainwave was it to start a fight with harmless squatters?'

'Seb, have you got your sergeant's notes in front of you?'

'Of course I have.'

'You'll see we didn't start the scrap. We drove down to talk to them, and …'

'I read all that, but I also know your brother. Loves punching folk.'

'He was sober, and he was with me. They taunted us.'

He sighed. 'Tom, we're not charging either party, so calm down. The only unchallenged fact seems they were camped on your land without permission. But my instinct tells me your brother hit first, and you're covering for him. The O'Connor Protocol. You've probably heard the expression.'

I didn't have an answer. Over the years we had shielded each other — white lies, small deceptions — but this was the first time that police had alluded to it.

'You there, Tom?'

'Yes, Seb. Does ring a bell. Only a vague notion what it means. You'll have to explain one day.'

'I'll send you the book. Now this other business. I took a call from a mutual friend, Todd Steele, who says you are running a fear campaign. Drug labs, drug couriers. Has he spoken to you?'

'Just this morning. The meths story is not a rumour. It came from one of your officers who had run out of leads. We're doing the town a community service.'

'I'll have to remember that line. But semantics aside, I checked with CIB and they also suspect Airlie is a clearing house for drugs. How much do you really know?'

'Last Friday a witch phoned in anonymously and said there's a boat here trafficking in the hard stuff, and there's also a woman who knows more than she's letting on. Does that make sense to you?'

'Well, the boat sounds possible. Hundreds of yachts touch in at Airlie every year. As for a woman keeping secrets, you can include my wife in that.'

'I was referring to drugs.'

'I know what you meant. Go easy how you handle these stories, and tell that brother of yours to keep his hands to himself.'

When Friday's edition landed on the streets I expected nasty phone calls, but apart from the usual 'Where's my paper?', the lines were silent. Perhaps drug trafficking was more smoke than mirrors in Airlie. I congratulated Billy and Pixie on the story, and told them to switch their energy to other matters.

'The drugs are out there, Tom, I know they are,' Billy said.

'I don't disagree, Billy, but we've played our part. Remember our decision that if no new evidence, no more articles.'

Soon after lunch, the *Calvados* returned to berth. I was so busy in the office that by the time I reached the marina, the yacht was secured and the crew gone. I hailed a man washing the deck of a boat next door.

'Hey, mister, did you see the crew leave?'

'Nope. They'd be at the pub I expect.'

'Didn't see a tallish, well-tanned girl? Dark hair, cut short?'

'Yeah, nice-looking piece. Come to think of it, I saw her go below. Fifteen minutes back. She might be still there.'

How interesting. Lisa had entered the yacht alone, which was not the kind of behaviour Jade would approve. When the man returned to his hose, I slipped onto the deck and checked the main hatch. Secure. The sails hatch. Also secure. When I inspected the small, amidships hatch I found the padlock open. Lisa had somehow found a key and gone below. Curious, I slid open the hatch and lowered myself inside. A faint rustle of paper came from aft. I inched along the carpeted deck, down a short flight of stairs to Jade's cabin where Lisa sat casually on the bed, her back to me, reading a chart.

'Hi, Lisa.'

She flew up from the bed, cracking her head on a beam. For an instant her eyes were wide with fear. Slowly, recognition dawned.

'Tom,' she said.

'Yes, I wanted to ask for a date.'

'You what?'

'Does Jade know you are here?'

'Um … no, what about you?'

'Lisa, what are you doing? What's special about that chart?'

'I'm … um … checking the route for Sunday. My turn to navigate.'

'Pull the other one.'

She rushed forward and took my hands. 'Please, Tom. Don't tell on me. I … I think Jade is cheating on us. Our trips to the reef, wages, everything. He's so secretive. Ask him a question and he treats you like a nuisance. That's why he doesn't sleep with the crew. They might learn too much.'

'Okay, tidy up, and let's get out of here.'

Lisa rolled the chart, slipped on her shoes and followed me out Jade's door, which she locked carefully. After filing the chart into a drawer at the navigator's table, she slung a bag over her shoulder and led the way to the centre hatch. Once the hose man was out of view she climbed on deck and I followed. Sliding the padlock closed, we jumped onto the marina where we held hands and sauntered along the marina to my car.

'I'll give you a lift home.'

'No thanks, Tom, I have shopping to do.'

'How about Magnums tonight?'

'Sure thing. We can meet at your flat after work. Maybe cook up a meal and practise a few moves.' As we kissed, she rubbed her pelvis against me. 'Nothing hard there, Tom. Haven't you pined for me?'

'Lisa, if that had been Jade, not me, you'd be lying unconscious in the hold. You took a big risk.'

'Nobody gets a chance to see anything when he's on board. In any case, I watched him all the way to Captain Morgan's. He wasn't coming back.'

'I'll take your word for it. See you at six.'

She kissed me and hurried past the chandlery shops to the boardwalk that led into town. By sneaking into Jade's cabin, she was either brave or stupid. Or was she? I had the feeling she knew precisely what she was about, and I doubt it related to wages. Not to mention she had somehow found a key to his cabin.

Apart from the handful of people finishing lunch at Captain Morgan's, the area round the marina was empty. Most cats were still out in the islands, and the passengers from half-day trips had already set off towards their accommodation. I was about to start the car when one of the elderly shop owners came out to see me. Dylan Vogel, who ran a tour boat in addition to his chandlery, was around seventy and had skin like a leather vest that's spent months in a tanning vat. He always wore immaculate white ducks and ironed shirt, white shoes and long white socks. He affected the title Cap'n Dylan, even had the name embroidered on his shirt, but most people knew him as Silly Dilly for his extravagant, sea-dog mannerisms.

'Yo, Tom, heard ye've been fightin' them natives.'

'You heard wrong, Dylan. The natives are asleep in the village.'

'Ah … maybe they be sleepin' now.'

'True. Anyway, must dash.'

'Hold right there, young Tom. I'm not finished yet.'

'You're upset, Dylan. Go back to your galley.'

'Ye're a cheeky pup, but I'll have my say. That matter with the natives is bad for Airlie … real bad. Ye should know better. Poor defenceless blighters against two hotheads. I hear tell they be takin' ye name off the plaque. Well, I say, let 'em.'

'Good for you.'

'Why'd ye do it, Tom? Can ye answer me that?'

'Dylan, I've not harmed a Black man in my life, nor said a bad word against him, and hope I never will. But should he come at me with a stick, I'll defend myself. So, if a single, misreported incident makes you think I'm racist, you're a waste of common courtesy.'

He shook his head and wrinkles marched across his face like waves on a brown beach. 'By Jove, Tom, steady on. There's no gain in insultin' folk.'

'No? You've insulted me, assuming I'm guilty without checking your facts. We have served your shop loyally for years, yet not an ounce of loyalty in return. See you, Dylan.'

That was one client we had just lost. Lenny's clever provocation was costing us business, and Vogel wouldn't be the last. I had hoped the issue would blow over with the *Mercury*'s apology, but the scud was turning into a cyclone. I had no option except to publish the O'Connor version of events.

CHAPTER 24

Pixie was at her desk when I returned mid-afternoon. 'Any feedback on the drugs story?' she asked.

'No, Pixie. The topic seems to have died a quiet death.'

'That's good, I suppose. Look, I have an idea for next week's paper. A positive story.'

'I'm listening.'

'I'll take an outing on a tourist boat and write up the experience,' she said.

'It does have merit, I agree, but at whose expense and when?'

'The trip won't cost anything. I would depart Sunday and return early Monday.'

'An overnight boat?'

'Yes.'

'What's the name of this boat?'

'The *Calvados*.'

I frowned. 'Pardon?'

'The *Calvados*. A two-master that sails twice a week out of Abell Point.'

'I know the boat. What gave you the idea?'

'The owner. He phoned in after lunch and suggested we meet at the marina. He's a lovely man and has an all-girl crew. The plan is I'll go out for the night, try not to enjoy myself, and next morning write up a story about tourism in the Whitsundays.'

'I'm getting bad vibes here, Pixie.'

'Tom, don't be a wet blanket.'

'You don't know Jade Wilson like I do. Sorry, but it's out of the question.'

'Is that because he objected to the drugs story? You're upset.'

'Pixie, I know this fellow.'

'Okay, what's he done wrong?'

How do I tell an eighteen-year-old reporter about Jade's addiction to casual sex? She sat before me crestfallen. I could imagine her seated excitedly on a marina bench as he detailed a night's sail through the islands.

'Pixie ...,' I began awkwardly, '... I have a lot of respect for you and your parents, and you'd know that. What you do on Sunday night would normally be none of my business, but this affects your work and … well, Jade is different. He … (and I felt myself redden) … prides himself on sleeping with a different woman every night. That's why he wants you on his boat.'

She threw back her head and laughed. 'Do you think I can't look after myself? That Pixie is a dumb little schoolie?'

'He's twice your age and very experienced. You wouldn't even know it was happening.'

'Tom, you sound like an old fuddy duddy. You're not twenty-five. You're fifty-five.'

Huffily, I stood up from her desk. 'Okay, have it your way.'

Damn the girl. Maybe I am an old gecko, and too bad

if she wants to be deflowered by Airlie's great white shark. That's growing up. She has to learn the real world sooner or later. I returned to my office trying to thrust her out of my mind, feigning I couldn't care less. I spent an hour on administration, then tackled the story about Lenny Watkins trespassing on our land. A few paragraphs, nothing more.

POLICE are investigating claims that an Aboriginal family camped illegally on a cane farm in Proserpine this week.

The family from Woodwark Bay were instrumental in the recent decision to build a heritage centre in Airlie's main street.

They were also behind the registration of a site of cultural significance on Conway Road. Police are concerned that when the land owners approached the illegal campers, they were threatened with violence. A spokesman for the landowners said nobody was injured in the dispute, and the Aboriginal family left the property soon afterwards. No charges are expected to be laid.

When I finished the story, I glanced out the office window where shadows from the afternoon sun extended across the vacant land behind Shingley Drive. Buses and taxis sped towards the marina while workers fled in the opposite direction to their homes in the valley. The clock on the wall said nine minutes past five. Pixie was still at her desk sorting faxes and Heather could be seen moving through the office, shutting down machines, closing windows, putting the *Post* to bed.

Minutes after Heather's departure, fingernails tapped on my door. 'Night, Tom.'

'Night, Pixie.'

'Are you still upset with me?'

'Pixie ...' I began wearily, '... What can I say? Just — um — have a good time on the boat.'

'I've decided not to go. Not worth the hassle.' Her eyes were wide and accusatory.

'Pixie, your idea for a news article was commendable. I mean that. But the material can be sourced other ways.'

'Why don't you come with me?'

'There's a thought. Since Jade will be at Captain Morgan's, go to him and suggest you would like me to join the party. Say you need help with your article. See how he takes it. If he's thrilled, I judged him wrong. If he's less than thrilled, you know what to expect.'

'I'll do that,' she declared, and left.

After finishing the tasks left on my desk, I climbed upstairs where I mixed a drink and waited in my favourite chair for Lisa. The sun had turned to a deep bronze when I heard a voice below the balcony.

'You there, Tom?'

'Sure, Lisa. The door's open. Come on up.'

She wore her Magnums attire of colourful skirt and blouse, and carried a pack that revealed a bottle of pinot grigio, a hot chicken and a pair of lace knickers.

'Three little offerings for Thomas,' she said.

'I like a considerate woman.'

As we kissed, I took the bottle. 'Start with a wine?'

'No, rum mixer, please. It makes me warm and fuzzy.'

The evening lay before us. I poured the drink and while we sat on the balcony, feet up, Lisa ran her fingers through my hair.

'Jade will finish the season early this year,' she said. 'Told us last night.'

'What does he call early?'

'October.'

'Why the rush? Tourist numbers don't fall until November.'

'He didn't say.'

'What will you do?'

'Haven't planned that far ahead.'

'How far have you planned?'

She yawned. 'Oh dear, my little chronometer has stopped. Give me your hand.'

Thoughtfully, Lisa had offered her pants as an arrival gift, and was guiding my finger to the reset button when a delicate cough sounded behind us.

'Excuse me.'

We were out of those chairs like corks at a wedding. Pixie stood on the top step.

'Shit, Pixie. Why don't you knock?'

'The door was open and I didn't know you had company. Sorry.'

'What is it?'

'Nothing,' she said, retreating down the stairs.

'Pixie, come back here!' When she stopped mid-step, I took a breath and calmed my voice. 'Sorry, what did you want? You may as well come in. This is my friend, Lisa. Lisa, this is my journalist, Pixie.'

The two women nodded to each other. What a bloody disaster. Another minute and I would've been tobogganing down the canyon. As it was, I had Abdul Nader's complaint.

Pixie gazed at the sky over my shoulder. 'I told Jade what you said, and he suggested a short cruise tomorrow. Both of us can go.'

'Fine, what time?'

'Ten o'clock. He will speak to his crew tonight. He asked you to see him at Magnums.'

'Thanks, Pixie. Well done. See you tomorrow at ten.'

She kept her eyes averted. 'Night, Tom. Night, Lisa.'

Turning, she hurried down the staircase, and slammed the door.

Lisa pulled a face. 'Looks like we both have an early morning. I'd better be off.'

'Don't you start. We'll eat the chicken and open the wine. Then we'll walk to Magnums.'

'Just like that?'

'Exactly like that. Pixie didn't know I had company. She had been out on an assignment.'

'An assignment with Jade?'

'Yes, he wants her to do a tourism article featuring his boat. An overnight trip. Knowing Jade, I wasn't keen.'

'Pixie is beautiful. You must be fond of her.'

'I am. Her old man has worked for the O'Connors for years. She's just out of school and I have a responsibility to the whole family. Anything else?'

'She comes to your flat late in the day, expecting you to be alone. Do you think I was born on another planet?'

I set the bottle of pinot grigio on the table and rubbed

my temples. What the hell had I done wrong? Everyone imagined that because Pixie was young and attractive — and somewhat naive — Tom O'Connor was working her over.

I was angry and said as much. 'She's on my staff, we don't have sex, and she thinks I'm an old fossil.'

Lisa smiled. 'That's cool, Tom. She's gone home and Jade has allowed you back on his yacht. So, guess what? I'm yours for the taking.'

We embraced, then sat on the balcony to eat the chicken and drink the wine. After helping tidy the dishes, Lisa retrieved her pants … 'Got to keep the oven warm' … and took my arm for the walk to Magnums, where we found Jade and his crew. Once the crew had agreed on a full day's pay, Jade confirmed a departure time of ten. Lisa and I then shared in a round of drinks and returned to my flat where we underwent the formality of making love. Around nine I drove her back to her house to organise for a day at sea.

CHAPTER 25

While I ate breakfast, I thought about the previous night … about the two women, but mostly about Jade. I was convinced he had targeted Pixie deliberately. Because the man had access to more playmates than a Chinese emperor, he didn't need the *Post*'s junior reporter, no matter how pretty. He intended debauching her as a lesson to Tom O'Connor who thought he could escape with the reputational damage he caused.

Around nine-thirty I threw togs and towel into a pack, dragged on my faithful Panama hat, and strolled down to the marina where the *Calvados* was the only late boat preparing to sail. Jade was unexpectedly cheerful.

'Hi, Tom. Welcome aboard. You know the drill. Tea and coffee in the saloon.'

'Thanks, Jade. Am I the last?'

'Yes, everyone is below getting acquainted.'

'Pixie?'

'Ah, young Pixie. She's with Lisa. Seems they know each other.'

'They do. Met at my flat last night.'

Since I had a few minutes before cast-off, I wandered below deck where I was surprised to find Todd Steele perched at the navigator's table. He was drinking from an oversize whiskey flask.

'Hello, Todd. Didn't know you were a sailor?'

'Hate stupid boats. If God meant us to float, he'd have given us paddles. Came on board only as a favour.'

Todd wore what he imagined to be nautical gear. Because I only ever saw him in outdated linen suits, his idea of marine fashion was comical. He wore long, baggy shorts fastened too high at the waist, a loose-knit, blue-and-red striped shirt, and white socks with sandals. On his head was a skipper's cap, but most obvious was the yellow life vest.

'You wearing that all day?'

'That's what they're here for.'

Because the saloon was partially occupied, he drew me to one side. 'You shouldn't have run that second drugs story, Tom. Some folk very angry.'

'Not the ones taking my name off the plaque?'

'Pretty much. You gone troppo? First an obsession with drug labs, then a boxing display on helpless Blacks. What's next? Making bombs for Gadaffi?'

'Don't use that 'b' word here. You could get thrown overboard.'

'Who by?'

'You mean, *by whom*. Changing the subject, what do you know of the O'Connor Protocol?'

His eyes became watchful. 'Sorry, you've got me there.'

'I'll refresh your memory. The protocol harks back to an Aboriginal death at The Leap. Apparently, a Steele found himself in prison while an O'Connor walked free, thanks to his brother.'

He drew hard on his whiskey. 'Hell, this is good stuff.

Listen, mate, The Leap is ancient history. Only a fool lives in the past.'

'My sentiment exactly.'

Recapping the flask, he said, 'Tom, I thought we had ended hostilities. I believe you've hatched another conspiracy theory.'

'What do you mean?'

'The illegal camping on your farm. That it was prearranged. All part of an evil plot against the O'Connors.'

'Well, it is rather odd. Why would Lenny abandon a perfectly good home at Woodwark Bay to live under a tarp?'

'Tom, you know what Blacks are like. They prefer an outdoor camp to four walls and a roof.'

I snorted. 'That's a myth. They want to sleep warm and dry as much as you do.'

We made our way to the deck as the *Calvados* eased along the channel that led to the break in the rock wall. Once through the gap an incoming swell pitched the ketch like a frisky horse.

Todd groaned and said, 'I need my friggin' head read.'

Lisa and a second crewmember were setting the main sail. Another two were further back hauling on a lighter rig. As the sails billowed in the wind, the ketch stopped pitching and relaxed into a long plunging stride. I looked around for Pixie. She was on a bench at the stern writing up notes, and in appearance was not dissimilar to the crew. She had fastened her hair under a cap and wore a checked blue shirt, white shorts and a pair of sandals.

I felt Todd beside me. 'That your girl, Tom?'

'She works for me.'

'Thought as much. Saw you together at the Council meeting. Spunkiest chick I've seen in years.'

'She's here on assignment, Todd, so leave her alone.'

I wandered back to where Pixie was seated. As I approached, she shifted across to make space.

'How's the research going, ace?'

'Tom, I didn't know you had a lover.'

'Is that a statement or question?'

'I was surprised, that's all.'

'If you walk through a back door, you have to expect surprises.'

'She's very attractive. I thought you lived upstairs like a monk.'

'I'm wishing I did.'

Lisa had finished tying off the main sheet, saw us together and came across, her bare feet padding on the teak.

'Interrupting anything?' she asked.

'Not if you include last night.'

Lisa laughed. 'I won't tell, if you don't.'

We made room on the bench between us.

'Tom, I read that article you did on the meths lab,' Lisa said. 'Any response?'

'No, although we half expected another threat.'

'What threat?' Pixie said.

'I didn't take it seriously. Some bloke warned me of an accident headed my way. But there was one call that keeps coming to mind. Anonymous witch who said somebody is keeping secrets from me. We think it's a woman.'

'You know lots of women,' Pixie said.

'Apart from you and Lisa, I know my mother.'

'And Heather, Roberta, Ethel, Mandy …'

'Thanks, Pixie. That's enough.'

'What about the woman who cuts your hair? Carmelita. She's always high as a kite.'

We left the conversation at that. The sun was hot as the breeze danced across the timber deck and stroked our faces. Three metres in front of where we sat, Jade's broad shoulders blocked out the wheel, which he spun to counter the waves that curled and broke like living creatures. I could understand why people loved the sea, why the ocean was in a mariner's blood. For me, however, the world I desired was found on dry land where you could walk to a pub, eat at a café or plant a tree.

Leaving the two women, I clambered forward to Jade. 'Have a rum,' he said. 'This is your day off.'

After breaking open his stash of mixes, I drank straight from the can and told my story of growing up on the farm, people I'd met, things I'd done. One rum later, I fell asleep against the cockpit. When I awoke the boat was at anchor, the sails furled and Jade nowhere in sight. Two of the crew in blue stood at the rail monitoring swimmers, who I could hear but not see, Lisa was laying a table with sandwiches, and Todd sat on the coaming reading a paper. Rising stiffly to my feet, I ambled across to the rail. Some eight or nine people were in the water. Among them was Pixie in a yellow bikini, and Jade teaching her to snorkel.

I leant on the rail watching friendly Jade instruct the willing Pixie, his hand under her midriff raising and lowering her. Both the instructor and instructed laughed as they made a game of this nautical art. When Lisa finished at the table, she walked to my side. In her hand she held a can of bitter.

'Hair of the dog, Tom.'

I gratefully took the can and drank.

'Beautiful day,' she said.

'Yes, couldn't be more perfect.'

'Except …' and she nodded towards the couple in the water. Jade had taken off Pixie's mask and rolled her onto her back; still friendly, still helpful. Pixie thrust her arms above her head, her dark hair floating about her face, her white skin contrasting against the green of the ocean and the yellow bikini. Jade laughed comfortably, opening and closing his large mouth of even white teeth.

'You care for Pixie's family. Isn't that what you said, Tom?'

'Right now, she's my only concern. The water looks inviting. Feel like a dip?'

'I'd love nothing better.'

It would be fair to say Jade was not pleased when I swam across.

'Piss off,' he muttered.

Lisa dived and bobbed up between them. 'Sorry, thought it was someone else. But since I'm here, shall I blow the whistle. Lunch is ready.'

'Oh, yes please,' Pixie cried. 'I'm starving.'

As the girls paddled ahead of us, I said, 'We should get a terrific article out of this, Jade. Whitsunday tourism at its awesome best.'

'You're a friggin' menace.'

'Jade, I just saved your bacon. The girl is barely eighteen and her old man is a gorilla.'

'Good try, mate. What's her name again? Mary?'

The sail back to Abell Point went quietly. When Pixie changed into dry clothes and retired to the saloon to write her article, I helped Lisa with her chores. We then sat on the foredeck, close and companionable. Behind us, Jade stood alone at the wheel, like a junkie whose daily hit has been snatched from his mouth. Once at the marina, Pixie collected her pushbike while Todd Steele complained about the absence of cabs and public toilets. He wagged his finger at me.

'What a queer world we live in, Tom.'

I ignored him.

'I hate sailin' one minute, love it the next.'

'You're still wearing your life vest.'

'There you are. That's how much I love it. If you're doing nothin', come up to Morgan's for a drink. I'll buy you one. For old times' sake.'

'Sorry. Diary's full.'

'Then make space. I'll tell you the story behind the O'Connor Protocol.'

I eyed him coldly. 'Four hours ago, it was news to you. Go home. You're drunk.'

'You interested or not?'

I swallowed the hook. 'This had better be genuine.'

When Lisa arrived at my side ten minutes later, I said, 'I'm sorry, Lisa, but Todd's got information on my family. I need to hear it.'

'Your family? Now?'

'That's right. He's meeting me at Captain Morgan's.'

She muttered. 'Two buddies with no wives to go home to.'

'It's nothing like that.'

'So, what's the hurry?'

'He has info that might explain the Lenny Watkins business.'

'And where do I fit in? Sit on your doorstep until midnight.'

'No, Lisa, cook yourself a meal, open a bottle of wine. I'll be home before you know.'

Taking her by the arms, I kissed her. She barely thawed.

'Don't ever say you love me, Tom. I couldn't stand it.'

Without a backward glance, she threw her pack over her shoulder and walked morosely up the street. Turning in the opposite direction, I bypassed the chandlery shops towards Captain Morgan's where Todd sat alone at a table drinking thick black espresso.

I ordered a Coke and pulled up a chair beside him. He had cast off the drunken veneer.

'Okay, Todd, what do you know of the O'Connor Protocol?'

'I could start with your grandpa's uncles who went to war. They were a great pair.'

'No, go back earlier. Tell me about The Leap.'

'The bloody Leap,' he sighed melodramatically. 'As you'd already know, that was in the 1860s when farmers were doing it tough. Blacks were spearing herds, burning down huts and wrecking fences. In hindsight, the Blacks had every right to be mad. Chased off their land without so much as a hello. Most Whites tried to find the middle ground, but not a chap called John Barnes. He was so bent on demonising Blacks that one day he copped a spear in the arm. Of course, he went to the law, who decided enough was enough, and set up a charter to *disperse* the local tribes. When a Native Mounted Police contingent was sent in to do the job, two friends of Barnes — Paul O'Connor and Blake Steele — rode along. They shouldn't have been there because it was a police matter, but they were local farmers and keen to help. Most of the tribe melted into the bush but the posse chased a woman and baby up Mount Mandarana. Paul O'Connor had barely reached the foothills of the mountain when his horse threw a shoe. Since he was the better rider, he and Blake swapped horses, and Blake led the lame horse back to the meeting point near Farleigh. Now riding his mate's horse, Paul rejoined the police who, well ... let's be honest ... forced the woman and her baby over the cliff. The woman died, but the baby survived. Johanna, I believe her name was. Anyway, when Paul heard the mother scream, he fled the mountain. As you can imagine there was an uproar, even in the 1860s. Somebody had to pay for the woman's death. Things didn't look too good for Paul until his magistrate brother, Michael, stepped in. Michael discovered Paul had ridden Blake Steele's horse, which was very convenient. Because the native police didn't know the two white men but recognised their horses, the finger was pointed at Blake. Michael took control and sent his brother to New Zealand for a six-month holiday while Blake stood trial for manslaughter. At the first trial he was found guilty, but on appeal the verdict was quashed because the evidence was unreliable. One constable said the white man had a beard, another said he was clean shaven, one said he was a good rider, another said he was hopeless. Meanwhile, under Michael's direction Paul's story never wavered that he pulled out of the chase because his horse was lame. So yes, there was bad blood between the two families.'

'Whose story made the history books?'

'That depends on the author, but residents at the time felt both men should've been charged. In any case, that's how the protocol began, brothers defending each other. A generation later, it was a set of twins in the army. Now the tradition falls to you and Patrick. Do you lie for him, or is it the other way round?'

I ignored the last remark. 'That's not Grandpa's recollection.'

'What do you expect? An O'Connor standing before a judge? How ridiculous.'

CHAPTER 26

When I arrived at the flat, Lisa was seated against the pillows, reading a book. To my surprise, she greeted me warmly.

'You weren't long, Thomas. How did it go?'

'Not quite what I expected.'

'All right, no more questions. I'm hungry and there's fry-up in the pan. Serve two plates and I'll join you.'

I set places on the balcony, uncorked a half-empty bottle of wine and dished out the meal. As Lisa was still in the bedroom, I poured myself a mouthful and gazed across the lapping water. Henry O'Connor and Todd Steele were two of a kind. They came from an age when slights were remembered and a tarnished name never cleared. For my part, I had no idea if Todd had family in Proserpine, and I didn't really care. One Steele in my life was enough.

'Happy anniversary,' Lisa said behind me. 'Turn round.'

She wore a sheer, red silk gown that rippled in the light from her neck to her ankles. Two oriental dragons breathed fire onto each breast, and their tails curled to her thighs.

I stared in awe.

'Wait, you haven't seen everything.'

She swept open the gown to reveal a beautiful naked body, but the chestnut thatch was dyed a deep, dark red.

Pushing me onto the sofa, she said, 'Let's see if colour makes a difference.'

Ten minutes later I came up for air. 'What anniversary?'

'It's three months today since we met. Had you forgotten?'

Unable to think of a convincing lie, I dragged her to her feet. 'Here, drink your wine while I reheat the food and tell you about Todd.'

'What a romantic beast you are. Shall we do the mayor's story next?'

Sunday dawned warm and clear. As the sun climbed over Mandalay, fishermen launched their tin-bottomed craft and shouted to each other across the burble of exhausts. Plovers took to the air, and Lisa walked semi-nude to the kitchen where she lit the gas under the coffee pot. Stretching lazily in the dappled light, she turned to me. 'We should go away together, Thomas.'

'I thought this was your vacation.'

'I mean at the end of the season. You could join me in Sydney. Forget all our worries.'

'How would Sydney change anything?'

She cupped my face in her hands. 'I meant what I said last night. Don't ever say you love me.'

'It hadn't crossed my mind ... well, not exactly.'

'That's because you don't know what love is, or that a woman in love wants to be sat on a pedestal. You love the Whitsundays, the newspaper, your family, and even Pixie in a grouchy way. I would have to trail along in their shadows, and I couldn't.' Her bottom lip trembled. 'When I'm with you, I live in a fantasy world. The two of us, man and woman, in a perfect heaven. It's like we're characters in a love song. When the track ends my life returns to normal. I pull on my uniform and spend the day with tourists who have invaded my paradise. But somehow the dream doesn't crumble for you. Your personal universe remains — the who and what of yourself — and the fate of this little waif is immaterial.'

Unasked, the endorphins flowed out of my brain and returned to their home in the pit. I had always associated Lisa with sex because, to be honest, that's what fuelled our relationship. This morning, however, she had unearthed a fresh sentiment. Love had not been mentioned before … now it was being tossed about as the natural order of things. When I had raised the idea of sharing my flat, she had objected because, quite rightly, familiarity could breed contempt, not to mention she enjoyed the company of her female crew. In the space of weeks, stage one of the relationship (the sex) had passed through stage two (the affair) into stage three (the love). Meanwhile, I was still locked in stage one. In October, when Jade's yacht departed, I had imagined she would be aboard looking forward to Sydney and a new partner with whom to practise sexual gymnastics.

We sat at the table, drinking coffee, watching the sun burn mist off the distant forest. Lisa took my hand and held it under her chin.

'I'm just being silly,' she said. 'You make breakfast while I prepare for work.'

As I toasted crumpets on the gas, she showered and changed. Later, I drove her home where she said, 'Tom, I'll be away two nights. Will you reflect on what I've said?'

'Of course.'

'I just wonder if it's … well … best to stop now or …'

'Bye Lisa,' I said, and kissed her. 'See you Tuesday.'

She smiled. 'Behave yourself,' and she ran into the house.

What did she expect me to say? It seemed she was asking me to dump everything and follow her to Sydney. Sorry, Lisa, but the north is my home and the *Post* is my livelihood. More to the point, who was she really? An English girl who had accompanied her boyfriend to Australia where the relationship had inexplicably died. Now she followed the sun. That's all I knew.

Maybe it's correct that some men only need a plate of stew and a good screw, but I never subscribed to that theory. Deep down, hidden from everyone, was a vulnerable side. At Hervey Bay I had fallen for a girl named Melanie whose father owned the coffee shop frequented by *Observer* staff. The affair had started pleasantly under her father's eye, until one night I asked her for a drink. Two hours and several drinks later we found ourselves alone in the spare bedroom of a friend's house. She only needed to touch my skin and I had a call to arms, and she obliged with her own manoeuvres. Next morning, we were madly in love. I was the young manager going places and she was the daughter of a coffee shop owner. Six months later, the dream evaporated. After blaming an overpriced dollar, her old man closed the shop, packed the car and took his wife back to Melbourne. I found a job on the paper for their daughter so she and I could remain together, but when rumours surfaced that my chiefs intended merging the two regional weeklies, I knew my time in Hervey Bay was limited. I applied for the job running a new paper in Mackay, but was placed in a queue. Apparently, they had plans for me in distant Toowoomba. Our roles were reversed. Melanie had a job and I didn't. While waiting for the ultimatum, I took two weeks leave and drove to Airlie where I hatched the idea of starting my own paper. Somehow, I thought Melanie would travel with me, a romantic belief that love would prevail as we grappled with our new venture. In time we would be successful entrepreneurs, enjoying the exquisite lifestyle of the tropics.

As it turned out, Hervey Bay was the furthest north she had travelled and she dreaded the unknown. Over the next few weeks, we argued and made up, repeating the cycle daily, while ignoring the fact that a glass barrier had risen between us. After one such evening in bed (when the rows were most heated) I handed in my notice. A fortnight later, Melanie stood beside the bright yellow Moke I had bought at the height of our romance, and told me she would always love me. We kissed and held hands, then I let out the clutch and was gone, taking an entire week to drive north. We didn't stay in touch except for a Christmas card I received (via the farm mailbox) with a Victorian postmark and no return address. However, the yuletide greeting did end with *Love, Melanie.* I carried that card in my pocket all through January, but as the first cyclones battered the coastline and tore holes in my fledgling income, I forgot the card and any idea of a revived affair. Her photo stands on the sideboard in my living room, and not once has Lisa asked about it. That was four years ago, and although I've enjoyed the company of women since, Melanie reminds me that normal relationships can exist.

CHAPTER 27

I turned left out of Lisa's street, then across to the farm where Mum was in the kitchen peeling vegetables to the music of Sting. Patrick was in the shed welding a hitch, and Grandpa was on the verandah reading the Sunday papers. I wanted to approach Grandpa about the O'Connor Protocol following Todd's account, but was reluctant to do so. He had been through a lot in recent weeks, and with his feet up and the sun shining, he seemed at peace.

'What are you reading, Grandpa?'

'How to make a fortune by ripping off morons. Listen to this story. A bloke in a suit comes to a pensioner's door with fake ID and claims he's from tax. He gets taken inside, allowed to ask lots of questions, even about the pensioner's bank account, then a week later the house is done over and the account emptied. How do they get away with it?'

'It's something to do with old men.'

'If the bastard came here, I'd set the dog on him.'

'Grandpa, I want to ask a question. You remember how that Aboriginal mother jumped off Mount Mandarana with her baby, and the baby survived. Do you know what happened to her?'

'Why should I?'

'Please, Grandpa. Billy and his family are descendants of

the same tribe as the woman. The baby's family could live here.'

'That's unlikely. Nobody even knows her name.'

'It was Johanna.'

'Where did you hear that?'

'Todd Steele.'

Grandpa almost exploded. 'Why the hell are you talking to him?'

'I was out on the boat with him yesterday. He drank too much and told me about The Leap. I don't believe everything he said, but the baby got a mention.'

Grandpa stood from his chair and walked to the edge of the verandah. Below him, Mum's roses were in bud and the camellia bushes that had sheltered his dead father were alive with flower.

He turned to me. 'Pour me a whiskey.'

When I had done so, he said resignedly, 'You're right. The baby survived and her name was Johanna.'

'Does Patrick know this?'

'No.'

'Then wait. I'll fetch him. He needs to hear.'

I jumped over the rail and brought Patrick up from the shed where he had been painting the weld. Once we were seated, I said, 'Okay, Grandpa, the floor is yours.'

'Don't get too excited. I only know bits and pieces. When the mother fell, they located her body at the base of the cliff and the baby curled up in the grass like a possum. Since the rest of the tribe had dispersed and nobody in the party knew how to look after babies, she was delivered to the base hospital. My great uncle Michael O'Connor, the magistrate, arranged for her adoption to a family at Finch Hatton. When Johanna grew up, she married a local chap who was part Juipera. What happened to them afterwards God only knows. Why is the baby so important?'

'It might shed light on Lenny's involvement.'

'Well, the baby can't help. For a start she was Juipera while our mate Lenny is Giya. Two different tribes. And I can't see how the Juipera would mix themselves up in a Lenny escapade that attracts the police. No, it's that rat-faced Todd Steele. He's still smarting from a crime his ancestors committed.'

'Sorry, Grandpa, but there's an element in Todd's story that needs clarification — the horses they rode. Apparently, Paul O'Connor's horse went lame, but since he was the better rider he took Blake Steele's horse, and rejoined the hunting party. Meanwhile, Blake walked the lame horse back to Farleigh. Had you heard about the horses?'

'Vaguely.'

'Sounds like a Steele fairytale,' Patrick said.

'Is it, Grandpa?'

It was fortunate Mum came onto the verandah to announce lunch as the conversation had stalled. At the table the mood was very different from the previous Sunday when Lisa had stirred Mum's romantic instincts. But she wasn't giving in.

'Tom, where's Lisa?'

'At work. Her boat sailed this morning.'

'Are you two serious?'

'Serious? What's that?'

'Don't get her pregnant and walk away,' Mum said.

'Why do people think that's all we do?'

'Because of a letter from a girl called Melanie.'

That straightened me up.

'Sorry Tom, I opened the letter by mistake. On the front I saw what I thought was *J. O'Connor* but the J. was actually a T., and there was no address on the back. It came before you arrived home from Hervey Bay … three pages about sex … so I burnt them. You never told us about a girl called Melanie, and I could see why.'

The letter had come four years ago. Mum had to be reading my mind as only an hour earlier I was thinking of the girl.

Patrick seized his cue. 'Mum showed me the letter, Tom. I wanted to discuss it with you. Honestly, some of the stuff was out of our league. Like, what's a vulva?'

'I'm sorry I opened it,' Mum retorted.

The best defence was to share the joke. 'You should've gone to Marvin. He studied Latin roots.'

'Sounds more like an O'Connor root,' Patrick said, straight-faced.

Mum slammed her fork on the table. 'Enough. I hope you and Lisa are genuine, that's all. She's a nice girl.' And closed the subject.

When I looked across at Grandpa, his head was down, cutting slowly through his roast. He appeared to have lost his appetite.

'You okay, Grandpa?'

'That Juipera baby. Often I think about her. Her mother dead and nobody knowing what to do next. Paul O'Connor should never have been near that mountain, but his brother did the right thing. He saved an innocent man from facing trial, and he organised adoption for the baby. Now the family is smeared with the O'Connor Protocol. Brothers looking after each other is natural, but what people said about Michael and Paul is downright malicious.'

. Patrick and I exchanged glances and said nothing. The rest of the meal was eaten in silence.

*   *   *

Monday morning in the newspaper office was like any other; staff arriving in dribs and drabs, noisily unloading their weekends onto each other. I wasn't excluded. First through my door was Heather, her hair a mass of tight curls.

'Don't stare,' she said. 'I took Mum to dinner at La Cucina last night. It was her seventieth birthday.'

'What curled your hair? The food?'

'No, Giancarlo's stories.' She closed the door. 'Tell me about Pixie. How did it end with Jade?'

'I spoilt his day and he's furious.'

'Does Pixie know about you and Lisa?'

'What's there to know?'

'She's not blind, Tom.'

What brought this on? Before I could ask, she disappeared, leaving a contrail in the air. Five minutes later Pixie arrived and breezed into my office with her tourism article. She sat on the chair in front of my desk while I read it.

'This is well done, Pixie, excellent use of language and sentence construction, but the content is a bit fluffy. Lots of the information is conjecture and you've only spoken to one operator. You need a few quotes from the tourist office and maybe the Chamber of Commerce. It will give your article body.'

'Thanks, Tom. I'll do that right away.'

'Good. Anything else?'

'I want to thank you for coming with me on Saturday. You and Lisa were kind even though Jade didn't try anything. I think he's lonely.'

'When you go home tonight, Pixie, ask your mum to read the story of Red Riding Hood. Near the end, the wolf disguises himself as her grandma in bed, waiting for the girl to appear.'

'You could ask your mum to read the story of King Lear and Cordelia,' she replied. 'It's about a feeble-minded old man and a sweet young woman. He misjudges her ... to his deep regret.'

Billy was the third person through my door. Since the *Mercury* article on the punch-up at the river bank, Billy's advertising portfolio had gone into freefall. He wanted me to spend the day convincing traders that ours was not a racist paper. To his mind, the sight of an Aboriginal sales manager and his Anglo-Saxon editor walking through the door together would create an impression of racial harmony to those firms who wrongly assumed the newspaper's pioneer heritage had upset their enlightened customer base.

'Where did you get that gobbledygook, Billy?'

'You. Ages ago. I wrote it down.'

And Billy's plan did work. First customer that morning was Dylan Vogel from the chandlery. When he saw Billy's hangdog face, he was full of apology for thinking we could be racist. No, he hadn't seen the *Mercury's* retraction. Yes, he had read our response and he was pleased everything had been cleared up because the *Post* was a respected newspaper. We spent the day listening to this kind of drivel, but at least our advertisers were back. On the way through the main street of Airlie, we saw council staff attaching a plaque to the outside wall of the heritage centre. I pulled in and inspected the plaque over their shoulders. The *Whitsunday Post* was there in its rightful place.

'Looks like common sense has prevailed,' Billy said.

'Thank heavens for that.'

Once back in the car, he handed me a sheet of paper. 'On a separate topic, Tom, I've narrowed down the list of boats that could be trafficking drugs. If we leave aside the permanently anchored and the overnighters, there are seven that do mysterious trips. Vogel's yacht is one of them.'

'Dylan Vogel?'

'Don't be fooled by his manner, Tom. He's a wily bastard.'

'I agree, Billy, but what do you call mysterious?'

'The boat has to be absent two or more days. Gives it time to collect drugs from a ship in the Whitsunday Passage and sail to a remote port where it won't be noticed. Shute Harbour or Bowen come to mind.'

'Why Vogel's boat?'

'The skipper has to know these waters, which Vogel's man does. He also needs a small, regular crew and a flexible timetable. I've identified all the boats in this category.'

'So, we have six possible boats and one probable. Go easy, Billy. I've already been threatened with a nasty accident.'

Fortunately, the world righted itself over the following

month. Lenny Watkins disappeared, presumably back to his home in Woodwark Bay, drug dealers vacated the main street, and Grandpa and Todd resumed their prickly truce. On the home front, Mum and Glenda (and sometimes Patrick) continued with preparations for the wedding, and Lisa dropped any further references to love.

Unlike my family, who couldn't leave the subject alone.

'Lisa has let her hair grow out, Tom. It's lovely now. Ask her where she gets it done,' Mum said one Sunday afternoon while Lisa was at the river with Patrick, looking for crocodiles.

'You ask.'

Grandpa had been slyly decanting the whiskey from his five-hundred-year-old bottle, and replacing it with new spirit. He couldn't trust relatives at a wedding. 'How did she get that bang on her head?' he asked. 'Spoils her face.'

'Don't know. She'll be back in ten minutes. Ask her. One question each.'

'You and Lisa could make the announcement at Patrick's wedding. Wouldn't that be marvellous?' Mum crooned.

Grandpa replaced the cap on his whiskey bottle. 'Tom won't marry the girl. Bet money on it.'

'Why so, Grandpa? I thought she ticked all the boxes.'

'Well, for a start she's English. As soon as the weather turns muggy, she'll clear out. Second, she's a nosey one. Notice how she queries everything? Why this? Why that? And third, once marriage enters the conversation, goodbye to fun. The sex boat wallows.'

'Your grandfather doesn't care who he offends,' Lisa said as we drove back to Airlie around four. 'He asked about my scar. Bold as brass, he was.'

'And …?'

After a silence she said, 'I cut my head on my first date. Talk about impatient. In our rush to strip in his tiny flat, I hit my head on a lamp. Blood everywhere. So, I went home a bloody mess and a virgin. When Dad learnt how it happened, he was furious and refused to take me to hospital until next day. By that time everyone decided the wound could heal naturally. Some say it looks cute. What do you think?'

'Well, um, it wouldn't hurt to …'

That is how the month went; feints and parries, followed by sublime delights and an assumption that our last day together in Airlie would look after itself.

CHAPTER 28

Our lives changed forever on the afternoon of Friday, 10 August. I was in the office waiting for Heather and Pixie to finish at their desks when the phone rang.

'It's your grandfather,' Heather said.

'Hi Grandpa.'

'They're here, damn them. They've come back.'

'Who has?'

'Lenny. Lenny and his family. They've moved into Pop's Place.'

'When?'

'Just now. They drove their Land Cruiser up from the river and moved in all their junk.'

'Have you called the police?'

'No. I've called you.'

'Where are Mum and Patrick?'

'In town. Patrick will kill them when he gets home.'

'He'd better not.'

Leaving instructions with Heather to lock up, I jumped in the car and drove across to the farm. Grandpa was alone on the verandah watching Lenny's family thrust open windows and doors at the old house. Kids were already running about in the yard and women could be seen moving from room to room.

'Just what I predicted,' Grandpa said.

I lifted the phone and dialled Chief Inspector Seb Gudinski.

'Seb, it's Tom O'Connor. Remember that Lenny Watkins family who camped on our river land? They've moved into my grandfather's old house. We need you to chase them out.'

'Hold on, Tom. That's the sacred site, isn't it? We can't barge in on people at a sacred site. I'll have to get advice. Call you back.'

When he hung up, I looked at Grandpa and shrugged. 'He's unsure what to do. He'll phone me.'

'That useless damn Marvin Fumbleton,' Grandpa said and dropped his face in his hands. 'I'll wring his bloody neck.'

'Stay here, Grandpa. I'll go down and talk to them.'

The original farm house was less than two hundred metres from the new house, but that afternoon it felt a mile.

'Hey, Lenny,' I called. 'Can you come outside.'

'What you want, Tom O'Connor? Give me beating with a stick?'

'No, I want to talk.'

He appeared at the window. 'Okay, talk.'

'This is my grandfather's house and a sacred site of the Giya people. What are you doing?'

'I'm a caretaker for the Giya. My family will live here to protect the site. This is my job.'

'When we agreed not to contest the registration, you promised you wouldn't interfere with the house. I trusted you, Lenny, and still do. Your word means a lot to me.'

'You don't care about my word, Tom O'Connor. You are

a white prick like your brother.'

'Have you ever heard of The Leap?'

His face was at once sly. 'Of course. Everybody who drives to Mackay knows The Leap.'

'Do you know the story behind it?'

'Sure do. All Black people know that story. And yes, I know Mr Paul O'Connor push lady and her baby off the cliff. So what?'

'Paul didn't push the lady. He was walking home with a lame horse when it happened.'

He shrugged. 'Like I say, so what?'

'Lenny, I hope your action today has nothing to do with that time. My grandpa has always respected your people. I think of the Giya and the Juipera as my brothers. What do you want from us? Would you like to camp on the river bank?'

'No, Tom O'Connor. We ask for nothing. My job is to care for this site of cultural significance. That's what my family will do.'

He tried to close the window that was stiff from years of inaction. Gripping the frame in two hands, he reefed inwards. With a loud crash the window broke from its frame.

'Bad maintenance,' he said, and threw the window onto the grass.

When I returned to the house, Mum and Patrick were on the verandah with Grandpa.

'Any luck?' Patrick asked.

'He's not leaving. He's the caretaker for the Giya.'

'I'll kick the bastard out.'

'Like you did at the river? No, we wait for Seb Gudinski to ring.'

Glumly, we sat on the verandah as the light faded from the sky. Soon it was almost dark. The sun melted into the distant ranges and kerosene lights glowed at the open windows in Pop's Place. Laughter drifted up the hill towards us.

Night had fallen when the phone rang.

'Is that you, Tom? Seb Gudinski here. Look, there's not a lot we can do at the minute. It seems Blacks are entitled to provide caretakers for their cultural sites. Is that how you read it?'

'So Lenny says. He's had legal advice from someone.'

'Maybe, but don't take the law into your own hands. That's a police direction. If they have no right to be there, we'll sort it through the courts.'

'That could take forever.'

'Possibly, but the house was empty I understand. That complicates things. Tell your legal people to liaise with the attorney-general's office. Sorry I can't be more help. Night, Tom.'

When the others read my face, they knew the news was bad. Lenny Watkins had us on the ropes.

'Four generations,' Patrick said quietly. 'It took four generations to get even.'

Supper that night was eaten in silence, nobody willing to express the despair we felt. How could one sacred site be desecrated to protect another? At the washing-up, I said to Mum and Patrick, 'I'll phone Marvin first thing next week and try to make an appointment. In the meantime, watch Grandpa. He might be tempted to do something foolish.'

When I arrived back at the flat, I was bothered by the silence, a feeling I had never encountered before. Lanyards slapping on masts were not playful reminders of boats on water, but tiny drums summoning dark forces into our paradise. It was also the first time since meeting Lisa that I needed someone who was not family. Despondently, I showered and climbed into bed.

*   *   *

Saturday morning, the weather changed. A strong south-easterly, loaded with rain, blew in from the Conway Range. The big reef cats hunkered at their berths, waiting for the tourists who were reluctant to spend a rough day at sea. In two days the weather would return to its tropical best, but in the meantime video stores would call in extra staff. As I sat over a bowl of cereal and the newspapers, I heard a voice at the back door.

'You there, Tom?'

'Yes, Pixie. Come on up.'

'Not disturbing anything?'

'No, I'm alone.'

She shook her hair from under a cap and tossed a wet raincoat over the railing. Despite the cool change, she wore a denim skirt and a pair of trainers. In her hands she held the briefcase she had received for her birthday.

I pointed to the briefcase. 'No work on weekends, Pixie.'

'Is that coffee I can smell? And look, I've called at the bakery. Croissants.'

In a whirlwind, she made herself a coffee, refilled my cup,

then placed the croissants with jam on the table. When she was seated, I asked, 'What's this all about?'

'I'm here to cheer you up. Dad learnt this morning about Lenny and his family.'

'Thanks, Pixie, but our hands are tied until Monday.'

'That's where you are wrong. Last night after work I went to the library and researched the history of The Leap.' She pulled a sheaf of papers from her briefcase. 'Look, this is written by the Mackay Historical Society. I photocopied it.'

I gazed at her in amazement. In all the years I had known about The Leap I never once thought of the library.

'Your family is also mentioned, though they're careful to say it's a rumour about Paul O'Connor's guilt. Go ahead and read.'

'Thanks, I will.'

For the next half hour, I was absorbed in the story of Mackay's early settlement; from 1860 when Captain John Mackay named the Pioneer River, through the initial years of farming to 1864 when sugar cane was introduced. Until then, Blacks and Whites had managed an uncomfortable, though peaceful, coexistence. However, the push towards cultivation resulted in the isolation of tribes from their food supply. The fight for survival turned ugly. This led to the deployment of the Native Mounted Police and the chase across Mount Mandarana. When Brisbane politicians heard about the woman and child who had "leapt" off the cliff, they demanded an inquiry. Initially, the magistrate Michael O'Connor was involved, but when it emerged that his brother was among the chasers, he stood aside. Paul O'Connor was cleared of any wrongdoing but the second farmer in the party, Blake Steele, was charged with manslaughter. Although vindicated at a second trial, the stigma remained.

At this point in the documents, the word "rumour" is introduced. The rumour was that both men hunted the woman to her death, but the magistrate Michael O'Connor "conspired" with Paul to muddy the facts. As a result, Paul was never charged, and the phrase O'Connor Protocol was coined. The document concluded:

IT IS an undisputed fact that Paul O'Connor and Blake Steele set out with the Native Mounted Police to disperse the Aboriginal tribes north of the Pioneer River. However, following an inquest and two court cases, some basic evidence is still contradictory. The O'Connor brothers always protested their innocence, and there is no question that Paul O'Connor's horse was lame when inspected the following day. Although it is possible the horses could have been exchanged, this author believes the police made the right decision. Blake Steele's family-owned farms at the base of Mount Mandarana (where the tragedy occurred) while O'Connor's farm was south of Farleigh, some distance away. He had everything to lose and nothing to gain by forcing the woman over a cliff. The truth may never come to light.

I lifted my head from the papers. 'Hey Pixie, the writer gives Paul O'Connor the benefit of doubt.'

Her voice came from the kitchen. 'Dad always said he was blameless. Now we have confirmation from a third party.'

She emerged drying her hands. 'The kitchen was a mess. When's Lisa due back?'

'Tomorrow. They've sailed up to Gloucester Island.'

'Then don't eat alone. Come over for a meal. Make it six. Dad likes his Fourex and Mum likes chocolate.'

'Thanks Pixie, but I'm having dinner here.'

'What's wrong with my home?'

'Nothing, but you work for me, and your dad works for Patrick. It would be awkward.'

'That doesn't make sense.'

I stared at her. Her eyes were steady, begging the grumpy master to get out of his chair.

'Okay, see you at six.'

She smiled. 'We'll fix that troublemaker, just you see.'

I walked her downstairs and opened the door. The scuds had passed leaving watery clouds that hid the brow of the Conway Range. Pixie shoved the raincoat into the basket at the front of her bike and mounted the seat. As she perched, one foot on the ground, I noticed the wren she had stitched on a pocket. She followed my eyes.

'I like fairy wrens, don't you?' she said. 'They're happy little birds.'

When I didn't argue, she said, 'See you later,' and cycled from the rear of the building into Shingley Drive. From there she turned right, then vanished over the hill towards the modest farm house where her parents lived.

Upstairs, I again read through the story behind The Leap. Even the name given to the cliff implied the woman had jumped and not been driven. But did she have a choice? Shivering with terror at the edge? Miraculously, or perhaps bravely, her child had survived — a little girl named Johanna, who in time would have married and had children of her own.

I rang Patrick with the information from the Mackay Historical Society. Like me, he had never considered there might be a report in the library.

'It doesn't improve the chaos out here,' he said.

'I guess not, but tell Grandpa anyway. Where is he?'

'He hasn't left the verandah all morning. They're wrecking the place, Tom. They've knocked out the inside walls and put a sheet of iron on the floor to light a fire. By the time they are evicted there'll be nothing left.'

'Patrick, take Grandpa for a drive. Get him out of the house.'

'Easier said than done. He won't move.'

'Okay, I'll see you tomorrow.'

CHAPTER 29

With the afternoon sun breaking through the clouds, I took my hat and set off along the shore for a cleansing walk. Two boys with bicycles sat on the sea wall casting for bream. When they waved, I responded, but in my heart I felt terrible for Grandpa, who believed, rightly or wrongly, that his grandfather was innocent of Kowaha's death. Although historians tended to agree, the truth was no longer relevant.

At five-thirty I drove into Airlie village for beer and chocolates, then five kilometres out of town to the acreage where Pixie's folk lived. Many years earlier, Terry Hanson had managed the farm that belonged to his parents, but a series of droughts and tough calls by the bank had forced them to sell. Since then, he had worked for the O'Connors, always with a gentle nature that seemed unaffected by life's vagaries. When I arrived at the small, weatherboard house, the front door was open and the scent of climbing roses filled the air. Pixie, still wearing her denim, came from the side of the house in a pair of gumboots. She carried a bucket of feed in one hand and bunches of greens in the other.

'Hello Tom, you're a bit early but that's good. Dad's toying with an old car in the shed. It's time he cleaned up.'

If fate had treated Terry more kindly, he would have

completed a trade as motor mechanic. Apart from fixing tractors on our farm, he restored classic vehicles, the latest of which was a 1940s Morris.

I wandered into the shed. 'Hi, Terry. I've been told to drag you out from under the bonnet.'

'Hello, Tom. Nasty business with your granddad's house.'

'Yes, we hope to get it sorted Monday.'

After washing his hands, he opened two beers then walked me around his garden. Neat little beds of carrot, tomato, lettuce and spinach were fenced off from the fowls and hares. A gravel road ran down the right of his land to properties along Crofton Creek, while down the left, three hectares were set aside for a cow and her calf, who was still wobbly on its legs. He watched as Pixie rubbed the feeding calf with an old towel.

'She'll be my next milker,' he said. 'Best stock I've ever had.'

When Pixie heard our voices she turned, 'Tom, come and smell the calf. She's gorgeous. Like milk and warm oats.'

I sniffed the soft hair and smelt … calf.

She laughed. 'Dad's the same. All he can smell are greasy engines.' She drew yellow ribbons from her pocket and tied them round the calf's neck. 'Now take a photo please, Tom. Do it properly, please. Come on, Dad, stand beside me.'

Upstairs, I met Pixie's mother, Irene, who complemented her husband in build and personality. Both were lean and had country smiles on sunburnt faces. My meetings with Irene were rare because she only ever visited our farm for the harvest party, which invariably fell on a *Post* production night. A quiet woman, she spent three days a week at an accountant's office and the other two days with St Vincent de Paul. The interior of the house reflected the exterior. Clean, tidy and comfortable. From where I sat at the dining table, I could see a bureau laden with photos of Pixie growing up. From there the view was through an archway into a sewing room filled with bags of material. Down the narrow corridor, two bedrooms led off to the right, while a living room with TV and sound system adjoined the dining room on the left.

Sitting in the chair opposite, Pixie watched me eat.

'What are you gazing at?' I asked.

'You.'

I nodded at her plate. 'Your vegies are getting cold.'

'Tom, can I write up what's happening to your farm?'

'No, thanks. We've suffered enough publicity.'

'I didn't mean like that. I meant in a diary. If Michael O'Connor had kept a diary, none of this speculation about his brother would exist.'

'That's a good idea,' Irene said. 'Otherwise, people will only remember what suits them.'

'Okay, Pixie. You be the record keeper.'

We finished eating early as happens with country folk. After helping to wash up, I said my goodnights and walked down the stairs to the Moke, which stood glistening under the porch light. Pixie followed me.

'Tom, thanks for coming over. Mum and Dad enjoyed your company.'

'And I enjoyed the night too. Surprised myself. Thanks, Pixie.'

She leant up and kissed me on the mouth. Twice now she had done that.

'That's a dangerous habit to get into,' I said.

'Since when?'

Climbing into the vehicle, I turned in the yard and exited through the gateway onto the road. In my mirror I saw Pixie wave from the porch. I tooted once and motored back to my flat at Shingley Beach.

*   *   *

On Sunday morning around ten, the *Calvados* returned to its berth. I drove down to the marina, and collected Lisa who was tired from a rough two-night sail to Gloucester Island.

As she settled into the car, I said, 'I'm lunching out at the farm today. Want to come?'

'Thanks, Tom, but I need a sleep.'

I studied her. Dark circles had formed under her eyes and her hair was a mess. 'Sure thing. My place or yours?'

'Yours please. Will you stay with me?'

'I'd love to, but …'

'What?'

'There's bad news at the farm. Lenny Watkins' family has moved into Pop's Place.'

'Oh, no.'

'I'll put you to bed, then return as soon as I can.'

'No, I'll join you. I can sleep later.'

At the flat I carried her bag upstairs while she hurried into the shower, where she washed then dried her hair. Ten minutes later she called from the bedroom. 'Come and talk to me.'

She stood at the mirror brushing her hair. In the strong

light, blemishes showed where an unforgiving sun had ravaged her skin. Her nails needed trimming and a band-aid on her wrist had come unstuck. When her eyes caught mine, she dropped the brush and embraced me. 'I so wanted you today, Thomas, in bed … holding me … promising not to let go because … well … last night I dreamt the party was over. Somebody had blown out the candles.'

'That's daft, Lisa. Nothing is over between us.'

'Sorry, the bleak sky has made me weepy.' She released her arms and opened the wardrobe where she had stored a few outfits. 'What shall I wear? You choose.'

'It might be cold coming home. Wear jeans.'

'Baggy jeans? Not likely. Your mother liked this dress. I'll wear it today. Help everyone feel normal.'

We drove out to the farm in a mood best described as forced lightness. The rain over the past thirty-six hours had settled the dust, freshening the entrance to the house and garden. Mum waved from the kitchen window and pointed to the verandah where Grandpa and Patrick sat with the unopened papers. After greeting Mum and a quick hello from Glenda, who was setting the table for six, we drew up chairs next to Grandpa.

'Has there been any change, Grandpa?' I asked.

'They have wrecked the place. Apart from that, no.'

Patrick motioned me to the rail where he handed me a pair of binoculars. 'You can see right through the building. There's nothing left inside.'

'I don't see the logic in their behaviour, Patrick. They could've turned Pop's house into a nice little home.'

'They don't intend staying, Tom. Their pleasure is in

making us drink our own medicine.'

I returned to my seat. 'Grandpa, we'll see Marvin tomorrow. File a court injunction.'

'It's too late, son. That room at the back, the one near the kitchen, was called Joe's room after your father. I built it six months before he was born, then I lined the walls and made him a cot. When the time came, his mother moved into the room because it was cooler than the main bedroom. Old Mrs Camilleri was the midwife. She and Mrs Reardon. Your father came out sleek as a seal and lived in that room until the day he married. But look at it now. I don't need glasses to see the destruction.'

'Grandpa, come inside. You're torturing yourself.'

'Somebody will pay for this. Some prick, somewhere.'

When we sat down to lunch, even Glenda was subdued. A doorway opened into the wedding showroom where boxes and materials were piled a metre high. I felt for her.

'How are the preparations?' I asked.

'Fine thanks, Tom. The dress is finished. Mrs Brunetta sent it out for a fitting. Looks beautiful, doesn't it, Mum?'

Mum. Three weeks ago, it was Mrs O'Connor.

'I'd love to see the dress,' Lisa said to her.

'I'll show you after lunch. It's from a Milanese pattern.'

Wedding talk bumped along the ground like a half-inflated balloon. We tried a few other topics but they all collapsed. Grandpa said not a word until near the end when he muttered, 'Uncle John's chest is in that house. He brought it back from the war. I'll walk down this afternoon and rescue it. Before I'm too late.'

'No, Henry. That'll only worsen the situation.'

'Don't be silly, woman. I'm fetching my chest.'

'That's all right, Mum,' I intervened. 'Patrick and I will go with him. There'll be no crazy stuff, I promise.'

After lunch we waited until the women had retreated to the wedding room before we trudged down to the house to collect the chest.

'Leave the speaking to me,' I said. 'If anything goes wrong, we'll be thrown into the watch house. As far as Inspector Gudinski is concerned, this place is sacred to the Giya. Okay?'

When they agreed, I strode to the back door. 'You there, Lenny?'

He came to the door holding a thin stick on which sizzled a piece of meat. Wiping his hand across his mouth, he said, 'What youse want?'

'My grandfather has a box here that belonged to his uncle from the First War. The box is a valuable keepsake. He would like to fetch it.'

'No box here, Tom.'

'It stood in the first bedroom. Mind if I have a look?'

'You not making this up?'

'Of course not.'

'Okay, just you.'

Leaving Grandpa and Patrick near the rock garden, I entered the house. It was a wreck. Walls had been torn down and a hole punched through the ceiling to allow smoke from their cooking fire to escape. Lenny's family sat around the fire like hippies at a fondue, roasting squares of meat, which they then dipped into a spicy tomato sauce. Nobody raised their head or offered a greeting. The first and second bedrooms were stripped bare. The timber bed-heads had been broken into firewood while the frames were in a line against the wall. Back in the living room, Lenny watched as I searched through the wood pile for Uncle John's chest. After a time, I came upon the remains of the ornately carved lid. I picked it up.

'Thanks, Lenny. I can't see anything more.'

'Good. Piss off and let us eat in peace.'

Returning to the rock garden, I handed over the lid. 'Sorry, Grandpa. That's all there was.'

'Thanks, Tom.'

'Grandpa, we have to stay calm. Wait until we talk to our solicitor tomorrow.'

Impulsively I hugged him, but the old body remained hard and unhappy.

CHAPTER 30

With the coming of Monday, the southerly front blew out to sea and the world again sparkled under a warm sun. At the flat, Lisa was still asleep when I walked down to the shop for milk. After making coffee and toast, I took them into the bedroom.

She stirred. 'What time is it?'

'Half past six.'

'What are you doing out of bed?'

'Serving breakfast.'

She took my hand and tried to draw me close, but I was not in the mood. Grandpa's beaten face kept appearing before me, and I feared we would have no luck with Marvin Fumbleton. When eventually Lisa gave up, she wrapped a sheet around her and strolled through to the kitchen with her tray.

'Your mum been here, Tom? Everything is nice and clean.'

'I hired a fairy. Put your feet up while I make some calls.'

She snapped off a piece of toast and layered it with butter. 'Tom, I have news of my own. At least, it's an answer to one of your questions. Remember how a woman told you that a boat in the Whitsundays was trafficking drugs. You called her a witch. Well, your description was pretty close. Her name is Mad Michelle and she lives off the Strathdickie

Road. We had local boys on the yacht last night. They said she loves giving people the creeps.'

'Thanks, I'll tell Billy. He might have to search for his trafficker elsewhere.'

'Sorry, Tom. I shouldn't be talking drugs.'

'That's all right, I have a newspaper to run and drugs are on the front page.'

Downstairs I cleared up the work from Friday, then at eight phoned Marvin Fumbleton who didn't welcome the early call.

'Damn it, Tom, I use this time for good reason.'

'This is kind of urgent. Our friend Lenny Watkins … that's correct, the Giya man … has moved into Pop's old house. Apparently, he's within his rights because he's the custodian.'

'What are you expecting me to do?'

'Evict him, Marvin. He has already trashed the place and Grandpa is beside himself. We need a meeting this morning. What time can you fit us in?'

'How about eleven?'

'That's too late. Make it ten.'

'Tom, I have an appointment at ten.'

'Then move it. Please.'

By the time I had rung Patrick and spoken to the staff about their work, the clock showed nine-thirty. Pixie overheard my conversation with Heather — that I had a meeting in town — and asked to join me, but I wouldn't hear of it.

'Tom, you said I could keep a diary of events.'

'You also have work to do. I could be away most of the day.'

'I can finish my work later.'

'Pixie, I said no.'

Lisa appeared at the bottom of the steps. 'Tom, are you driving into Proserpine?'

'Yes, right now.'

'Can I bum a lift?'

'Okay, but you'll have to catch a bus home.'

'That's fine. I'm ready.'

I grabbed my files on the sacred site and strode out to the car. Lisa threw her bag into the rear and jumped in beside me.

After ten minutes of silence, she said, 'What's bothering you, Tom?'

'Lots of things on today.'

'Nothing to do with Pixie?'

'Lisa, get this straight. Pixie works for me. She's not my girlfriend.'

'She was upset. Like she expected to go with you.'

'She's researching a story in town, but today I'm on private business.'

'Tom, I like the girl. Don't be hard on her for my sake.'

'I won't.'

After dropping Lisa off at one of the banks, I met Grandpa and Patrick outside Marvin's door. Again, the three of us filed into his office.

'*Manus in mano*,' he said brightly, unlike his tone of two hours earlier. '*Hand in hand*. Lawyer and client.'

'Cut the crap,' Grandpa replied.

'Well, Henry, I've had another look at the Act, which to be honest is far from complete, though it's getting there. If the custodians want to alter anything, they are meant to consult the property owners. Are there sacred artifacts at or near the house?'

'Yes, my Uncle John's chest.'

'I mean Aboriginal artifacts.'

'Nope.'

'How can you be sure?'

'I'm sure. So, what can we do?'

'Negotiate. There's no precedent for throwing a custodian off a site of cultural significance, which is the quarter hectare including the house. You've already accepted the place is sacred. If it goes to court, the judge is unlikely to sympathise with you.'

'You say we are defeated?'

'Not quite, but you have to face reality.'

'Thanks, Marvin. Thanks a bloody lot.' Grandpa jumped out of his chair and left the office.

Marvin was alarmed. 'Tom and Patrick, you have to take control. Make sure your grandfather stays away from them. You must negotiate.'

'We tried,' I said, 'and were told to piss off.'

'Oh dear, I hoped it wouldn't come to this.'

'Marvin, start court proceedings. Whatever it takes we want that house back.'

I followed Patrick out of the office to where Grandpa leant against the car.

'We are stuffed, lads. Well and truly.' He looked down the street towards Conway. 'Might as well burn the joint.'

'No, Grandpa, we'll work through the law, and when Lenny is evicted, we'll rebuild. Okay?'

'Whatever you say, Tom.'

As nobody felt like coffee, Patrick drove Grandpa home while I did a U-turn and headed out past the golf club to see Harvey and Thelma Nicholson. Vaguely, I hoped Aboriginal lore might step in where European law had failed.

The fibro houses were as neat and tidy as my previous visit. I drew to a dusty halt outside their gate and walked up to the door. Before I had knocked, the door opened and Harvey stood in the entrance.

'Tom O'Connor, I've been expecting you.'

'So, you know what Lenny Watkins has done?'

'Yes, I am sorry.'

He led the way to the verandah where he motioned me to a chair and asked Thelma to make tea, but she remained in the doorway arms folded.

'You expected me, Harvey. Why?'

Awkwardly, he toyed with a vase, avoiding eye contact.

'Tell him,' Thelma said.

'Tell me what?'

'Lenny is our … um … son.'

'Beg your pardon?'

'Lenny is … Juipera … like us, but married a Giya woman. Because he starts trouble willy-nilly, the Giya elders washed their hands of him. We have to put up with his nonsense.'

'So, there may not be a sacred site?'

'That's not for me to judge. This is Giya country.'

'I, well, thought these things went through a land council.'

'As a rule they would, but this registration is new. The council wouldn't meet unless there's a dispute. And there wasn't.'

'That was our advice. Tell me, Harvey, is this related to the death of the woman at Mount Mandarana?'

He shrugged. 'My great aunt is a third cousin of Johanna, the baby who survived. Lenny believes his duty is to make amends.'

'Why single out our family? There were also the Native Mounted Police and Blake Steele. His descendant, Todd, lives in Airlie.'

'Lenny has talked to the spirits of the Rainbow Serpent. They told him that Paul O'Connor pushed the woman.'

'With all due respect, Harvey, that's rubbish.'

He frowned. 'The Rainbow Serpent is real.'

'That's not what I meant. Sorry.' I changed the subject. 'Where did Lenny get his Land Cruiser? I've been told his boys work in the mines, yet I've never seen them. Do they?'

'He has no working-age sons. Somebody gave him the Cruiser. I think it was to do with his house at Woodwark Bay.'

'He was bought out for the price of a car?'

'Maybe. But he didn't own the house. That was an empty building he moved into. He's been there so long, doing no harm, nobody tries to kick him out.'

'Until now?'

'Yes.'

'Another question, Harvey. Would you consider taking revenge against my family?'

'They were bad days, Tom ... real bad, but they're behind us. Thelma, love, where's that book of words?'

Thelma crossed to the sideboard where several heavy, rather tattered books stood upright between two painted rocks. One book was the *King James Bible*, another had *The Fall of Rome* in gold lettering along the spine, and a third — the one she selected — was titled *Maxims of the Ancient World*.

Harvey put on a set of wire-framed glasses and thumbed through the book. 'Listen to this, Tom. It comes from Chinese proverbs. *Before setting out on revenge, a man must first dig two graves …*' He closed the book 'We are too old to dig graves.'

'And so is Grandpa,' I said, rising from the table. 'Thank you, Harvey and Thelma, for your hospitality. I'm sorry that your son Lenny is a troublemaker. But rest assured, whatever he does will never come between us.'

After shaking hands, I drove back through town then along Conway Road to our farm. From the road the scene was no different to last month or last year. When I stopped the engine, I heard Patrick's tractor working the ploughed ground along the river flat. I turned the car in his direction and flashed the lights. After a time, he flashed a response, then I saw him drive across to the farm ute and make his way up the headland. I met him at the shed.

'Patrick, I've been to see Harvey and Thelma Nicholson, the old couple in Proserpine. They've been a real surprise. Lenny is their son. Harvey and Thelma are Juipera, same as Lenny, but he married into a Giya family, so he can claim descent from both tribes. The other thing is that the Nicholsons are distant relatives of the woman who died at The Leap. Lenny's got a reason for payback.'

'I knew it. Grandpa will go berserk. Why didn't we learn all this before signing the papers.'

'I don't know, Patrick. A lot of it is my fault. I took people at face value. Another thing — the Land Cruiser that Lenny drives was bought for him. Somebody with money is funding his payback.'

He punched a tractor tyre. 'Todd Steele. What a surprise.'

'Patrick, I have to return to work. Mind what you tell Grandpa. And don't do anything rash.'

'Rash? We've done everything your way, Tom. We should've paid for a specialist lawyer.'

'What difference would that make? This is not law, it's a vendetta.'

*   *   *

When I arrived at the office, close to three in the afternoon, I was met with a derailment, which in hindsight, I should have anticipated. Ethel's computer had died and she was manually sorting through the ad copy, attaching pieces of artwork to the copy sheets. Heather met me at the door. 'I've phoned the Apple dealer in Mackay, Tom, but he won't be here until morning.'

I walked across to Ethel. 'How far are you behind?'

'There's a mountain of ads pouring in. A lot of it is fresh copy. I've finished the community news but I haven't started on the TV Guide.'

'I thought that was Friday's job.'

'As a rule it would be, but I did the sugar feature on Friday. I wanted to get ahead before the weekend.'

'Damn.'

'Look, Tom, with a clear run at my copy tomorrow, I

should finish by six at the latest. Pixie's spent the day reading faxes. She could help with the TV Guide.'

I glanced across at Pixie behind a pile of faxes, sports draws and manila folders. She squinted intently at the old-fashioned monitor, oblivious to the drama two desks away.

'Give me a minute,' I said to Ethel, 'I'll come up with a solution.'

I called Heather into my office. 'This is a bloody ambush. How did her computer break down at a critical moment? Two hours left in the day and she's smirking.'

'Lend her yours, Tom. Secure the private files, then activate the drivers for the printer and scanner. She can be back at work in ten minutes.'

In no time I was standing beside Ethel's desk with my computer in hand. 'Thank God we had a back-up. Plug in your cables and you're away. Aren't you relieved?'

It was now three-thirty and I was hungry. After checking the flat upstairs and finding Lisa absent, I walked down to the café for a burger.

'Eating in or taking away, Tom?' the girl called at me from behind the counter.

'Eating here,' I said.

While the meat sizzled, I sat at a table and filled out the football tipping competition we ran in the paper. Over the years I had put my weekly dollar into the competition, but never scored higher than mid field. Luck was not one of my strong points. When the girl finished the burger, she brought it across. 'Want tomato sauce?'

'No. It's fine, thanks.'

The burger smelt good and bulged with healthy salads. I was still admiring it when Billy came through the door and settled himself opposite. 'Got a minute, Tom?'

I nodded.

'I've spoken to Lisa and we could be onto something. Remember what I said about seven local boats that go on mysterious trips? Well, I found out today that when Vogel's yacht is not taking tourists to the reef, it sails towards Hook Island with three crew on board. Night trips only.'

'How far does it sail?'

'No idea, nor does Lisa. She was studying charts when you caught her.'

'What interest would a deckhand have in tracking yachts?'

'Curiosity, I guess. These blokes are so secretive. And the other night as the *Calvados* left harbour, Lisa saw lights flashing in the direction Vogel had sailed.'

'They could've been fishermen checking their lines. Did Lisa tell you she unmasked the witch? Apparently, the woman is a known mischief maker.'

'She did, but I'm keeping an open mind. I've played darts with Mad Michelle. She's loopy, but she hangs out with the whisperers.'

'Keep me informed, Billy, and mind your step.'

When he left, I finished the burger and returned to the office where Lisa was seated on the bench, eating sushi with a plastic fork. I moved her to one side and sat beside her. 'You and Billy have been busy.'

'You mean with Vogel's secretive trips?'

I studied her. 'Lisa, who are you?'

She concentrated on marshalling grains of rice. 'Sorry, Tom?'

'For a deckhand enjoying the tropical sunshine, you're very inquisitive. Jade's charts, flashing lights, drug dealers. Is there a purpose behind all this?'

'Tom, I hate drugs as much as Billy does. I come from Sydney and I've seen kids vomit their guts out in a back alley. Billy has told me his story, and if we can stop one ounce of poison going into a kid's blood, we've achieved something. When we find our boat we'll go to the cops, and Pixie can have her scoop.'

'She doesn't want a scoop. Keep her out of it.'

'Whatever. But that's my so-called *purpose*.'

'Okay, I believe you. Now go upstairs and open a shiraz. I won't be long.'

By five-thirty all staff had departed. After locking the doors, I trudged up to the flat. Lisa had showered, and was seated on the balcony in my *Mercury* tee that had somehow been relocated to her end of the wardrobe. She poured a Jameson's and ice. 'Here, Thomas. First things first.'

I sipped the nectar and closed my eyes. What a day it had been.

But it wasn't over yet.

CHAPTER 31

I was in a deep sleep around nine Monday night when the phone rang. An incessant *brrr-brrr, brrr-brrr*. For a minute I didn't know where I was, or what caused the noise. Lisa lay sprawled across my arm. Pushing myself free, I reached for the handset.

'Tom O'Connor,' I mumbled.

Patrick's voice. 'Hell, Tom! Grandpa has lit the house. He's inside. Come now for God's sake. Hurry!'

Throwing on clothes, I ran down the stairs and into the Moke. Lisa was behind me. 'What's happened?'

'Grandpa. He's in trouble. Stay near the phone.'

The car wheels spun as I tore onto the Proserpine Road then swerved wildly around traffic to the Conway Beach turnoff. From the crest of the hill above Palm Creek I saw the glow in the sky, then I was across the bridge, over the tramlines and down the gravel track to where two women stood near Pop's Place. Flames roared into the heavens against a background of roiling smoke.

I skidded to a halt. 'Where's Grandpa?'

'In the house. Look.'

Grandpa stood in Joe's room near the broken windows. He carried his old whiskey bottle and punched the air like a cyclist crossing the line. Fire had taken hold in the main section of the house, and slivers of flame darted through the openings. Two empty fire extinguishers lay on their side in the grass.

'Where's the fire brigade?' I shouted.

'It's coming.'

Patrick hurried from the shed with sacks drenched in water.

Draping one of the sacks over my head, I ran to the side of the building. 'Grandpa! Can you hear me? Grandpa!'

For a moment he turned towards me. Fire had taken his eyelashes and brows, and his face was like a hairless skull. He tipped the bottle to his lips and drank hard. Whiskey flowed down his chin and caught fire.

'Grandpa, please. Come to me. God no! Please, Grandpa, don't do this!'

Dropping the bottle, he raised both arms in the air and bellowed. Then the fire had him. As he fell to one side, he looked at me and mouthed the words, 'My son.'

I felt Patrick beside me. Wrapping ourselves in the wet sacks, we forced our way to the edge of the building. The heat and smoke were intense.

Mum screamed. 'No! Not you two. Get back. It's too late.'

I plunged towards the vacant window. Patrick grabbed me by the arm. 'Don't Tom. Come back. Please, brother.'

Sanity returned and I lurched away from the house to collapse on the ground, weeping and choking.

Then I recall men lifting me to one side and noisy pumps throwing water over the flames. An ambulance officer was trying to force me onto a stretcher while he treated my burns, but I refused to lie still. Grandpa's spirit was in that house pleading with me. 'My son,' the spirit said, over and over. Rolling on my side, I stared at the flames. They were red, hungry, relentless. I shut my eyes and climbed to my feet. Dear God, why, Grandpa?

Although the pain was severe, I insisted on returning to the main house with Mum, Patrick and Glenda, who were suffocating under their own torment. Somebody in uniform made tea and brought it to us in the dining room. The ambulance officer sat to one side. 'You ought to come with me to hospital, sir. Get those burns dressed properly. That one on your shoulder is deep.'

'No, I want to stay.'

'Go with him, Tom,' Mum said. 'There's nothing can be done tonight.'

Patrick had his arms round Glenda who was crying like a child. 'Go, brother, leave everything to me. We can talk in the morning.'

'A toast to Grandpa before I leave.'

'Yes, we'll do that.'

Easing Glenda into Mum's arms, Patrick opened the drinks cabinet and took out the small decanted bottle of Grandpa's ancient whiskey.

'I'd advise against that, sir,' the ambo muttered.

Patrick poured two glasses and said, 'To Grandpa.' I hardly tasted the stuff. I remember falling into Patrick's arms where I bawled shamelessly.

*   *   *

At the hospital they dressed my burns, then around six in

the morning I cadged a lift to the farm with a wardsman who was ending his shift. Patrick was outside filling his mind with tasks necessary to keep the farm operating, Mum was in her dressing-gown in the kitchen, and Glenda was in the shower. My car stood at a crazy angle down the hill where I had left it last night, and the stinking ruins of Pop's house smouldered in the pearl light of dawn. Mum made coffees and brought them out to us in her slippers.

'You should be in hospital,' she said.

'It's a bit painful but nothing serious. What about yourselves?'

'We're okay. Shocked, of course. Lisa's rung twice asking for you.' She nodded towards the house. 'Better let her know you're all right.'

'I will. Shortly.'

As we drank our coffee, I asked for details about yesterday evening.

Patrick spoke in a monotone. 'Not long after your visit, Lenny and his family jumped in their Land Cruiser and drove off. Probably no connection, but they seemed in a hurry. Grandpa had been quiet ever since our meeting with Marvin in the morning. Hardly ate any food, sat on the verandah staring at the old house. Around eight-thirty he said that as the house was empty, he'd go down and cut a few camellias. Mum wanted him to wait until morning, but he said Lenny might be back by then. Some fifteen or twenty minutes later we heard a fire crackling. I thought it was a cane fire, but Glenda said no, it's the old house. My first thought was to let it burn. Good riddance, sort of thing. Then Mum said, "Where's Grandpa?" We all assumed he must've lit the fire, but didn't imagine he'd be inside. When I saw him from the verandah, I rang you, then the fire brigade and ambulance. By the time we got down there with two extinguishers, it was well ablaze. I was chasing up wet sacks from the shed when you arrived. The rest you know.'

'What happens now?'

'Grandpa's body is in the morgue, but the police say we can't go near the house until their investigation is complete. Might take a week. After that? Well, the Giya have their sacred site and the custodians will need a new home.'

'They'll probably return to Woodwark Bay,' I said, then pointed to the charred remains. 'We can't look at that forever.'

'Don't worry, I'll bulldoze it clean when the police have finished.' He threw his coffee dregs on the grass. 'Todd Steele is behind all this. He should be a happy man this morning.'

We turned to watch a ute pull into the yard. It was Terry Hanson arriving for work. As the motor died, he stepped from the driver's door and Pixie from the other, dressed like she'd been called from bed. While she waited at the front of the vehicle, Terry walked down to us.

'Terribly sorry to hear about your grandfather,' he said. 'Dreadful business.'

We all shook hands. 'Thanks, Terry.'

'I didn't know what to do, but thought it best we carry on as usual.'

'You're right,' Patrick said. 'Those river blocks need finishing. You okay with that?'

'Of course.'

I nodded towards his ute. 'Pixie ought to be readying for work.'

'She wanted to come over, see if there was any way to help.'

'Thank her from us, but we're all right.'

'Go up to her,' Mum said. 'And be gracious. You'll need that over the next week.'

I followed Mum's advice and walked slowly up the hill. I didn't want Pixie's nice words. I didn't want anyone's. I needed to grieve for my grandfather in private, to be alone with his spirit.

'Sorry, Tom. I didn't know whether to come or not.' Her hair was unbrushed, and a faded jacket was buttoned over cotton pyjamas.

'That's all right, Pixie. Thanks for coming. I won't be at the office for a while, so you'd best shoulder the load. Glenda can give you a lift.'

'May I stay a minute? I won't talk to anyone.'

'Yes, that's fine,' I said, and moved away.

'I didn't mean to intrude, Tom, but I knew your grandpa from when I was little. I loved him in his gruff way.'

When I returned down the incline, Patrick and Terry had gone to the shed, and were bolting implements to one of the tractors. Mum called out to Pixie, 'Join us for breakfast, love. Tom can drive you to work afterwards.'

'I've got breakfast at home, thanks Mrs O'Connor.'

'You can eat with us,' Mum said, and strode to her kitchen.

After a light but subdued breakfast, I left instructions for Patrick to stay in touch, then dusted soot from the car seats and motioned Pixie aboard. As we drove wordlessly to her house, she said, 'Leave me at the gate, Tom, and

I'll collect my bike.'

'It's no trouble. I can wait.'

In her driveway, I loaded the bike then sat calmly at the wheel, engine running, waiting for her to change. Twenty minutes later she emerged and jumped into the car.

'I'm surprised you didn't blow the horn,' she said.

'Seatbelt, Pixie.'

She bit her lip. 'Before we leave, Tom, I have a small … um … gift.'

Opening her briefcase, she offered a little green and white wreath that had a yellow flower glued at the centre. The green was the green of a eucalypt forest, the yellow was a flower in bloom, and the white? White for serenity, white dove, white challenging the darkness? I didn't ask.

'They're all Heaven's colours, Tom, and I'm wearing the same colours today. To remind us that beyond grief there is hope. And, well …' She shrugged self-consciously. '… with hope comes joy.'

Maybe it's what she said, maybe how she said it, but I couldn't answer. I rested my head on the steering wheel and sobbed. She didn't try to touch me, just waited. After a time, I lifted my head and rubbed my eyes. 'Thanks, Pixie,' I said and slipped the wreath into my pocket.

I dropped her at the office and climbed the stairs where I recounted to Lisa the events of the night. As she'd done nurse's training in England (another surprise), she inspected my burns then drove the car into Airlie Pharmacy where she bought more bandages, ointments and pain killers. When she returned, I looked at the clock. 'Staff will arrive in ten minutes. I need to be out of here.'

'Good idea,' she said. 'Where shall we go?'

'I want to be alone. Sorry.'

'Is that healthy? You've suffered nasty trauma. Remember our first afternoon together? We took a catamaran across the bay. Let's do that again. It's peaceful out there.'

'I'm not up to that sort of thing.'

'I'll be the skipper. You sit up front and sleep.'

Since it was impossible to object further, we bundled together warm clothes and sneaked out the door for a morning's sail off Airlie Beach. While the boat tripped across the placid water, I reflected on Grandpa, who had been a man of his times. Wilful and unapologetic, he had defiantly gone down with his ship. The pain of immolation would've been horrible but the more powerful the exit, the greater the statement. But to whom was the statement addressed? Surely not to the original inhabitants or their difficult son. No, I believed it was anger with the law, with people harbouring resentment, and with the shadowy men who used vulnerable people for their grubby ends. Grandpa's triumphant cries at the finish were addressed to those who thought he was beaten, that he would suffer his humiliation in silence.

When we returned to the sand in front of Mick's Cat Hire, Lisa said, 'What's your favourite place in all the world, Tom?'

'Whitsundays, I guess.'

'Anywhere in particular?'

'Yes, the mouth of the river. I always loved it there.'

'Then let's go for a drive.'

Because the day was well advanced and I had no intention of returning to the office, I agreed. The route would take us past the farm, but fortunately Pop's Place — what remained of it — was invisible from the road. Lisa drove while I gazed at the scenery. In every tree, in every rock, I saw my grandfather. Perhaps we are closer to the Dreamtime than we imagine. The God of Abraham is also the God of the Dreaming. Soon after crossing Saltwater Creek, we turned towards the boat ramp, and stopped above the high-water mark. The river was in full flight out to sea, tugging at mangrove stems that bobbed and swayed in the current. Sea eagles cruised over distant flats, and egrets grazed on molluscs at the waterline.

'Any crocodiles here?' Lisa asked.

'One or two.'

'Right now?'

'Probably not this minute. They're shy creatures. If we had a boat and motored upriver, we'd find them sunning on the mud.'

'Patrick showed me one at the bottom of your farm. Ugly brute. Why do they eat people?'

'Easy prey. Sweet flesh.'

'You won't find me near the water. Did you come here with your grandfather?'

'Often. With both Grandpa and Dad. We brought folding chairs and cast on the incoming tide. Never went home without a meal. Some days we caught enough fish for a month.'

'Tom, your grandfather said frightful things, but that wasn't the real him.'

'You're right, Lisa, it wasn't.'

She checked her watch. 'We're taking the *Calvados* on

a sunset cruise tonight. Depart at five and return in the morning. I have to go and make ready. Will you be okay at the flat on your own?'

'No, leave me here. There's a chair, cast net and lines in the back of the Moke. Leave them behind. And if you use the grey key on the ring, open the steel box. You'll find a bottle of whiskey and a torch. I'll stay here, do some fishing and think of Grandpa.'

'Why don't I drive you back to the farmhouse? Spend the night with your mum and Patrick.'

'I need to be alone. Just one night of grieving then it's over.'

'What if I tell Patrick you're here? He can bring some food at dark.'

'No, Lisa.'

CHAPTER 32

After reluctantly dropping off the goods, Lisa reversed up the boat ramp and onto the road. For a time, I heard the car grinding through the foothills of the Conway Range, then there was silence. Total mud-sucking, fish-jumping silence. I took a slug of whiskey, unfolded the chair, and rubbed insect repellent on the exposed patches of skin. As the tide slowed, I cast a net from the bank and hauled in a dozen prawns, handling them carefully to keep my bandages dry. Around five-thirty, the tide stopped moving and began to retrace its path upriver. Meanwhile, the alcohol was hot in my belly and the bottle half empty. I threaded a prawn on a hook and cast into the river. The line jerked twice then was still. I reeled in and baited the hook a second time. Dusk was now lowering its mantle across the mangroves, birds winged for home and a bandicoot led her juvenile to higher ground. A half moon rose above the trees and cast a low-wattage glow on the river. I drank more whiskey. Soon it was dark. A big croc nosed up to the bank and watched me, his eyes two pale red beacons in the moonlight. When I threw a rock at him, he slid beneath the water. I drank more whiskey and felt bad, like all the years of family anguish were being dumped on me, drowning me. I lay back in my chair and closed my eyes.

Grandpa dancing in the flames would stay with me forever. The old man crazy with grief over his beloved home. I finished the whiskey and threw the bottle into deep water where it dipped and glinted like metal on fire. My line snaked taut. I took the weight, and for ten minutes I drew the fighting barramundi to the shore. He was beautiful, silver gleaming in the dark, kilograms of sweet flesh. Tomorrow's dinner. After throwing him high on the bank, I returned to my chair. Grandpa had caught barramundi right here, on this very spot. He and my dad, both gone, both had taught me to fish, both were wonderful men. My head slumped on my chest. My dad and my grandpa, I loved them. I dozed.

Screaming. Screaming broke through my skull like cold blows at night. Jackhammers, men running with pneumatic drills, forcing the wall. The scream persisted. Grandpa's last cry. I shook myself awake. Car headlights burnt the night and Lisa was there, screaming at the big ugly snout crawling up the mud to my chair. She threw rocks but the primeval brain was locked on food.

'Tom! Tom! Wake up. Tom!'

She had the arm of the chair and was pulling me backwards. My legs wouldn't move. The big croc came hard and Lisa smashed the torch on his snout. She grabbed me under the armpits.

'Tom! For God's sake, help me!'

We were stumbling backwards in the mud. The croc had retreated in the noise and light. Then Lisa dragged me into the car and reversed crazily up the boat ramp. On the road, she pulled over until the shaking stopped, then drove me in silence back to the flat where she showered me and changed the bandages. Afterwards she held me in bed, rocking me, telling me to cry. It would be all right.

But I was silent. Even if the croc had taken me, I wouldn't have cared.

*   *   *

In the early hours I fell asleep and slept until midday. Warm smells from the kitchen woke me, somebody braising steak and onions. I sat up, hungry and alert.

'You awake, Tom?'

Lisa came to the door. 'How do you feel?'

'Famished.'

She shuddered. 'Lord, that was close.'

'I thought you had sailed on the *Calvados*.'

'At the last minute I decided I couldn't leave you at the river. I was already in uniform, helping prepare the yacht, when I told Jade. He wasn't pleased about sailing short-handed, but his three crew are experienced and the sea was calm. Besides, he's not that callous he doesn't sympathise. The roadside was very dark when I returned, missed the exit to the boat ramp and ended up at Conway Beach. By the time I found you it was almost too late. Never again, Thomas.'

'Thanks, Lisa. You were brave.'

We sat in the bed for some minutes when there was a knock on the door.

'You'd better answer it,' Lisa said.

I dressed slowly and went to the door. Heather stood at

the top of the stairs like a rent collector, not wanting to be there but not leaving empty-handed.

'Thank heavens you're safe. First your grandpa, now you and the crocodiles. I hope that's the end of it.'

'Me too, Heather. What do you want?'

'The police are downstairs. You available?'

'Yes. Give me a minute.'

After closing the door, I told Lisa that life was back to normal. While she renewed my bandages, I suggested she walk down to the marina and make amends with Jade. She had a job to keep, and she couldn't exactly claim she was my personal nurse. I shaved, then descended the stairs to where the two cops sat in my office spinning the propeller of a little plane Nana had given me when I was ten. They were the same cops, Phil Manning and his constable, and the same mountain of gear hanging off their belts.

'Afternoon, Tom. Sorry to disturb you. We want to tidy up the details of your grandfather's death.'

'Yes, burnt the sacred site with himself in it.'

'I assume you mean the house.'

'Yes, Phil.'

'The house was occupied by the family of …' he checked his notebook '… Lenny Watkins. Were they present at the time?'

'I don't believe so. Their car had gone.'

'It was reported Henry O'Connor set fire to the house. Why do you think that?'

'My brother phoned to say the house was on fire with Grandpa inside. When I arrived, the place was ablaze and Grandpa … well … like Patrick had said.'

'Could the fire have been lit by a person or persons unknown, and your grandfather was trapped?'

'He wasn't trapped, Phil. Lenny Watkins had trashed the house, but he didn't set fire to it. Poor old Grandpa did.'

The cops stood up. Phil Manning, who had asked the questions shook my hand and said, 'Sorry to hear about your grandfather, Tom. He was a good man, one of the best.'

While they let themselves out the door, I decided I had to face the staff sometime. Walking into the centre of the office, I sat on an empty chair.

'All right, guys. You've heard what happened to my grandpa. Died in a house fire two nights ago, and I guess you heard that I nearly made a croc's supper. That's all in the past now. The sooner we return to work the better. I'll be tied up over the next few days with legal matters, so I'm relying on you to bring out a paper. Okay?'

Everybody agreed but said nothing. What was there to say? Heather came across with a condolences card they had signed, then she turned and said, 'Right gang, back to the coalface.'

When I passed Pixie's desk, she collected a news folder and pen and followed me into the office. Dusting off a chair that didn't need dusting, she sat and crossed her legs like a secretary about to take notes.

'This looks formal,' I said.

'I could lounge against the door frame.'

I allowed a smile. 'You would need a lounge suit.'

'With embroidered pockets, of course.'

I found myself studying her. It wasn't so many weeks ago she had sat in that very chair: unadorned though pretty, miserable yet defiant. 'Pixie, do you mind if I … um … ask a question? The birds and flowers you wear, …' I nodded to the embroidery on her skirt '… are they your own creation?'

'Is that scepticism I detect? Then you would be right. The needlework is all Aunty Joan's effort. She gave it to me when I was little. A whole box of Australian plants and animals. But I was at a loss what to do with them. You see, I …' she paused '… Are you okay?'

Without warning I had begun to cry. Embarrassing trauma tears. I brushed them away. 'Sorry, please go on.'

'You sure?'

'Yes, I'm listening.'

'Well, I was always academic and never appreciated handicraft, until the end of last year. As a reward for matriculating, Mum took me on the overnight train to Brisbane. It was my first visit to the city and we had a great time. One day we went shopping at David Jones where there were all these amazing departments: clothes, shoes, underwear, perfume … everything for the modern woman. We each bought a couple of dresses, then I saw this separate rack of women's briefs. They were printed with motifs of Australian flora and fauna — banksia, koalas, rosellas … you name it. The store called them the Australiana Collection. I bought a dozen or so, then a few assorted pairs like the tartan. I like them, they're fun, and they complement my aunt's embroidery.'

'Don't have an accident. Somebody might think you're odd.'

'Do you?' Her eyes were amused, waiting.

'No, Pixie, you're not odd … different yes, but never odd. And thanks for the explanation. Mum's bound to ask.'

Awkwardly I blew my nose. 'Right, back to business. Is this our page one lead?'

'Yes, the airport. Li Yang is not happy. The contract to deliver gravel for the airport extension went to an interstate firm, who then sub-contracted to a Bowen company. Despite Li's best efforts his trucks missed out. The council CEO said the budget overrun was caused by three months' flooding last year, and a lot of work had to be redone. Li claims Council is being rorted by the big contractors who use a cheap road base, then get paid to repeat the mistake.'

'Li needs to be careful. Rort is a powerful word. If he has suspicions, he should take them to the authorities. In the meantime, do your story that the extension has gone over budget by two million, and give the CEO's explanation. Let me see a proof before it's dropped on the page.'

I was about to return upstairs when Billy took me to one side. 'There'll be one hungry croc in the river tonight, Tom.'

'Yes, very stupid of me.'

'You were heartbroken, nothing stupid in that. And I feel terrible about what happened to your grandpa. He was one of a kind.'

'Thanks, Billy.'

'On a separate note, Tom, there's something interesting about the *Calvados*. Hope you don't mind talking about it. As you may know, she did a sunset cruise last night. That's common. Most of the boats try it on a calm sea. Anyway, I launched my tinny with the intention of shadowing Vogel's yacht, but it was tied up and going nowhere, so I chose the

Calvados. Like you'd expect, Jade sailed across the front of Airlie, but instead of returning to the marina, he headed north. An hour later, lights flashed at him from the shore. That's right, not from the south where Lisa saw a light, but up near Woodwark Bay. Admittedly, I was too far back to be certain. The *Calvados* didn't appear to respond, but kept on track until around nine, then turned about, and anchored off Airlie. After that I left her and went to bed. What do you think?'

'Could the torch be someone at the huts taking a leak?'

'No. Two steady flashes.'

'I don't know, Billy. Might be a coincidence.'

'It's a pity Lisa wasn't on board. She could've given me a clue.'

'Well, swap notes but keep it low key.'

When Billy returned to his desk, my conscience told me to call Patrick. Since Grandpa's death I had been immersed in my own grief, yet it was Patrick who had buoyed Grandpa in all the months following Dad's accident.

The phone had almost rung out when Mum's voice came on the line.

'Hello, Mum. Tom here. How is everyone?'

She was silent for a long time. 'Dreadful. And I received a call from Heather. You were nearly eaten by a croc last night. What in God's name is going on?'

'Sorry, Mum. I was an idiot. Fell asleep at the boat ramp. Lisa woke me in time. I'm okay now. How is Patrick?'

'He's hardly spoken. Poor Glenda is distraught. The

wedding is less than three months away and the world has gone mad.'

'Is Patrick in?'

'He's out in the paddock. Come over and eat with us tonight. I'll expect you early.'

It was now mid-afternoon Wednesday as I remounted the stairs. Even though I had slept well the previous night I was tired; so much spinning through the head, so many troubled dreams. I lay on the sofa and stared at the ceiling, mesmerised by the crocodile's eyes. After ten minutes of this torture, I returned to my office where I tackled a stack of letters. At five, staff popped their heads through the doorway and said goodnight. I heard Heather say, 'Move along, Pixie, I'm locking up in two minutes.'

Pixie thrust her story into my hand and squeezed through the door that Heather held ajar like a prison guard. After collecting her bag, Heather said, 'Any word on a day for the funeral?'

'We meet the undertaker tomorrow.'

'The sooner it's over the better. Have you heard from that Lenny Watkins fellow?'

'Not a whisper.'

'I hope he receives his due,' she said vehemently.

'We might never see him again.'

'His type doesn't disappear. Find him, and get answers.'

CHAPTER 33

Heather gave me a brief hug, and left through the rear door where her car was parked. Suddenly the office was quiet and still. In recent times I had enjoyed this hour of the day, but not this week, not even the past month. Upstairs, I took a lemon soda onto the balcony where, despite everything, the view was still impressively beautiful. I had finished the drink, and was preparing to leave for the farm when Lisa returned.

'I've been to see Jade. All is forgiven. Apparently, the sunset cruise last night was so popular he's organised another for Friday night. You'll have to cook and find other means to amuse yourself.'

'I'll survive. By the way, I learnt a curious thing about Jade's sunset cruise. Billy followed in his fishing tinny and saw a light flash twice, like a signal. This time it came from the land.'

She grimaced. 'Billy needs to be careful.'

'That's what I said.'

Because I was eating with family, we skipped our usual drinks. I dropped Lisa off at her house, and motored down Conway Road to the farm where Mum had switched on an outside light. Patrick was on the verandah hanging a shade cloth between the posts.

'Every time we walk down the hallway we see the old house,' he said. 'It's bloody terrible.'

'Any word on the funeral?'

'Seems like Grandpa's body will be released on Monday. We'd like to do the funeral Tuesday. All that will be discussed with the undertaker tomorrow.'

He gestured to a chair. 'Have a beer with me, Tom. I hear you've tried to keep a family tradition.'

'How do you mean?'

'Fill yourself with whiskey, then kill yourself. Not clever.'

'You're right. I'm not coping too well. How about you?'

'Oh, busy all day. I've got Mum to worry about and Glenda moved in this afternoon. That wasn't to happen until after the wedding, but stuff the niceties. As soon as the police give their approval, we'll clear the site. Plant flowers and native trees. I don't think the Giya will object to that.'

'I'm sure they won't.'

'Then I'm going after the bastard who killed Grandpa. Somebody started this war, and it wasn't Lenny.'

'You still think Todd Steele?'

'Who else? I'll burn down his house, maybe even a car or two.'

'Patrick, listen to yourself. Is that your wedding gift to Glenda? A life in prison.'

'He hired Lenny to do his dirty work. I can be clever too.'

'I'm familiar with your cleverness.'

'So, what's your answer, Tom? Let Grandpa's death slide by like it was an accident?'

'No. Our investigations can be transparent — use the paper's resources. If we find evidence of wrongdoing, we'll go to Seb Gudinski.'

When Mum called us to dinner, Patrick clapped me on the knee. 'You take the high way, little brother, I'll take mine.'

At the dinner table, everyone made an effort to lift spirits. Glenda told a hoary joke she'd heard at the bank, and we laughed like we were in the best seats of a comedy festival. Mum then told her only joke, which featured an Irishman flying to America. He asks the steward, 'How high is this plane?' The steward answers, 'Thirty thousand feet.' And the Irishman says, 'That's incredible! How wide is it?' One day I'll buy Mum a book of jokes from which she can choose a second party stopper. Meantime, Patrick managed only the first line of his joke when Mum silenced him. She knew where it was headed.

'Tom, what's your joke?'

'There was this Welsh referee, see ...'

They dutifully laughed. Afterwards, we washed up together and retired to bed. For the first time in years every bedroom door in that house — apart from Grandpa's — was latched wide open.

*   *   *

Next morning, Thursday, was production day at the office. All hands were on deck as we set the paper for its five o'clock run to the printers. Pixie's story on the airport went in with a

262

few minor corrections. Even Todd Steele's copy was on time and intact, no missing photos to chase up and no sudden alterations. Around nine, Patrick and I met the undertaker who confirmed the funeral would be on Tuesday. With that information we added a notice in the classifieds, then boxed a piece on the front page, announcing that the office would be closed Tuesday due to a family bereavement. As we dropped the final page in the box, Lisa came through the door. She shared a coffee with us then asked to see me alone.

'Tom, I told Jade you were traumatised and under doctor's orders for another five days. So, I requested compassionate leave until Sunday, our next trip to the reef.'

I frowned. 'Go on.'

'Billy and I have had a chat. He wants me to help shadow the *Calvados* on its cruise tomorrow night. The moon will be around quarter full; perfect for the job. I'm convinced the *Calvados* is innocent, but if the lights appear, we'll take a fix.'

'You think they're related to drugs?'

'Not really, but it begs the question.'

I still felt the lights were innocuous as every boat at night carried a torch, and campers would need a torch to move around, but I didn't express this view. Lisa and Billy were on a mission. Besides, while they investigated mysterious lights, I intended driving out to Woodwark Bay to see if Lenny Watkins had returned to his home.

CHAPTER 34

Friday morning was business as usual. I sat at my desk taking early calls from residents who had not received their *Post*, from the SOWs who were chasing nudists off the foreshore, and from a boy who had lost his dog. With the boy, I phoned my delivery coordinator, and asked him to organise a search. 'Please, Kim, could you make it urgent.'

'Right away, Tom.'

Strangely enough, I received no calls on Grandpa's death, which was a relief as dozens of people had already offered their condolences. No, that's a lie. I was upset that not one person rang me that morning. 'I miss you, Grandpa,' I said aloud and unhappily. I was at Heather's desk leaving a note, when I heard bicycle tyres. I looked at the clock. Not yet eight.

'What is it, Pixie?' I said, without lifting my head.

'Council meeting at nine-thirty. Remember, Tom?'

'Ah ...,' I said blankly. Council meetings were normally the second Monday of the month. This Monday, however, was a Council audit, and the meeting had been moved forward. Which indeed I had forgotten. 'We don't ... um ... leave until nine. People are still in bed.'

'I want to be ready for it. Last time I didn't think of

questions until we got back to the office. They escaped with too much.'

'Listen Pixie, this is not federal parliament. It's a shire council. Apart from the occasional big story — like we're pursuing — the minutiae is barking dogs and rubbish bins. Only a handful of nutters expect reams of Council news.'

She was piqued. 'Tom, I'm learning. One day I might be an old cynic, but not yet. Shall we start afresh? Good morning.'

Over the next half hour, the remainder of the staff trickled in. Again, it was congratulations on a first-rate paper. We talked briefly about work matters, and yes, Ethel's computer was a temporary fix and she would receive a new one later in the day. At eight-thirty I sat with the sales reps to discuss upcoming features and the run-of-press ads that needed attention, then at nine I collected Pixie for the drive to Proserpine. Apart from a black condolence ribbon on her blouse, she wore the skirt featuring a koala.

'Tell me, Pixie, is the koala significant?'

'Not especially. I wear this skirt most Fridays. Why?'

'It might give the mayor flashbacks.'

'Then his day is not busy enough. And before you ask, the matching garment continues the koala theme — eucalyptus flowers. All good?'

After a short silence, I said, 'Yes, Pixie. All good.'

'Thank you, Tom,' she said quietly. 'That's how it should be.'

With an effort I dragged myself back to Council issues. 'Anything of interest in the agenda?'

'Ten pages on barking dogs and rubbish bins. Relax. Bad

joke. There was one item, though, that caught my eye. You've been to Woodwark Bay. What's there?'

'Not much. A few huts, Lenny's house and a fantastic view. Why?'

'Council has received a development application.'

'Oh. From whom?'

She opened the agenda on her lap. 'A company named Tagula Enterprises. Do you know them?'

'I will before the day's out.'

When we drew into the Council premises, councillors of my grandpa's vintage came forward to offer their sympathy. They had all known Henry O'Connor, who was a feudal lord of the Proserpine valley. Many of these councillors had fought him, others had admired him, and some were secretly glad he was dead. After a few quick handshakes and murmured condolences, they turned to Pixie who had become their favourite daughter.

Abdul Nader was no exception. 'Good morning, Pixie. Glad to see you've returned to our humble chambers.'

'I like it here, sir.'

'Call me Abdul. Everyone does.'

'Hattie taken the day off?' I asked.

'No, she's around somewhere.'

'Great secretary,' I said. 'Always keen to give the boss a hand.'

'You'd know, of course. Anyway, must dash.'

When Pixie turned to me, she caught my grin. 'It wasn't that funny.'

'Yes, it was. He thought he had seen rabbits.'

As we entered the chamber, the *Mercury* reporter met me at the door. 'Look where they've shoved us, Tom. Right up the back. We can't even see who's talking.'

She was correct. In the rearrangement of furniture, the secretary's table sat alone at the centre, winged either side by the public gallery. Behind them the press table was squeezed into a corner like a detention desk.

'I'm not sitting there. It's humiliating,' she said.

'You're damn right,' snorted Herb McBride from the *Proserpine Gazette*. A round, dapper man of my grandfather's era, Herb had not missed a Council meeting in fifty years. 'They can go to buggery.'

'And all because of one kind act last month,' I said. 'How values have changed.'

At nine-thirty when Abdul banged his gavel to open proceedings, the three newspapers walked out the door.

Pixie was horrified. 'You can't do this, Tom.'

'Relax, Pixie. Once we write a few crap stories we'll get our table back, plus cushions on the chairs.'

'I thought you wanted to hear about Woodwark Bay.'

'I'll phone Abdul after three. In the meantime, we'll do a local feature, then drive across for a look.'

From the corner of my eye, I saw Herb McBride approach. 'Tom, spare a minute?'

'Sure, Herb.' I turned to Pixie. 'Why don't you source a feature of your own. Take the camera and return inside an hour. I'll be at the *Gazette*. You happy with that?'

'Yes, Mr O'Connor. You rest up like the doctor said.'

With a theatrical sigh in my direction, she shouldered the camera and walked down the street.

'Attractive lass you have there, Tom. She seems to respect you.'

'She's showing off.'

Herb led me through reception to the back of the *Gazette* where he had a cubby hole behind the presses. Three battered chairs faced each other over an ancient formica table. After selecting chipped mugs from a hook, he made instant coffee, added sugar and milk, then sat in one of the chairs.

'Tom, I read your story on the airport budget this morning, and I can guess your source. Li Yang.'

'That's right. He's annoyed about losing a contract.'

'Speaking as an old friend of your grandfather, mind how you go. Councillor Yang strides where angels fear to tread.' He leant closer. I could smell Brilliantine on his still-dark hair. 'Tagula Enterprises. Did you see that name in the agenda?'

'Funny you should ask, Herb. Who are they?'

'A crowd from down south. I'll tell you more, but promise the story is mine.'

'It's a promise. I don't want a news story, I want information about Tagula because they're connected to Woodwark Bay. As you might recall, the man who trashed my grandpa's house, Lenny Watkins, lives there.'

'All right. Two weeks ago, Tagula submitted a development application. Li Yang will make sure it's approved because he's got the contract to supply material for the road.'

'Is that in writing?'

'It was a handshake, which happens to be stronger than law. The conversation was secretly taped.'

'How do you know this?'

'I have a reliable source.'

'Tell me, Herb. I'll not reveal it.'

'I trust you. The source was Todd Steele.'

I nearly fell off my chair. 'Bloody hell.'

I then detailed the bad blood that existed between Todd Steele and Henry O'Connor. 'The dots are starting to join up. Todd needed to remove Lenny from Woodwark Bay, and he also wanted payback against Grandpa. *Whammo.* He's killed two birds with one stone. The crafty old bastard.'

'That's conjecture, Tom. Li Yang is the real crook in this story.'

'They're both crooks. So, what do you know about Tagula Enterprises?'

'They're a Sydney mob. Seems like they go round the country sniffing out developments that stall for no apparent reason. The same with prime land. If it's sitting vacant, they dig into the history. Up here, Todd Steele would be their man on the ground.'

'So at this minute, with no press in the chamber, Li will push through the application. Later, he and Todd will open a bottle of champagne. Me and my smart mouth handed it to them on a platter.'

'Remember, Tom, you heard nothing about a secret tape.'

'Of course. Any chance you know who the Tagula directors are?'

'You'd have to do a company search. Give your lass the job, and leave Councillor Yang to me.'

For the next half hour, Herb showed me through his premises. Although his *Gazette* was printed on colour offset in another location, he had three small presses for commercial work in Proserpine. His son now operated the business, allowing Herb to do what he liked best; reportage of local government. After a time, Pixie wandered through from the front, having been directed by *Gazette* staff, and sat in one of the chairs.

Following introductions, she said, 'My feet hurt. I've walked all over town for people who are never where they're supposed to be. Can I have a glass of water, please?'

Herb fussed about looking for a glass, but when he sniffed at a clear liquid in the fridge, Pixie changed her mind.

'I'd rather stop at a creek,' she muttered.

'There's water in the front office,' he said. 'Are you the daughter of Terry and Irene Hanson?'

'That's right.'

'My granddaughter Sue is your age. She sponsors an Australian wildlife refuge.' He nodded at the koala on her skirt. 'Young people wear their hearts on their sleeve. Pity we hadn't done likewise.'

'You still can,' she replied. 'It's not difficult.'

'Come, Pixie,' I said. 'We have a busy day.'

After pausing at the front office to receive a bottle of water, Pixie and I returned to Cannonvale. I told her about Li Yang and that he was off limits until the *Gazette* had finished with him. I also explained that Tagula was a Sydney firm, and the development of Woodwark Bay was likely to be sold through Todd Steele.

CHAPTER 35

As the time was barely eleven, we swung left at the Paluma Road intersection and drove over the hills north-west of Cannonvale. After skirting the three inlets, where houses mushroomed against the slopes, we plunged onto the rough terrain that isolated Woodwark Bay. Minutes later my heart sank. The site where Lenny's family had once lived was now empty: not so much as a child's toy or spent tissue. A demolition unit had scrubbed the place clean. Wherever Lenny had gone after trashing Pop's house, it wasn't to Woodwark Bay. I parked the car and studied the landscape. Even the five huts that had squatted along the beach were gone. All that remained were Jade's deep-water jetty and the shed he had built. Shrugging at Pixie, who had not known what to expect, I walked down to the shed that had one tilting door secured by padlocks. It was impossible to know what lay inside.

Pixie joined me. 'What are you looking for, Tom?'

'I'd say Tagula knew their development application would receive the green light. Lenny's place has disappeared, so have the huts. Nothing left but this shed. Once Lenny had moved into Grandpa's house, Tagula Enterprises — or their agent in Airlie — made sure he wasn't coming back.'

'It's beautiful land.'

'Yes, and more valuable than ever.'

'So what next?'

'We'll take a few photos then research Tagula.'

I gazed out over the water, trying to picture the location of Billy's tinny when he saw the torch. And where was Jade's yacht at the time? Sailing imperturbably north. That was three nights ago. The huts and Lenny's house had been demolished sooner than that.

*   *   *

Researching Tagula Enterprises came easier than expected. I had just parked the car when my office phone rang.

'Hello, Tom. This is Abdul. No reporters at the meeting today. I hear you don't like the new seating arrangements.'

'Correct, Abdul. Nothing to do with last month's little drama?'

'Of course not. We're trying to make the public more inclusive.'

'Is that joke of the day?'

He paused. 'All right, next month you're back where I can see you. And everyone is fine as they are. Not your fault.'

'Thanks, Abdul. Now for more pressing business. Did you approve the application for Woodwark Bay?'

'Yes, subject to the usual conditions.'

'What do you know of Tagula Enterprises?'

'Not a lot. Big investors from Sydney. Good luck to them, I say. A sealed road into that place will cost a fortune, not to mention power and water. There's already a glut of sites with ocean views.'

'Who are their directors?'

'Wouldn't know off the top of my head.'

'Abdul, can you send across what you have?'

'Sorry, Tom. That material is commercial in confidence. It can't leave the office.'

'You owe me one, remember.'

'I could go down for this.'

'I'll courier it straight back. Tagula are not as squeaky clean as they appear.'

'Okay, Tom. Tread carefully for both our sakes.'

When the call ended, I walked through to Pixie's desk.

'Do that story on Woodwark Bay but remember, no mention of Councillor Yang just yet. All the information in the agenda is correct, and the mayor is sending over what he knows on Tagula Enterprises. Next month's meeting has been sorted. I'll phone Herb McBride and the *Mercury*.'

'If I caused the ruckus, Tom, I'm sorry.'

'Don't be. The place needed a shake-up.'

Late that afternoon a courier delivered the papers on Tagula's application. The large buff envelope held more dull material than a hospital laundry. Endless pages addressing the pre-conditions on a development greater than ten hectares, lists of council fees, documents from government agencies on land classification, water rights and freehold title. One single sheet declared the land free of environmental issues, and another sheet noted that five illegal squatters' huts had been erected above the high tide mark. There was also one jetty attached to a substantial metal shed. No mention was made of Lenny Watkins' abode that evidently had never existed. At the back of the file was a brief outline of the company Tagula Enterprises. The first name I saw was J. T. Wilson whom I guessed was Jade, skipper of the *Calvados*. I had seen his watch inscribed with J. T., his surname was Wilson and his involvement made sense; he already owned the jetty and shed. If my assumption was correct, Tagula hadn't sniffed out the land for development. They had held it for years.

When Billy arrived at work mid-afternoon, I reported to him what I had discovered.

He lay back in his chair, staring at the ceiling. 'Where have I heard of Tagula before? I know. Todd Steele's office last week. On his desk was a stack of colour brochures advertising Tagula Estate. The front page was an ocean vista with a happy family picnicking on the grass. That's all I saw. I didn't touch anything, but I do remember the name Tagula.'

'When you go back on Monday, grab one. Don't let Todd see you. I want to know more. Do you agree this J. T. Wilson must be Jade?'

'It has to be. Lisa and I will shadow his *Calvados* tonight. If another torch appears to make contact, I think we have proof he is up to mischief.'

'No risks, Billy. They could swamp that tinny of yours with a bucket.'

'They won't catch us. I have borrowed my cousin's Quintrex with seventy horsepower on the back. The boat can do thirty-five knots provided it doesn't flip.' He handed me a sheet of paper. 'We leave from the sailing club at six, and hide among the moored yachts while Jade sails across the front of Airlie. By then it's dark. After that we stay behind him — how far back depends on what lights he's running. Can you drop Lisa to the sailing club at five-thirty?'

'Sure.'

'Hey, Tom, if you're not busy, join the party. Three people won't slow the boat, and an extra pair of eyes will come in useful.'

'I'll think about it.'

When three-thirty approached, I strolled through the office. All desks were vacant except those of Heather and Pixie. I thumbed through the pile of mail on Heather's desk.

'Anything exciting?'

'If you mean big cheques, no.' She nodded towards Pixie. 'Why don't you send her home. Everyone else has the afternoon off.'

Retracing my steps, I stopped at Pixie's desk. 'How is the Woodwark Bay story making out?'

'It's finished. I'm onto the sport now.'

'Why don't you go home'

'Does my presence bother you?'

'No, you've worked a huge week. Take a couple of hours off.'

'Thanks, Tom. I'd appreciate that.'

'So what is Pixie's idea of Friday night entertainment?'

'You asking for a date?'

'No. I'm curious.'

'Now that I'm eighteen, I sometimes go for a drink with friends. Maybe Magnums or the Beach Hotel. We might drive into the RSL in Proserpine and play the machines. A couple of girls have been on a sunset cruise. I'd enjoy that.

They say Airlie at night is very pretty. Anyway, I can guess what you do Friday nights.'

'Try me.'

'Take Lisa to Magnums.'

'Not even close. Nowadays she works on Friday night.'

'Sunset cruise?'

'Yes, they're flavour of the season. Mostly I stay home and listen to country music with a stray dog — if there's one about.'

'I'm sure you could find one.'

After wishing Heather and myself a breezy goodnight, she picked up her bag and left, which gave me no option but to evict Heather as well. Next, I closed the office and wandered upstairs to the balcony from where I could see the *Calvados* preparing for a sunset cruise. I checked the time and poured myself a mineral water. Soon Lisa would arrive, and I would drive her across to the sailing club to meet Billy for their night reconnaissance. He had asked me to join them but I wasn't keen on a wet night in a plunging boat. To be frank, however, I had limited choices. I could prop up Magnums' bar, I could spend the night with Mum and Patrick grieving Grandpa's death, or I could listen to country music with a stray dog. Discarding all three, I fished out a pair of black jeans and black shirt, and waited for Lisa, who strolled down the hill from her lodgings.

'Dressed for dinner, Tom?'

'You'd better hurry. Billy wants us at the boat ramp at five-thirty.'

'Us?'

'Yes. Another pair of eyes. His suggestion.'

Following a stop for hot chicken and chips, we drove the Moke into the sailing club carpark. Billy then helped carry our gear to the ramp where his cousin's boat was idling in the water.

'Glad you joined us, boss. Jump aboard.'

CHAPTER 36

The sun dipped towards the mountains, and the sea breeze shifted more easterly, where it chopped at the surface of an outgoing tide. After inching to a spot among the moored yachts, we anchored and waited for the *Calvados* to appear. The horizon had dissolved into molten red when she slipped out of the breakwater and rounded Abell Point. Several minutes later, the crew set a light sail, untroubled by the guests who assembled along her deck admiring Airlie at sundown. At a leisurely pace, Jade crossed the mouth of the bay, staying about a kilometre out to sea and parallel with the shore.

'This is where we learn if our night is wasted,' Billy said. 'At Mandalay he can either keep heading south, or turn and sail north.'

We motored further out of the inlet to watch.

'He's coming about,' Lisa said.

Sails flapped, the boom swung across, the jib tightened, and the *Calvados* pointed north.

Billy eased open the throttle. 'Okay, my hearties, let's follow that cab.'

For more than an hour we trailed the *Calvados*. The occasional cloud swept over the moon, masking our quarry. At one anxious point the sky cleared, and we found ourselves less than two hundred metres from her port quarter. From that distance we could hear music and the voices of guests. Billy idled back.

'Where are we?' I asked him.

'It's hard to know. We passed Bluff Point fifteen minutes ago, so I'm guessing the *Calvados* is about level with Woodwark Bay.'

At that instant we all saw it. Sharp and clear. Three flashes followed by another three. The shore was closer than we thought. Billy eased the boat seawards.

'That's a new code,' he said. 'The one I saw had two flashes. Any response from the *Calvados*?'

'Nothing,' I replied.

'Listen,' he whispered. 'I can hear a motor.'

We froze. There it was. Out to sea, an engine coming to life. The sound drew nearer.

'I didn't expect this,' Billy said. 'We're out of here. Hang on.'

He turned the boat one-eighty degrees and slammed the throttle forward. Seconds later we were up on a plane racing back to Airlie, white foam arching from the bows.

'Crikey, they have some power. They're closing the gap.'

'What did your cousin say about this boat? Thirty-five knots?'

'Give or take.'

After ten minutes of hard running, the spray of our pursuer was now visible. 'He'll catch us before Airlie. What's our choices, Billy?'

'Pretend we're fishermen?' Lisa offered.

'Not likely. We don't have a line between us.'

'Well, they're chasing us for a reason,' I said. 'And when they arrive, they won't ask about fishing spots. They'll tie chains to our ankles and chuck us overboard.'

'That's a bit macabre.'

'Do you want to chance it?'

'No.'

Billy pointed towards land. 'I have a plan. That inlet to starboard is protected by a shoal of rocks. I've been there before, in daylight I admit, but I remember it well. A double dog-leg … left, then right. The opening is when you line up the nearest island in Double Cone with Mount Marlow. Okay Tom, up the front with a pole in case we get stuck. Lisa, watch our backs.'

As we drew level with the first Double Cone, Billy gently reversed the throttle. Mount Marlow appeared black and distant above the Goorganga Plains.

'Right, take a bearing.'

'We're spot on,' I said.

'No, a bit further,' Lisa responded.

Billy split the difference and eased the boat forty-five degrees to his right. We were close to stationary, inching forward.

'Okay, we're in the channel,' he said. 'First dog-leg is one hundred metres to the left.'

I counted to one hundred then said, 'Turn now.'

Billy swung left. No crunch of metal on stone.

'Second dog-leg. Eighty metres to the right.'

Again, I counted to eighty. 'Now.'

Billy slid the boat to the right. Crash. He cut the throttle. I felt the water with my paddle. Solid rock.

'Bloody hell. Where's the gap?' I could see our hunter

approaching, It was big and fast. Men were standing on the deck.

'More to your left,' Billy said. 'I think we turned too soon. Find that hole, Tom.'

I thrust down the paddle. Rock. Again, I pushed it down. More rock. Again and again. Rock after rock. Suddenly nothing. The paddle went out of sight.

'We're there, Billy. Turn now.'

Billy manoeuvred through the opening, and shortly we were hunkered inside the mangroves. We cut the motor and lowered anchor. Silence.

We heard the engines of our pursuer drop a note, the boat slowed, voices. 'Where the hell have they gone?'

'Through the shoal. There must be an opening. What's the depth sounder read?'

'Solid mass to our right. Nothing behind us.'

'That's useful. Where's the gap?'

'Seems we're on it.'

'Sure you can read the thing?'

'Just do as I say.'

Crunch. 'Damn it.'

They made several attempts at finding the gap but each time the hull scraped on rocks. Finally, they gave up and retreated to open water. The roar of the powerful engines vanished northwards.

Billy watched them with his binoculars. 'We wait until the *Calvados* returns, which should be around eleven. That's high tide. We can escape from here and trail the yacht into Airlie. They'll anchor somewhere for the night while we mosey off home.'

'Sounds good to me, skipper,' I said.

For the next two hours we dozed fitfully until the lights and music of the *Calvados* appeared from the north. When it had passed, we sneaked into open water and followed her. The marina lights of Abell Point came into view, and soon we were among other craft that were out partying or fishing. Using the cover of numbers, Billy increased throttle and slowly overtook our quarry. One of the crew was at the wheel, several people sat around in groups, and the lights of Jade's stateroom glowed on the moving water. Through the open portholes, I could see two figures. A girl's cry drifted onto the night air. 'No. Please, no.'

The voice sounded uncannily like Pixie's.

CHAPTER 37

By one-thirty in the morning Lisa and I had our feet up, drinking whiskey neat from the bottle. We had helped Billy load his boat on the trailer, seen him off to his cousin's house, then returned to the flat.

'Who do you think they were?' I asked.

'Don't know, Tom.'

'No clues at all?'

'Only that our snooping wasn't appreciated. Three angry men in a powerful boat.'

'Not somebody watching Jade's arse?'

She shook her head. 'Jade's arrival at the scene was pure accident. Think about it, Tom. He wouldn't have risked a crowd on board if he was up to no-good.'

'The trip could have been a rehearsal. See how long it takes from A to B.'

She sat upright in her chair. 'Tom, will you make love to me?'

'That's been my intention all night.'

'I mean right now. Tomorrow will be so different.'

The tone of her voice alarmed me. 'What do you mean, Lisa?'

Taking my hand, she led me inside the flat where the only light was from a street lamp. While still fully clothed, we caressed and kissed like in a 1950s movie. I lifted her onto the bed. She was the lonely, hungry woman I had first met: Lisa of the awesome body and forehead scar, Lisa who had been a companion through my darkest hours. We made love — a wonderful, powerful, emotional experience in which the outside world faded to a dot in the night.

Afterwards we lay awake.

'Would you like a cup of tea, Tom?'

'Not really.'

'I'm sorry, but I have to get up.'

In the darkness, she climbed out of bed and pulled on a gown. Then the kitchen flooded with light and a tap ran as she filled the kettle. Soon she returned to the bedroom holding a steaming mug.

'Lisa, you said tomorrow will be different. What's up?'

'I have a confession, but first you must promise to tell nobody.'

'I promise.'

'I'm serious. Say it properly.'

'I swear to you, Lisa, that my lips are sealed. Okay, out with it.'

'Tom, I'm a member of the Australian Federal Police. I'm in the Whitsundays under cover. Sorry I didn't confide sooner, but I couldn't. We've suspected for years that drugs were coming into the country through Airlie. Initially the *Calvados* was one of our suspects, which explains why I got to crew her from Sydney. Although we have since ruled her out — yes, that's why I was inspecting Jade's charts — we had few other leads until I saw the torch flashes to the south. Tonight's appearance of the power boat has confirmed our suspicions that the Whitsundays is a contraband gateway.'

She paused and studied me. 'I'm truly sorry, Tom.'

'Do you have an identity card?'

Taking up her small bag, she unpicked the lining and drew out a laminated card that had her photo and the AFP insignia. I examined it. Lisa Dawson. Funny really, but her surname had never entered the conversation.

'How much of the past few months was real?'

'Everything except my identity. I struggled not to become attached because one day I would be exposed and have to return to my office in Sydney. If you want to kick me out, I'll understand.'

I climbed out of bed. My alter-ego didn't know what was happening. Although still high from the past few hours, it was wounded by the deception. Pouring myself a mug of tea, I returned to the bedroom where Lisa waited.

'I'm not upset, Lisa. Well, not unbearably. We always assumed you were returning to Sydney with Jade and the *Calvados*. I can't pretend I wouldn't miss you, but the end has arrived sooner than expected. You're a cop and you're here to catch drug runners. I'm pleased to have made your cover look authentic.'

She wiped her eyes. 'I'll never do this again. Ever. Right from the beginning I should've talked Billy out of his little escapades. We could've been killed.'

After a time, she recovered, and we sat at the kitchen table.

'So, Lisa, what's next?'

She sniffled. 'I guess no more cosy dinners.'

'No. I meant … you're a cop and I'm a journalist. I want

to break into Jade's shed. See what he's hiding. Best to do it in daylight when nobody's around. My theory is the boat that chased us had picked up a consignment offshore, and dropped it at the shed. Now the light could've been a tip-off about us, but I reckon its main purpose was to inform Jade the task was complete. When he leaves in October, the stuff will be packed into the *Calvados* hull.'

'Tom, you need to put a lid on your imagination. This obsession with Jade is growing tedious.'

'I just don't believe in coincidences. Same place, same lights. Let's ask Billy.'

'No, you promised. And another thing. No local cops.'

'If all hell breaks loose, we'll need them.'

'No, not yet. Local police have a habit of warning the baddies, even if they don't intend to. Liaison is done at superintendent level.'

'Sergeant Phil is rock solid. He was kicking my arse before I was nine.'

'No, please. Just us and the AFP.'

'Billy has to know.'

'Please, Tom, I've sworn you to secrecy. And no more cloak and dagger stuff. Leave the boats and shed to the federal police.'

'A quick squiz won't hurt. We'll drive there first thing tomorrow.' I studied my watch. 'Today, actually. Join me for the ride and help pick the lock.'

Although she was less than excited, we finished drinking our tea and returned to bed like a married couple whose thoughts have moved on from sex. I don't know if we had ever imagined settling down together. She had always deflected talk about herself, and I don't think she wanted to live this far from Sydney. But a cop? Apart from the scar, Lisa was an attractive young lady. Maybe that's how she received the head wound. Nothing to do with a boyfriend on her first date. I didn't expect I would discover the truth and, with a tinge of sadness, I removed truth's chair from the table.

Minutes after sunrise on Saturday morning, I roused Lisa and led the way downstairs to the car. We called at a hardware store where I bought small metal picks which, I explained to her, I had seen cops use in a hundred movies. With half a day to ourselves, I was certain we could crack at least one of the locks. If not, I would return with a young offender who had learnt his trade at prison school. In the centre of the bay the *Calvados* sat at anchor and people could be seen moving about on deck. Knowing Jade's routine, he would have his guests ashore first thing after coffee and rolls. We motored over the hill, then around the inlets to the gravel track leading into Woodwark Bay. I pulled over and studied the track.

'Somebody has driven here in the past few hours,' I said. 'You can see where their tyres lifted the damp gravel.'

'Have they gone in or out?'

'Out. The car is a four by four. Big one. And look, different tyres on the front and back. Should be easy to find.'

'I didn't know you were a Black tracker.'

'We both have our surprises.'

At the entrance to Woodwark Bay, I braked suddenly to avoid crashing into a steel gate. It was padlocked with a freshly painted sign that read, *Private Property - Trespassers Prosecuted.* Since the gate had not been there the previous morning, one had to ask why the haste? We skirted the barrier on foot then continued to the edge of the clearing. After ten minutes in which there was no sign of movement, we strolled down to the shed where Lisa took the pouch and set to work on the padlocks. 'AFP electives are not all dull and boring,' she said. Talk about surprises. This woman was full of them.

Patiently, she sprang the first lock then the second.

'Right, Tom. The door's open. Remember, whatever we touch must go back precisely as it was.'

The shed was around six metres square, bolted to a slab of concrete. At the back were several empty pallets and a variety of tools one might use for repairing boats. The left wall was vacant, but against the right wall was a single pallet loaded with boxes the size of a wine carton. Every box was plastic wrapped, bound with a steel strap and carried the label, *machine bearings - does not grease.* Short of cutting the straps, it was impossible to verify the contents.

'There may be other clues,' I said. 'Check the walls, behind the tools, everywhere.'

We spent twenty minutes in that shed. Not a thing. Not even a dead cockroach. Finally, we retraced our steps to the door, brushed the concrete with my hat, and reset the padlocks. After returning to the car, we drove to a secluded coffee shop in Cannonvale.

'Any ideas?' I asked.

'Sorry, Tom, I have to be honest with you. On today's evidence I could not recommend an AFP raid. The shed appears to be private storage. Believe me, it's not uncommon to find a room full of boxes sealed against corrosion — especially machine parts.'

'Don't you think the labels are a bit contrived? *does not grease*. Somebody is taking the piss. Surely we can't eliminate drugs?'

'Drugs held in an exposed shed like that? Maybe the locked gate will frighten off nosey parkers, but not someone intent on mischief. The risks are too great. AFP investigations say we are chasing the wrong fox. Remember Vogel's yacht? Where was it at the time of the torch flashes?'

'Lisa, we can only follow one trail at a time. If this one runs cold, we'll go after Vogel. So, let's pretend Jade is our man, and he's planning a night trip to load the cargo. That'd be the next new moon, right?'

She grimaced. 'You and your grandpa have a lot in common — bloody stubborn. Yes, one would load contraband when the light is poor.'

'Are you likely to be on board?'

'I am his crew, remember.'

'So what now?'

'Wearing my AFP cap, I strongly urge you and Billy to back off. Please Tom, leave it to the professionals. One clumsy move on your part and years of surveillance will go up in smoke. Despite my reservations, I'll ask for more AFP personnel to join the ones already on site. With the extra resources, they can watch the shed and put tabs on suspicious activity. Bear in mind they're unlikely to pounce here. Far better to track the boat to Sydney, and arrest the whole syndicate.'

'Where do these drugs come from?'

'Asia. Thailand most likely. We know they come in by ship then are dispatched offshore at night. Boats like the one that chased us would deliver them to a prearranged location, where they are loaded straight into a van. Shute Harbour fits their crime perfectly, and is being monitored even as we speak.'

CHAPTER 38

By the time we finished coffee, the *Calvados* was in its berth at Abell Point, and I was hungry for a good meal. After dropping Lisa at her house, I drove across to the farm where I hoped breakfast might be still on the table. As I swung into the carport, I heard the familiar roar of a tractor in harness. Mum shouted above the noise and gestured to where Patrick was bulldozing the last of Grandpa's house. Once done, he poured fuel over the debris, and set it alight.

'Thank God for that,' Mum said.

'Three O'Connor men were born in that house,' I said. 'I feel we should toast its destruction.'

'I beat you to it. The whiskey is down the sink. I assume you've come early for lunch.'

'Breakfast if there's any left. And here, I've baked an apple pie.' I lifted a packet from the seat of the car. 'Where's Glenda?'

'Spending the day with her granny. Tom, you'd better talk to your brother. He's forgotten about the wedding.'

'Mum, wait until after the funeral. He's still in shock.'

'We all are, but life can't stop for the dead.'

When Patrick came up to the house, we stood on the verandah drinking coffee while the second fire consumed what the firemen had saved.

'Next week I'll dig a hole and bury the lot,' he said. 'Poor old Grandpa. I suppose we should never love anything to excess. Have you made headway since I last saw you?'

'I have actually. Tagula Enterprises. Firm of developers from Sydney. They're behind this trouble with Lenny Watkins. And I'll tell you whose name is mixed up with the firm.'

'I can guess,' he said grimly. 'Todd Steele.'

'Right.'

'He thinks he's so bloody clever.'

'One other name is Jade Wilson who owns a yacht at the marina.'

'Do you know him?'

'Yes, he's the bloke Lisa sails for. All tan and white teeth. We have a suspicion he may be into drugs.'

'Anyone else?'

'One minute. I have the folder with me.'

I took a shoe box from the car, and dug through to the bottom page. 'Let's see now. The second director is S. M. Carney, also from Sydney. The name rings a bell. I'll ask Marvin to chase up the company register.'

Patrick squinted at me. 'Carney was one of the lawyers who helped Lenny Watkins. I've still got the files.' He dived into the small room that served as an office, and returned with the Giya dossier. 'Here it is. Seamus Martin Carney. He signed on behalf of the firm, Mason Edelstein and Birch.'

'Of course,' I said. 'The same Seamus Carney whose card was in Jade's wallet. There has to be a law against this. Once Carney has completed the legalities for a sacred site, the

Tagula mob bribes Lenny out of Woodwark Bay, locks the gate behind him, and submits a development application.'

'It's useless complaining to the police, Tom. We'll have to sort it ourselves.'

'Don't worry, we are,' I said, ending the conversation.

After the three of us sat down to an early lunch, I happened to reach across for a dish when I caught Mum's eye. She had been staring into space and her eyes were moist, which was unusual. Mum was a strong, no-nonsense woman who had buried her grief in Dad's coffin years earlier. Recent events, however, had cracked the lid open. I rose from my chair and embraced her. Patrick came from the other side and took Mum's hands in his. We remained in that tableau long after the food had gone cold.

*   *   *

Sunday morning early, I picked up Lisa and drove her to the marina where she reported for work. She apologised that as the *Calvados* was on a two-night cruise to Whitehaven, she wouldn't be back in time for Grandpa's funeral.

'Tom, I'm sad about that. I'd like to be there for your family. These past few months have been special.'

'I'll miss you too,' I said.

Grabbing her duffel bag, she hurried down the ramp to where the *Calvados* lay at berth. At the rail where she turned and waved, I conceded that she did indeed have the qualities of an undercover agent: lithe, attractive, smart …

and deceitful. Once she had gone, I drove back to the flat, stifling the temptation to buy coffee and the Sunday papers. Instead, I returned to my desk and started on the creditors that Heather seemed to breed in that little office of hers. Around two in the afternoon, I was about to toss down my pen when I heard a bicycle outside. No guesses to my visitor's identity. After a big stretch and yawn, I unlocked the door to reveal Pixie leaning her bike against the wall. Her face was crumpled as if she had spent the morning in tears.

I softened. 'You okay, Pixie?'

'Yes. May I come in?

She walked through and sat at her desk.

'Don't sit there, Pixie. This is Sunday. Come upstairs.'

'No, it wouldn't seem right with Lisa away.'

'How did you know?'

'Jade said.'

'Well, I'm hungry. Let's buy fish and chips and eat in the park. You can tell me about it.'

Soon afterwards, we sat at a picnic table and toyed with the wrapping of a meal that lay between us. Pixie left her food untouched, and sipped half-heartedly on a vanilla milkshake.

'What's happened?' I asked.

Suddenly she was crying. Not just tears running down her face, but full heaving sobs she made no attempt to hide. From the bench opposite I handed over my serviette and waited until the sobbing eased.

'Let me guess. It was Jade?'

She blew her nose. 'Last Friday night I took a sunset cruise on his yacht. Don't stare at me like that. I thought

Lisa was on board and it was a lovely night, and, yes, you weren't interested in being pleasant. So, I booked a night on the *Calvados*. About ten of us plus the crew. And it was a beautiful night. We talked, we had a few drinks, and I avoided a boy who fancied his chances. All evening Jade was the perfect gentleman. Around eleven I went to sleep in one of the bunks downstairs. I slept for an hour or so, I don't remember, but around midnight Jade woke me with a coffee, saying I wouldn't want to miss a cruise ship out to sea. He sat with me talking for a couple of minutes, then when he stood up to take coffee to the girl on watch, he tripped and spilt drink over my jeans. It wasn't hot but I was a mess. He told me to use the shower in his cabin and he'd borrow clothes from one of his crew. Tom, this is horrid, and I guess I've been an idiot. I locked the cabin from inside then went into the shower. Suddenly, I was so drowsy I couldn't keep my eyes open. I stepped out of the shower, not even a towel around me, and Jade was sitting on the bed with a smirk on his face. Then I realised he had put something in my coffee. He had deliberately got me naked into his cabin. I fought him, and he was on top of me, calling me awful names, and trying to, you know, have sex. When I screamed, people banged on the door from outside. He guessed it was all over because he let them in, then stormed onto the deck. I saw him at the wheel as we came ashore, but we didn't make eye contact.'

When Pixie finished her story, she sat facing away from me, gazing across the bay that I had once remarked was always beautiful.

'Have you told your parents?'

'Yes, but not everything.'

'Maybe you should. I can drive you over now.'

'Tom, do you think I deserve what happened? Been the foolish little girl? The whore?' she added bitterly.

'Not with Jade. He has an appalling reputation.'

'Go ahead, say it. You warned me. Yes, I was friendly with him, but I am with everyone. And no, I didn't encourage him, not by so much as a glance.'

'Do you want to lay charges?'

'What good would that serve?'

'It might help other women.'

'Humiliate myself in court on the chance it might save others? No thanks.'

'Pixie, he tried to rape you.'

'I don't care if it was attempted murder.'

I pushed the food to one side and held her hand. 'I'm really sorry, Pixie. You told me about wanting to do a sunset cruise. If I had been more sensitive, never mind that crap about Red Riding Hood, we could have prevented this.'

Her face was down, concealed behind a curtain of hair. 'No, Tom. I was taking that boat on Friday, right or wrong.'

After a while I removed my hand that, somehow, she had taken in both of hers.

'So, what now?' I asked.

'I'm older and wiser, if nothing else,' she murmured, lifting her face. 'And I've learnt new things.'

'Like what?'

She smiled ruefully. 'What the head is on a boat. It's the bathroom. I thought it was a poor attempt at a joke.' Then, straightening her shoulders, she added, 'I'll tell you one thing, Tom. Jade has to be taught a lesson. He's a menace.'

'That's my girl. And maybe it will come sooner than he thinks.'

She rose from the bench. 'Thanks for listening. I'm okay to go home now. See you on Monday.'

After a brief hug, she walked through the park to her bicycle and rode home.

CHAPTER 39

Monday morning was uneventful except that I phoned Marvin Fumbleton and asked him to do a search on Tagula Enterprises. Within the hour he rang back. Two directors, as we already knew, were Jade Wilson and Seamus Carney, but he discovered a third shareholder whose name was listed as the Deboyne Trust.

'Marvin, who is Deboyne?'

'Family name, I guess.'

'You are on the ball today. Leaving kinship aside, isn't it also an island in the Pacific? Made the news last year. Tidal wave or something.'

'Sorry, Tom. Never heard of it. Many of these islands were named after seventeenth-century pirates.'

Somehow I couldn't envisage our Sydney gang as pirates of the high seas; rogues maybe, but not pirates. Still, the word Deboyne intrigued me. I looked up the encyclopaedia and found Deboyne was an island in the Louisiade Archipelago. Checking an atlas, I discovered the archipelago was a group of atolls and islands between New Guinea and the Solomons. Abruptly, the name of the largest island, Tagula, leapt off the page.

I went to my office door and summoned Billy.

'I think I'm onto something. Two names keep popping up

together: Tagula and Calvados, and now a third, Deboyne. And they all happen to be islands in the Louisiade Archipelago. Do you see the link? Calvados is Jade's boat, Tagula is their company name, and Deboyne is one of the shareholders.'

'Good work, Tom. I'll tell you something else. Todd's house at Mandalay is called Deboyne Place.'

'At last the pieces are fitting together. This is clear proof that Todd, Jade Wilson and Seamus Carney are behind the development of Woodwark Bay. They are equally responsible for Grandpa's death.'

'And what about the drugs? Do you think they're a sideline of Jade's?'

'The jury is out on that. Last Saturday morning Lisa and I broke into Jade's shed where, among other things, we found sealed boxes. They were labelled as machine parts. Lisa thinks the labels are genuine.'

'And you, Tom?'

'I know it's a big call, but drugs have to be considered. Why a padlocked gate and shed? Why signals off the jetty?'

'I'm of the same mind. Then how do we prepare for their next move? Too dicey sitting out there in my tinny every night.'

'You're right. It has to be a crescent moon. Maybe the next one. Problem is, a couple of nights either side of the crescent is just as dark. So, let's start some action in the newspaper. I'll do a lead story that fishermen saws lights at sea and reported them to authorities, then I'll do a second story naming the entities behind the Woodwark Bay development.'

In the afternoon, Patrick rang with more details on the

funeral. After a requiem mass at St Catherine's, he and I would accompany the casket with Mum and Glenda while cousins on Mum's side would serve as pall bearers. Once at the graveside, Father Desmond promised to keep the ceremony short, then following the committal, mourners would be invited to a wake at the farmhouse.

'Is there anything I've forgotten, Tom?'

'No, but I have firm evidence that Todd's gang is behind Grandpa's death.'

'How firm? Enough to get out the whip?'

'Not yet. I'll explain tomorrow.'

The funeral was one of those ghastly events that humans put themselves through for the solace of the living and recent dead. Indeed, we had said our prayers for Grandpa who had danced in the flames while still on earth. Father Desmond's eulogy was brief, though powerful, touching on the life of an O'Connor who had been one of the great men of the Proserpine district, a man who had been a Christian in deed if not in word. As a family, we sat in the front pew, listening to the rustling and murmuring behind us. Was Grandpa's end cowardly or brave? We should have a bronze plaque screwed to the lid of his box: *I Died As I Lived*. My suit was tight across the waist, and my tie was a knotted relic from an era when sobriety was measured by the weight of one's clothes. As we stood for the Lord's Prayer, I felt a touch on my shoulder. Reaching up, I made contact with a young woman's fingers. After the service the mourners processed slowly to the front of the church where the family shook endless hands. Todd Steele was one of the last.

'My condolences to you and your family, Tom.'

'Thanks, Todd. Anything else?'

'Like what?'

'Revenge is sweet.'

'Sorry, Tom. I don't follow.'

'It took four generations, but it's done. The O'Connors, the Steeles, The Leap.'

'You've gone troppo.'

'That's possible. Too much sunshine and rum. But try these names for size: Calvados, Tagula, Deboyne.'

He was startled. 'Don't be a fool, Tom.'

Our right hands remained in the condolence grasp as we talked. 'What's the connection, Todd? Drugs?' His face had gone white. 'I'll test my theory with a story in Friday's paper.'

'Don't, Tom. Damn it. What do you want from me?'

'Tell me what you know about Seamus Carney and Jade Wilson. We know the code is Louisiade.'

I felt a tug on the sleeve. Others wanted to shake my hand. Todd let go. 'We have to talk. My office after the wake.'

'No, the mouth of Palm Creek at two o'clock. And don't drive up to the farm, somebody might shoot you.'

They had closed the back door of the hearse and were waiting. Pixie emerged from the crowd and came towards me. She wore a black-and-white dress, black shoes and black hat; an outfit that would have done justice to a state funeral. Taking my arm, she escorted me to the undertaker's lead car where Mum, Patrick and Glenda were inside enduring the heat.

'Thanks, Pixie,' I said, and climbed into the front seat, pulling the door shut.

'That girl's in love,' Mum said.

'Tom is the only one blind to it,' Patrick added. 'Where's Lisa?'

'Minding her business.'

Patrick wasn't giving up, funeral or no funeral. 'Which of the two is your favourite, Tom?'

'Well, they both show promise on a wet track. Lisa has the experience but Pixie has the pedigree. Lisa's carrying extra lead in her saddle whereas Pixie hasn't been tried at the distance.'

Mum reached across and clouted me with her handbag. 'Show respect, the pair of you.'

'Was that Pixie in the black-and-white?' the driver asked.

'Yes, mate. What's your opinion?'

He shrugged. 'Never been to a race meeting.'

The ceremony at the graveyard went as reasonably as could be expected. A small wind had risen, blowing cane trash in from a neighbouring field. White, bustling clouds screened the sun from the clay that broke from the edges of the hole, thudding remorselessly on the lid of Grandpa's coffin. The earth was impatient to bury the man who would have no equal in my life. Glenda showed why she will make a great daughter-in-law, guiding Mum to the basket of rose petals, which we fluttered into the hole. Despite the lovely symbolism, Grandpa wasn't rose petals. He was rough language, raw sugar cane and weathered hands. At the end of the service, Father Desmond advised mourners of the wake at the farm house, acknowledged the undertakers and family, and hurried off to a meeting at St Catherine's school.

Formalities over, Glenda ferried Mum and her sisters home in one car, while Patrick and I followed in mine.

'Tom, what's the evidence on Todd Steele?'

I told him about the Louisiade Archipelago and the three islands that found their way into the business. 'The *Calvados* worked those islands before Jade bought her, when she was still called the *Torres Mail*. The name would have sentimental value.'

'I'd say they go to the islands every year and screw the natives. And if they're into trafficking, there will be a drop-off point.'

'You could be right. Ships sailing from Asia would be clean before entering Australian waters. Okay, this is my plan. Todd is meeting me at the mouth of Palm Creek at two. If he doesn't spill the beans on his mates, I'll splash his name all over the *Post*.'

'Look, Tom, I'm sorry, but this is where I back out. Not great timing, but I've promised Glenda. All my focus is to be on the wedding.'

I glanced at him. This was not the Patrick of old.

'God's honour,' he said.

At the house, we dragged out cooler boxes of beer, soft drink and white wine. Tables and chairs were scattered about the verandah and teapots filled with boiling water. Cars pulled into the driveway; the men in suits, the women in stockings and hats, unsure if they were still in mourning or at the wake.

'Come on in,' Patrick shouted from the kitchen window. 'Plenty of food and grog.'

As the crowd built, the coats came off, beer and wine

unlocked awkward throats, and the verandah echoed with bush yarns and unaffected country laughter. While Glenda and Pixie ferried trays of sandwiches from the kitchen to all parts of the house, Patrick and Terry kept up the supply of ice and drinks.

At five minutes to two I drove to the mouth of Palm Creek where Todd stood beside his Mercedes. In my mind he had always seemed like a wrinkled old turkey, marked by the starched collars on his thin, pale neck. Even at a distance I could see the tremor in his hands.

'Okay, Todd, what do you know?'

'You got a tape running?'

'Not today.'

'I'm clean of this drugs business. It's all Jade and Seamus. They've been doing it for years. I just want the bloody land for development.'

'How do you know they've been at it for years?'

'At the end of the season, drugs are stockpiled in Jade's shed. Two weeks at the most. Lenny Watkins was given a retainer to watch over it, and keep his mouth shut. But he was becoming unreliable. Too much women and silly games. So, we decided to clear out all inhabitants, apply for development, then lock up the place for three years. Just keep Jade's shed and the jetty.'

'So how did you move Lenny out of there?'

'While planning for the heritage centre, we discovered he was part Juipera and that he was a descendant of the baby who survived at The Leap. Wasn't hard to fill his head with the O'Connors and the injury they caused. We bought him a Land Cruiser to facilitate his work as an elder, then paid him another five thousand dollars to camp on the O'Connor river land. Next, Seamus drew up quasi-legal documents that showed Lenny was an Aboriginal caretaker and entitled to live on or near the sacred site. It didn't take Lenny long to understand he could move into your pop's old house. The day he vacated Woodwark Bay we sent in a bulldozer and removed every trace of him. We did the same to the squatters' huts after buying out the occupants for a fortune.'

As Todd spoke, he doodled with his shoe in the dust. Crooked arrows and coiling snakes; meaningless patterns except to a psychiatrist. Or an O'Connor.

'Tom, I never meant to harm your grandfather. Honestly, how was I to know Lenny would trash the house?'

'Bullshit, Todd. You didn't care what Lenny did. It was you who killed Grandpa, not Lenny.'

'Don't say that. Come on. Be reasonable.'

'Okay. You're off the hook if you tell me when the drug transfer is due.'

'I don't know. The drugs are Jade and Seamus's business.'

I stepped into my car. 'You had your chance, Todd, and you blew it. When the police call, tell them you're innocent.'

He ran to the driver's side and grabbed the steering wheel. 'Please, Tom, I know nothing about the drugs.'

I started the engine. 'Go screw yourself.'

He covered his face with his hands. 'All right, I do know, but they'll kill me. The next new moon, plus one night. Don't tell anyone, please.'

I let out the clutch. Tough luck, mate. The AFP have to be in on this.

By the time I returned to the house, the wake had almost died. A handful of steady drinkers guarded the only cooler box that held beer. Terry, Billy and Patrick were at the centre of the group.

Patrick came across to the car. 'How did you make out, Thomas?'

'We've nailed our man.' I threw off my jacket and tie. 'And I've got a thirst.'

Between trips to the bushes behind the shed I told Patrick the latest revelation from Todd.

'That prick's not finished yet,' he slurred. 'He'll rue the day he crossed an O'Connor.'

'I thought you were done with revenge.'

'I'm givin' moral support, bro'.'

By dark only four of us remained on the verandah while the women moved about inside cataloguing items in the wedding pavilion. A half moon glided through the heavens, airbrushing clouds that blew in with the north-easterly. The pile of ash from Pop's house was a grey-black mound that stood as a plinth to Grandpa's last stand.

Mum strode onto the verandah. 'Right, boys, the wake is over. Tom can stay here tonight. Glenda will drive the others home.'

As we gathered ourselves, Pixie came to the doorway. 'Goodnight, Tom. Goodnight, Patrick.'

'Night, Pixie.'

When the car lights had faded, Patrick opened two beers and lowered himself to the step beside me. 'She's top shelf, that one, Thomas.'

'So is your Glenda. You chose well there, brother.'

'Too right,' he burped. 'Ace women, both of them.'

CHAPTER 40

True to my word, I wrote a story on drugs in the area, and I had Pixie write a second story on Council approval to develop Woodwark Bay. I also made sure she included the three names: Todd Steele, Jade Wilson and Seamus Carney, and their link to Tagula Enterprises. In my drugs story I made no reference to the trio but said police had their concerns.

A SENIOR police officer told the *Post* this week that shipments of drugs were believed to be entering Australia through the Whitsunday Passage.

'We understand the drugs originate in Asia and are being smuggled under the cover of a tourist enterprise,' the officer said.

'Fishermen have reported unusual activity during the hours of darkness. We fear this activity could be a drug cartel at work.

'Our belief is that the off-loaded drugs are taken by road or sea to Sydney where they are sold on the street.

'We ask residents to report suspicious behaviour to their local police as a matter of urgency.'

When the *Calvados* returned to harbour late Thursday afternoon, I left my desk and watched Lisa follow the pathway to the flat. She had that easy stride, which is athletic and graceful, and her face was happy. Like a cheetah in love. I met her under the mango tree where she dropped her bag and threw her arms around me. Minutes later, at the top of the stairs, she discarded her uniform.

'What do you think, Thomas?'

At first glance Lisa was naked apart from white lingerie. However, upon closer inspection the lace revealed itself as carefully applied body paint. Astonishingly, some dude had painted two sheer, white garments on naked Lisa.

'Can I touch you?'

'Not yet. You might spoil it and this is my underwear for dinner. Now pour me a wine. Look, there are even clips on the bra strap.'

Giancarlo found a space at his bar where we had pre-dinner drinks, then later moved us to a private table. He was in an expansive mood, lighting the candles with grand gestures, pouring the wine with a flourish, selecting music full of mandolins and Italian bravura.

'Don't be in no hurry,' he said. 'Kitchen open 'til late.'

'Giancarlo, I'll have the red emperor,' I said, reading from the menu, 'herb marinated and garnished with julienned lemon peel. Served on a bed of fresh garden salad.'

Lisa hadn't taken her eyes off me. 'I'll have the same.'

Tenderness enveloped us like the first night at La Cucina; the warmth, the magical indifference to time.

'Who painted you?' I asked.

'One of the young men on the boat. He works in television

and paints the faces of clowns and pantomime actors. He had his paints with him and was returning from a workshop on Long Island. I was in a daring mood, and he obliged. In the sail locker.'

'I wouldn't know how to do that sort of thing. Paint a nude woman.'

'I've got his number.'

While waiting for the courses to arrive, our fingers explored the zones that wept with anticipation, smudging the lace, igniting nerve ends. We told harmless anecdotes and made love with our eyes. That night, after the cab had driven us home, we fell into bed, knowing we were mortal and that the end was perilously close.

*   *   *

Friday morning's paper lay on front lawns, headline screaming: *Whitsundays To Fight Drug Traffickers*. We didn't have much of a story to go with the headline, but we expected it to startle our crooked mates. Lisa saw things differently.

'I wish you hadn't done that, Tom. It might blow the operation.'

'If the trafficker is Jade, he's too committed. A shipment is already enroute.'

'How do you know?'

'Todd Steele in a rare moment of cooperation.' I told Lisa about the three men and their connection with the islands in Louisiade Archipelago. I also told her about my meeting with Todd after the funeral.

'We agreed to leave this to the AFP. Todd could be lying.'

'He was too frightened to lie. Besides, I promised not to use his name in the story.'

'They'll guess where the information came from. His life will be in danger.'

I shrugged. 'He should've thought of that earlier.'

As anticipated, the office phone ran hot. Todd was furious.

'You're an arsehole, O'Connor. You gave your word.'

'Is your name mentioned?'

'It might as well. And what about that crap on Woodwark Bay? Todd Steele is splashed all over it.'

'Do you think I care? My grandpa is dead, his home is burnt to the ground and our farm is a dubious sacred site. Cry on Jade's shoulder.'

When he slammed the phone in my ear, it rang again immediately. Chief Inspector Seb Gudinski was on the line.

'Who is this senior officer, Tom?'

'Nobody in particular. A generic title.'

'Why doesn't that surprise me? I've had a call from Brisbane. Yes, you heard, freakin' Brisbane. The chief super wanted to know what's going on. Am I playing a lone hand up here? I didn't know what the bloke was on about. Where did this story come from?'

'We're playing a hunch, Seb.'

'A hunch? This is not a horse race. It's the real thing. Big money and big players. Dangerous bastards. According to the boss, Drug Squad have been watching this place for months. They're worried the traffickers might vamoose.'

'I don't think so.'

'What do you know that we don't?'

'Like I said, Seb, it's a hunch. If they bolt from cover, be ready.'

'No wonder I've got a freakin' ulcer.'

Throughout the day we fielded a dozen curious callers. Chamber of Commerce president, Steve Redmond, was near the front of the queue.

'Tom, this kind of story will be the death of us.'

'Death of who, Steve? I don't see any tourists dying, but I see plenty of kids who might live to old age.'

'Do you have hard evidence?'

'The cops are on to it. They expect to flush out the cartel in the next few weeks. Then Airlie becomes the carefree little town it used to be.'

'Meantime we all sweat. Is that the plan?'

Around mid-afternoon, Lisa left the flat to prepare the *Calvados* for an overnight cruise. Even though she was vague about Jade's intended course, I promised faithfully that Billy and I would make no attempt to follow.

'If Todd is correct with his dates, this will be Jade's last rehearsal,' I said.

'Tonight's cruise is no rehearsal, Tom. It's a regular sail with twelve people on board.'

'Maybe so, Lisa, but watch yourself.'

'You and Billy are the ones I'm worried about. You're seriously out of your depth. Stick to newspapers, Tom, please.'

CHAPTER 41

As the afternoon wore on, I kept myself busy while waiting for Billy. Since the funeral we'd had little opportunity to review progress on the paper, or the development with Tagula Enterprises. I also needed to be sure he wouldn't attempt to follow Jade. When four-thirty came, only Heather, Pixie and myself remained in the office.

I walked through to the front counter. 'Heather, have you heard from Billy?'

'He's finished for the day.'

'Finished? He's been gone since lunch.'

'He works long hours, Tom. Don't be unreasonable. I told him to make himself scarce.'

'Thanks a lot.'

'You need to unwind as well. Here's an idea. Take Pixie out for a drink.'

'No.'

'Any reason why?'

'I don't need one. You're not my mother.'

'I'm guessing the reason is Lisa. To make it look proper I'll tag along as a threesome. One round of drinks at Captain Morgan's.'

'Heather …' I began.

'Just fetch your car keys, and throw Pixie's bike in the back. We'll see you there.'

With that, Heather told Pixie to grab her bag, and the pair sailed out the door leaving me to lock up.

Parking spaces near the marina were at a premium with the boats coming in from the islands. Youngsters with backpacks stood in groups waiting for buses while older tourists dawdled near the shops, catching their sunburnt reflections in the glass. Under the stern of a chubby trailer-sailer, I parked beside Heather's sedan, adjusted my Panama, and strolled up to Captain Morgan's which was overflowing with office workers and marine types. Heather and Pixie occupied a table near the back.

'I'll have a schooner of bitter,' I said.

'Drink what you like, Tom. The shout is yours. I'll have a lemon soda, and Pixie a vodka and orange.'

I forced a passage to the bar, avoiding Maggie Morgan, who had opened a fresh complaint since my last visit. Didn't the woman ever yearn for peace? Her husband Dan had to be a saint — or deaf. After ordering three drinks, I returned to the table where we talked about the benefit of computers over linotype, and scanners over process cameras. Safe topics, both of them. When Heather said it was time to depart because she had a mother to cook for, I stood as well.

'No, Tom. Pixie hasn't finished her drink. I'll see you Monday.'

Directly she left, Pixie reached for her handbag. 'It's all right, Tom. I don't want this vodka. The ice has melted. Let's go.'

'Sorry, Pixie. I'm in no rush,' I said, feeling a heel. 'I

planned to try the new tapas bar in Airlie Village. You interested?'

She was hesitant. 'I'm not sure. I mean, I'd like to, but don't think you're obliged to ask. I offered to help Dad with his new garden.'

'No, let's do it. Ring your parents from the office. We'll leave the car there and walk. Afterwards, you can catch a cab home.'

We drove back to the *Post*, parked under the lean-to and sauntered into town along the trail that followed the water's edge. In the east, a mass of cumulous filled the horizon from Hayman Island to Daydream, while in the west a still-warm sun bounced off the glass-fronted units. Since Pixie had gone back to stitching embroidery on her clothes, she now wore a dress that featured the corella. She had swapped court shoes for sandals, and pinned her hair above the nape. As we strolled along, men admired her openly, but she was oblivious to their attention, pointing out little things — a fish skipping, a gull with paint on its wing — and gave the impression she'd rather be nowhere else in the world.

When we entered the main street, she said, 'Tom, what's a tapas bar? Sorry, how silly of me. A bar that serves tapas.'

'Tapas are light Spanish dishes that bars serve with drinks,' I said, quoting from an advertorial I had written. 'They're the exotic alternative to wine bars. Modern youth prefer them to the pub.'

'Modern youth? Is that us?'

'I trust your question is rhetorical.'

Inside, I pushed through to the front where I ordered a platter of tapas and two spirit mixes. Drinks and food in hand, we found our way to a small outside deck where the atmosphere was less stuffy. Pixie located two seats in a corner and urged me to sit. For a time we were silent, watching the crowd, and I found the privacy surprisingly relaxed.

She nodded at my glass. 'Another drink?'

When I made to stand, she pressed my arm. 'It's my buy.'

After returning with the drinks, she said they had cleared tables from the centre of the room and people were dancing. Did I dance?

'Depends on how much I've drunk.'

'I like to dance,' she said. 'Years ago, when Mum and Dad went to socials, they took me along. I couldn't keep still.'

'Patrick gets married in a few months,' I replied. 'I'll dance then.'

'You will need to practise.'

I shook my head. 'All eyes will be on my brother.'

When the music changed beat, she set down her glass and jumped to her feet. 'Come, one dance, then we'll find somewhere proper to eat.'

I threw back my drink and followed Pixie onto the floor. Elbowing out a metre of space, I impersonated an eighties rocker until Pixie seized me by the wrists.

'Dance with me. That's how it's done. As a couple.'

After placing my hands on her waist, she held my shoulders and began to sway. I had never been this close to Pixie before, never felt her skin through her clothes, her eyes into mine.

'It's time we ate,' I said.

She leant her head against me. 'Sure. At the end of the bracket.'

'You've drunk too much, Pixie. Let's go.'

Leading her out the door, I took her to a creperie in a quiet part of the village where bright fluorescent light replaced the dangerous music. Oddly enough, it was like the dance had never happened. She told me about the awards her father had collected for restoring English cars, and how her mother washed and mended clothes for the homeless.

When the food arrived, we ate in silence, cutting the crepes into slivers to eat like pieces of raw meat. The meal over, we walked up the street towards the taxi rank opposite Magnums. Pixie felt for my hand. 'Can we have a last drink before going home?'

I released my fingers to glance at my watch. 'It's almost nine.'

'I'm a big girl.' She took my hand again. 'And you're no Jade.'

We crossed the street into noisy, smoky Magnums where I forced my way to a table inhabited by a group of youths. Carefree and rowdy, most of them were perched on the table, resting their feet on the benches. As we approached, they made room for us. I occupied a seat at the end leaving space opposite for Pixie, but she chose to sit on the table facing me, her knees level with my chest.

'What will you drink?' I asked.

'The same.'

After ordering two mixes, I carried them back. Her eyes followed me.

'Move across and I'll join you.'

'No, Tom. Stay on the bench. I never get to look down on you.'

'Do you look up at me?'

'Always.'

'It's not obvious,' I said.

'You wouldn't notice.'

As she sipped the drink, her eyes darted to the nearby groups. Even though young and vivacious, she no longer seemed at ease among her peers. The outing in Jade's boat had dented her confidence.

'Did Jade hurt you?' I asked.

'He tried.'

'I can imagine. He's strong.'

'Too strong for me. Look, the bruises haven't gone.' She exposed the inside of her thigh where an ugly black thumbprint contaminated the white skin. 'And other bruises I can't show here.'

We were close, physically close. I felt like I clung to the edge of a vortex: the allure of flesh, Eve's flesh — innocence masking the taste of forbidden fruit. Shutting my eyes, I asked her to sit beside me.

She slid off the table onto the bench. 'Tom, are you in love with Lisa?'

'We're loyal to each other.'

'That's not the same.'

'It ought to be,' I said.

'I suppose so … though I think you are in love. Your eyes glow when she comes into the office.'

'We are happy in other ways.'

She giggled. 'Don't I know it. You went so red that night on the balcony.' She was serious again. 'In the meantime, you mock Pixie. Like the morning you declared you had seen a beaver. There's Pixie, wide-eyed and trusting, while Tom merrily describes Lisa's vagina. To you I am just a schoolgirl.'

I shook my head. 'In some ways you're very adult, like with the Aboriginal matter and at Grandpa's funeral. You are also … well …'

'Well, what?'

'Um … young and pretty, as my family keeps telling me.'

'You make it sound like a character flaw. Would you prefer I left town?'

On impulse I drew her into my arms. A wise man would say, 'Go wherever the cage door is open.' But I couldn't. Her heart beat warmly against my chest as I tried to imagine Shingley Drive without her.

After a time, she looked up and kissed me. 'Even if you send me away, I won't leave. I'll work for you forever, like Heather does.'

'She's become impossible. Needs retrenching.'

'You love her, Thomas.'

I forgot about time then, about the need to go home, about what was right in Pixie's company. Meanwhile, I felt she still basked in the awe of the O'Connors, the nearest of whom was Tom.

Around ten-thirty I hailed a cab and accompanied her back to her house. A quick peck on the cheek, then she was through her gate and up the stairs. After turning to wave, she closed the door. Within seconds, like in a stage play, the verandah light went out. Pixie was gone.

CHAPTER 42

When I opened the door to the back of the *Post*, all thoughts of Pixie disappeared. My first impression was that a tornado had ripped through the newsroom. Computers, books, papers lay everywhere. I switched on the light in my office. The chaos was worse. Somebody had gone to the effort of upturning my desk and dumping the computer and files on the floor. I slid to my haunches unable to absorb the scope of the devastation. What animal would do this? I tried my phone. Useless. After finding the one on Roberta's desk intact, I rang the police. Sergeant Phil Manning came on the line.

'Phil, it's Tom O'Connor here. My office has been trashed. Can you take a look?'

'No worries. See you in twenty.'

When Phil and his offsider arrived, I rose to greet them.

'Holy Toledo,' Phil said. 'Somebody's had fun.'

'Fun's not the word. I came home just before I rang you. Found the place as you see it.'

'Any idea who it might be? A name misspelt in the bowls results?'

'Get serious, Phil. We've covered four big stories of late.' I listed them on my fingers. 'Sacred sites, rorts in council, the development in Woodwark Bay, and drug trafficking. It has to be among that lot.'

'Which narrows it down to a few hundred. Mind if we look around?'

They tromped across the floor, sticking their big hands on any surface that might've left a print. After searching every desk, Phil entered my office.

Five minutes later he strolled out. 'You touched anything yet, Tom.'

'Only the handset, and it's dead.'

'Come inside.'

As I walked into the office, he pointed to a small transparent bag that held white powder and lay among the rubbish in a bottom drawer. 'What's that?'

I peered at the bag. 'Salt? Sugar? My God, they're drugs!'

'You ever seen them before?'

'Never.'

'You being straight with me, Tom?'

'I swear I am, Phil.'

'My boss tried to caution you, and you wouldn't freakin' listen.' He glanced through the door where his constable was rooting among papers at Mandy's desk. 'I should call CIB down here tonight, but instead I'll disappear the evidence until Sunday, which gives you forty-eight hours to establish they're not yours. In the meantime, I'll seal your door. Nobody in or out, including you.'

Shortly afterwards, Phil Manning whistled to his constable and the pair crunched out the door.

'Freakin' vandals are a menace,' Phil said, pausing at his car. 'Should nail their balls to a tree. We'll get the fingerprint mob onto it tomorrow, Tom. Don't touch a thing until we're through.'

When they had left, I sat on the steps reflecting on the two men most likely to have orchestrated the crime: Jade Wilson and Todd Steele. With Jade's rendezvous night so close I didn't think he would be that stupid. All the evidence pointed to Todd. Exhausted, I was about to climb upstairs when I heard a tap on the back wall. Billy's head appeared.

'Where have you been?' I asked.

'Out and about.' Then he gasped. 'Crikey, Tom! Anything pinched?'

'Impossible to say. Staff will have to check their own desks.'

'I know one suspect. Todd's car was here at seven-thirty.'

'You kidding me, Billy?'

'Nope. His Merc was out front all right. When I ran into Heather at the supermarket, she said she had left you and Pixie at Captain Morgan's. Twenty minutes later while taking a bus into the village, I saw Todd's car near the front door. Couldn't tell if your Moke was here, but since the place was in darkness, I assumed you had sent Pixie home, and joined Todd for a drink. Down in the village, I spot you and Pixie at the tapas bar, but no sign of Todd. So, after sinking a few beers with mates, I'm on the way home when I notice the office lights on, and the cops pulling out. Didn't expect this.'

'So, it was Todd, the old prick.'

'Maybe not Todd himself. He's over eighty.' He gestured at my door where Sergeant Manning had placed a seal. 'What's in there?'

'An even bigger mess. Worse still, they left a calling card.

Small bag with white powder. Drugs of some kind. Phil's given me until Sunday to prove they're not mine.'

'Surely that's obvious.'

'Not to the police. I have to find Lenny Watkins. He is Todd's hit man. Get him to admit that Todd arranged for this damage, and that we are being set up. I'll try Harvey Nicholson first thing. He should know Lenny's whereabouts.'

'And I'll keep a watch on Jade. He'll be involved, you can bet.'

While Billy walked to the bus stop at the corner of Shingley Drive, I climbed the stairs expecting more chaos, but the flat had not been touched. After our second drugs article in the paper, a caller had warned me to expect a *friggin' accident*. He was a man of his word.

*   *   *

Soon after daylight next morning, I drove to the house of Harvey and Thelma Nicholson. Harvey didn't break any records answering the door.

'Sorry, Harvey, I won't keep you long. I need to find your son, Lenny.'

'He's not here, Tom. I haven't seen Lenny in weeks.'

'Where is he?'

'Don't know. After your grandpa's house burnt down, he took off.'

Harvey was unceremoniously thrust aside. Thelma stood in the doorway, her lips pursed. 'Tom, you find that no good Lenny and give him what-for. Nothing but trouble, that boy.'

'Where is he, Thelma?'

'Greenvale. When he left your house, he tried the brothers down south. They chased him to Greenvale where he can do no harm.'

*   *   *

Because the mining town of Greenvale was six hours north-west of Proserpine, I wasted no time filling the tank and heading up Highway One. At Townsville I swung west towards Charters Towers, then north along the development road to Greenvale where the mining company had built a town to accommodate the families extracting nickel from the hot, hard earth. Parts of the mine had since closed, leaving houses to a group of citizens who chose to live beyond the reach of civilisation.

At the pub I asked after Lenny.

'Is he a Black man?' the elderly barmaid lisped. Because her front teeth were missing, top and bottom, she afforded a direct visual route to the tonsils. Not pretty.

'That's right. Aboriginal family. Three women and maybe seven kids.'

'You from the government?'

I pointed to the dusty Moke. 'Does that look government?'

'You could be in disguise. Cops do it all the time.'

'I want Lenny for personal reasons. It's about my grandfather.'

'Well, he'll be here on Sunday for lunch. If you need him sooner, his house is last on the Mount Garnet Road.'

Afraid that Lenny might recognise the car, I parked it behind a clump of wild lantana and clambered through a paddock to the house where I could see him reclining on a director's chair in the shade, his feet propped on a machinery case. A mug of tea sat at his right hand, while scattered around him was the flotsam that appeared to follow him through life. I waited until I was at his back fence before raising my head.

'Good day, Lenny.'

The response was gratifyingly dramatic. He sprang from the chair toppling it backwards, two dogs barked the sky down and his family scrambled into the house. He attempted to follow but I cleared the fence, seizing him by the arm.

'Hold on, Lenny. We're mates. Sacred site and all that.'

'Piss off, you bastard.'

When one of his dogs lunged at me, I smacked it on the head with a crank handle. 'Settle down or I'll crack you too,' I told him.

'What you want? I didn't burn no house down.'

'I know you didn't, but I need your help. You have nothing to fear from the O'Connors, that's all in the past.'

'Bullshit. An O'Connor pushed a Black woman over the cliff. She was a great-great-aunt of my granny.'

'Todd Steele told you lies. There is no quarrel between our families. Todd wanted you out of Woodwark Bay so he could develop the land. Make millions of dollars. If everything he said was true, why did he need to pay you money, buy you a Land Cruiser?'

'He called it hardship money, to make up for all the bad times.'

'Lenny, you're welcome to whatever cash comes your way.

That's your break in life, but I have a bone to pick with Todd. He destroyed Grandpa, now he's destroying me.'

Lenny relaxed and uprighted his chair. In an instant he was the genial host. 'Sit down, Tom, and have a cuppa.'

He called to one of his women who brought out two mugs of tea. I drew a sheet of paper from my pocket. 'Lenny, how well can you read?'

'I get by.'

'Okay, read this, and sign it.'

'I don't put my mark on nothin'.'

'Lenny, I have evidence you were paid to watch over the shed at Woodwark Bay. Because unlawful stuff is kept in that shed, you could end up in prison. Two years. Maybe more.'

'You're a big prick.'

'Not like others I could name. But if you help me now, your role at the shed goes with me to the grave.'

'Let me see it.' He read laboriously, 'I, Lenny Watkins, do solemnly swear that Todd Steele paid me to cause trouble with the O'Connor family, and to trash the house of Henry O'Connor. The O'Connor family has done me no harm, and I apologise sincerely for taking Todd's money and causing injury to the O'Connors and their property. Furthermore, Todd Steele paid me cash to leave evidence of drugs at the *Whitsunday Post*.'

He threw the paper on the ground. 'Damn you, Tom. What's this about drugs? I never touch the filthy stuff.'

'That windscreen on your Land Cruiser is covered in bugs. Did you drive from Airlie last night?'

'Course not. Those bugs been stuck there for weeks.'

'The cops think you are the villain in this.'

'It wasn't me. Cross my heart.'

'Okay, I believe you.'

I took the pen, reflected a moment, then added to the bottom: 'I, Lenny Watkins, declare Todd Steele had drugs in his hand when he asked me to junk the *Whitsunday Post*. I didn't harm the newspaper office or take the drugs.'

'Now sign this paper, Lenny, so I can demonstrate we are both victims.'

'No sweat, Tom. Mr Steele needs takin' down a peg or two.'

When he scratched his name on the document, I called one of his women to sign as a witness. I also signed and added the date.

'Um … Tom, do you mind? … one other thing.'

'Yes.'

'The sacred site. I'm sorry, bro', but will you … um … care for it?'

'I promise, Lenny. That place is sacred to me too.'

We shook hands. 'Thanks, bro'.'

Climbing over the fence, I returned to my car. Although I couldn't pretend to love him for his treatment of Grandpa's house, we were brothers in a way: two pawns in a Todd Steele crusade to remedy an old grievance. In any event, Lenny had signed a document that hopefully pointed Sergeant Manning in the right direction.

As it was now almost four on Saturday afternoon, I bought a can of refreshment from the toothless barmaid and returned to Charters Towers where I booked into a motel for the night.

*   *   *

Next morning, I left Charters Towers at daylight, arriving in Airlie around nine. Lisa was in the flat anxiously awaiting me. She pointed to the chaos downstairs where officers were still collecting evidence.

'Tom, are you okay? You weren't here when it happened?'

'No, I was in the village with Pixie.'

'Who did it?'

'We think Todd or Jade, or both. Todd's white Mercedes was seen in the street.'

'That sounds a bit dumb, even for Todd. And don't forget Jade was on the *Calvados* all night. What about your drug dealers? Vandalism is their favourite sport — after killing people.'

'There's more to the story, Lisa. A bag of white powder was planted in my desk. Luckily Sergeant Manning found the bag, and has given me forty-eight hours to prove it's not mine.'

'Sorry, Tom, but I don't share your confidence. By next week the AFP will be asking serious questions. Vandals aside, I have my own news. Jade has told us that he's finishing the season early. When he learnt his brother has cancer, he decided to make tomorrow his last trip. He'll pay off two of the crew when he returns on Thursday, and keep the other two for his run to Sydney.'

'So Thursday is party night.'

'Maybe a drink or two. Nothing more. He's leaving first light Friday morning.'

'That's not possible. He has a shed full of drugs to collect.'

'Tom, whatever the contents of those boxes — greased or ungreased — they are not Jade's. It was Vogel's power boat that monitored the torch flashes, and it's Vogel who has rented the shed for six weeks. I have an AFP briefing this afternoon in Bowen and two of my chiefs are flying up from Sydney. They've planned an operation for Friday night … AFP, Customs, everyone.'

'Who's driving you to Bowen?'

'Nobody. I'm hiring a car. It'll arrive soon.'

At that very moment two cars pulled up. One of the drivers joined his companion in the second car then accelerated away, leaving the first car at the kerb. Lisa kissed me. 'You be careful, Tom. No silly stuff.' And ran down the steps.

I watched as she expertly did a U-turn and joined the traffic for the run to Bowen. So that was that. Sighing, I fetched my hat and walked up to the police station where I found Sergeant Manning.

'What's this?' he said.

'It's a signed statement from Lenny Watkins. He declares that Todd Steele tried to bribe him into planting drugs.'

'This'll get laughed out of court.'

'Phil, I also have a witness who saw Todd's car here on Friday night.'

He shook his head. 'I've been busy myself. Todd was at a Rotary dinner and his car is a red herring. Now do me a favour. After dark tonight, open your office and destroy the bag. You'll find it hidden inside the light cover. There's funny business going on, but you ain't a drug dealer and the plant was freakin' clumsy. In the meantime, stay off the drug stories until my boss gives the all clear. Okay?'

'Will do, Phil. And thanks.'

Around five Sunday afternoon I drove out to the farm where I cornered Patrick, and told him the latest developments.

'Red herring? What a load of crap,' he said. 'I ought to pay Todd a visit.'

'No, Patrick. Remember your promise to Glenda. Besides, I've got information that the federal cops are planning an operation Friday night. It's all hush hush. We've been told to keep out of their way.'

Customarily I would stay for tea, but I was edgy about the drugs and returned to Shingley Drive. By seven o'clock the building was dark and ghostly quiet, like a creature that is wounded but refuses to yield. After removing the bag from the light cover, I dropped it into my shorts and strolled to the rock wall where I tossed it into the current. For a short, frightening minute the bag floated, then the powder liquefied and the bag sank.

CHAPTER 43

Sometime during Sunday night, emergency sirens woke me, but after their wail faded over the hill into Airlie I drifted back to sleep. An interesting thing about dreams is that I never remember them in the morning. The canvases on which they are painted always seem to dissolve before I can stretch them into a frame. But that night the sirens woke me mid-dream. I was on a fast yacht sailing through the gloom, chased by creatures that dived out of the mists to tear at the sails. Lisa was at the wheel heaving the boat from side to side, and Pixie stood at the mast lunging at the creatures with a bread knife. Sharp claws were shredding her clothes over torn flesh. She cried for help but I was paralysed. I couldn't move. I saw her raw, bleeding body and I was helpless.

An hour after the sirens had passed, I was woken a second time by a handful of stones bouncing off the bedroom window. Pushing open the window, I saw Patrick in the reflected glow of a street light.

'Let me in, Tom, quick,' he whispered hoarsely.

I hurried downstairs and unlocked the door. 'What's up?'

'You won't believe it but Todd's dead and his house is burnt down.'

'You what?'

'Not me. Someone's killed Todd and torched his house.'

'How do you know?'

'I was there.'

I sat him in a chair and made coffee. I was speechless.

'It wasn't me, Tom, I swear. I was angry I'll admit, but I thought if I could see how the man lived, see his house, it might settle me down. I left the car in the street and walked up his driveway. A small hatchback was parked outside the door, a Barina or Suzuki. Something like that. Then I heard a noise from inside the house. A fella came running out dressed in black and wearing a balaclava. He jumped in the car and was gone. As the front door was open, I crept inside. Then I smelt it. Smoke. Not a tobacco smell, but acrid … like carpet burning. I sneaked into the living room. Somebody had pushed furniture against the wall and lit a fire. That wasn't as bad as seeing Todd on the floor with a cane knife in his back. I panicked and bolted out the door. By the time I'd driven back to Airlie fire engines were screaming past. So I came here.'

I stared at him. 'You've just fled a murder scene, you and a man in black who drives a hatchback. Your own car would've been seen, your fingerprints are on everything, and you've told half Proserpine you'll get even with Todd. You're off your rocker.'

'I swear I'm innocent, Tom. And I touched nothing or walked in nothing. Look at my shoes.'

'Why in God's name did you leave the farm? The cops will be out there now.'

'I know it doesn't look smart. But I meant no harm.'

I took several deep breaths. 'Okay, any other clues about this man in black?'

'No, it happened too sudden.'

'Does he know you were there?'

'Probably not. My car was down the street.'

'You are lying, Patrick. I'm your brother. Look at me.'

He fidgeted with his cup. 'Sorry, Tom, but … um …'

'Um, what?'

'This sounds ridiculous, but I was to … well … keep it to myself. Todd rang me. He asked me over for a chat.'

'Todd wanted to clear his conscious before getting murdered? Try harder.'

'I promise, it's true.'

'All right then.' I sighed. 'You are certain the caller was Todd?'

'It seemed genuine.'

'When did he ring?'

'Around eight maybe.'

'And you left home at once?'

'Yes.'

'Where do Mum and Glenda think you are?'

'Checking Jack Pollock's irrigator. Glenda had gone out.'

'That's a pathetic alibi. What else are you hiding?'

'Nothing. I swear.'

'Okay, we'll go with this for a story. You drove to my flat worried that I'd been showing signs of depression. You spent the night on the sofa. I'll vouch for you and so will Mum. Now take a shower while I wash and dry your clothes. At daylight we'll eat breakfast together in an Airlie café, then you drive back to the farm. Pretend you're innocent.'

'Damn it, Tom, I am.'

'Phil Manning has already swallowed one O'Connor yarn

this week. His belly might be full.' I looked at the clock. 'It's past midnight. Get some sleep.'

After I had made up the sofa, he climbed into the sheets while I put on the wash and returned to my empty bed.

'Tom, apart from us, who wanted the old fella dead?'

'I don't care. Go to sleep.'

*   *   *

Early Monday morning we drove in Patrick's Holden to one of those waterfront cafés that serves breakfast for boat crews. I loudly greeted everyone I knew. Seated alone at a table was Dan Morgan from Captain Morgan's Bar. His eyes were dark and his face sullen, which was out of character for a man who loved working the crowds.

'Morning, Dan,' I said. 'This is my brother, Patrick.'

After ordering bacon and eggs, we chose a central table. 'He's a merry little gannet,' Patrick whispered.

'Yes, runs the bar at Abell Point. His wife packs a mean whinge. Speaking of moods, how is Glenda? I didn't see her yesterday.'

'She and Mum are like that,' he said, crossing his fingers. 'They can't wait for the big day. Same with me, Tom. Kids will be popping out before you know it.'

In twenty minutes we had finished our breakfast and stood to leave.

'Bye, Patrick. Many thanks for staying the night.'

'No worries, little brother. If you need me, ring the farm.'

I patted him on the shoulder and watched as he drove across the hill towards Conway. Why had God in his wisdom given me an idiot for a brother? Meanwhile, my theory that Todd was at the root of our troubles lay in tatters now he'd been killed. Maybe old Vogel did have a case to answer, though I couldn't see it. Tagula Enterprises, dead shareholder or not, simply had to be the bad apple in Airlie's barrel.

Back at the office I began the tedious job of salvaging records. Although four of our seven computers were smashed, I was confident a technician could extract valuable data from the hard drives. I rang the Apple outlet in Mackay and told him he was needed in Airlie again and to bring four new computers. Next, I called a glazier to repair the windows. When staff arrived to start their working week, they stared horrified at the mess but settled readily into the clean-up.

Somewhere on the floor a phone rang. Heather answered it and rushed into my office. 'News has just come in. Todd Steele was murdered last night and his house burnt down.'

'Thanks, Heather, I'd heard earlier. We have to try and carry on as usual. When the office is shipshape, Pixie and I will visit the crime scene. If anybody asks about the *Post*, say we were vandalised, which is the truth.'

Heather shook her head, releasing her jowls, which flapped like a boxer dog's. 'It was those drug stories, Tom. Nothing but trouble since drugs entered the conversation.'

'Talking of drug stories, where's Billy?'

'Hasn't come in yet.'

'Why am I not surprised?'

Within two hours the *Post* was back on its feet, tidier if anything. The glazier had repaired the windows and the Apple tech was busily replacing computers. I happened to glance out the window and saw a police car ease over the crest of Shute Harbour Road.

'Come, Pixie. Grab a camera and notebook. We'll do that visit now.'

Before she could argue, I pushed her into the car and sped towards Todd Steele's house at Mandalay. In the mirror I watched the police turn into our street. Heather, bless her soul, would say: 'Sorry, he's following up a news story. You should've phoned.'

Todd's burnt-out house was surrounded by emergency vehicles and a community huddle that parted to let us through. After taking several external photos, we interviewed a bored detective constable who said firemen had discovered the body of a male person whose death was being treated as suspicious.

'How did he die?'

'I'm not at liberty to say.'

'Give us a break, Detective. I bet you told the *ABC*.'

'I could've done. So what?'

Taking Pixie to one side, I said, 'I want a quick peek through the back door. Distract him. Ask silly questions while showing some leg.'

'That's demeaning, Tom.'

'He's only a cop.'

When silence followed, I said, 'We could swap places?'

After giving me the *look*, Pixie adjusted her hem and sat coyly on the bonnet. 'Detective, what would police do if they found drugs at the murder scene?'

While the cop did his best to concentrate, I slunk round the corner of the house. Most of the fire seemed to have been at the front with little damage to the back. I let myself through the kitchen door and into a room where two officers photographed the murder scene, and another two plucked samples of evidence from the floor. Todd Steele lay on his side in pyjamas, his upper body covered with a sheet. Todd's wearing of pyjamas intrigued me. Why would an old-fashioned conservative dressed in pyjamas invite a stranger to his home? In which case, if he hadn't phoned Patrick, who did?

Quietly I returned to the front of the house where Pixie had run out of questions. When she noticed me, she slid off the bonnet unlocking the detective's gaze.

'Where the hell have you been?' he said.

'Needed a leak. Sorry.'

He eyed me suspiciously. 'What's your name?'

'Tom O'Connor.'

'O'Connor? I should've freakin' guessed. Piss off, both of you.'

As we reversed down the driveway, Pixie said, 'I make his morning, then you go and spoil it. He'll be all confused.'

Two minutes later, while driving through the leafy suburb, she asked, 'Why did he explode at the name O'Connor?'

When I tried to fob her off, she went dangerously quiet. The silence lasted from Mandalay, through Jubilee Pocket to the village. As we slowed for traffic, she demanded we pull into an empty parking space on the foreshore.

'Please, Pixie, can't it wait? I have a mountain of work to do.'

'I've backed you this far, Tom,' she snapped. 'And I've just played the flirt, so what's going on?'

Monday morning at the beach was peaceful. Council had sprinklers flicking water onto the grass while a team of workers raked paths and gardens. A dozen backpackers sat under the shelters, some with books open, others cutting their toenails. We found a vacant bench on the point.

'Pixie, this is not for general broadcast. Do you understand?'

'You trusted me before, Tom.'

'We're on tricky ground. Very tricky.'

'Who are *we*?'

'Patrick, Billy, myself, others.'

'How tricky? People could get hurt?'

'Or die. One already has. Todd Steele.'

With that, I told her everything, even that Lisa was an undercover federal agent, and how we expected a major drug delivery on Friday night. Half an hour later she had trouble keeping still.

'Tell me how I can help.'

'We might need a liaison. A person who is above suspicion. Right now, Patrick is in trouble with the law, I'm trying to juggle a dozen separate tasks, and Billy is a lone vigilante.'

'I'll do whatever is needed,' she said, and extended her hand for a manly shake.

'Thanks, Pixie, but nothing risky. Promise?'

As I strode through the office door, Heather handed me two messages. The first was from Lisa who had returned from Bowen with orders to proceed directly to the *Calvados*. She would not be back at Airlie until Thursday.

The second message was from Sergeant Phil Manning.

'He wants you right away, Tom. He doesn't sound happy.'

I climbed into the car and drove across to the Cannonvale Police Station. After letting me stew at the counter for ten minutes, Phil emerged from behind a glass door. 'Tom, this is looking grim. Arson and murder. We need an explanation. Come through.'

He sat me in a plain, grey room that contained a table and four chairs. The cold light bouncing off the walls came from a single fluorescent tube and two small, barred windows. The room was over-airconditioned.

'This looks official, Phil.'

'No, it's an off-the-record chat. Nothing formal.'

He paused as the door opened and Chief Inspector Seb Gudinski entered. Seb threw his cap on the table. 'Don't mind me, fellas. Go ahead, Phil.'

The sergeant turned back to me. 'Right, Tom, you would know Todd Steele was killed last night and his house set alight. Well, guess what? Your brother's car was seen at the house about the same time the fire started.'

'You're kidding me, Phil. My brother owns a white VK Holden like a thousand others in the north.'

'A Broncos sticker on the rear window and a nudge bar? Not many like that. Where were you last night?'

'In my flat above the office. With my brother.'

'I freakin' told you,' Seb Gudinski snorted. 'The O'Connor Protocol. Tom has to cover for Patrick who is in deep shit. I could write the freakin' script myself. Your brother is our chief suspect, Tom. Do the right thing by the law, your faithful readers — even your mum — and tell the truth.'

'I am, Seb. If Patrick was guilty, I'd hand him over. Is that your only evidence? A white Holden?'

'A cane knife, footprints and a powerful motive.'

'We all own cane knives, footprints on a cement driveway sounds dodgy, and we say things in the heat of the moment. Have you talked to Patrick?'

'We have,' Sergeant Phil said. 'And you know what? Same story.'

I leant forward on the table. 'I'll tell you where to look for the culprit. Three men — Jade Wilson, Seamus Carney and the late Todd Steele — are part of a drug trafficking syndicate. You should know that through the AFP in Sydney who are already talking to your bosses. Sadly for Todd, he wanted to back out of the syndicate. Land deals were more his scene. The problem is he knew too much. Somebody wanted him dead before the next big delivery.'

Seb Gudinski looked uncomfortable. 'Careful what you say, Tom. We have detectives chasing the drug link. And it has nothing to do with Todd's murder.'

'I bet it does. Either way, my brother might be a numbskull but he's not a murderer.'

They asked more questions about the night but the interview was going nowhere. Finally, they gave up and told me to leave. As I walked to the car, they stood on the front steps of the police station like two forlorn parishioners. Why had God dumped on them a high-profile murder, an arson attack and a drug scandal in the space of a month? It was more fun dealing with the devils they knew, which included the O'Connor brothers.

CHAPTER 44

At the office, the staff thrived on the emergency as if they had sided with Lord Thomas to man the battlements. Even Ethel's fingers danced across the keyboard making up for lost time. Sergeant Major Heather walked from desk to desk (a word of support here, a tone of admonishment there), and junior reporter Pixie had taken on the mantle of senior editor. The only face missing was Billy's.

Shortly after eleven he wandered through the back door with a satchel of advertising copy.

'Sorry, boss. I've been out flogging my shoe leather.'

'That excuse is not even original, Billy.'

'Didn't know it had to be.'

He checked nobody was within earshot. 'I've got information. See you outside in ten minutes.'

He walked across to Ethel's desk where he dumped his copy and instructions; all pleasantly given and received. Next, he saw Heather, who chewed his ear over a handful of bad accounts, then he strolled out the door with a coffee in hand.

I joined him on the bench near the lean-to. 'Have you heard about Todd?' I asked.

'Yes, the town's buzzing with the news.'

'So, what else is there?'

'The drugs delivery has been changed to Thursday.'

'How do you know?'

'By being a good detective. After I left you on Friday night, I spent the weekend staking out the shed in Woodwark Bay. That place is our only lead, Tom. All was quiet until yesterday about an hour after dusk when two fellas in a small boat motored through the channel and parked in the lee of the jetty. No lights were shown, nothing. I crawled to within fifty metres of the shed and lay there. At nine when it was pitch dark, they opened the door and disappeared inside, pulling the door shut after them. So I crept closer. Around ten they re-emerged, locked the shed, and sat on the jetty talking about dogs and stuff. Then one fella said to the other, "Have we given it enough time, George?"

'George answered, "No, we haven't. And don't forget the code. Two by two flashes if all going to plan. Three quick flashes, the drop's been called off."

'The first fella then said, "Anything else changed?" "Nope," said George. "Same times on everything, but get into that bird brain of yours — Thursday, not Friday."'

When Billy finished mimicking the voices, he turned to me. 'That's exactly what they said, fair dinkum.'

'What happened next?'

'They stayed another hour, then hopped into their boat and motored south.'

'Well, something forced them to reschedule.'

'Todd's death, I'd reckon. Cops are jumping everywhere.'

'Maybe. Our problem now is that Lisa's on the *Calvados* until Thursday morning.'

'Tom, we don't need Lisa.'

For the second time that day I revealed Lisa's identity.

'I'll be damned,' Billy said, shaking his head in disbelief. 'She's an undercover fed. Shouldn't we tell Phil Manning? He'd know what to do.'

'Lisa told me not to approach anyone. The AFP have it under control.'

'When exactly does she get back?'

'Late morning. She'll have to contact her boss the minute she's in. Tell him to dispatch his troops, pronto.'

'Doesn't give them much time. The boat will have a radio. Send her a coded message through the Volunteer Marine Rescue.'

'Too dangerous.'

'We don't have a choice, Tom. What's their call sign?'

Because I didn't have a clue, we tramped upstairs to locate a diary I kept on boats using the marina. The *Calvados* was there, of course, but no radio details. In one corner of the room sat Lisa's duffel bag, which we opened guiltily. Apart from some washing and a change of clothes, the bag contained nothing of value, likewise the pockets of two dresses hanging in the cupboard.

'She shares a house on Border Drive. Most of her gear is there,' I explained to Billy. 'She keeps personal items in a small pack. Even her AFP identity.'

'That house will be locked. If she's not back by late morning we approach Phil Manning. Right, Tom?'

'I don't know, Billy. I gave her my word, and besides, the federal police are not novices. They would have contingency plans.'

*　　*　　*

Over the next few days, we put our shoulders to the wheel. Apart from Pixie, who was a co-conspirator, I told my staff a credible lie. I said that as the presses in Mackay would be shutting for maintenance on Thursday night, our paper had to be print-ready five hours earlier than usual. No excuses for late copy or late page completions.

Meanwhile, detectives kept quizzing me about Patrick's whereabouts on Sunday night. They were certain he had murdered Todd, and only a lying, two-faced brother stood between him and justice. Mum was also fed up with police knocking on her door.

'When's it going to end, Tom?'

'Mum, our Patrick has nothing to worry about. Unfortunately, police work on the theory that a man is guilty until proven innocent. We're doing our best to clear his name.'

'Have you spoken to Mr Fumbleton?'

'You serious? Marvin is still waiting for Grandpa to ring.'

'Well, get legal advice somewhere.'

On Thursday at noon, as Mandy flipped the last page into the courier's box, I thanked staff for their effort under trying circumstances and gave everyone the afternoon off.

Heather wouldn't hear of it. 'Tom, the invoices are a week overdue. We should spend an hour bringing paperwork up to date.'

'No, Heather. Right now, I'm the boss. Believe me, everything will return to normal by Monday.'

'That's a brave call.'

'The police are close to a breakthrough. Go home, go shopping, whatever. Tomorrow is a new day.'

With that, I walked to the back door and held it open. Inside ten minutes, staff had collected their belongings and raised dust leaving the carpark.

When the building was empty, Pixie wheeled out her pushbike and leant it against the wall.

'What's the plan tonight, Tom?'

'Where's Billy? The three of us need a chat.'

Within minutes Billy made his appearance and we sat on the bench.

'Okay,' I said, 'when Lisa returns to port, which should be about now, she has to phone her AFP mates with the changed timetable. Let's hope they can move fast. Billy, I think you and I ought to commandeer your cousin's boat, and watch for any yacht that leaves harbour, including Vogel's. We can shadow it to Woodwark Bay. Meantime we still watch the *Calvados*. Lisa believes Jade is above suspicion, but after Todd's death, we can't rule him out. Regardless of whose boat we follow, no heroics from anyone. If the AFP are late, we note details and ring the police immediately we get home. Pixie, take this phone and your bike to the end of the track into the bay. Stay hidden in the bushes. Should a vehicle go in or out, try to record its number. Billy and I will have the other phone. Call if anything happens. Whatever you do, keep the volume low and stay under cover.'

'Tom, why not speak to Sergeant Phil? You won't find a man more trustworthy.'

'No, Pixie. Lisa said the police cage has a rat. I know Phil is honest but once he's informed, the whole station will start humming. It wouldn't be long before the traffickers are in the loop.'

'What about Chief Inspector Gudinski?'

'Seb wouldn't believe me. Besides, this is a job for the feds. They can decide who is in or out.'

'Let's compromise,' Billy said. 'You thought Lisa should be home by midday. If no word from her by two, we phone Sergeant Phil.'

'Okay. Two o'clock is her deadline. Now remember, we are observers only.'

After Billy and Pixie had left, I returned to the office where I sorted accounts for an hour to take my mind off drugs. I was about to shut the computer when the phone rang.

I picked up the handset. 'Tom O'Connor speaking.'

It was Lisa's breathless voice. 'Tom, can you hear me?'

'Sure. Where are you?'

'At the marina on a payphone. We dropped off our guests, now Jade wants to retrieve some dive gear we lost at Pioneer Rocks. Probably take a few hours. When we get back to Airlie, we'll pack for an early start in the morning. See you at the flat around five.'

'No, Lisa, listen to me. Are you alone?'

'Yes. What's the matter?'

'The delivery date is moved forward twenty-four hours. Ring your bosses and tell them it's happening tonight. Can they get to Woodwark Bay in time?'

'That won't be a problem. They can be ready in thirty minutes. You absolutely sure?'

'Yes. Billy overheard two men talking at the shed.'

'Okay, I'll phone my boss now. And tell Billy to stay at home. I repeat that. Stay at home.'

'Lisa, you be careful. Jade's trip to Pioneer Rocks could be a diversion.'

'The trip is genuine. Dive gear isn't cheap. Promise you'll wait for me at the flat.'

'I'll uncork your favourite red.'

'Thanks, darling. I look forward to it.'

With three hours to fill, I drove across to the farm to see Patrick, who had always been my confidant, despite the troubles he created. He listened as I explained our plan, and even the complications that included Lisa's role as an undercover agent.

'You joining the action, little brother?' he asked.

'Only from a distance.'

'If you need muscle, you know who to call.'

'Patrick, your responsibility is to Glenda.'

'No harm in offering.'

When I returned to the *Post* around five, there was no sign of Lisa.

I rang Billy at his cousin's house. 'She phoned in earlier and has contacted her AFP boss. He needs only thirty minutes to mobilise. I hope she's safe, Billy. She could be alone with Jade on the boat.'

'Cops know how to look after themselves. Are you ready?'

'We can't just abandon her.'

'Leave a note. Our plan is to watch for a suspicious yacht. You can't do that from home, and remember, Pixie is already up at the gate.'

I scribbled out a semi-plausible explanation for Lisa and packed a few essentials. Next, I donned my commando jeans and shirt and drove up to the sailing club where Billy was launching his cousin's boat. The sun had melted into the hills beyond Abell Point and the crimson glow suggested darkness was less than twenty minutes away.

'Any sign of Lisa?' he asked.

'Nothing. I'm worried about her.'

'Listen, Tom, if Jade is innocent, he could be still at Pioneer Rocks. If he's guilty, he'll be headed for Woodwark Bay with Lisa on board alive and well. He can't sail the *Calvados* alone.'

'That makes sense … I guess. The AFP should be in position. Odd that Pixie hasn't made contact.'

'Try the phone.'

When I rang, Pixie answered immediately. 'Yes, Tom,' she whispered.

'Any sign of the cops?'

'Nobody has been in or out.'

'Lisa said they could move in thirty minutes. That was four hours ago.'

'They didn't come this way.'

'There's no other entrance. Keep your head down and stay in touch.'

When I ended the call, I said, 'Okay, Billy, it seems the federal cops are a non-event. Lisa may have misunderstood me. What do you suggest?'

'Stay to the plan. Look, Tom, I owe you an apology. I

took it on myself to ring Phil Manning after lunch. Sorry, but I thought we had left too much to the feds who are playing silly buggers. Phil has decided to make his own arrangements. He will have a team on standby. Four-by-four vehicles, bolt cutters, the lot. I gave Pixie his number.'

'I hope we don't end up with egg on our faces.'

'Better than being dead in the water. Let's prepare for a long night.'

'I have.' And showed him the bottle of rum, coffee flask and meat pies.

CHAPTER 45

Billy motored into the channel in the twilight, avoiding the dozens of yachts that lay at anchor. The occasional television set flickered in a half-lit saloon, but mostly yachtsmen sat on their decks enjoying the close of day. By the time we reached clear water, the sky was black with the first stars burning holes in the velvet. Double Cone was just visible and Pigeon Island had dissolved into the background. Billy idled across the bay, then continued northwards hugging the inlets.

'Aren't we supposed to wait for a yacht leaving harbour?' I asked Billy.

'They could come from anywhere. We'll anchor at Woodwark Bay.'

'That wasn't in the plan.'

'Tom, we are here to stop heroin reaching Sydney, even if that means delaying their boat until Phil arrives. Our advantage is surprise. Todd told you tomorrow night is the drop, but we know better. By tomorrow the traffickers will have vanished into thin air. I won't be upset if you order me to turn around. I'll come back on my own.'

'Of course I'm staying.'

'It could get dangerous.'

'That's what the rum is for.'

At the southern bluff protecting Woodwark Bay, Billy unscrewed the anchor from its chain, tied the flukes to a rope and lowered them silently overboard. Pouring two coffees, we sat on the thwart, ate the cold pies and listened for noises above the relentless slap of ocean. My head dropped onto my chest. Billy was nudging me.

'They're here, Tom.'

'Where?'

'See that dark shape. It's barely moving. That's a deep-sea cruiser. Feeling its way into the channel.'

I could hear the rhythmic beat echoing faintly across the water. The cruiser was two hundred metres to our starboard. I crouched against the side of our boat. A soft glow reflected off their wheel, a man's voice gave short commands. Then a beam of light exposed the jetty and was gone. Soon a weak, second light opened the darkness to reveal people bustling along the jetty from the cruiser to the shed. Fifteen minutes later the light was quenched, followed by an engine cranking to life. The cruiser inched down the channel to deep water where the helmsman opened the throttle and steered northwards.

'Gone to Bowen, I expect.' Billy said.

'The cops will never find it.'

'I bet they do. Didn't Lisa meet her friends in Bowen?'

'True. What now?'

'We wait for the pick-up.'

Around nine-thirty we heard the faint throb of a diesel. Within minutes, starlight revealed a two-masted yacht chugging towards the bay like a ghost ship.

'Look, Tom. That's the *Calvados*.'

'You sure?'

'Damn sure. The ketch rig and high prow. No others like it.'

There was not a light, not a visible soul on board. Suddenly two quick flashes from the shore followed by another two. Two flashes in reply. The *Calvados* turned forty-five degrees and began nosing towards the channel. The chug of the diesel died to a flat burble as the ship felt its way through the hazards. Then it was at the jetty and the motor fell silent.

Billy picked up our handset and dialled Sergeant Manning. Shaking his head, he put his mouth to my ear. 'I can't get a signal, Tom. Cops won't be any help. Just you and me. Better pass that bottle.'

We each took a slug of rum and clasped hands like rugby pals.

'Go well, mate.'

'You too, brother.'

Raising the anchor, we paddled into the channel. A dull light showed five people moving between the shed and the *Calvados*. Five people. Where was Lisa? Seated below deck, or at home fuming over my hasty note?

We eased the boat to the opposite side of the jetty and climbed onto the decking.

'What's the plan?' I whispered.

'Grab a gaff hook each,' Billy hissed. 'As a man reaches the *Calvados*, I crack him on the head and you drag him into the shadows. Do that three times and we've squared the odds.'

'Why don't we just set the yacht adrift?'

'That's Plan B.'

The first man was like stunning a cow. When he turned to climb onto the yacht with a package, Billy struck him with the blunt end of the gaff. I caught him and the package, and dragged him two metres along the deck into shadow.

The second man was a stunning failure. In the poor light, Billy's gaff took the man's cap and pony tail, but no skull. Dropping his package with a roar, he lunged at Billy who tripped over the uneven deck. Coming off the bench, I swung my gaff at the man's right ear and pitched him headfirst into our boat where he lay still. All surprise had gone from our attack. Lights were doused. The only sounds were our heartbeats and the lapping of water. Abruptly there was an explosion and a bullet ripped through the air between us.

'Holy shit!'

We dived for the jetty as Jade's voice carried from the shed. 'O'Connor, I know you're there. You and your Black mate. In ten seconds, we start shooting. Stand up with your hands on your head.'

'Where is he?' Billy whispered.

'He can't see us either. I'll make him think we've jumped in the water.'

I pushed our first man off the jetty with a loud splash. Billy leapt off the other side.

'What the …?'

I was left alone facing Jade and two others, all of whom were likely armed. Seizing the gaff hook, I crept along the jetty towards the shed. Beneath me, Billy swam towards the shore. Another two rapid bursts of fire. Jade had stepped onto the jetty and was firing at swirls in the water. With each gun flash his face was lit, exposing the open door of the shed. I was crouched apelike, ready to spring at Jade when bright light flooded the scene.

'Drop it, Tom.'

I let go the shaft and straightened, covering my eyes from the glare.

'Lisa?'

'Yes, it's me. You were told to stay home.'

'You've caught them?'

'No, I've caught you. Sorry, Thomas, it wasn't supposed to end like this.'

'Like what?'

Jade had returned to the shed where he was reloading. 'Damn it, Shirley. Finish the prick so we can move. His mate is still in the water.'

'Shirley?'

'Sorry, Tom. I'm not a federal cop. Nor am I Lisa.'

Surprises were coming from everywhere. A familiar male voice echoed from the darkness. 'This is the police. Drop your weapons. Now.'

Jade had two alternatives: fight or flee. He chose the latter. When he ran for the trees, Pixie stepped from the shadows with a hockey stick. Like a veteran pro, she took a short backswing and drove into his groin. Apart from the awful thud of wood into soft leather, there was silence. Then Jade bellowed, white teeth gleaming in the light, and collapsed in a writhing, yowling heap.

'You little bitch,' Lisa said, firing at Pixie who clutched her side and fell backwards on the grass.

'No!' I cried and dived for Pixie.

Lisa turned the pistol on me. 'You're a fool, Thomas. Such a hopeless … impossible …' She sighed unhappily. '… frustrating fool. But the most gorgeous fool I ever met. You and your Whitsundays. Why didn't you listen?' As she paused, finger on the trigger, a gun barked in the darkness. A bright red hole appeared above her left breast. She stared at it, then as she turned to gaze at me, she slumped lifeless against the door of the shed.

'You all right, little brother?'

Patrick walked into the light holding the farm rifle, which he pointed at the final member of the gang who stood quivering in the corner. It was Captain Dan Morgan.

'I'm a cop in plain clothes,' Patrick said to him. 'I'm allowed to shoot dirty crooks.'

'Don't you dare,' I said as I reached for Pixie who was seated on the ground holding her side.

'Pixie, love, you okay?'

'I think so. Hurts a bit, that's all.'

I switched on the torch that had fallen from her pocket. Blood soaked her shirt and ran into her jeans.

'I know some first aid. Let me see.'

I eased open the shirt to reveal a wound near her hip and a small exit hole. 'Bullet's gone right through. You could be lucky.'

'Why is that?'

'I don't have a knife.'

'Please stop the bleeding,' she winced. 'How's Lisa?'

'Gone, I'm afraid.'

'And Billy?'

Billy. In the excitement I'd forgotten Billy. 'Wait here and

I'll find him.'

'No need, boss. I'm right behind you.'

Just then the hillside was flooded with the roar of four-by-four vehicles and bright lights.

'Real police, I'm guessing,' Pixie said. 'Hold me, Tom.'

CHAPTER 46

Pixie's guess was right. Sergeant Phil Manning and six constables had arrived to take control. As I discovered later, Pixie had seen the yacht sneak into the channel and dialled Sergeant Manning with the news that Billy and I were missing, presumably fallen foul of the motor cruiser. She added that she was now in the company of Patrick who, having failed to contact me earlier, had rung and obtained her location. At first the pair had stayed under cover, but soon realised a police follow-up would need more detail on the gang's activities. They were halfway to the shed when Billy and I climbed onto the jetty and set a cat among the pigeons. Meanwhile, Sergeant Manning had departed with his team for Woodwark Bay where the fight was almost over, apart from the two accomplices with loaded guns and massive headaches.

After bandaging Pixie, I rode with her to the Proserpine Hospital in the rear of a police vehicle while a second vehicle took Jade, who had thankfully lapsed into a coma. Patrick drove Billy home and the remaining cops processed the crime scene. At the hospital I sat on a hard bench waiting for news on Pixie. Around midnight when a nurse came to say she was not in danger, I was given a mattress in the wardsman's store where I promptly fell asleep.

Woken by kookaburras at sunrise, I dodged past the duty nurse and called on my patient who reclined in bed, gazing through the open door. Although her eyes were heavy with medication, she did her best to smile as I crept into the room.

'How's my ace reporter?'

'All right, I think. I can't move for bandages.'

'Don't try. You've earned the rest.'

Tears welled into her eyes. 'We almost failed, Tom.'

'Rubbish. You were magnificent.'

'Come a bit closer, please.'

When I drew near, she took my face in both hands and kissed me. 'Promise to kiss me every day. Please, Tom.'

'That will lift Ethel's brows,' I said, then added, 'Yes, Pixie, I promise a kiss every day. And more, if you want.'

'I love you,' she whispered.

At that moment I was sprung by the duty nurse who drove me out with a sharp tongue.

At eight-thirty when official visiting hours began, I called on Pixie but she was asleep. A nurse pointed me to a canteen that served bacon rolls, and as I departed the hospital, she handed me a note.

'Sergeant Manning wants to see you when convenient.'

Climbing into the Moke, I drove to the police station where Phil Manning treated me more kindly than last time.

'How is she, Tom?'

'Fortunately, no serious damage. She'll be home in a few days. What's happened at your end?'

'We've had a busy night. First up, you don't need to

cover for your brother anymore. He didn't kill Todd Steele. That crime belongs to Seamus Carney who is otherwise known as Dan Morgan.'

'You for real?'

'Yes. It appears Seamus — alias Dan — was a former employee of the Sydney law firm, Mason Edelstein and Birch. Nine years ago, Seamus was caught with his hand in the till. To avoid embarrassment, the firm showed him the door, but as a trade-off for years of service he was allowed to keep practising law. Very convenient. He adopted a new identity, Dan Morgan, and came to Airlie with his wife where they bought a bar and renamed it Captain Morgan's. Once here, he joined forces with Jade Wilson and Todd Steele to make money however they could, which included drug trafficking and land deals. He and Todd concocted the sacred site registration to get Lenny Watkins out of their hair. They relied on your lawyer being overwhelmed by the application, which he was. However, they underestimated the O'Connors. Their first shock came when your grandfather took his own life rather than be drubbed by his enemies. Their second shock was the O'Connor Protocol. They thought they could rid themselves of Todd Steele by using Patrick as a scapegoat. … (Sergeant Phil mimicked my voice) … *Your honour, my brother slept in my flat all night. He never left my side.* What a laugh. No, not funny really. Their ruse almost succeeded. On the night of Todd's murder, Jade was off sailing his boat, and Dan Morgan, alias Seamus, was never on our radar. So it was easy. Dan disguised his voice and invited Patrick — who he rightly guessed was impulsive — to Todd's house for a chat. While Patrick was still on his way, Dan knocked on Todd's door and got invited inside. Once there he sank the cane knife into Todd's unsuspecting back and set fire to the house. Next thing, bumbling Patrick was all over the crime scene.'

'Where did Dan get the knife?'

'He pinched it from your farm during your grandfather's wake. Thought a knife might come in useful. Luckily for Patrick there were dozens of fingerprints on it, even your mother's.'

'And who vandalised my office?'

'Our friend Dan again. The white Mercedes was a bit clumsy, but the trashing was genuine. So too were the drugs.'

'How did Lisa fit into the picture?'

'Not Lisa. Shirley Delaney. Last year you and Billy almost sprang the syndicate with your newspaper. You don't know how close you went. So, they decided to plant somebody on the inside. One of Jade's old girlfriends, Shirley, was ideal. Meanwhile, she created the AFP cover so that if you became a nuisance, she could swear you to secrecy. I would've exposed her cover in minutes.'

'She did say Airlie had a corrupt officer.'

'And you believed her?'

'I did, Phil. Sorry.'

'That's okay, you were under her spell.'

'Where is she now?'

'In the morgue.'

I sighed. 'That is terrible, really. She saved me from a croc … among other things.'

'So I heard.'

'Where's Jade?'

'Under guard in Mackay Base Hospital. They say staff are queuing at his door. Never seen coconuts so big or black.'

'What will happen to Pixie?'

'Nothing, she acted in self-defence. Brave girl. I wouldn't take on a man running at me with a gun.'

'What about Patrick?'

'We've confiscated the rifle. There'll be an inquest, but police evidence will say Shirley had tried killing one person and was about to kill another. At worst, I imagine he'll escape with a rap on the knuckles.'

'Billy should be pleased. He's smashed the drug syndicate.'

'He did, but in future trust your local police. You especially.'

*　　*　　*

The following Monday afternoon I received a call from the hospital to say Pixie was ready to go home, and had asked me to collect her. We eased her gently into the seat, and wrapped her shoulders with a cardigan for the twenty-minute drive. Although her face was drawn, she was as pretty as ever and her eyes glowed as she admired the scenery along Shute Harbour Road. Near the turn-off to her house, she asked me to pull into a rail siding.

'Tom, the other morning when I said I loved you, did you think I was delirious?'

'Why do you ask?'

'I never know what you're thinking.' She reached into her bag. 'I had promised myself I would wear these today. The eucalyptus flowers. They've been special to me … to us.'

She paused. 'Do you love me?'

I looked out the window and pondered my reply.

'Surely it's not that hard,' she said.

'Yes … I do love you.'

'You sound hesitant.'

'I feel awkward after how I've treated you. You know … Terry Hanson's daughter, copy setter, ex-schoolgirl …'

'Go easy on yourself. You're not God, you're an O'Connor.'

'Whatever that is.'

'I'll explain it like this,' she said. 'A simple little creature that builds walls. Then hides behind them.'

EPILOGUE

As it turned out, Sergeant Manning's optimism was misplaced. Detectives in Mackay decided Patrick did have a case to answer. They laid charges of unlawful killing and of going armed in public. Fortunately, the judge determined that the killing, though tragic, had prevented further deaths. However, on the second charge he found Patrick had indeed gone armed in public "without lawful occasion in such a manner as to cause fear". When he received a two-year suspended sentence, Glenda said she had no choice but to postpone the wedding. In the meantime, Pixie and I settled into a comfortable pre-marital relationship that included a makeover of my bachelor flat. As the paper was growing rapidly, I promoted myself to managing director and, with Heather's solid approval, Pixie to the role of editor.

On the day Glenda and Patrick announced their new wedding date, I put THE question to Pixie.

She cupped her hand to her ear. 'Sorry, can you repeat that?'

'Pixie, will you ...?'

She laughed. 'Yes, you idiot.'

Consequently, Mum got the double wedding she longed for. The invitation cards were printed with the heading, *The*

O'Connor Protocol — two brothers' names entwined on the one card, two brothers in the middle covering for each other … as it ought to be.